CHILDFINDERS

A NOVEL

HUGO N. GERSTL

ChildFinders

A NOVEL

HUGO N. GERSTL

PANGÆA

Publishing Group

CHILDFINDERS – A NOVEL

ISBN 978-1-950134-28-1
Pangæa Publishing Group
www.PangaeaPublishing.com

Editor: Richard Peaks

Cover images:
Forest background @ Aliaksandr Makaranka - DepositPhotos.com
Teddy bear @ Milan Radulovic - DepositPhotos.com
Open chapter fleuron images from
@Truemitra - FreeVector.com

Cover design and typesetting by
DesignPeaks@gmail.com

For information contact:

PANGÆA PUBLISHING GROUP
25579 Carmel Knolls Drive, Carmel, CA 93923 – USA
Telephone: 831-624-3508/831-649-0668 –Fax: 831-649-8007
Email: info@pangaeapublishing.com

Hugo N. Gerstl Collection

See below some of Pangæa Publishing Group's bestsellers by the same author:

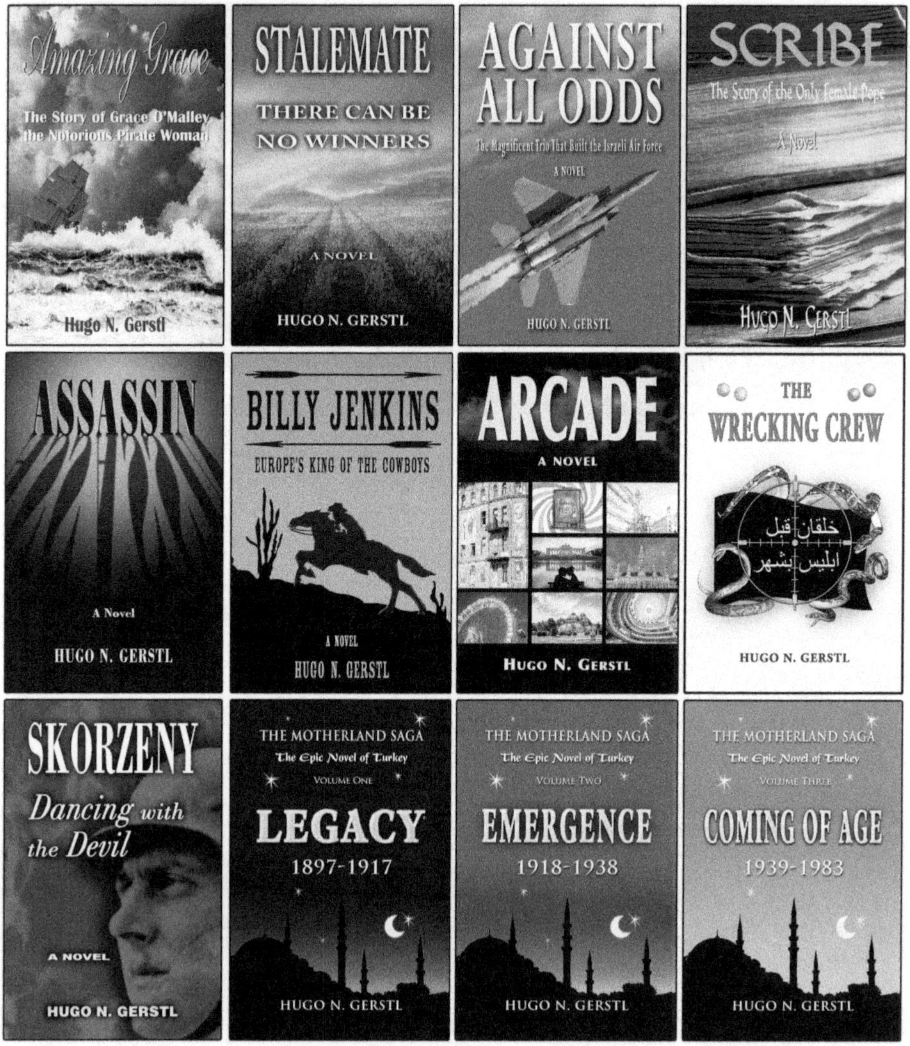

Do not miss them on your shelf!

For Hugo N. Gerstl's complete novels list and descriptions, go to www.HugoGerstl.com

PANGÆA

PANGÆA PUBLISHING GROUP
25579 Carmel Knolls Drive
Carmel, CA 93923
Email: info@pangaeapublishing.com

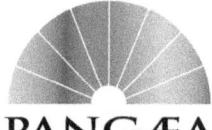

FEBRUARY - MARCH

1

"What'll we do now, Melissa?"

"I dunno, Becky. It's almost five. My mom's gonna' call me home for dinner any minute. Have you got any ideas, Tiffany?" Melissa asked, turning to her other friend.

Amy Roth stood in her kitchen, chopping vegetables for the evening salad. She stopped for a moment to glance at the three youngsters. The scene made her smile. Spring had not officially arrived, she thought, but the oak and alder trees surrounding the yard seemed to care as little as the girls. They were budding, girls and nature alike. Melissa was fine. A strong, healthy eight-year-old. Hard to believe that five years ago she had disappeared.

"We could make up nutty nursery rhymes like teacher taught us this afternoon."

"Yucch!" Becky said. "That's too much like homework!"

"It's not either," Tiffany replied. "Watch. I'll do one right now. Hey diddle-diddle, the cat and the fiddle, the cow jumped over the other cat—. Hey, Melissa, you're all pale. Is something wrong?"

"N-no," Melissa said. "I'm fine."

"Maybe we should play jump rope," Becky suggested. "Melissa, you be in the middle."

The rest of the girls' conversation was too quiet to reach Amy. She stared out the window as Melissa started jumping.

As Tiffany and Becky started turning the rope, they sang, "Ice cream soda, lemonade punch. Tell me the 'nitial of my honey bunch. Melissa, Melissa, silly little goat, Melissa, sta—"

The telephone rang, obscuring the last line of the jump-rope rhyme. Obedient to habit, Amy answered the phone.

"Hello?"

"Hi, Amy. It's me," her ex-husband's voice said through the phone.

"Uh-huh."

"Oh, real glad to hear from me, eh? I thought you wanted me to take care of Melissa while you were off taking depositions."

"Uh-huh."

"Amy, is something wrong? Are you feeling okay?"

"I feel fine."

"Well, set an extra place for me at dinner, will you? I'll do the dishes and put Melissa to bed, so you can get to sleep early. I know you have to be on the road by five."

"Okay."

"I'll see you in an hour or so. 'Bye."

"'Bye." She hung up the phone.

"Was that Daddy?"

Looking over the island counter where the phone was sitting, Amy saw her daughter trudging in. "Yes, dear." She walked over to the cupboard and pulled out three dishes, set them around the table, and placed silverware beside each plate. When she finished, she walked back over to the counter to continue cutting vegetables for the salad. "Where did I put that knife?" She glanced at the dishwasher, then grabbed another from the rack.

"I washed my hands, Mommy. Is there anything I can do to help?" Melissa said, returning to the kitchen.

"You could set the table."

The little girl looked up at her with a funny grin. "Mommy, you just set the table."

Amy looked at the plates on the table. *I really need to take a vacation*, she thought. To her daughter, she said, "Oh, right. Why don't you go do your homework, honey?"

"Okay." Melissa headed down the hall to her room.

An hour after dinner, Daniel Roth walked into his daughter's room. The clownfaced clock above the child's small desk, its eyes shifting left and right in time to the wooden tick-tock, read eight. Amy had already gone to bed. Melissa was dressed in her pink flannel nightie.

"Read me a fairy tale," she said.

"Aren't you a little old for fairy tales?" He put her down on her bed. She burrowed into the covers.

"I'll never be too old for fairy tales, Daddy. Please."

He smiled and pulled a well-worn book off the shelf by the door. His voice was soft and soothing as he read.

"'—and all the other princesses danced at the wedding. They danced so much, they wore out their shoes, and they all lived happily ever after.'"

"Another one, Daddy? Please? I'll be your best friend."

Daniel looked down at the tiny, elfin face, framed by honey-colored curls, the huge green eyes surrounded by impossibly long, dark lashes. "Nope. I promised your mom."

"O.K.," she said, yawning. "Kiss me g'night, Daddy."

"Sure, honey," he said. He bent over and brushed his lips against her forehead.

Suddenly, his eyes went wide with terror as she pulled the kitchen knife out from under the blanket. Before he could stop her, she plunged the blade into his throat, severing the carotid artery, killing him almost instantly.

The law enforcement agencies were stymied. Despite every known polygraph and psychological test, despite hypnotherapists, and a staggering dose of sodium pentothal, they concluded that Melissa Roth was perfectly sane. And that she had no memory whatever about what she had done.

The telephone connection to Maui was instantaneous. "Hitoshi, we've got a problem," the tall man said, his voice tight. "There's been a foul-up. A few hours ago, one of the weapons misfired, right in my own backyard."

The day had not begun well for Henry VanBurgh. Karl, that bitchy little rabbit, had rolled in at six thirty, just about the time Henry had finished showering and trimming his beard.

"Welcome home, Queen," Henry had greeted his lover. "Look, if you want to go hunting all night, that's your business. If you bring home AIDS, that's mine. Or haven't you heard we're high risk?"

"Screw off, Henry," Karl responded. "Just because you work for the almighty Center for Disease Control, you think you've got it all down. You can't die if you've never lived." He poured himself a cup of coffee and sat down at the kitchen table.

Henry worried more every day about Karl's need to cruise the bars at least three nights a week and try to prove he could pick up any so-inclined male over the age of thirteen. He knew the odds against tomorrow increased with each new liaison.

After a few angry words, Henry drove off in the Toyota Prius he and the NCDC Federal Credit Union had purchased the month before. His anger had begun to abate by quarter of twelve, when his supervisor, Dub Slimmon, buzzed for him.

"Now what?" Henry muttered out loud. "Probably ask me to stay late again tonight."

He'd no sooner gotten to his boss's office when Slimmon said, "Sit down, Henry, I've been meaning to talk to you about your work."

Henry felt a cold chill. People were getting laid off left and right. "If it's something I've done wrong, sir—?"

"No, Henry, it's not that at all. Stop worrying all the time. You're doing fine. As President Roosevelt once said, 'We have nothing to fear but chastity itself.'"

Henry stared at the man blankly.

Slimmon continued. "Henry, I want you to take the 1:54 Delta flight to Mobile this afternoon. Here are your tickets. There's a very bad man named Benjamin Blackston, who'll be giving a talk to the White Christian Heritage Society at the Threepenny Opera Restaurant this evening. After that, he'll return to the Hyatt Regency. You are to kill him, Henry, then come back on the next flight. Do you understand?"

"Yes, sir."

"I've packed a briefcase for your trip. Everything you'll need is in there. Blackston's a little guy. You shouldn't have much trouble with him."

The Delta CRJ arrived back in Atlanta at 9:22 the following morning. Henry had slept for an hour during the flight. When he awoke, he was genuinely surprised to find himself on board. His last recollection had been of going to work the previous morning.

He was even more surprised when he deplaned, carrying a small briefcase, and found two strange men approaching him.

"Henry VanBurgh?" the taller of them asked, a country drawl apparent in his voice.

"Yes."

"FBI," he said, flashing a card case. "You're under arrest for the murder of Benjamin Blackston. I must advise you that anything you say will be used against you."

"I can't understand it, sir. VanBurgh was caught with the rope in his briefcase. There was a round trip ticket in his pocket. He was seen by four witnesses at the Hyatt Regency the night of the murder. His supervisor swears he sent the guy to Mobile. Still, VanBurgh denies it all."

The section chief sat back in his chair and asked, "How'd he make out with the polygraph?"

"Passed."

"A good criminal can do that."

The first agent nodded and flipped a page in the folder on his lap. "He also passed voice stress analysis and hypnosis. Volunteered for an

MRI, PET scan, EEG. Hell, he even told us to cut open his brain, if we thought that would prove him innocent."

"Background?" The chief laced his fingers under his chin.

"Gay. HIV negative."

"Nothing unusual in his history?"

"He disappeared from home for two weeks when he was eight. He has no recollection of anything that happened during that time."

"Anything else?"

"According to his teachers, VanBurgh was so quiet he almost faded into the woodwork. Never got into trouble, never dated. They seemed surprised he had any relationship at all. Came to work on time, never advertised his sexual preferences. Holst was his first emotional experience, man or woman."

"Dennis, don't tell me you've still got your nose in FBI business."

"Old habits never die, Ezra. Since they made me a paid consultant, there's no reason I shouldn't justify the millions they're paying me. And don't roll your eyes like that, my Israeli semi-retiree. Thanks to WhatsApp, I can see the hairs growing in your nose even from 7,230 miles away. Ah, to be in Tel Aviv in the spring."

"Millions, Dennis?"

"Well, I admit that in U.S. dollars, I'm probably making substantially less than our esteemed president. Still, I'll go out of my mind if I don't do something more exciting than watch the grass grow."

"May I respectfully ask why you'r calling? And stop shifting your eyes as though you're trying to see something behind me. Rachel's at the beach."

"So say you, Mister Caen. Unless that glorious redhead behind you is an apparition … Actually, I am calling for a reason, Ezra. When I was giving a guest lecture at Hamilton University last week, I met a professor of actuarial science, a fellow named Jeff Savage. We got to talking and when he heard I was ex-FBI, he asked me some provocative questions. Seems he and a buddy of his are amateur computer sleuths. Long story short, he invited me to lunch with his friend and they filled me in on a farfetched idea they had about some funny stuff going on. Only, after they showed me how much work they'd done, it didn't seem so farfetched to me."

"And your point is?"

"If there's anything to what they say, this looks like the kind of bone you might like to chew on. How'd you like to watch the grass growing in someone else's backyard?"

"As I've heard said by people more knowledgeable than me, the grass is always greener on the other side of the pond."

2

For the first few days after Daniel's death, Amy felt numb. It seemed her house was occupied all day long by friends, colleagues, police investigators, and, of course, the ever-present media.

The authorities insisted that the child be kept under observation at Border House, a supervised home. The place had lovely grounds and Amy's regular school, Hillcrest, provided a private tutoring program. But it was an institution nonetheless. Amy slept fitfully, only a few hours each night, before she awoke in hot and cold sweats. So many thoughts assailed her.

What kind of parent am I that the State has declared me incapable of caring for my own daughter? What kind of monster did I carry inside me for nine months? Was there something in my genes? Dan's?

She couldn't reconcile any of it. In the end, she cried herself into an exhausted few moments of sleep, or she tossed, turned, and hyperventilated until the gray-black night turned to morning, leaving her with ever-deepening dark circles under her green eyes.

Amy had immersed herself so deeply in the practice of law that she had few friends in whom she could confide. For the first week after Daniel's death, she spent every day, from breakfast to bedtime, with her daughter. The people at the home were very patient, very solicitous, but she felt their stares boring into her back when she couldn't see them. And she heard half-whispered voices that she could never identify.

"There's the mother of that poor little girl who killed her father."

"What kind of mind poisoning could she have inflicted on the child to make her do that?"

"You know how it is with these divorces nowadays."

"Yes, but even so, you have to admit that's going over the line."

She wanted to turn and shout at the voices, tell them it wasn't that way at all, that she, Daniel, and Melissa had all been friends. But, of course, she did none of those things. She simply listened. And took it all inside. And bled.

The most difficult part came three days after Daniel's death, when Melissa asked where her daddy was, why he didn't visit her. Amy was able to choke out that daddy was "away," and that appeared to satisfy the child. On the fifth day, she summoned the courage to tell her daughter that daddy had died and gone to heaven, and that he wasn't coming back. Melissa appeared stoic about the whole thing.

"How did he die, Mommy? An airplane crash? A fire?" Trust a child to find the most spectacular and heroic means for her father to die. If only she knew the truth.

"He died in an accident, darling," Amy replied. At least that was not a complete lie.

"Are we going to be all right, Mommy?"

"Of course we are, darling." She hugged Melissa to her breast, relieved at how easily the explanation had gone.

"When can I go home?"

"In a while, darling. The doctors want to do some tests."

"Am I sick, Mommy?"

"No, darling, of course not."

"Why can't I go home then?"

At that moment, a large, African-American woman of about sixty ambled into Melissa's room. She reminded Amy of Nana Mae, the woman who'd helped raise her when her parents were both working in the store.

"Don't you worry, child," the woman, whose name was Willie, said. "You're gonna' go home when it's the right time for you to do so, and that'll sure be soon enough. Your mama has to work hard with all that lawyerin' stuff, and she's out of town a lot. You'll see, honey. You'll go home just as soon as you're ready. It's almost past your bedtime and your mama's too, so I'm gonna' tell her to scoot, y'hear?"

Willie had been a godsend, and the god who'd sent her had been Charles Cunningham. Not for the first time in her life, she was grateful for all he'd done for her.

She often thought she wouldn't have made it without his strength. He'd been one of the first to call. He'd spent hours talking patiently with her, telling her there was no way she could be held to blame; that she'd been a warm, loving, caring mother. What had happened was totally aberrant, a freak of nature. Most of all, though, for some reason she could never quite fathom, the media coverage was suddenly gone.

She must remember to purchase a small memento for him, but what in the world did you buy for the man who *really* had everything?

Two weeks after Daniel's death, Amy returned "home," to her fifteen by twenty-foot office at Cunningham, MacLeish, Durgan & Whyte. She was grateful to find that her associates had relieved her of the bulk of her work during the time she'd been gone, and that her desk looked, if anything, less like a war zone than she'd left it.

During her first hour back, Amy reflected on how her relationship with Charles Cunningham had evolved over the years she'd known him.

Amy's parents had owned a dry goods store in Minneapolis. Her mom and dad barely managed to keep their heads above water while she struggled through junior college, then the University of Minnesota, with passing but unspectacular grades. She mused, not for the first time, about the incredible good fortune that had brought her to this time and place.

Amy had attended University of Minnesota Law School because it was the only one of six she'd applied for that accepted her, and because it was affordable. As in her undergraduate studies, she received passing grades, but little more.

"Oh, well," she told her study partner, a short, roly-poly young man named Arthur Dohrmann, who'd tried unsuccessfully to get into her panties during the first year of law school, "I guess if you believe the old saying, 'The "A" students become professors, the "B" students become judges, and the "C" students make money,' I'm going to be a wealthy woman someday." Now, Arthur was doing Legal Aid work in Chicago's inner city, and Amy was a partner at one of the most prestigious law firms in the world. At least one of them was making good money.

During her second year at law school, she had been surprised to receive an unsolicited letter from a suburb of Washington, D.C. The letterhead read, "Cunningham, MacLeish, Durgan & Whyte." She'd seen attorneys' stationery in the past. The larger firms in Minneapolis often had lines and lines of tiny little names in the upper left-hand corner. She dreamt that one day her name would be one of those small entries above the dividing line between partners and associates.

Cunningham-MacLeish's letterhead did not contain names. Rather there were fifty different *cities* throughout the world where Cunningham-MacLeish maintained offices. She had looked on a map to find their headquarters—Winchester Township, a small community on the Beltway near the nation's capital. The letter, addressing her by her maiden name, had read,

Dear Miss Klein:

You have been recommended to us as a young woman of singular drive and ambition. We understand you will be completing your second year of law school within a few months.

Cunningham, MacLeish, Durgan & Whyte is instituting a program of summer internships for deserving law students, particularly minorities and women. We would like to invite you to attend a meeting at our headquarters during the weekend of March 7, to discuss the possibility of your applying for such an internship. Naturally, should you be interested, we will furnish air transportation and cover all of your expenses.

Your acceptance of this opportunity does not imply that we are tendering you an offer of employment, but generally we have found that a high percentage of pre-screened candidates such as yourself ultimately accept positions with our firm.

The weekend had been a dream come true. Amy had stayed at the Sheraton where she was treated as a treasured guest. When she returned to school, she increased her grade point average dramatically.

After she graduated, Amy spent the following summer cramming forty hours a week for the bar exam and performing twenty hours of "grunt" work each week at Cunningham-MacLeish.

Amy was so certain she'd "aced" the bar that the night before the results were announced, she held a small, celebratory party at her apartment. By that time, she was engaged to Dan Roth, who was just starting his own architectural practice. The sun was starting to rise on a perfect life.

Tom Riley, her supervising partner, called her at eight the following morning. "Amy, I don't know how to say this," he began, "and I don't want you to feel that we at Cunningham-MacLeish have lost the slightest faith in you, but—"

The color drained from her face. Her hands felt momentarily numb with the prescience of what was to follow. She barely heard the next words. "—so sorry. We found out you missed by just two points. Two lousy little points. Of course, we expect you'll stay with Cunningham-MacLeish while you study for the bar again and I'm sure that—"

After two hours of sobbing, she knew what she'd have to do. The rule at Cunningham-MacLeish was very clear: flunk the bar, you have thirty days to clear out your desk and look elsewhere.

She'd presented herself to the hiring partner, Leonard Weinshenk, the following morning, her written resignation in hand. He smiled gently at her and said, "Mister Cunningham wants to see you in his office for a few minutes."

The golden goodbye, she'd thought, from Charles F. Cunningham himself. The unapproachable senior partner, the man you met *once* on the day you were hired. They never referred to him as "the old man." He was always "Mister Cunningham," to all but his own senior partners. Behind his back, they called him "the iron lion," a nickname passed down since time out of mind. Charles F. Cunningham III occupied his own suite of offices on the top floor of the Cunningham-MacLeish building. You never went into the lion's den unless you were summoned.

When she'd exited the elevator, she'd been awed, even in her emotionally drained state. The double doors leading to Cunningham's outer offices were framed by gray, black-and-white polished marble. The walls of the reception area were burnished walnut. Matching leather sofas faced one another in a small alcove, off to the side of the room. Photographs of Charles Cunningham in informal poses with three former presidents, the present chief executive, two Supreme Court justices, and an assortment of world leaders hung in discreet groupings.

Cunningham's private waiting room was large enough to hold four of her own cubicles. Its old, genuine oak floors were covered by richly colored, tightly woven Persian carpets of the highest quality. Cunningham's administrative executive's desk was twice the size of her own. A discreet sign at its right front corner read, "Sharon Graham."

"Good morning, Miss Klein." The tall, attractive, red-haired woman, ten years Amy's senior, smiled warmly. "Mister Cunningham's expecting you. Let me show you in."

The office was forty by forty feet. A polished, ebony desk was balanced by a matching conference table and soft-grained leather furniture. The view of the world was endless.

There were three photographs to the left of a small wet bar: an aerial shot of a huge complex, a view of an exquisite greensward leading up to a palatial mansion, and a shot showing a smiling Cunningham warmly shaking hands with a shorter black man.

Cunningham stood as she entered, a tall, handsome, patrician man in his mid-fifties, the face one expected to see on a Supreme Court justice or the president of the American Bar Association. If anyone had ever looked the part of attorney and counselor at law, it was Charles F. Cunningham III.

"Won't you sit down, Miss Klein?" he said. His resonant voice was fatherly and personal, as though she were the only person that mattered in his life. Small wonder he'd impressed so many juries. "May I offer you some orange juice, Perrier water?"

"No, thank you, sir," she said, trying to maintain her dignity. After all, this was the last time she'd ever be in his office.

"I understand you'll be marrying Daniel Roth in the next few months?"

"I hope to, sir." She was amazed that this friend of presidents had taken the time to know about her personal life.

"Fine man," he said. "I hear he's recently opened his own architectural firm. I'm certain he'll do quite well with a woman like you beside him."

"Thank you, Mister Cunningham," she said, biting down on her lip. How could she have let a man like this down?

"I understand you had a small problem with the bar," he continued smoothly.

"Not really small, Mister Cunningham. I failed."

"Well now, young lady, the word 'fail' is rather a harsh word, wouldn't you say?"

"I can't think of a gentle way to say it, Mister Cunningham. I truly appreciate your taking your time with me. In fact, I'm quite surprised you even wanted to talk to me. I've been with Cunningham-MacLeish—"

"Two summers, and the better part of this fall," he interrupted gently. "And yes, I know the general rule that if someone fails the bar we expect resignation. But that's a *general* rule, Miss Klein. There are always exceptions to be made. Occasionally, when one finds a truly deserving young person, rules can be bent a little."

"What do you mean?" she asked, scarcely believing her ears.

"I would consider it a personal favor if you'd think about staying on at Cunningham-MacLeish, at least for one more try at the bar. If you don't pass the second time, well—"

On her second attempt, Amy Klein Roth passed the Bar easily.

Cunningham, MacLeish, Durgan & Whyte, "Cunningham-MacLeish," as it was more familiarly known in the legal community, was an old-line firm, highly rated by the legal establishment, and, of course, deserving of the AV rating in Martindale-Hubbell, the self-appointed arbiter of the *crème de la crème*. The firm represented large insurance companies, the state's foremost banking and trust organizations, and several Fortune 500 companies. The "Cunningham" in Cunningham-MacLeish had been the present senior partner's *grandfather*. The firm's partners included a former vice president, two senators who'd lost their bids for reelection, the recently retired judge advocate general of the Air Force, and the former general counsel of one of the "seven sisters" of international oil. In the past quarter century, the firm had sent two partners to the state supreme court, three to its courts of appeal, ten to the trial judiciary, and five to Congress.

At first blush, Cunningham-MacLeish's universe appeared to be one of gentility. However, Amy soon became disabused of her notion that the largest law firms were nothing but clean, honest elegance. When you got right down to it, the legal profession was, first and foremost, a business. Cunningham-MacLeish exercised great prestige and power. But it took five million dollars a month to keep the doors of that prestigious and powerful office open, and without money generated by paying clients, all the power and prestige in the world wouldn't be worth much in front of a bankruptcy judge.

During her first year as an attorney, Amy sometimes worked on cases for clients that Charles F. Cunningham III did not know existed *and did not want to know existed.* Occasionally, the most notorious of these types were quietly referred elsewhere.

Amy had been an associate with the firm just over four years when Cunningham summoned her to his office. It happened so quickly, she didn't have a chance to become nervous until the interview was over.

One moment, she was sitting in her own cubicle working on a set of interrogatories. The next, her phone buzzed with an interoffice call. "Mrs. Roth, this is Charles Cunningham. Might I see you for a few moments, please?"

"Mrs. Roth—may I call you Amy?" he said, when she'd sat down across from him.

"Yes, sir."

"You've been with us four years, thirty-six days if I'm correct?"

"Yes, sir." She was not surprised at the precision of his remark. Cunningham had unquestionably been briefed before this meeting.

"Let me get right to the point. I've looked over your briefs from the Standard Insurance and Continental Petroleum cases." Cunningham motioned to a set of files lying open on his desk. "They're quite impressive.

I've also spoken with the head of your department, who had fine things to say about you. You've justified the faith I have in you. I'm convinced you're one of our finer young litigators."

She wasn't sure how to react.

"The reason I asked you to come into my office today," he continued, "is to invite you to join what we euphemistically call the 'A-team.'"

Amy reddened. She'd heard those words used before. Joining the A-team meant you carried Charles Cunningham's briefcase for a few years, sat around a huge conference table on the top floor, exchanging ideas with the best and the brightest, and that you were on career fast track toward partnership.

"I . . . I don't know what to say," she stammered.

"My understanding is it's probably the first time you don't," he said, smiling warmly. "There'll be some immediate changes. You'll have a month to clean up your present caseload and transfer your files to various associates. Office administration will be advised of your promotion to Senior Associate. I'm sure you'll be more than pleased at the difference in remuneration. Of course, you'll have to give up your somewhat spartan office." He smiled. "As a member of my team, I'd like to have you a bit closer to me."

Three years ago, Amy had been promoted again, this time to junior partner, responsible for substantial cases of her own.

Charles Cunningham remained the stern but approachable father figure. She soon learned that he spent four months a year out of the office, engaged in his passion for world travel. Even when he was in residence, much of his time was devoted to meetings with the celebrated and influential elite of the world.

Only rarely did the litigation department actually go all the way through trial. Cases were resolved at pre-trial conferences where the overwhelming quality of Cunningham-MacLeish's preparation demonstrated to the opposition the inherent wisdom of settling without the risk—and indignity—of dirtying one's hands in the courtroom.

Charles Cunningham had slowed down some, but at sixty-two one didn't expect him to come in as often as in the past. Cunningham-MacLeish was a well-oiled machine. The presence or absence of the highest among equals made little difference.

Since Amy's father had died of cancer just after she'd passed the bar, and her mother followed a year later, Charles Cunningham had become a surrogate father figure to her. She'd gone to Charles when Melissa had disappeared, six years ago. And Cunningham had quietly counseled her when her marriage to Dan came to an end.

Amy's mind returned to the present.

Now, there were only two things that mattered: getting Melissa back home as soon as possible, and burying herself in work so that somehow life could return to "normal."

The first folder she read contained a single page memo prepared by her intake assistant. She silently thanked Cunningham for assigning her a case that would involve travel, aggressiveness, and creative effort.

TO: AKR
FROM: JVW

C-M has been retained by the government of Portugal, one of the major reinsurers of the western world. The adverse party is Lloyds of London as indemnitor for The Great Atlantic Insurance Consortium (GAIC).

GAIC, one of Lloyds' underwriters, hedged its bet by having Portugal carry the reinsurance. Under this system, national governments bolster their treasuries by insuring insurers, for a piece of the action. The risk to the reinsurer is usually minimal, but occasionally, when there's a really heavy loss, the reinsurer may be asked to cough up.

Our client reinsured GAIC which, unfortunately, filed for bankruptcy in the Cayman Islands two weeks after the Hanagasa Maru, which was insured by GAIC, spilled three hundred thousand gallons of sweet crude petroleum off the coast of Cape Town. The Hanagasa Maru had no business being anywhere near Cape Town because Chesterfield

Oil, which had commissioned the ship, knew of the dangerous cross-tides in the area. Cunningham's called in an actuary from Hamilton University, Jeff Savage. Cunningham wants us to meet with him.

JACK W.

Amy spent the afternoon researching the law of the high seas, international insurance law, and sovereign immunity. By the time she looked out her window, it was getting dark. The electronic thermometer on the First National Bank building alternated between thirty-four degrees Fahrenheit and one degree Celsius, time six-forty.

She wondered if Charles Cunningham was still here. Early evenings were a good time to talk. Since it was only one floor up from hers, she ascended the inner stairway.

Cunningham's reception area was dark except for the faint glow cast by a table lamp.

She heard Cunningham's voice on the telephone. "I'm still rather disturbed about the misfire. Keep trying to get the weapon back."

She knocked on his inner door. "Mister Cunningham?"

There was a sudden change in his voice. Did she detect a hint of nervousness under the urbanity? "Why don't I call you back in a few minutes? One of my partners is waiting in the outer office."

Cunningham emerged moments later, his smile warm as ever. "Amy! I certainly didn't expect you'd be staying late. Have you been out here long?"

"Fifteen seconds. I couldn't help but hear you talking about a weapon misfire. Am I intruding?"

"No, not at all," he said. Did she sense the briefest hesitancy in his voice? "One of our Japanese manufacturing clients is trying to get around a forty-year-old embargo. When the experimental weapon goes off, the lawyers are left to clean up the mess. Nothing to worry about. But tell me, Amy, how come you're here at this hour? It's only been a week since Daniel—"

"Two weeks," she said. Something in the back of her mind was disturbed by his mistake. He was always so precise and knowledgeable about everything. Like four years and thirty-six days to her elevation to senior associate.

"I'm sorry. Of course it's been two weeks," Cunningham said. "I fear that at sixty-two I'm starting to lose it." He smiled, ruefully. "Oh, to have the years you do, young lady," he said, winking. "Did you plan on staying at the office all night?"

"Only long enough to see how many alligators are snapping at my legs." She couldn't help but smile.

"I'll tell you what. I've got a few telephone calls to return. Why don't you come back up in an hour and let me take you to dinner?"

"I'm not really in the mood to go out fancy."

"Neither am I," Cunningham said. "I know a nice, casual Italian place. They serve the best pizza in town."

"Perfect. I'll be back in an hour." Cunningham turned toward his desk. "Oh, and Mr. Cunningham?"

He stopped and looked back at her. "Yes?"

"Thanks again. I know I've said it before, but I truly mean it. Thanks so much. For everything." Amy walked to the elevator and listened to the door to Cunningham's office close.

An hour-and-a-half later, they drove separate cars to the small, Italian restaurant. From her seat in the corner of the room, Amy could see the door and most of the restaurant. She watched a mother trying to get a teenager to stop eating long enough to talk. Turning slightly, she watched the door open. A man wrapped in a heavy down coat walked in and headed for the takeout counter. He was nothing special, yet she found herself staring, observing his every move. Until that moment, she hadn't noticed how much she had needed to be out among people.

"As usual, 'Doctor' Cunningham has the right prescription," she said.

Charles looked at her for a moment, then smiled gently. "Might I also prescribe one of Mama Rizzini's small combination pizzas?"

"You were serious about the pizza." She said it half as a question, half unbelieving. It was not a food she would have expected a man like him to eat.

A young, dark-haired man wearing a white apron walked up to their table and pulled out a receipt pad. "Good evening, sir," he said to Cunningham. "Are you ready to order?"

Charles looked at Amy again, then turned to the waiter and said, "We will have two of the deluxe combination pizzas, small please, and a carafe of your house red." The waiter moved smartly away. Cunningham turned to his junior partner and asked, "Amy, how are you getting by—?"

Before he could finish his sentence, she blurted out, "I've always meant to ask you about those pictures on your office wall. The ones taken on your estate. It really looks beautiful from the photos." She paused a moment, trying to figure out what she could say to get some harmless conversation started. "I've always wondered about the man with you in the third picture. I recognize most of the ones out in the foyer, but—"

Cunningham stared past her shoulder. "His name's Guillaume M'bele," he said, shifting his eyes back to meet Amy's glance. "He's been a very special friend for more than twenty-five years. Guillaume started out with nothing and rose to be the interior minister of what was then called Zaire—it's called the Democratic Republic of the Congo once again. Most presidents and prime ministers had a lot handed to them. M'bele struggled to get everything he has."

Amy saw a passion in her employer and friend she'd not seen before. "He sounds fascinating. How did you meet him?"

"Now that's an interesting story." He smiled and took a deep breath. "I was about the same age you are now. My wife had decided we should take a safari in Zaire. No sooner we got there, my wife decided it was dreadful and she wouldn't leave the hotel. I ended up spending my time in the bar." Charles' grin broadened and his eyes lost their focus. "That's where I met Guillaume. He invited me to a party for some dignitaries." He chuckled. "The party was terrible, but we became great friends. I've visited him almost every year since."

"That's one of the places you go for those four months?"

He looked at her, appraising. His smile was no longer as open. "Yes, I keep a small villa there."

The waiter arrived with their wine and a basket of hot garlic bread. He poured two glasses of wine and placed the carafe in front of Cunningham. "Your pizzas will be ready in a few minutes," he said, turned, and walked away.

"I've talked enough about me." Charles broke off a piece of the garlic bread, handed it to her, and broke off another for himself. "How are you doing, Amy? *Really*, I mean?"

She took a breath, sighed, and said, "It's been rough. I don't have to tell you that. You know, I absolutely believe Melissa has no recollection at all about—" Her voice trailed off, and she picked up her wine glass.

He patted her hand gently. "I'm certain you're right. Have you even a hint as to why she might have done what she did?"

She took a sip of her wine before answering, "None whatsoever. We had no warning at all. It was an ordinary day in every respect I can think of. She went to school in the morning. I picked her up at three-thirty."

Cunningham paused to chew his bread. "Nothing unusual at school?"

"Not that I know of."

"After school?"

Amy thought a minute, swirled the wine in her glass. "You know, I can't remember much about that evening. It wasn't anything special. Melissa played with friends and Dan came over for dinner so that I wouldn't have to leave her alone in the house when I left the next day."

"What exactly happened after dinner?" He set down the bread and steepled his fingers, concentrating on Amy as if he were taking a deposition.

"She did her homework. Dan did the dishes. I went to bed early. I was supposed to leave at five the next morning."

"What about the knife?"

Amy looked away. "Most likely she took it from the kitchen and hid it before dinner. I can't think of any other way."

"This defies logic," Charles said, his intensity evaporating.

"I agree." She ate a piece of her bread, savoring the sweet bite of the garlic and trying not to relive her memories of that night.

They were silent for a time. Amy watched people make purchases at the takeout counter. Watched clouds puff out of their mouths as they walked into the cold night air.

The waiter returned with a large tray. He placed a plate in front of Amy and she stared at it. Nearly falling over the edges of the dish, the pizza was covered with olives, peppers, several types of cheese, a few kinds of meat. She looked over at Cunningham.

He smiled and picked up his knife and fork. "I don't want to hear another word from you until you're finished with that whole thing."

"The whole—"

"Ahah." He wagged a finger at her. "Eat."

Cunningham ate his pizza and washed it down with the wine. When he was finished, he said, "I'm stuffed. How are you doing with yours?"

Amy looked up from her empty plate and reached for her glass. "I guess I was hungrier than I thought." She sipped her wine.

"Good. Now, tell me, outside of the two-week disappearance and the divorce—more than enough trauma in a young life—has anything unusual happened to Melissa?"

"That's it, although God knows what might have happened to her during the time she was away. The police psychologists thought maybe something had happened during that time to cause a—" she thought back to what they had called it "—a delayed traumatic neurosis or a displaced rage. They've done a lot of speculating, but they've come to no conclusions. What seems to frustrate them most is that whatever caused Melissa to act the way she did appears to have been totally erased."

"Surely the psychologists know about retrograde amnesia? That she'd be able to blot something as horrible as this out of her mind?"

"I asked about that. They say Melissa absolutely defies conventional wisdom." Amy smiled ruefully. "Heck, she even defies *unconventional* wisdom. Whatever was there simply isn't there anymore."

"Strange," he murmured and refilled his wine glass. "Did you ever try to get in touch with those people who brought her back?"

"*ChildFinders?*"

"Yes."

"That was one of the first things I thought of. The rental agent in the building where we picked her up said they'd been gone for over a year. Do you think *ChildFinders* might have had something to do with—?"

"I doubt it," he said. "I just thought you might ask them if they'd noticed anything when they brought her back."

"Tell me, Mr. Cunningham—"

"I told you, Amy," he raised his hand and interrupted, "when we're not at work you can call me Charles."

"Sorry." She smiled. "Charles, have you ever heard of *ChildFinders?*"

"Yes," Cunningham said. He picked up his wine glass and looked thoughtfully at the dark red liquid. "It's a very quiet, almost secret organization. I'm told they provide a great humanitarian service, but they're most insistent on their privacy."

"Do you think you might be able to contact someone involved with *ChildFinders?* Perhaps they'd provide you with information?"

"Not likely, Amy, but I could try."

"I understand. I just thought there might be a chance."

Cunningham looked at her for a moment, and said, "If you could find someone with access to a large enough computer database, you'd probably make some headway. And by that, I don't mean your standard internet stuff." He glanced at his watch. "Looks like it's time to go home, young lady. For you and me both. I'll see you safely to your car. You head right on home and try to get a proper night's sleep. What I said still goes. Take off as much time as you need."

"I don't think I'll have to. The work will do me good," she said.

"Well then, welcome back." He helped her on with her coat. "As I pointed out some years ago, you're one of our better litigators. Meanwhile, if I can think of anything to help you unravel the mystery, or if I find out anything more about *ChildFinders*, you'll be the first to know."

As she climbed into bed, Amy felt a vague sense of unease. Something she had overheard Cunningham say on the phone was totally out of character, but she couldn't quite put her finger on what it was.

Then, she concentrated on something else he'd said. If she wanted to locate *ChildFinders*, the best way would be through someone with access to a lot of computer information—but "not your standard internet stuff," he had said.

ChildFinders was the missing piece of the puzzle. If only she could find someone who would have access to "a big bank of computers." She drifted off into a long, satisfying sleep.

Charles Cunningham, however, did not sleep well that night. Amy Roth had come in too soon after the phone conversation she had overheard. Had she appeared half a minute before, who knows what she might have heard? She was a bright, perceptive woman, who was looking for the same answers he was—and not getting any closer to them.

3

"Come on, old man, a couple more minutes on the Stairmaster, then it's time to jog around the track. I can't believe you young people today. Thirty-eight years old and you're already pooped. Why, when I was your age—"

"Yeah, I know, back when Lincoln was president and Barney Oldfield was still in diapers." Jeff Savage grinned at his mentor and closest friend. Ron Ames, ten years his senior, was chairman of the computer department and had been his campus sponsor when Jeff had first came to Hamilton University.

More recently, his friend had been there to celebrate with him when Jeff made full professor and finally started getting lucrative consulting assignments with insurance companies and big law firms.

"I still can't figure why Dana lets you come to the gym every afternoon and mentally undress these incredible student bodies," Jeff said, grinning.

"It's the old story," Ames said, thin beads of sweat gathering on his forehead as his breathing became more labored. "She says I'm like a dog chasing a car tire. Wouldn't know what to do with it if I caught it. Speaking of which, I'll bet the witty and urbane Professor Savage catches more than his share of campus fish."

"That's for me to know and you to dream about," Jeff responded equably.

"Uh-huh, with the university providing you a two-bedroom, rent-free love nest, gym privileges, the latest laptop and desktop computers. I've had enough of the Stairmaster. Two miles tonight?"

"One's plenty, but I think I'll do another ten minutes on the Stairmaster first," Jeff said. "Believe it or not, I'm starting to get my second wind."

"OK, Mister Athlete," Ames said, grinning. "I'll walk the track to cool down, then we'll do a quick mile. You should be appropriately bushed by then."

"Sounds good to me."

No sooner had Ron departed, a tall blonde in a leopard print leotard started using the machine next to his. Jeff stared straight ahead, into the mirror on the far wall of the university weight room.

The blonde met his look in the glass and smiled. "Good afternoon, Professor Savage," she said to him without turning.

Jeff watched her legs pump up and down a few times before he responded, "Afternoon," and smiled back. She took a few more steps. "You seem to have the advantage, here," he said.

"How's that?" He watched her reflection move to look at the real him.

Turning his head to meet her gaze, Savage said, "You know who I am."

She smiled, forming deep dimples in her round cheeks. Jeff's legs worked the pedals marginally faster. "My name's Tanya. Tanya Davies."

"Nice to meet you, Tanya." He looked back at the mirror. Maybe Ames was right, he thought. This exercise regimen had its advantages. The girls hadn't flirted with him back when his greatest effort was lifting a Whopper and a bag of fries.

He spoke again, looking back at the mirror. "What are you studying?" He watched in the glass as the girl looked him over.

"You mean right this moment?"

Jeff glanced at her from the corner of his eye, and said, "I mean, what's your major?"

She giggled. "I'm undecided at the moment. What do you teach?"

"Actuarial science."

"Is that in the physics department?"

"No. It's part of the math department. I deal with statistics."

"Oh."

The conversation was not going well, Jeff thought. He thought about how he could explain what he did and make it sound interesting. His job was figuring out risks and odds for insurance companies. How could he make that sound glamorous?

"Hey, it's not that bad. Have you ever been to a horse race?"

"Yes. My father took me to the track when I turned eighteen. He said he wanted to teach me to be careful what I bet on."

Jeff turned and looked at the girl. "Well, that's almost exactly what I teach. I just show how to do it mathematically."

"So your students go out and figure odds at race tracks?"

"Not quite." Jeff chuckled. "Most actuaries work for insurance companies. We figure out the risks on different types of insurance so that the company knows what to charge."

"So, you can't use it at a race track?" She sounded disappointed.

He thought a minute, knowing that in fact what he did could help him design a betting system. Maybe he could impress her by—. He pushed the thought out of his head. He had enough troubles without getting into gambling.

"Most people don't use it that way, but it could be done."

"Great. You teach students how to be better gamblers. Maybe I'll take one of your classes."

"That wouldn't bother me at all. Right now, I'm getting tired of walking in place, here." Jeff stepped off the Stairmaster.

"How about going to relax in the Jacuzzi?" Tanya said as she stepped off her machine.

"I'm sorry, Tanya. I promised a friend I'd run a mile with him. Then it's sauna time!"

"Well, maybe I'll see you here tomorrow." She walked toward the women's shower room. Before she passed through the door, she looked back at him and smiled.

"Just what you need, Savage," he chided himself out loud. "A coed half your age."

Ron was waiting patiently for him when he got to the track. "You're a whole five minutes late, buddy boy," he said. "A blonde distraction I suppose?"

Jeff grinned. "Yep. But I told her that I had a date on the track with a friend."

"All right, actuary man. One dollar says I beat your—"

"You're on!" Jeff said. Jeff glanced over at his friend. Ames might be ten years his senior, but he was two inches taller than Jeff's five-ten, had a full head of dark hair, and there was not an ounce of fat on him. As usual, they raced the last quarter mile. Not unexpectedly, Ames beat him by ten yards.

Afterward, they luxuriated in the dry heat that made the day's stress evaporate. "You ever get job burnout?" Ames asked.

"Not yet," Savage responded. If I do my job right, there's a fairly big pot of gold at the end of the rainbow."

"Meaning?"

"Other than teaching, my hours are my own and not much competition. There's only sixteen thousand actuaries worldwide. One for every three hundred thousand people in the world. And it's fun. I get paid to find out all the information available in the entire universe that would affect the odds. Then I plug that information into every available database I can get my hands on, and use my allegedly inventive brain to come up with the percentage chance for the company to win the bet.

"If I guess right, the term policy comes to an end or Harold Wimberly dies one week *after* canceling his policy with the company, having faithfully paid premiums for fifty-six point seven years to the day. When that happens, the insurance company makes a *lot* of money. If Harold dies the day *before* he cancels the policy, the Great Fidelity Insurance Company coughs up a bundle. While it won't break their back, since they've been able to invest old Harold's premiums for several years, it would have been much more profitable for them had Mister Wimberly had the decency to die after the policy had lapsed."

"Don't you feel ghoulish plotting poor old Harold's demise?" Ames asked.

"Not me. Anyone who buys life insurance is betting on how soon he'll die. The only way to beat the house is to kick off as soon as possible after buying the policy. Now, you tell me, who's the ghoul?"

"Speaking of odds-plotting, I need your help. Are you doing anything for dinner tonight?"

"Matter of fact, I am. Remember when Dennis O'Brien, the retired FBI guy lectured here a couple of weeks ago?"

"Uh-huh. We spoke at lunch about our sleuthing games. He seemed interested in what we had to say."

"Turns out, he took it one step farther. Called a high-powered law enforcement guy in Israel, of all places. Fellow named Ezra Caen. What's with the look, Ron?"

"Ezra Caen." It was a statement, not a question.

"You know him??

"I know *of* him. I read about him in the *New York Times* on line a couple of years ago. Supposed to be the best counterterrorist in the world. He was the one who foiled the plot to assassinate the Ayatollah."

"How did Dennis O'Brien ever get to meet someone like that?"

"I haven't the faintest idea. All I know is Dennis called me a week ago and told me he'd run our ideas by Mister Caen, that the man had to be in the D.C. area for some business, and that he wanted to meet us."

"You're serious?"

"I am. He got in about ten this morning and we're supposed to go to dinner in an hour. Doesn't Dana have her Wednesday night bridge game this evening?"

"Yeah."

"Why don't you join Ezra and me? I'm sure he wouldn't mind 'cause Dennis O'Brien told me he wanted to meet us to talk about our theory."

"I'll give Dana a call," Ames replied, extracting his cell phone. "No reason we can't give Mister Caen the full treatment.

To see Ezra Caen on the street would have been to have forgotten him a moment later. He was an unprepossessing man of fifty, five-and-a-half feet tall, and lean. His carefully dyed hair was dark, but he hadn't bothered to disguise a balding crown prevalent in males his age and older. Ezra Caen's slightly rumpled appearance and his bifocals were neither stylish nor flattering. In short, he was everyman, not as everyman liked to portray himself, but as everyman truly was.

Three days before, Dennis O'Brien had telephoned Savage and told him what to expect. He'd added, "Don't let Caen's mild looks deceive you, Jeff. Everywhere he's worked, they refer to him as 'the plodder.' He comes off as mild-mannered, deferential, even a bit overwhelmed by people, but they seem to tell him things they wouldn't tell anyone else, and when the bad guys find themselves convicted and in prison, they would never have believed he was the one responsible."

Jeff Savage and Ron Ames met Caen in the reception area of the Montclair House, where Ezra was staying, and they seemed comfortable with one another from the first handshake. At dinner in the Montclair's lounge, conversation was amiable.

"Is this your first trip to Hamilton University, Mister Caen?" Ames opened.

"First to the university, but I've been to the States several times in the last decade. While we're at it, shall we drop the Mister This and Mister That and use first names? I'm game if you guys are."

"Sure thing," Jeff rejoined. "Did Dennis tell you anything about our computer games?"

"In generalities," the older man responded. "He said something about a higher number of strange deaths than usual among high-and-mighties. Both Dennis and I have wrestled with conspiracy theories for so many years that our bullshit meters have gotten pretty sensitive, but we've also learned to consider the evidence before shooting off our mouths."

"I'm glad you said that," Ames said.

"Have you talked to anyone else yet?" Caen asked.

"No, Ezra, for the exact reason you just pointed out. We've got pretty respectable jobs, but even in academia the powers-that-be don't want to get the reputation of employing a bunch of looney tunes."

"Like the old Bugs Bunny cartoons?" Jeff cut in.

"Ah, yes, Warner Brothers'1950s answer to Disney's Mickey Mouse."

"You really remember that stuff?" Savage asked, aghast.

"Nope. By the time I was born that was passé even in South Africa."

As they finished their meal, Ames said, "Ezra, I don't know how eager you are to look at what we've got, but this is my wife's 'girls' night out,' and if you've got the time, this is the evening Jeff and I generally play explorer. D'you think you might want to join us over at my house for some boys' fun and games?"

"I don't see why not. I'd be interested in knowing if I'm dealing with a couple of looney tunes or if what you've found may be as intriguing as Dennis seems to think it is."

4

The Ames home, twenty minutes' drive from the Montclair House, was nestled among gently rolling hills. Like planned communities all over the United States, as many houses as possible were squeezed onto a minimum plot of land. The development, which had been conceived and built by a major insurance company, boasted common greens, artificial lakes, and a community center, complete with swim-gym, tennis courts, two Olympic-sized swimming pools with adjacent kiddie pools and hot tubs, and several large clubrooms.

By seven-fifteen, Dana had left on her half-minute drive to the conference center and the three men had retired to the den. One wall was covered with charts stuck to it with pushpins. Two computers, their fans humming quietly, sat next to each other on a double-sized desk. Ezra had brought his own laptop to the meeting and Ames and Savage had connected him to their programs.

After awhile, Savage asked Ezra, "I assume you've seen the reports about the increase in political killings?"

"Political killings are a dime a dozen everywhere. To tell you the truth, I hadn't really noticed."

"There's been a threefold increase over last year in political killings or suicides during the last three months. Since I have access to the insurance companies' private databases, I can pull up a lot of private information. Look at these figures, Ezra. See if you notice anything out of place."

	January-March This Year	January-March Last year	Entire last year
Murders or suicides With apparent direct Political connections worldwide:	29	8	40
Deaths where close Associates of those who died were found dead less than a week later:	22	1	5
Deaths noted above where suspect was immediately identified and taken into custody:	7	4	33
Deaths noted above where the suspect taken into custody denied killing the victim:	7	1	13
Deaths noted above where the suspect passed all known lie detector tests	7	0	0

"Looks a little bit unusual," Caen remarked.

"Maybe more than a little bit. All seven killers were positively identified by eyewitnesses. The police didn't even have to obtain a confession. Yet in each case, the suspects not only denied being involved in the deaths, but every test they took supported their statements."

"There's all kinds of reasons for that."

"Not that often and not in such close proximity. The chance of twenty-two people involved in twenty-nine deaths dying within a week of those deaths seems more than coincidental."

"Perhaps, but I still don't see enough figures to excite me. Not yet, anyway."

"So, you're willing to give it some more thought?" Ames asked.

"If you mean would I be willing to be withhold my judgment until I have more information, I can only go so far as to say I'd be receptive to more data."

"I'm glad you committed even to that. In the last couple of days I've learned of one other death that ties in with the others, immediate identity of the suspect—by her own mother in fact—and complete denial followed by the suspect passing all tests. The only difference here was that the victim was no one with political connections. In Winchester Township, about a hundred miles from here, an eight-year-old girl, Melissa Roth stabbed her father in the throat."

"Sounds like a job that could easily be handled by the local constabulary."

"Yes, but they have a micro-view of the universe. They investigate whatever affects their own little corner of the world. Both Ron and I believe there's more to this story than meets the eye."

"Ever hear of your FBI? As in Dennis O'Brien?"

"He's retired."

"So am I."

"From what he tells me, if I went to them with this information, they'd brush me off with a 'Thank you so much, Professor Savage, we'll call you when we know anything for sure. No, you don't have to bother to call us back, we'll call you.'"

"Maybe, maybe not."

"As an actuary, I gather a whole lot of information, then make one blind leap of faith, and give the insurance company my guess on the odds. I'm working on a huge hunch. I think there's something very strange here. Something that might be far bigger than Ron or I suspect."

"Just a hunch?" Ezra asked.

"How long has it been since you've done anything exciting?"

"Five, six months."

Caen returned to his computer and studied the figures once again. Just a hunch they'd said. But neither Ames nor Savage seemed the type to go out on a limb and saw the limb off the tree. They spoke simply, without any salesman's pitch or unsupportable conclusions.

For more years than he'd care to admit, Ezra Caen had relied on hunches when others dismissed them. There was something about this handful of figures that seemed more compelling than he thought they'd be.

And what if there was something to what they'd said?

"Tell you what, gentlemen. I'll be here another week visiting Dennis. If anything comes up in that week, you can reach me at Dennis's home. After that, I'll be in Tel Aviv. Here is my private number."

THREE MONTHS EARLIER

5

Like most men, Charles Flanders Cunningham liked toys with moving parts. Unlike most men, he had the means with which to indulge himself. Of his many worldly possessions, his single-engine 1963 Cessna 205 Stationair—the TLC—was his favorite. He had said more than once that he would sooner give up sex than give up his plane. His wife, Margaret, believing him, came up with the name TLC. If he gave her half the tender loving care he gave it, she said, she'd be more than satisfied.

By sheer coincidence, shortly before he'd purchased it, he'd become secretly involved with the Trilateral Commission; in fact, he had used that involvement to rationalize—if only to himself—the purchase of the plane. Amused by the irony, particularly since only he would understand it, he'd had the letters TLC painted on the nose of the Cessna.

The Stationair didn't have sleek lines or retractable gear, and it was an orphan. The geniuses in Wichita had built four hundred sixty-two Stationairs during 1963 and 1964. Then they'd quit making them. Just like that.

They'd replaced the 205 with something called the 206, but it wasn't the same, he thought. It was exactly different. The 206 had a larger engine that gulped half again as much fuel as the 205, not that expense was any object to him. It didn't go any faster, nor did it have the large-wheeled, heavy-duty landing gear that made the 205 look so ungainly. Most of all, it just plain wasn't as much *fun* to fly as the Stationair.

Now, Cessna wasn't even making single-engine aircraft anymore. Incredibly high jury verdicts by salt-of-the-earth men and women who thought all small planes were death traps had made manufacturer's insurance impossible to obtain. Building single-engined aircraft had become so risky that the company was all but bankrupt. Even today, Textron Aviation, which produces aircraft designated as Cessnas in China, blanches any time a Cessna, even one built sixty years ago, goes down. Unlike automobiles, trial lawyers have managed to convince juries that light airplanes are supposed to keep flying forever. Miraculously, for the most part they do, so long as their engines are replaced every two thousand hours and corrosion hadn't set in.

Cunningham had made certain his green-and-white six-seater had been pampered throughout its life. He'd hangared it, had it meticulously painted every five years to preserve its skin, and cared for it as if it were his only son. The Stationair looked as if it had just rolled off the assembly line.

From ten thousand, five hundred feet above the rainforest of eastern Congo, it was hard to believe he was traveling one hundred fifty miles per hour over the ground. He had a greater sensation of speed when he drove the Land Rover ten miles an hour over a rutted road.

He'd departed nearly three hours ago, at sunup. Before takeoff, he'd removed the rear seats and installed the eighty-gallon inboard reserve tank, which ensured he'd have enough fuel for the round trip.

Charles Cunningham did not trust the garbage they'd have available at Kamina, most likely stale automotive fuel sent upriver from the capital. He smiled wryly as he remembered his flight instructor's words, "It's probably all right to use plain old auto gas in the plane. Nine times out of ten you'll be just as safe as if you used AvGas." No, thank you. Better to carry his own fuel, brought in by private aerial tankers.

December 22 was a typical midsummer's day at Kamina, blazing sun, a slight wind coming out of the east, temperature in the low eighties. The town was located at eight degrees, five minutes south latitude, twenty-five degrees east longitude. A branch of the Lavat River, not much more than a sluggish wash, debouched into the muddy Komami River, a mile south of this provincial backwater.

Just after ten thirty, Cunningham greased the aircraft onto the short runway at fifty miles per hour, bringing it to a stop fifteen hundred feet later, then taxied toward the rickety, wooden terminal building. He spotted two other planes on the field, a dust-caked, red-and-white Skyhawk parked in front of a small Quonset hut adjacent to the terminal, and an ancient DC-3, its nose pointed high, facing the runway, ready to taxi out and take to the skies, the words, "Air Shaba," painted in faded gray on the side of the fuselage. He'd flown into this field each December for the past twenty years. He'd wager the Goony Bird hadn't moved in the past decade. The flaking, peeling paint on the sign outside the terminal read, "Kamina, Congo, Elevation 1,115 meters."

Cunningham descended from the Stationair and walked stiffly toward a short, plump black man dressed in a cream-colored suit, a size too small for him, that did not conceal the fresh perspiration stains at the armpits. The two men embraced and kissed one another's cheeks, Continental-style, as they'd done at this time every year for the past two decades.

Each had grown old gracefully. More important to their own welfare, each had advanced quietly—and safely—into the highest echelons of power and influence.

"So, we renew the lease again, Mister Minister?" the tall Caucasian said in French, the formality belied by a wink.

"Indeed, my friend," the silver-haired Black replied. As he looked at the deposit book from the Union Bank of Switzerland, its number matching the one in his wallet, his eyes widened. "I see you have increased the annual payment by fifty thousand."

"Only appropriate, Guillaume. It's not every day one deals with the interior minister himself."

"I'm grateful, Flanders," the minister replied. "Those in the new government who hold the purse strings watch ever more vigilantly where money goes. Our revered egalitarian leader promises more reforms each month. It becomes harder than ever for a servant of the people to arrange for retirement. It never ceases to amaze me that you continue to make any payment at all. Any nation on the continent would cheerfully give you land and facilities for nothing."

"You flatter me, Guillaume," Cunningham said. "Don't worry, it's well worth what I pay you. Every man needs privacy. Unless you're in my position, you can hardly realize how much it means to be able to get away—totally away—from the world, to have more land than the whole country of Liechtenstein to yourself."

"Alone?" The black man chuckled. "You house three hundred of our poorest malnourished orphans at a time. The Children's Institute is the largest, best-equipped hospital in Central Africa, years ahead of anything we've got in the capital."

"The Institute occupies two square miles. The rest is truly mine. A very small price to pay, Guillaume."

"My people say that for a man to argue over whether or not he owns land is like a group of fleas arguing over which one owns the dog."

"Well, said, my friend, but my little bit of the dog is well fenced, well protected and, thanks to you, well insulated from the outside world. Cigarette, Guillaume?" he asked, holding out a pack of Marlboros.

"Thank you, yes. We rarely see American cigarettes except on the Kinshasa black market."

"Follow me out to the plane," Cunningham said, smiling. When they got there, he opened the baggage door and handed the appreciative minister four cartons of Marlboros, then glanced at the plain, functional Rolex on his left wrist. The minister caught the hint immediately. "Must you take off so soon?"

"I'm afraid so, Guillaume. I've got less than an hour to climb to altitude before ground winds make things unpleasant on takeoff. Do you plan on getting back to the capital in that Air Shaba luxury liner?" he said, pointing toward the ancient DC-3.

"That coffin wouldn't get me as far as the next village. Its engines haven't turned for the past eight years. No, my friend. The 737 our government requisitions from Air Congo every so often will bump along the cobblestoned skies of our beautiful homeland until it puts me down in Kananga. Next week that same jet will pick me up in Lumumbashi. I still can't understand why you'd want to meet at Kamina."

"Privacy."

"Ah, yes, your privacy," the black man murmured. "How are things at the Preserve? It's been five years since I've been there."

"You've always got an open invitation."

"You and I are close enough that we need not mince words. It discomforts me to see my countrymen posturing as slaves to the great, white 'bwana.' You insist on reliving the life of a 'Massa' in the *antebellum* south of your own country. Not that I begrudge you that. It's just that I need not be part of it."

The white man felt the hairs prickle uncomfortably on his forearms. "As long as they all know it's a game, what harm does it do, eh, Guillaume?" he said smoothly. "Those 'slaves' are paid five times what they'd make working anywhere else in Congo, not to mention the food and clothing they manage to steal when my back is conveniently turned."

"Ah, yes, the white man's burden," M'bele murmured. "But come, my friend, I've neglected my manners and I truly apologize. You may yet see me at the door of your Preserve, humble though it may be." The last remark broke the tension and they laughed, two old comrades quite a way down life's long road.

"Apology unnecessary, Guillaume. It's always good to see you, but I must be getting back to my little part of the dog."

6

In the twenty years he'd been doing business with Guillaume M'bele, no uninvited guest had crossed the frontiers of Charles Cunningham's private preserve. The minister made certain the local tribesfolk firmly believed there were evil spirits in the mountains north of Manono, and that to cross the Lavat River would almost certainly mean joining one's ancestors immediately. On the other hand, the Children's Institute, just south of Manono, dispensed very good medicine indeed. The poorest, sickest orphans, the unwanted, came to the white man's hospital, where many were miraculously cured.

Three hours, fifteen minutes northeast of Kamina, he spotted the red tile roofs and white buildings of the Institute, standing out in bold relief against the green and dun rolling hills below. The U-shaped main building housed a two-hundred-bed hospital that would attract any physician or surgeon of worth in the world. From its direct visualization cholangiopancreatoscopy system to its four state-of-the-art operating theaters, the Institute would have been a showpiece anywhere.

The main building was surrounded by a series of smaller units— the Orphans' Residence and the School. Children who would otherwise have been illiterate ciphers, sucking at the thin blood of a poor nation, obtained a first-class education. The school had one computer terminal for every student, a gymnasium that had produced four Olympic bronze medalists, and a vocational training facility that would have aroused envy

---

in the boardrooms of many Fortune 500 companies. What was more impressive still, the Preserve's ample endowment fund provided its graduates
with full scholarships to attend universities throughout the world.

Erecting these facilities in the foothills of eastern Congo had not
been cheap, but it had been more than worth it, he thought. It was his
Maginot line, defending the outer perimeters of his empire. No one
crossed the thin ribbon of river that was now passing immediately below
his aircraft.

Cunningham adjusted the constant speed propeller so that it beat
a smooth, quiet twenty-one hundred RPM, and switched to both fuel
tanks in preparation for landing. The Cessna's high wings shielded his
head from the sun, provided shade in the cockpit while flying, and gave
him an almost unlimited view of the ground. More important, unlike the
more rakish-looking low-winged aircraft, which required electric pumps
to ensure that fuel reached the engine, the Stationair provided AvGas
by the simple expedient of gravity. Throughout his life, he had taken no
more risks than were reasonable and prudent.

Thirty-five miles north of the Institute, the 205's instruments
homed in on the GPS Radio from the Preserve's private airport. Moments
later, Cunningham spotted another large building, almost invisible, its
colors replicating those of the surrounding countryside with unerring accuracy. The Center. Exactly halfway between the Institute and the Preserve.

The plane dropped ten degrees of flap to lose altitude more quickly.
The man experienced a flash of intense anger. *The Trilateral Commission
had metamorphosed into something called "World Security Watch," but it was
only a change of name. The oh-so-high-and-mighty kings of the world still
ran the show, as they had for so many years. Sanctimonious bastards.* Twenty-
two years ago, he'd done everything possible to gain entry. There'd been
an opening. They couldn't help but invite him to join. From every con-
ceivable aspect, by exercise of logic, he should have been the unanimous
choice. Instead, they'd chosen that goddammed, snot-nosed fledgling just
because his last name was Rockefeller.

Actually, he thought, by rejecting him they'd done him and humanity a great service, for out of his rage and humiliation—discreetly

masked, of course, for that was how one operated in polite society—he'd conceived the idea of the Project.

The plane entered its final approach. Unlike the patchy, asphalt-and-dirt strip at Kamina, the runway at this field, unmarked on any charts, was a hundred-fifty-foot wide concrete boulevard that left a two-mile gash across the adjacent land. The airport was equipped with an all-weather instrument landing system, GPS-capability, high-intensity landing lights, tower and the latest development in radar.

When Cunningham landed, he noticed one of the periodic visitors, a super-long-range Boeing 767, unmarked except for the word "Luftleben" discreetly stenciled in small letters on its tail, parked at the terminal building. A smaller craft, a Cessna Citation XLS, sat in a large, open hangar. A third, unexpected sight, brought a broad grin to his face: an ancient DC-3, painted in the red, gold, and green colors of Congo's flag, bearing the bold logo, "*AIR SHABA TOO!*"

Cunningham shut down the engine and alighted from the Station-air. The youngest of his four associates, Hitoshi Kono, waited outside the boxlike terminal building, bowing in stereotype imitation of an Asian servant. "A most unworthy welcome, Potentate-Sama," the Japanese said humbly. "Your loyal servant seems to have misplaced the keys to yonder modern structure, and if I don't get in there within two minutes, I'm gonna' pee all over your red-carpeted entryway."

The taller man laughed out loud. "Does a serious word ever pass your lips?"

"Oh, yes, Papa-Sama, but only after I use the facilities."

"Just make sure you stay two paces behind and to the left of me," he said.

They entered the building together. From the outside, the rectangular, two-story structure looked like the kind of passenger terminal to be found at any of fifty regional airports in the United States. "It sure ain't like Des Moines," Kono said when it had been completed a decade ago. The ground floor contained executive suites, a central library, and a large bar stocked with the finest spirits.

"I'll call Shari to arrange for our transportation," Cunningham said. "Shall we take the tram?"

"I've got time on my hands," the Japanese responded. "Let's have the full treatment."

The upper floor housed a modern office complex, equipped with computers, scanners, image-producing cell phones, three one-bedroom suites, and a large, sumptuously furnished observation center. The air conditioning was so quietly efficient it could not be heard above the soft music that issued from the Bose acoustic sound wave speakers conveniently placed throughout the terminal.

Cunningham entered one of the offices and said, "7-2-3-5-1," without removing the handset from the base of the phone.

"Yes, sir?"

"Shari, I'm back. Kono is with me. Could you have M'tumba pick us up, please?"

"Of course, sir." Crisp, professional, no nonsense, filled with private warmth for the lord of the manor. His wish was her command, no questions asked. What a shame there weren't more women like her. Sharon Graham was the only other American at the Preserve, one of the few human beings he implicitly trusted. She had been his aide for nineteen years. At forty-four, she maintained a strikingly attractive figure and a lightly freckled face that still turned heads. She was punctiliously correct in her speech and manner, efficient, calm in any crisis. And damned good in bed.

The two men could have descended by elevator to the basement level of the terminal, taken the underground tram that connected the airport directly to the Residence, and been home within five minutes. Instead, they'd elected to take the extra time and the personal service that went with it.

Kono appeared in the doorway. "All set?"

"Our transport will be here in fifteen minutes."

"How about the rest?"

"They're due in tomorrow. I didn't think you'd arrive 'til then."

"You know me better than to assume the expected. My money says the nymphomaniac gets here first."

The tall man raised his eyebrows. "Rather a sexist way to talk about a colleague in today's politically correct world, isn't it?"

"If the shoe fits, wear it. Don't get me wrong, Charles, when it comes to brainwashing—"

"You *are* rather old fashioned," the man said. "The word 'brainwashing' went out some time ago. We've used the term 'programming' or 'intracranial reconstitution' for years."

"Brandy?"

Cunningham said, "5-1-5-3-2," then addressed his colleague. "Since we've got a quarter hour, we may as well be comfortable."

They adjourned to a corner of the conference room. Cunningham sat in an overstuffed, tan leather chair. Kono kicked off his brown loafers and sank into a dark-gray, fabric, swivel rocker. A white-maned black man, dressed in tuxedo, brought each a snifter of Courvoisier VSOP cognac. The host lifted his glass in silent toast. After several moments, Kono asked, "Do you mind if I make a few calls to make sure everything's in order back home?"

"Suit yourself." After his guest left the room, Cunningham gazed meditatively into his snifter. His thoughts went back twenty years, to the time when he'd first brought his four associates together.

Lee Chung Lien was an only child, whose father had honed a unique set of skills and knowledge during the years immediately following the Korean War. The Chinese government had used that knowledge to great advantage. Chung Lien was three years old in 1985 when her father was sent to a specialized laboratory in Liaoning Province, fifty miles from the North Korean border. During the next two years, he worked first hand with every technique developed by Chinese, Soviet, and German practitioners, on young human beings from a dozen nations.

Intracranial Reconstitution was in its infancy then. Its methods were crude by today's standards, but the Liaoning group made quantum leaps of knowledge.

From the very first, Chung Lien became fascinated with her father's work. He treated her more as a treasured student than a silly child. By the time the term 'brainwashing' gained a certain horrific popular appeal and wise men in the West began to take I.R. seriously, the Chinese were decades ahead of their Western counterparts and Lee Chung Lien, all four-feet-eleven inches and ninety-six pounds of her, was years ahead of most of her Chinese colleagues.

The tall man stood up, stretched, cracked his knuckles, and bent to touch his toes. He'd become stiff from sitting in the plane all day. After a few minutes, he gazed out the window and resumed his thoughts about Doctor Lee.

In 2003, he'd attended an international peace and trade conference in Shanghai. The Chinese had sent Lee Chung Lien, recently graduated from the university, as an observer. He had had a brief fling with the young woman, and although the conference ended in stalemated failure, as both sides seemed to know it would, he'd learned all about Chung Lien's other talents.

Just before he left Shanghai, he made her a business proposal, which she accepted immediately. At that time, Chung Lien was earning the equivalent of three thousand American dollars a year in *renminbi,* a currency that was not accepted outside of the Peoples' Republic, and the government provided her with a spartan, twelve-hundred-square-foot apartment in the middle of Beijing. Cunningham multiplied her earnings by a factor of one hundred, gave her a one-seventh share in the Project, unlimited funds and human beings to work with, and provided her with an elegant, fully furnished, five-thousand-square-foot villa in the middle of nowhere.

Kono reentered the room. "All done," he said.

"You know," Cunningham mused, "I've never regretted bringing Doctor Lee aboard. Despite her sexual, ah, proclivities, she's the ideal scientist in every sense of the word. There are no frontiers she won't cross."

"They said the same thing about Josef Mengele," the Japanese remarked mildly.

"Aren't you in an odd position to moralize, my friend?"

"I suppose you're right," Kono said, chuckling. "Who'd have thought I'd be where I am today? Forty-five years old and still having more fun than I ever thought I'd have. Not bad for a little kid born in Tokyo just after the Vietnamese war."

Cunningham looked out the window at the gaily-festooned aircraft in which Kono had arrived. He shook his head in wonder and smiled as he'd done so many times during the past two decades. He thought back to the time he'd met his youngest, brashest associate.

Hitoshi's parents were in their forties when their only child was born. His father had been a junior engineer at Toyo Kogyo, a small company that barely survived World War II and had started building a funny little tin-can car called the Mazda. His mother had been a classical singer of consequence before she married.

During the first seven years of his life, Hitoshi received as much love and affection as any child could hope to have. His world collapsed when his parents were killed in an automobile accident. Hitoshi was sent to the home of his maternal grandmother, who lived near the still-operational American Tachikawa Air Base.

Hitoshi Kono quickly learned not only American slang, but also how to deal with the denizens of New Rome. By the time Ronald Reagan was elected president of the United States, Hitoshi had ingratiated himself with the Americans in myriad ways. Did they want to meet a "nice" Japanese girl (or, perhaps one not so "nice")? No problem. Did they need to find a gift shop that wouldn't steal them blind? Young Kono was their man.

Although he might have gotten into the "right" schools had his parents survived, Kono knew that the way things now stood he'd never end up in the higher echelons of Sumitomo, Nissan, or Sony. Which, as it turned out, was a great loss to Sumitomo, Nissan, and Sony.

By the time he was in his mid-teens, in addition to his appealing charm, which had already landed him in bed with more than one bored American military wife, Hitoshi had an unparalleled penchant for organization. When he arranged for a client to shop anywhere within a fifty-mile radius of the base, he not only received a small rebate for himself, but ensured that his patron got his or her money's worth.

One of his lady friends, the wife of an Air Force colonel, goaded her husband into sponsoring Hitoshi's admission to UCLA. Kono capitalized on his good fortune by taking a degree in business administration in three years, with grades sufficient to earn him a postgraduate fellowship at Case Western Reserve under Professor Lupolo Nero, a pioneer in the field of organizational behavior.

By the time he'd graduated, Japanese industrialists were starting to see anyone from "Uncle Sugar" as a fat goose, waiting to be plucked. Hitoshi saw fat geese on *both* sides of the Pacific Rim.

It made sense to establish connections, not only in Japan and the United States, but also throughout Southeast Asia and Western Europe. Hitoshi eschewed involvement in day-to-day transfers, but made introductions, for a minuscule percentage of each shipment. Neither buyer nor seller ever felt cheated. After all, brokers had oiled the machinery of commerce for thousands of years.

"Every waterfall begins with a single drop of water," he often said. Soon the number of shipments from which he derived one-tenth of one percent was a torrent. By the time his twenty-fifth birthday rolled around, he was a multi-millionaire, but still single and bored.

"When you answered that ad twenty years ago, you certainly announced your arrival at Kamina in style. A candy-striped, chartered Skylane from the capital," the tall man said, chuckling.

"Huh?" the Japanese said.

"I was just thinking out loud. Hitoshi, have you ever regretted joining us?"

"Never."

"Nor I. Over the years you've surprised, delighted, and often frustrated me, but you've always delivered the goods in spades."

"Speaking of which— "

The master of The Preserve rolled his eyes in feigned exasperation as he watched the arrival of the carriage and six. The driver, M'tumba, looked like a coachman born a hundred years too late. He had iron-gray hair and was anywhere between fifty and death.

When the two men emerged from the door, the servant was all smiles and obsequiousness. Like nothing so much as a caricature from *Gone with the Wind* Charles thought.

God, was he really so old he remembered back that far? Before the war. Well, he smiled inwardly, not *quite* that old. He'd been born in 1958, thirteen years after the war, and when he was growing up, the movies had kept him enthralled on many Saturday afternoons.

His mind raced back. World War II had been the last honest-to-God, worthwhile war where there really were identifiable good guys and bad guys. John Wayne and Humphrey Bogart, Marilyn Monroe and Jayne Mansfield with that incredible chest. Gregory Peck in *Twelve O'Clock High*—what a tragedy he'd died back in 2003—eighty-seven certainly wasn't *that* old. It had been such a simple world back then. Where had it all gone so wrong? We'd been a nation whose hero had been Bill Holden, not Kanye West. Cunningham forced himself to return to the present.

M'tumba drove the horse-drawn carriage down the freshly paved road. The way wound through rolling savanna and climbed into richly forested highland. Just beyond the eight-hundred-meter elevation sign, the coachman turned onto a side road and entered an anachronistic scene out of the nineteenth century. A canopy of magnolia trees led to an oak plank gate in the middle of a twelve-foot high rock wall.

As they entered the portal, Kono whistled appreciatively. "This place gets more luxurious every time I see it! You must have three hundred acres of green lawn leading up the hill to the house."

"More or less, Hitoshi. When were you last here?"

"Six months ago."

"We've added the umbrella pines, twin rose gardens and a small orchard of dwarf fruit trees since then," he said, as they drove along the quarter-mile entry leading to the Manor.

The residence building, an imposing, neo-classical edifice, dominated the hill, its ivy-covered walls proclaiming agelessness. Kono knew the entire complex had been built less than fifteen years before.

"Would you mind if we walked to my quarters?" Hitoshi asked, as the carriage wheels crunched over the semicircular gravel driveway adjacent to the front entrance. "I need to get my blood circulating after sitting around all day."

"My pleasure," his host responded. They alighted from the conveyance. M'tumba clucked his tongue and the horses started toward the stable in the distance.

Cunningham was glad his associate had chosen to walk to the guest quarters. Although he was in his sixties, he maintained himself in top physical condition through a regimen of reasonable exertion. He hated the grunting and sweating of the gym and had given up that barbaric means of torture several years ago. In the past few months, he'd cut back on tennis, particularly after he'd read an article which claimed that the Swiss, who ate a diet rich in all manner of fats, had fewer heart attacks than most people in other western nations because they walked so much.

Something about the thighs being the largest muscles in the body and generating the greatest blood circulation.

The area at the rear of the mansion differed from the well-manicured front lawn. "My own Villa d'Este," he remarked to Kono, as they strolled through a walled forest of umbrella pines, rivulets, lakes, and rococo statuary, surrounded by the relaxing sound of splashing water.

"How many fountains are there?"

"Seven hundred, all gravity-fed. Not one mechanical pump. Even on the hottest days, it's more than tolerable."

Beyond the fountains the area featured sumptuous, multicolored orchid gardens, topiary, and small ponds stocked with rainbow trout, a park reminiscent of Vienna's Schönbrunn, precise down to the replica of the Belvedere statue half a mile from the manor house.

They weren't even breathing hard by the time they'd breasted the gently undulating hills and reached the eight villas strung like a necklace around the perimeter of the estate. Each house was constructed in a different style. Each contained five thousand square feet of living space, a swimming pool, Jacuzzi, and sauna.

It was paradise on earth, less than twenty miles as the crow flies, yet an entire universe away from, the Center.

Kono's Japanese-style house surrounded a central courtyard, exposed to the elements. "I haven't exactly planned your first evening here, since, as usual, you appeared rather unexpectedly," his host said, as they entered the villa together. "Were you in the mood for a kimono-clad Japanese maiden or a healthy, blonde California girl?"

"Surprise me," Kono answered.

"Why not both?"

Kono and Cunningham walked through the house, out to the courtyard. Designed by one of Japan's premier artist-aesthetes, it bespoke profound simplicity, nobility, and peace.

"Ah, Papa-sama, don't worry," the younger man said. "I am quite capable of entertaining myself. I'll probably spend the evening sitting on a tatami mat, meditating in complete serenity, and thinking about tomorrow."

"Right," his host said with a grin. "Will I see you for breakfast?"

"I guarantee it." He chuckled. "Sayonara, Papa-sama."

7

Cunningham rolled over and away from the woman and slept for an hour. It was dark when he awoke. He tossed and turned, trying in vain to find a comfortable position.

"Tomorrow?" she asked, sensing his discomfort.

"Yes."

"Do you want to talk about it?"

"You're sure you're not too tired?"

"I'm sure I can accommodate my lord and master's desire to talk," she said. She turned on the bedside lamp adjacent to the night table.

He rose, wrapped himself in a silk dressing gown, and walked to the nearest window. In the darkness, the dim planter bulbs from the garden below stretched almost to the horizon, a miniature city of lights. He turned and looked back into the room. Oak, walnut, teak, and mahogany. Soft, recessed lighting in one corner of the bedroom afforded a perfect setting for the two Rembrandts, the Tiepolo, the El Greco, and the small Hieronymus Bosch triptych. With the exception of the French Impressionists—he had a superb Monet, a Manet, a Degas, and three Van Goghs scattered throughout the mansion—not a damned thing of any value had been painted much after eighteen sixty.

Most of the furnishings in the room had been at Versailles the same year Marie Antoinette played milkmaid. He returned to the bed. Shari arranged the goose down bolster pillows to provide him with added support.

"All my life, I've been the ultimate insider and, conversely, the ultimate outsider, the man presidents and politicians turn to when they want wise, sympathetic counsel. The éminence grise who's embodied the American governing class. Ninety-nine percent of the people in the United States wouldn't recognize my name if they heard it.

"I've got all the right credentials, Harvard Law Review, senior partner in one of the world's most influential firms, governor of the Agency for International Development—"

"I can name a dozen more things you've been and done," she said, gently stroking his iron-gray hair.

"But how much of it really is my doing? What would my grandpa have said?"

"He'd have been proud of you, Flan. You're everything he wanted to be."

"That old reprobate?" the man said, his face relaxing for the first time. "God knows he kicked ass on his way up. Talk about being born on the wrong side of the tracks. He couldn't even have heard the train from where he was. Now there was a tough bugger who didn't give a damn what the world thought. I wonder what the Lowells, Cabots, and Lodges we number among our clients would think if they knew how that old bastard really made his money?"

"I doubt they've got enough blood left in their patrician veins to give it a thought. You might be servant class to them, but you've got enough money to buy and sell them a dozen times."

"What if the project fails, Shari? There goes my whole life's ambition." His head dropped back against the pillow for support.

"Don't you think that's pushing it? You'd be left with ten *billion* dollars, a law firm that takes in five million a month, not to mention the ownership of all his lordship surveys."

"Getting where I am wasn't hard, with a five-hundred-million-dollar nest egg at a time when money still meant something. Dear, lovable, weak-sister dad had the good grace to die politely at fifty, before he screwed up the firm or spent too much of what the old man left him."

"And all you managed to do was multiply what you had by a factor of twenty."

"Hensleigh's opposed to the Plan."

"He can't stop you," Shari said, moving her hand down his shoulder. "I doubt he'd try. After twenty years down the road together, you're all in the rather unenviable position of mutual trust or mutual blackmail."

"Artfully put." Cunningham turned to face his aide and lover.

"I've had a good teacher in more things than one." She smiled lasciviously. "As usual, you'll end up on top."

Sunlight streamed into the bedroom by seven. He lay still, trying not to disturb the figure sleeping quietly next to him. He listened intently to the chirping of a thousand tropical birds as they went about the simple joys of their lives. Did birds have nervous breakdowns? Did they find themselves in loveless, childless marriages where their wives lived in a separate part of the world for months at a time?

He was sixty-two, almost too late for an heir. Grandpa would have looked askance at him. "Flan," he would have said, "if a woman had tried to do to me what Margaret did to you, I'd have kicked her ass out of my home a year after I'd married her. And don't give me that shit about you needed to marry into society or that she was the prettiest and smartest Radcliffe debutante of that year. When it gets down to the bottom line, you've got to be a team in everything, or you're nowhere. If sex is good, you can overlook a lot, but if you ain't gettin' any, you've got a lot of explaining to do, mostly to yourself."

He wondered what granddad would have thought about Sharon Graham. He hadn't been surprised when he found out, shortly before the old man's death, that gramp had had a "special friend" for the last thirty years of his life. Father would never have understood, of course. He'd married young and been pussy-whipped all his life.

Grandpa had tried to warn Flan early on, when he had been courting Margaret. He'd ignored the old man's words. Grandpa'd been born with the dinosaurs. The world had changed. Bullshit, he thought, as he glanced over at Sharon. The more things change, the more they stay the same. *Until today, grandpa. Until today.*

Shari stirred and snuggled into his leg. "Time to get up, lover?" she mumbled, half asleep.

"Yeah, Mizz Graham," he said. "Time to sneak off to your own quarters lest the domestics get suspicious." Ever since she'd been at the Preserve, they'd played the game of, "We mustn't let the servants know." The household staff knew enough to keep their own counsel. What the Master did was his business. Had he slept with a baboon or one of the stabled horses they wouldn't have lifted an eyebrow.

Shortly after Shari left, there was a sharp knock on his door. "Good morning, Regina," he called cheerfully. "You may enter."

"Thank you, sir." Jet black, stern-visaged, forty-five-year-old Regina, whose last name he didn't even know, had been widowed ten years ago, just before she'd come to work at the Manor. She hadn't really asked for the job; she simply assumed it was hers, and appeared promptly at eight in the morning the day after she'd been interviewed, attired in a starched, white outfit. Since that time, he'd never seen her wear anything else. The other servants cowered when she walked by. It was obvious she considered herself the queen among a lesser grade of humans.

She walked directly into his bath area with barely a nod in his direction. She always made him feel he was in the presence of a sharp-tongued mother superior or a stern, spinster teacher. One of these days, he thought, I am going to get out of this bed buck-naked before she leaves, just to see what she does. But in ten years, he hadn't dared do so. He'd pictured a hundred times the withering look she'd give him. He did not need additional discomfort in his life. Better just to play the game and let Regina do her thing.

She emerged from the bathroom. "You may proceed," she said curtly, and left, closing the door soundlessly behind her. She was a witch, but a good one. He knew that when he went into the bath, he'd find freshly pressed, warmed bath towels, a facial cloth, a fresh bar of his favorite soap, a full bottle each of French shampoo and Australian hair conditioner, and a long-handled luffa.

He placed one of the towels on a side bar, pressed three buttons. The electronic door slid open. No sooner had he entered the shower then five shower heads, one directly above and one each at his front, back, and two sides, pelted him with fine, needle-thin jets of water, thermostatically preadjusted to his preferred temperature. The man luxuriated in the warmth of the shower for three minutes, then pressed the "off" button. The door reopened and he emerged to the automatic glow of five gentle heat lamps, placed in similar position to the showerheads.

Regina had turned on the sauna room adjacent to the shower when she'd made her morning rounds. Undoubtedly it would be warmed to one hundred eighty-five degrees, its wood sides freshly scrubbed to maximize the birch, camphor and eucalyptus aromas within. He lay supine on the smooth, wooden bench, his head cushioned on a fleece pillow, for several minutes until he felt his muscles loosen and the salts and sleep leave his body. Then he reentered the shower after pressing the appropriate buttons.

He applied the rich shampoo, rinsed, then rubbed the aromatic jojoba conditioner into his scalp, soaped and soaked his body. Afterward, with towel around his lean, hard midriff, he shaved, glancing at his image in the large, gilt-edged mirror. "Not too shabby," he murmured, grinning at the reflection of a man still striking by any standards. "Not too shabby at all."

8

———— ▸◂ ————

Cunningham emerged half an hour later, adorned in khaki shorts, shirt, and safari hat. Kono and Sharon joined him for breakfast on the closed-in veranda, which was kept at a constant sixty-eight degrees year 'round. The air was fresh with the delicate scent of orchids. The wall opposite the screened portion of the room had a floor-to-ceiling waterfall. The constant chirping of birds punctuated their conversation. A servant brought them freshly-baked croissants, smoked white fish, olives, feta cheese, rose petal jam, and steaming mint tea.

"Any news about when they'll be here?" Cunningham asked his aide.

"Prasad's expected to arrive from Johannesburg later this morning."

"What about Chung Lien?"

He saw the sour look on Sharon's face. There had been bad blood between Shari and Chung Lien from the first. "Doctor Lee spent the better part of last week in the Seychelles, obviously not working on her tan," she said, with thinly veiled sarcasm.

"Don't worry about Chung Lien, Ms. Graham," Hitoshi said. "She's probably exhausted even her own libido by making those huge, willing natives into the most wonderful lovers imaginable."

Sharon glared balefully at her boss. "Probably caught some sort of social disease."

————

"There's no room in this project for taking potshots at colleagues, Ms. Graham," Cunningham snapped. "We are a team. I want to know when Doctors Lee and Hensleigh are arriving."

"We've sent the Gulfstream to get them," Sharon replied, chastened. "They probably won't get here 'til five o'clock."

"How come so late?"

"The Gulfstream left for the Seychelles at dawn. Hensleigh was delayed in London last night. British Airways only got out this morning. The Gulfstream will land at Nairobi for refueling and wait for him there. He and Doctor Lee will make the last leg of the trip together."

"Damn!" the man pounded his fist on the table. "Why couldn't he have chartered a flight for once in his stingy life?"

"Come on, Charles," Hitoshi said, trying to lighten the tension. "Asking Will Hensleigh to change his habits would be like trying to teach a pig to sing. It wouldn't work, and it would annoy the pig."

The remark had its desired effect. Each had his or her own particular Will Hensleigh story. Like any oddball member of a group, he provided comic relief.

William Hensleigh was a thorough, fastidious man who wanted everything in its place, on time, precisely as ordered. When he was very young, his mother had purchased seven pairs of underdrawers for him, each marked with a different day of the week. This had pleased him. By the time he'd entered public school, such a thing would have made him a laughingstock, but his habits were as ingrained as though they'd been etched into little grooves in his brain. Will bought into the program of English society with a vengeance. English society, in return, paid him precisely the rewards due a diligent, nose-to-the-grindstone scholar.

When he was seventeen, Hensleigh had decided to become a neurosurgeon. He'd made that election based on reasonable, practical grounds. Medicine was well suited to his nature. As long as he was going to engage in that profession, he may as well stand on the top rung of its societal ladder. At the bottom were generalists and pediatricians, little more than witch doctors who held the hands of old ladies, crazy people, or sloppy young mothers on the National Health program who brought in dirty, malignant children, nasty little savages who sneezed and coughed all over you and had the manners of pigs.

Next up the ladder were physicians—internists, proctologists, gynecologists, obstetricians. Theirs was a messy job that involved digging around in obscene personal places.

Surgeons were the *real* doctors, of course. The more specialized they were, the higher echelon they occupied in the opinion of their colleagues. Neurosurgery and cardio-thoracic surgery stood at the apex of the profession. William Hensleigh was not interested in the heart, since it was nothing more than a large pump. One might have suggested, only half in jest, that this was because Will did not have much of a heart himself. By process of elimination, that left neurosurgery.

His decision made, he set about in as precise a fashion as he knew how, to achieve his goal. He attended the right public school. His grades earned him the right to attend a proper college at Oxford. Because he'd been fortunate enough to have been born in 1967, too late to have seen action in any war involving the Empire, Will found it unnecessary to delay his studies for something as mundane as military service.

"With your pick of the world's medical talent, what caused you to choose him?" Hitoshi asked.

"The fact that he was as brilliant as he was odd."

Early on, Will's father had experienced a mental depression and twice attempted suicide, unsuccessfully, but it rattled Hensleigh's perfect world. Will isolated a substance called corticotropin-releasing hormone, CRH. He demonstrated that CRH, when given in small doses, promotes vigilance and decreases interest in food, but when there's too much CRH in the system, there's a hyper-arousal, a permanent fight-or-flight response that creates anxiety and depression.

About that time, Sandoz synthesized clozapine, a drug that seemed to work wonders with schizophrenics and depressives. It was withdrawn after a small percentage of patients who'd taken it died of a sudden loss of white blood cells. Everyone in the medical community gave up on clozapine. Everyone except Will.

Hensleigh devised a theory that if one could inject a time-released, controlled portion of CRH and clozapine into the body, a supply that could be called up on demand, one could achieve control of passion, memory, or actions—anything that interfered with the mechanical perfection of the human machine.

"At thirty, Will became assistant professor at Brasenose College, Oxford," Cunningham mused. "This allowed him access to the world's finest laboratories at no cost. Two years later, he published his first paper on the theory of timed-release chemical implantation. His magnum opus was neither ridiculed nor hailed. To his extreme frustration, it was *ignored.*"

By everyone but me, Charles thought. He'd chanced upon Hensleigh's work by sheer accident, when he'd attended a conference of the Bio-Ethics Commission in London. He remained in England and went up to Oxford to meet the good doctor in person. Forty-eight hours after they'd met, they struck an agreement that had lasted two decades.

And that was how Will had become part of the Project.

Two nights ago, Rajendra Prasad had received a disturbing call from Will Hensleigh.

"Have you seen the Plan, Raj?"

"Are you sure we should be talking about it by telephone, Will? We're on an unsecure line."

"It's the only time we can talk before the meeting. Don't worry, Prasad, I won't compromise anyone. What do you think?"

"I'm not surprised by it, if that's what you mean."

"D'you think he can bring it off?"

"That's the gamble we all take, isn't it?"

He heard a slight wheeze at the other end of the line. Hensleigh's voice sounded uncharacteristically tense, his words delivered in a torrent much faster than usual. "Bloody immoral if you ask me."

"Don't tell me you never suspected?" There was no response. The Indian continued. "Will, we were not brought together because Charles thought we'd make good chums. Each of us was chosen for a reason. Did you ever wonder why you were ignored by the academy when your idea was twenty years ahead of its time? Or why Cunningham was able to give Doctor Lee the thing she needed more than anything else—total scientific and sexual freedom?"

"Why you, Raj? With your computer skills you could get a high-paying job anywhere."

"Not when he met me. Twenty-one years ago, my Cambridge degree in computer design didn't mean a damned thing. I was a very junior employee, working for Big Blue, living in Burnaby, just outside Vancouver. Do you have any idea what life's like for an East Indian there? I'll tell you. We have a bitter joke in Burnaby. An East Indian walks up to a Royal Canadian Mountie and asks, 'Excuse me, officer, can you tell me how to get to Princes Street or should I fuck myself now?' Worse yet, I was a smartass East Indian with a two-thousand-dollar-a-month paycheck and a twelve-hundred-dollar-a-month habit. I was within a millimeter of getting deported, and all I could think of was where I'd find my next fix."

"I didn't know. Are you sure you want to tell me this?"

"Why not? It might give you some idea why I owe Charles so much. Just about the time I was on my way out the door, IBM got involved in a lawsuit with Hitachi over an esoteric microchip. Charles Cunningham learned of my background and asked IBM to detach me so I could assist him on the case. I don't have to tell you how happy that made my bosses.

"Over the months, without judging me in any way, he asked if I really wanted to continue down the road I was going. I broke down and cried in his office. I really did.

"He paid for me to spend six weeks at a private detox center, another two months at a halfway house, and he never said a word to the IBM people. As far as they knew, I was working with him every day."

"It's hard to think poorly of someone like that, but don't you see the immorality of the Plan?"

Rajendra watched the relaxing images of fish swim across the monitor on his desk. "What's moral, Will? Does Israel think the Palestinians are moral? Do the Palestinians think the Israelis are moral? What did you think of the Irish Republican Army?"

"Bloody bunch of cutthroats."

"What do you suppose they think of you?"

"That's different."

"Oh?"

"What we've done over the years at the Preserve is truly reprehensible, now that I see where it's going."

"Is it?" the Indian asked sharply. "Cunningham gave you the same thing he gave me. You got to join a very select group of scientists in an adventure that stretched the boundaries of our intellects—and our morals, if you want to call it that—with a tax-free million dollar a year paycheck plus a one-seventh interest in the net profits of the Project, and the freedom to push back the frontiers of human knowledge with no limits. Rather a strange time for you to be moralizing, my friend."

"Well, I—"

Prasad could hear the doubt in Hensleigh's voice. "Think about it, Will." He reached over and gently set the phone back in its cradle.

Over the following nights, the Indian thought about what Hensleigh had said. Since the time he had accepted Flanders' offer, his soul had become enmeshed in the African project. He couldn't wait for the four months of every year he spent at the Center, supervising his portion of the work. He'd given up one addiction for another.

Rajendra Prasad was a small, unprepossessing man, who still felt discomfort at being the only passenger aboard the chartered Bombardier Challenger 350 that Cunningham had sent to pick him up at O.R. Tambo-Johannesburg International Airport. Despite the new government, now led by Cyril Ramaphosa after the resignation of the staggeringly corrupt Jacob Zuma, and despite Prasad's status as an international visitor whose annual income was over a million U.S. dollars a year, he knew he was nothing more than another "curry muncher" in the eyes of the poorest white Afrikaner. No matter he'd been schooled at Cambridge, no matter he was arguably one of the most brilliant computer geniuses on the face of the earth, to them he belonged in the Indian market and would never be a real human being.

Prasad silently loathed these six million ignorant whites, who'd managed to hold a nation of forty million hostages against the world, but, at the same time, he feared and admired their dogged determination, and had unprotestingly spent the last evening in Lenasia, the Asian section outside of Jo'burg, in the company of twenty-three cousins huddled in a two-bedroom house. They'd all insisted on coming out to O.R. Tambo to see him off and didn't quite understand why he'd been the only one to board the unmarked jet parked at the General Aviation terminal.

He explained that the jet had been sent by an American computer giant to bring him to a conference in London: "you know how the crazy Americans throw their money around." The explanation had satisfied them.

As the Bombardier took off, Rajendra Prasad glanced down and quickly lost interest in the monotonous brown landscape below. For the first hour, he played chess with the onboard computer. He did reasonably well, considering his opponent was an electronic Magnus Carlsen.

After he'd lost two games, he typed a series of keystroke commands into the computer. Within a few moments, he scrolled down the financials on the Project.

Cunningham's initial outlay: $ 700,000,000.00 (Loaned money to associates at 7% per annum). Initial participation of each partner:

Cunningham (3/7 of the operation)................ *300,000,000*
Prasad (1/7) *100,000,000*
Lee (1/7) *100,000,000*
Hensleigh (1/7).. *100,000,000*
Kono (1/7) .... <u>*100,000,000*</u>
                                                            $ 700,000,000

Less startup and development costs:
Construction costs -- compound........................ *50,000,000*
                      Airport 5,000,000
Children's hospital & institute.......................... *10,000,000*
Road construction *5,000,000*
Plant... *5,000,000*
Electric, gas, etc. installation........................... *15,000,000*
Contingency reserve... <u>*15,000,000*</u>
                      Total costs ....$ 105,000,000
Net available for use: *$ 595,000,000*

In the twenty years they'd been together, the annual return on income averaged fifteen percent, $ 89,250,000 per annum. Prasad noted the costs of doing business from the statements. Including the *Child-Finders* operation, which occupied the great bulk of outlay, it cost thirty million dollars a year, plus a million each to Chung Lien, Will, Hitoshi and himself, to keep the operation going. A few more keystrokes. The computer printed the following:

Income from Investments	*Expenses*	
Interest income ... $ 89,250,000	*Operations ... $ 30,000,000*	
	Principal reduction	
	on Charles loans	*8,000,000*
	Associates' salaries	*4,000,000*
$ 89,250,000	*$ 42,000,000*	

Available for distribution: $ 47,250,000
Available per 1/7 interest: $ 6,750,000

During the first years of the operation, Prasad recalled that in order to make up the deficit between the seven million in interest on his note and the available distribution, he'd had to give up $250,000 of his salary. Still, seven hundred fifty thousand a year was more than he'd ever seen in his life.

In 2009, the operations had started to yield income. Five hundred thousand dollars in each of the first two years. The project had produced five million dollars net income each year since 2010. Passive income supported the darker side. Prasad read over the current balance sheet. The present net worth of the operation was $2,100,000,000, which meant he was worth *three hundred million dollars*. Not bad for a boy from the slums of Calcutta.

After he finished his calculations, he took a nap and awoke refreshed when a crew member approached to tell him they'd be landing in less than half an hour. He looked down and saw they were over Lake Tanganyika. He willed himself into a self-guided meditation. He would be at peace when the plane landed.

The petite, middle-aged Chinese woman had totally enjoyed her five days in the Seychelles, sunning herself on Silhouette Island, gambling all evening at the vice dens of Victoria, and loving the nights away in the arms of handsome native men.

Her scientific practice had matured during the past two decades, she thought. Working with nearly eight hundred subjects from virtually every country on earth had provided her with an unprecedented living laboratory. Earlier in her career, Lee Chung Lien quoted the American inventor Thomas Edison, who'd said, "I've never had a failure; I have successfully demonstrated ten thousand times how to do a thing the wrong way." Nowadays, her mistakes had diminished, almost to nonexistence.

The Cessna Citation XLS had picked her up at Victoria Airport two hours ago. It was nearing noon in Kenya. Looking down, she saw the coast at Mombasa. In less than an hour, the plane would land at Nairobi to pick up the most totally asexual human being she'd ever met, and whisk them to the Preserve. The light vibration of the Citation felt good. She rubbed her thighs together in a motion that yielded very pleasant sensations indeed. Perhaps Charles would be good for some fun tonight if she were lucky, and if that red-headed cow were not around to interfere.

Had William Hensleigh known what Lee Chung Lien thought of his asexuality, it would not have disturbed him in the least. He would simply have accepted it as an accurate assessment. Hensleigh was not married, had never been married, and had no serious attachments, male or female. It wasn't a question of being homely, or of not having all the right appendages and equipment, nor was it a matter of lack of desire. It was simply that Will had properly and correctly loaded his life's plate with precisely the amount of activity he believed he could comfortably handle. An emotional attachment would hinder his getting things done in a fitting and prudent manner.

At the moment the Citation carrying Lee Chung Lien touched down at Nairobi, Will Hensleigh was thinking about how he'd voice his feelings to the others. Although the past two decades had resulted in unheard-of professional satisfaction and material wealth, he was disturbed by the Plan on two accounts. First, he thought it immoral. More important, he doubted the Plan would succeed. No undertaking of the type Cunningham proposed had ever worked in the past, and since it would not succeed, its failure would disturb the orderliness of his world.

It was the same logic that placed him on a commercial flight. Hensleigh saw no need to squander funds on such unnecessarily frivolous luxuries as chartering an aircraft, when British Airways could quite competently fly him to Nairobi tourist class for one-fiftieth the cost. Unfortunately, there'd been a freeze at Heathrow, last night. When coupled with the unavoidable shutdown of one of the runways at Cairo, this had caused an eight-hour delay. Hensleigh had insisted that British Airways agents text Nairobi to advise that he'd be late.

A reedy voice came over the Airbus 320's speakers, properly English, thank God. "Ladies and gentlemen, this is Captain Dunhill speaking. We're dreadfully sorry about the delays, and trust you'll understand. If you look out the porthole to your right, you'll see we're just making landfall. Cairo Tower has cleared us to land. We should be on the ground by ten thirty hours, local time. Please set your chronometers forward if you've not already done so. Thank you for your patience. We invite you to sit back and enjoy the rest of the flight."

Always obedient to authority, William Hensleigh glanced down at his left wrist and prepared to adjust his watch ahead. The timepiece showed eight-seventeen, Greenwich Mean Time. His last conscious thought as the explosion ripped through the plane, killing all one hundred forty-one passengers aboard, was, "This cannot be happening. If one plays by the rules, everything invariably comes out all right."

Cunningham walked into the small study and looked around. Kono and Prasad sat by a small table. They stopped talking and looked up when Flanders entered. Sharon Graham continued reading her novel until she heard him clear his throat.

"My friends," their host said, "I have some tragic news. The British Airways flight carrying Doctor Hensleigh exploded on its approach to Cairo Airport. The IRA and Hamas are both claiming responsibility."

Cunningham watched his colleagues' reactions. Prasad's face turned as white as his jacket. Kono reached for a tumbler of scotch. Sharon nearly dropped her book. Flanders continued, "His death is a great loss to us all. If there is any consolation, it is that he taught his techniques to the many fine surgeons here. His work will be continued."

Prasad and Kono exchanged meaningful glances. They didn't for a moment believe that the explosion was an accident. But there was nothing they could say or do except move forward, lest they themselves fall victim to similar misfortune.

9

Promptly at eight-thirty, the guests gathered in an intimate conference room. Cocoa colored leather chairs surrounded a mahogany table. Charles Cunningham sat at its head, Sharon immediately to his left. "Each of you has read the details of the Plan," he said. "Are there any questions?"

"Yes, Charles," the Chinese woman said. "Why now, at this moment? We've got a most lucrative business going. You could take a thirty percent annual return on your investment with no difficulty whatever."

"Are you opposed to the Plan, Doctor Lee?" There was the barest hint of coldness in his tone.

Lee returned Cunningham's frostiness. "Would I be here if I were?"

Kono and Prasad shot sidelong glances at one another. The unspoken message in the room was that Hensleigh was *not* here.

"I simply wanted to know why it was imperative that we start immediately," she continued.

"What better time?" their host replied. "The world's gone mad. Things simply cannot continue as they have. National governments are a thing of the past. Oil, banking, and electronics cartels have crossed every frontier with total impunity.

"Americans are led to believe that Iran, North Korea, and immigrants from Mexico—Mexico, for God's sake!—constitute the biggest menace to their security. And while the U.S. is busy trying to protect its 'national security,' it ignores the fact that it's the biggest debtor nation in the world and it's going in the same direction as the old Soviet Union. It is, quite simply, going to run out of money well before it accomplishes its goals. With a few computer strokes, all the money invested by the English, the Japanese, the Chinese, or the Germans in the U.S. could be instantaneously withdrawn, which, of course, would bring down the government within twenty-four hours. America is twenty-two *trillion* dollars in debt. Six hundred eleven thousand dollars for every man, woman, and child in the country. And that debt is increasing at the rate of sixty thousand dollars a *second*, every minute of every hour of every day. Even the most optimistic economists tell us the U.S. will owe forty-five trillion dollars by 2025.

"American politicians say they'll generate new programs, build new schools, new roads. *Where are they going to get the money to do these things?* The cupboard's bare and the guardians of the trough are looting it the same way the 'good citizens' of our inner cities are looting the half-empty stores of anything they can carry away before the store owner files for bankruptcy."

As each participant brought the problems of their own countries into focus, Cunningham smiled to himself. *Let them talk*, he thought. *They'll come to the same conclusions as me.*

After a while, he spoke quietly, but with conviction. "My friends, nine out of every ten human beings in the world live their lives in fear. Fear of disease, fear of losing their jobs, fear of offending someone, fear of foreigners crossing their borders, fear of *living*. Ninety-five out of every one hundred people are pushed around by the remaining five throughout their lives.

"Each of those leaders the world has perceived as villains throughout history—Hitler, Attila, Genghis Khan—had one thing in common. They understood the psychology of fear and made it work for them. They might be hated, vilified, and detested today, but not one detractor says they weren't effective when they were in power. The human animal is violent and self-interested. The only hope for the survival of humanity is tight control—control by a single, unquestioned authority."

There was more agitated grumbling. Cunningham continued, "On the other hand, the kindest, most well-intentioned leaders that ever lived invariably failed. Mikhail Gorbachev presided over the demise of his society. Putin held the whole thing together. Jimmy Carter failed as president. Roosevelt took the country by the balls and dragged it forward, despite the fact that he was, to all intents and purposes, a dictator. Rajendra," he said, turning to the Indian. "Mother Teresa may have been a saint, but is Calcutta any less a disaster for her efforts?

"The nations of the world simply cannot govern themselves anymore. It's time for a *real* change. The Plan is the only way to accomplish that change. The American economy is in shambles. The EU will explode the minute France discovers it's nothing more than a charade for Germany to dominate the Continent. Can any of you think of a more propitious time to put the Plan into action?"

No one said a word. Flanders stood at the foot of the conference table, leaning palms down onto the surface. His gaze examined each person in turn. Prasad stared at his own fingers. Chung Lien returned Cunningham's look. Sharon sat back, casually secure. Kono looked at the others before meeting his host's glance.

"I'm in for the duration, Papa-sama. I've often wondered what it would be like to play 'serious world leader'."

Cunningham chuckled and walked back around to his seat at the head of the table. He motioned to Sharon, who pushed back from the table and pressed several buttons on the wall. The lights dimmed and a screen descended from the ceiling.

"I have prepared the beginnings of a DVD program which we will show to the world leaders when the time is right," the tall American said.

"Just a moment, Charles," the diminutive Chinese woman said. "You have always told us that secrecy is the most important element in our program. Public disclosure is the last thing we want. Would you have the world look at us as megalomaniacal?"

The mood in the room became noticeably tense. Each of Cunningham's associates had silently thought the same thing when he'd made his announcement only moments before. Only Chung Lien had had the courage to bring their concern out in the open.

Cunningham arched his eyebrows for the briefest moment, then eased the tension immediately. "Of course you're right, my dear Doctor

Lee, and I thank you for bringing this to my attention. I have no intention of publicly showing this program except to a very few chosen leaders, and even then only at the appropriate time. Think of it as a small, personal memento, akin to a home movie—something a parent whose children have grown up likes to view occasionally to recapture his or her youth. Sharon, I wonder if you might start the DVD, please?"

The monitor came to life. Cunningham's face was centered in the frame. He wore a plain gray suit and a red tie, the picture of the kindly father. "The purpose of the film you are about to see is to invite you to join my colleagues and me in a great adventure." The voice paused. "World peace. Real security for everyone."

Kono gazed at the real Cunningham with the look of a man who has just heard a terrible joke and wants to repeat it. Charles' glance flicked over his youngest associate and returned to the film. Kono and Prasad glanced quickly at one another. This was not the type of home movie anyone kept in his or her closet. They looked back at the screen. Charles' open face and brown eyes invited the viewer to come closer as he spoke in a warm, confidential tone.

"Several years ago, I was a senior partner in one of America's major law firms, due to nothing more than a fortunate accident of birth. My friends were starting to come into positions of leadership and power. I could easily have run for public office, but campaigning had become disgusting and unpleasant.

"I lived in the shadow of a grandfather I'd worshipped. I'd never done a thing for which I alone could take credit, except invest wisely enough to increase the fortune left to me. Think of what would be like to go to the gaming tables in Las Vegas or Monte Carlo and know—*know*— that you'd win every time? I never had to wish I might one day win the lottery, because I won the lottery every day of my life. The world had been given to me with no effort on my part except to wake up in the morning.

"Twenty years ago, my cash assets were increasing at the rate of over one and one-half million dollars a day! There was no mountain left to climb. Indeed, there'd never been any mountains for me to climb at all." The camera backed away. Cunningham stood with a pointer in his hand. The camera homed in on a chart that contained a pyramid.

?
POWER
M O N E Y
L   O   V   E
S H E L T E R
F   O   O   D

He pointed to the apex of the pyramid. "Psychologists tell us we have an ascending series of needs, from the most basic, at the bottom of the pyramid, to those things each of us could choose if we could. I had filled in all the blanks but one. There must be something higher that a man could achieve. Power, in and of itself, must be used for the greater good.

"I retreated into myself. Finally, the answer came, slowly at first, then with a force I'd never felt before." He flipped the chart. The words, "***PEACE AND SECURITY FOR ALL HUMANKIND***," stood out in bold relief.

"The conventional wisdom of what was supposed to work had carried the world down the road to chaos. I don't have to cite many examples. Can you truthfully say you're better off now than you were ten years ago? Happier, more secure?

"Twenty years ago, I gathered together a group of colleagues with similar dreams." Prasad looked around at that line, but soon returned his attention to the screen. "We knew that our dream would not be an easy one to achieve. We also knew the only thing that mattered in our efforts was results. If we failed, life would continue to get worse. To succeed, we used some extraordinary means."

The screen cut to a cartoon showing a brawny caveman forcing a much smaller individual to trade him a fish for a carrot under threat of a beating. In the next scene, the little fellow knocked at the cave-door of a still larger man. He explained his dilemma by wordless gestures, then handed the huge man the carrot and ten shells. The large man waited 'til nightfall, dug a large pit, in which he placed upraised stakes, just outside the cave of the little man's tormentor, then set up a loud noise by beating on the mouth of the cave with sticks. When the first man came out to investigate, he fell into the hole.

"Throughout history, the most successful means of war has had many names: ambush, guerrilla warfare, terrorism. Some condemned these methods as unfair, but history was to prove this was the only way the little man could fight back. It became clear over the centuries that he who controls the element of surprise has an overwhelming advantage and can defeat almost impossible odds."

The camera returned to a close-up shot of the fatherly, white-haired man. "In my lifetime, with the exception of a few true professionals, every time there has been a particularly brutal political crime, guerrilla groups immediately claimed they'd done the deed. Their names have become familiar to us all. In each instance, the leaders of these cliques made one fatal mistake: by creating publicity for themselves they lost their anonymity and the ability to control the element of surprise."

The scene on the monitor changed. Doctor Lee was shown, standing in the middle of a lab, with a small child lying on a gurney in front of her. Cunningham's voice continued to flow from the speakers. "Doctor Lee Chung Lien, a pioneer in intracranial reconstitution, joined us in order to make the fruits of her father's teaching, and her own studies, available to benefit us all. Her techniques allowed us to gather an army of soldiers capable only of following our orders."

The picture changed to a similar lab. Will Hensleigh was shown injecting a rat. "The late Doctor William Hensleigh, dear friend and brilliant researcher in biochemical neurology, synthesized a substance that would help assure that our soldiers could and would carry out their orders."

The late Doctor William Hensleigh, Kono thought. He looked around again. He almost forgot to smile when he met Cunningham's gaze. It was not lost on him that the voiceover had been done long before six o'clock that evening. He had been with Cunningham for two of those hours. That left too little time for someone to have edited the change into the DVD.

"In order to ensure proper delivery of the drug when needed, Rajendra Prasad created a subminiature electronic device, or SMED. With his amazing ability in electronics, Rajendra made a device that could be activated by the simple expedient of sound.

"Finally, we needed to arrange for the gathering and dispersal of our army." The scene on the monitor showed Kono standing at the bottom of an airplane ramp, helping a younger man carry an unconscious child to an adjacent terminal. "This task was carried out by Hitoshi Kono, a man of incredible talents. Through the organization that we created, *ChildFinders*, Kono oversaw the recruitment and distribution of over seven hundred fully programmed soldiers."

Cunningham's face returned to the screen. "These last six months have merely been a demonstration of our capabilities. A program of political assassinations with no traceable link. An unstoppable army of hidden soldiers, perhaps in the very homes of many rulers. Indeed, this will prove to be an inspiration to all world leaders.

"No longer will despotism and corruption be a way of life. All politicians and pretenders have been put on notice. They must work together, toward goals that will truly be beneficial, or they will be replaced by more conscientious public servants. In a few moments, we will show you the workings of our plan in somewhat greater detail."

The monitor darkened and the lights in the conference room came up. "What do you think?" Cunningham's question was met with stunned silence.

Chung Lien was the first to speak. "You're absolutely certain this is for your private use? If such a film ever became public—"

"Doctor Lee," Cunningham replied, the slightest edge of testiness entering his voice. "I promised each of you this film was private. If you don't trust me, I'll happily place it in a sealed vault and give you the only key."

"I didn't accuse you of anything, Charles," Chung Lien responded just as firmly. "I simply want to ensure that this operation is successful. The scientist in me wants to omit all possible risk of error."

"Very well, Chung Lien, I understand perfectly. Tomorrow, we will complete the filming."

A servant entered the room with a bottle of Dom Perignon and a tray that held six goblets. The elderly black man poured the sparkling drink into the glasses and handed one to each of the associates. The sixth glass sat on the tray. "To our success," Charles said and raised his glass.

"And to the memory of our colleague, Doctor William Hensleigh. His name will gain immortality with the rest of us once the Plan succeeds." Cunningham swallowed his champagne. The others took their time drinking.

10

"It's been a hard day of filming," Cunningham said. "Shall we start from where we ended last evening?"

"Why not, Papa-sama?" Kono responded.

The screen descended and the lights dimmed once again. The first shots showed malnourished children, looking like skeletons of a great famine, being brought to the Children's Institute and emerging later on looking well-fed. This was followed by slides of these same children graduating from the Institute's high school, then a group of young adults being handed diplomas from universities. There were several closeups of a particularly handsome trio.

Sharon's soft voice narrated the first segment. "Phineas Kumba, his brother Woodrow, and Zahira Uwonna Kumba, Woodrow's wife. Phineas holds a master's degree in business administration, *summa cum laude*, from Stanford University. Woodrow took his doctorate in philosophy from Oxford. Zahira, a graduate of the Sorbonne School of the University of Paris, is one of the foremost educators now working at the Institute."

Lee Chung Lien appeared on screen. "Hypnosis dates back to the dawn of mankind," she began. "The desire of one human being to control another is universal. In the early years of the Twentieth Century, Pavlov and Freud made great strides in our understanding of human and animal behavior. During the fifth and sixth decades of the century, significant advances were made in the field of intracranial reconstitution. We tend to fear something we don't understand. It was this way with I.R. The uneducated public called it 'brainwashing.' Paranoia over its use peaked in the nineteen sixties and seventies. Twenty years ago, my colleagues and I sought to refine the practice of intracranial reconstitution."

Sharon, who was watching the video closely, noted that her rival not once mixed 'l's' and 'r's,' a problem experienced by many Asiatics of her acquaintance.

The recorded Lee Chung Lien continued. "The initial studies were done with youngsters from the Institute, since they were immediately available. As our successes grew, it became necessary to enlarge our sources."

The camera refocused on Cunningham. "In order for our Plan to succeed," he said, "it was essential that we recruit, train, and disperse an army such as the world has never seen before. No one was more critical to that operation than Hitoshi Kono, for once our soldiers had been selected, it was up to Doctor Kono to arrange for their coming in and their going out."

Hitoshi's disarming smile and engaging, sympathetic manner translated well onto the screen. "No one likes the idea of kidnap. That crime is detested in every society. Yet the disappearance of human beings has become an unfortunate, and tragic, fact of modern life."

The camera cut from Hitoshi's face to a blue, 2011 Buick sedan pulling into a parking lot. The parking area adjacent to the Safeway supermarket was three-quarters full. The driver parked the Buick between a white BMW 325i and a brown Lexus RX330, fifty yards from the market. An attractive, dark-haired woman in her late twenties emerged from the driver's side of the car, walked around to the right-side door, opened it and unbuckled a belt from the child seat. She lifted a blonde-haired little girl into her arms, carried the child to the nearest shopping cart, and wheeled the cart into the market.

"Winchester Township," Kono said. "A typical upper-middle-class neighborhood on the East Coast of the United States. Saturday morning, U.S.A. An ordinary day in the life of Amy Roth, lawyer, and her two-year-old daughter, Melissa."

"May I see that last series again," Chung Lien interrupted.

Cunningham pushed the "Pause" button on the projector, pressed the "Slow reverse" button, and held it at the point they'd just passed. Cunningham smiled at Doctor Lee. "Someone you think you might recognize?"

"Isn't that—?"

"You're absolute right, Doctor Lee," he said. "I thought I'd surprise you. I'm sure you of all people would be interested in watching history repeat itself."

"But—?"

"Come now," the tall man said, smiling genially. "Isn't that what science is all about? Shall we return to the film?"

On screen, the woman wheeled the shopping cart back to the car, removed the child, placed her in the safety seat, and closed the front door. She fumbled for the keys in her purse, unlocked the rear lid of the car, and put two paper shopping bags in the trunk. While the lid was still raised, the woman wheeled the cart back to the stacking line.

The camera zoomed in on one of the paper bags in the trunk. There was a picture of a light-haired girl and the words, "*MISSING! BARBARA LOGAN, AGED 10 YEARS. IF YOU HAVE SEEN THIS CHILD, PLEASE CALL NATIONAL CENTER FOR MISSING AND EXPLOITED CHILDREN, 1-800-555-HELP.*"

Kono's recorded voice continued. "Amy Roth has seen these kinds of pictures a hundred times. She's seen posters and TV ads. She's thought about those missing children in the past, but not really. That's something that happens to somebody else's kids. A runaway, a twelve-year-old who got hooked on drugs. Things like that don't happen to nice, little, pink-clad, two-year-old baby girls in the parking lot of Winchester Township Safeway market at eleven a.m. on a Saturday morning in January."

The camera zoomed in on the woman as she approached the car, slammed the trunk door closed, and opened the left-hand door. The frame froze on the woman's face as she saw the empty safety seat.

"Those things don't happen," Hitoshi continued. "It's just someone's twisted, gruesome idea of a joke, isn't it?"

Kono's face appeared on screen. He walked over to a chart. Using a pointer, he said, "In the United States, thirty children a day mysteriously disappear. That is a minuscule number, one person in every eight million. Over time, these tiny numbers add up. Ten thousand mysterious disappearances in a year, two hundred thousand over a span of twenty. Still not a horrendous number. Unless the person who vanishes is your own loved one.

"If you multiply the United States figure by a factor of twenty for the rest of the world combined, the number becomes more serious." Kono flipped the chart and continued. "Half of those who disappear are victims of abduction. One hundred thousand a year. The most horrifying type of kidnap is the unexplained disappearance. No calls, no ransom demands, no explanation. The kind of thing you see on Safeway bags."

The camera closed in on Hitoshi's face. His expression was serious, concerned. "Studies have shown that the chance of such a victim being returned has a definite track. Parents usually spend the first twenty-four hours conducting a private search. When police are brought in, they start their investigations in much the same way. As time goes on, they alert other agencies. The disappearance becomes a statistic on a nationwide computer.

"But there are only so many law enforcement officers around. The local policeman has to testify in court on a traffic ticket, or he must answer a call to break up domestic violence, or he must cruise residential streets because Mr. and Mrs. Jones, who are on vacation, requested that the Chief dispatch an officer to drive by the house once a day. There are only so many working hours in the day. The City Council doesn't have the money to pay for overtime."

The camera moved to another chart. "Historically, hope of return is highest on the eleventh through the fifteenth days after a kidnap. The chances of a happy ending diminish rapidly after that."

Cunningham appeared on camera, seated at a large, executive desk. He gazed directly at the viewer. "In order to arrive at where we are today, we performed certain operations that might seem 'irregular.' To recruit soldiers for our Army, it was necessary for us to 'borrow' a few children, for a very brief period. With the demise of the old Soviet Union and the anarchy we find around the world, we focused our operations in places where children would least be missed for a couple of weeks: Romania, Moldova, the fragmenting war zones—"

The monitor cut to a film clip of a busy airport. The voice over was Sharon Graham's. "Our Center is far from anywhere of consequence in the world. Yet, in order to succeed in our undertaking without raising suspicion, it was necessary that anyone we 'borrowed' be returned home within two weeks after he or she had disappeared." The image of the airport was replaced by a shot of the Preserve's private airport. One of the 767s was taxiing out to the runway for takeoff.

"All of our operations were handled by air," Sharon continued. "Our recruits had a long, restful, drug-induced sleep, so they would be spared anxiety either coming or going."

The camera returned to Hitoshi. "During our twenty years' operation, we borrowed a total of seven hundred fifty children between the ages of two and eighteen years of age, all of normal intelligence. Three children a month worldwide. In each case, these children were returned to their homes within two weeks after they'd vanished."

Cunningham appeared on screen again. "Since our guests' memories were softened by unconsciousness during their journey and reinvented during their stay with us, it became necessary to provide an unimpeachable vehicle for the return of those who'd been temporarily detained. Before we took even one child, we created a superb organization, *ChildFinders*, whose sole purpose was to locate and return missing children. *ChildFinders* cooperated with its sister agencies by giving them free access to its information. It soon developed an unparalleled reputation for integrity."

Rajendra Prasad, who'd kept *ChildFinders'* records, dropped his eyes from the screen and stared down at the floor, incredulous. That last statement was patently untrue. *ChildFinders* cooperated with *no one* and scrupulously fabricated all records it turned over to anyone.

The on-screen Cunningham continued. "Over the years, *Child-Finders* managed to locate and return thousands of missing children to their parents."

Another absolute lie, Prasad thought. *ChildFinders* had returned precisely seven hundred fifty children—seven hundred fifty programmed weapons—from whence they'd come.

"Among those children whom *ChildFinders* returned were those who'd enjoyed a brief stay with us at the Center," Cunningham's voice was now a soft buzz. "*ChildFinders'* representatives were invariably clean-looking, well-intentioned young psychology interns. No agent stayed with us longer than six months. After that time, they went on to better things."

Yes, thought Kono, glancing swiftly at Prasad, then back to the screen. After six months earning three times what they might have earned elsewhere, they were given other assignments. Within a year, two at most, they suffered unfortunate accidents, where they prematurely—and permanently—disappeared.

Before they had an opportunity further to consider Charles Cunningham's words, Lee Chung Lien's image returned to the screen, this time wearing a white laboratory coat.

"The goal of any scientist is to minimize the opportunity for error. But human beings possess an enormous variety of individual reactions. No one can guarantee a result with one hundred percent certainty. There must be a backup—a contingency reserve. If there's a second contingency reserve, so much the better.

"The barbaric methods used in brainwashing during the fifties and sixties were undependable. We needed to program the subject's mind to *want* to cooperate when the retraining was complete."

The monitor now showed a lengthy segment of the Center's mind reprogramming operation—a series of injections, hypnosis, repetition, reward—in detail. "When our subjects leave us, they have become weapons with a triple redundancy system.

"Each of our guests is assigned a discrete, randomly selected command sequence, generally in his or her own language and cultural milieu, so it becomes impossible to trace any act done by any of them to a common thread, a single command. The signal chosen is always changed just slightly from the expected. As an example, we might use the sequence, 'Sing a song of sixpence, a pocket full of *barley*.'

"The command sequence was the first element of control. To reduce the risk of error, we added two security systems."

The camera homed in on a chart that looked like a series of many-fingered tree roots trying to grab onto another series of ganglia-fingered roots. "These are greatly enlarged nerve cells," Chung Lien continued.

"Nerve cells transmit message signals throughout the body. Without them, you'd never feel pain if you cut yourself. You could lose a leg and never know it. A child first learns that fire is dangerous when he touches a hot stove. He wouldn't acquire that knowledge without nerve cells. Nerve cells don't merely transmit physical messages from the brain to the body and back. Everything from the greatest joy to a mental breakdown results from nerves passing signals throughout the human body."

The camera moved in much closer. Tendrils trying to reach for one another were greatly enlarged. Doctor Lee took a black marking pen and drew a circle around the point where the dendritic fingers came closest to touching. "In order to transmit signals, nerve cells use electrical impulses. Each one *almost* touches the next. There's a space between them so small the most powerful microscope is not able to detect it. This space is called the synaptic gap. Whenever there is a message to be passed through nerve cells, two chemicals, serotonin and norepinephrine, serve as messengers."

She flipped the chart. The next illustration portrayed what looked like two bodies of land separated by a river. A series of piers reached out from each of the land masses. Triangular red pieces and crescent-shaped blue pieces appeared to be swimming in the river.

"The red chips represent serotonin. The blue crescents are norepinephrine," she said. The piers jutting out are points from which chemicals are sent and received across the synaptic gap. The departure points are called releasors. The arrival piers are receptors. Not every signal successfully crosses this tiny gulf. Those that do, race on to the next nerve cell, and this journey continues a million times until the signal reaches the brain. The entire series of transmissions takes less than a thousandth of a second."

A series of film clips showed a woman petting a purring cat, a baby sitting on the floor at her feet, happily banging a wooden spoon against a pot. A moment later, the woman picked up the toddler and placed it in a playpen. The child howled lustily. The mother took the spoon and pot and placed it next to the child in the playpen. The child started banging the pot again, as happy as it had been a few moments before. As she started back toward the cat, the woman accidentally stepped on the animal's tail. The cat screeched and zipped out of the room.

"What you see here are emotions we experience every day. Everything we physically feel, everything we mentally feel, is a result of uncountable numbers of journeys across millions of synaptic gaps every second of our lives. Recently, scientists determined what causes nerves to act as they do. By interfering with the journey across the synaptic gap, we can control moods, memory, even the mind itself. While working with us, Doctor Hensleigh formulated the perfect combination of substances to do what we needed.

"Once I had accomplished the mind programming, the next step was to implant chemicals that would remain inert in the body for years, if necessary, before they might be triggered into action. They would be virtually impervious to detection and would not be dislodged or accidentally punctured by the body's normal activities."

Chung Lien held up a soft, plastic sac, half the size of a fingernail, with two tiny, square chips on top. "During his or her useful life, our weapon will need only one shot of the chemical. Thus, the dispenser need not be large. The heart of this backup system consists of two tiny chips, a Sub-Miniature Electrical Dispenser on the right, and a single element computer on the left. Each one is so small it is almost invisible to the naked eye.

"We found it most logical to inject the container directly into the area at the base of the neck for a number of reasons. First, if one of our weapons acted totally out of character, law enforcement investigators would almost certainly order a brain scan. Although the capsule is small and soft-structured, a magnetic resonance imager or PET scanner would pick it up. But if such a scan were centered on the brain, nothing unusual would appear.

"Second, the area at the base of the neck is close enough to the ear to activate the device. Third, the neck provides anchor tissue and room in which to maneuver. Fourth, there are so many folds of skin in the neck that a transverse incision in that area would hardly be noticeable a month after it was made. Finally, that area of the body is close enough to both brain and spine to make sure there is immediate and thorough coverage of all necessary nerve cells an instant after the chemicals are dispensed."

The monitor showed Dr. Hensleigh making a minuscule incision into the neck of an apparently unconscious child and implanting the device. "Because of its size and composition, there is no toxic reaction. The insertion requires no major cutting and leaves no apparent scarring. The capsule is lodged deep enough that the subject is not even aware of its presence."

Chung Lien pointed to a large chart with a series of simplified diagrams. "Let's see how the system works so far. The Sub-Miniature Electrical Dispenser acts when it detects a certain series of frequencies, set off by each subject's trigger phrase. When the pressure sensor in the dispenser detects the proper signal, its microchip directs a capacitor to shatter the chemical sac and discharge the chemicals.

"Now the program has kicked into gear and the subject is ready to receive the command. As soon as the command is given, the medication blocks every nerve message that interferes with obeying the command. From that point until the order is carried out, the subject is nothing more than a programmed robot."

The camera moved to Rajendra, who was also wearing a lab coat. "The second chip atop the sac is, perhaps, our most ingenious device. This microchip, a single-purpose subminiature computer, has only one function. It shuts down everything after the deed is done. *Everything*. The medication is dissipated. The mind is directed to disregard and completely eliminate any reference to the command that has gone before. The sequence that Doctor Lee etched into the subject's brain is totally erased. There is not one expert in the world, nor any machine devised by man that can retrieve anything that happened. Everything is, quite simply, annulled. Thus, each of our weapons can be used only once. Then that person is deprogrammed forever."

Cunningham returned to the screen. "The entire process consumes fourteen days, including the borrowing and return by *ChildFinders*. Two weeks. What nation has ever been able to build a foolproof, totally undetectable weapon in such a short time? A perfect weapon in the most positive war ever fought—a war to ensure the safety and security of all mankind?"

Cunningham signaled the lights to go up as the images on the screen faded.

"Now, my friends, as a reward for all the hard work you've done today, and the marvelous film we have produced, I have arranged a small, practical demonstration of how the weapon system works."

Prasad and Kono glanced at one another uneasily. If Cunningham noticed them, he gave no evidence of it, but continued smoothly. "This afternoon we had occasion to lunch with Zahira, Phineas, and Woodrow, those fine young people we saw on screen a few moments ago. I have asked them to join us this evening." He pressed a series of numbers on the speaker console. "Woodrow, I wonder if you could join us in the library-conference room for a few moments, please? It's down the hall from the dining room and to the left."

"I trust the demonstration you spoke of is about to begin?" Chung Lien asked. "Is it to be recorded?"

"Of course," Cunningham responded. "Naturally the cameras remain hidden. If any of you experience any discomfort during the demonstration, please feel free to absent yourself for as long as you need," he said.

Sharon felt a sense of foreboding, but said nothing. If the Chinese bitch could remain impassive, so could she.

Charles pressed a button on the intercom speaker next to the door. Within a minute, there was a knock on the door.

"Come in, Woodrow," Charles called out cheerfully.

The Cambridge-educated black man entered. Chung Lien noticed, not for the first time, what a handsome specimen he was. She rubbed her thighs together, feeling a warm flush.

"Sit down. You needn't feel uncomfortable among us. We need your advice."

"Happy to help," the young man grinned.

"I knew you'd be. Doctor Lee and I are having a debate. Are you familiar with Shakespeare?"

"You have to be when you're educated in England."

"Good. Then you're familiar with the statement, "Tis better to have loved and lost than never to have painted at all?'"

The young man looked blank.

"Woodrow," the host continued. "I am going to hand you a capsule filled with potassium cyanide, one of the deadliest poisons known to man. Its smell is not unpleasant. You will die within seconds after you bite down on the capsule. Please do so."

"Yes, sir." The black man wordlessly took the gelatin capsule and dutifully bit down. Moments later, his writhing stopped and he lay still on the floor in front of them.

Prasad's eyes widened. Sharon felt like gagging, but brought herself up short as she watched Chung Lien's inexpressive face. Think of something else, someplace else, she repeated to herself. This is not happening. This is only an exhibition, a play act. In a few minutes this handsome, intelligent young man will stand up and we'll all feel foolish.

Cunningham prodded the body with his foot. Satisfied that Woodrow Kumba was never going to rise again, he pressed the intercom buzzer again. "Zahira, we have a question about the latest method of teaching third graders at the Institute. Could you come up and assist us?"

"Certainly," she said. "I'll be up in a few seconds. The conference room, right?"

Cunningham met the girl at the door, before she could catch sight of Woodrow. Without preamble, he said, "Jack be nimble, Jack be quick, Jack jump over the shoe-box quick!"

As she entered the room, Zahira wore the same blank expression her husband had worn moments before.

"Zahira, I want you to take this knife I'm handing you. I want you to cut out your husband Woodrow's heart, his eyes, and his tongue, take all these things to the kitchen, chop them up, and feed them to the dogs immediately outside the kitchen door. When you've done that, please take a long, hot bath in the basement bathroom, clean yourself up, change into the new white frock I've laid out for you in the adjacent bedroom, and rejoin Phineas in the recreation room."

"Yes, sir," Zahira said, with no more emotion than had she been asked to remove the tea service from the room.

This is a ghastly joke, Sharon thought. *It's Charles' cruel game to see how much I can take. Look at the Chinawoman. She's in on it. She knows. There's no way I'll leave now. I'll stay, I'll stay, I'll stay. Think of roses, think of magnolias, think of your work. Keep your mind occupied, that's the secret. Like looking straight ahead in the middle distance when you're riding in a car so you don't get carsick.*

Yet, like someone who drives by a particularly gruesome accident, Sharon found herself sneaking glances at what was going on less than five feet from where she sat.

The young black woman calmly took the knife from Cunningham. It was pearl-handled, well-sharpened and serrated, but it was not a surgical instrument and it was somewhat small. Zahira was a strong woman, but it took her three hard punches before she was deep enough to start sawing through the chest cavity.

She took no notice of the visceral substances that spattered her white dress, nor the gases from the prostrate body that forced various liquids and food in a partially digested state onto her hands. As she sawed, she hummed tunelessly, as though she were a small child building a castle out of sand.

Sharon saw Woodrow's heart, still engorged with blood, since the young man had not long been dead. She heard the wet-sloppy swish-saw as Zahira cut through arteries and veins leading to and from the large, purplish muscle. Various organs started to ooze their way out of the body cavity, pressed forward by the pressure Zahira was applying with her other hand to gain leverage as she continued to swish-saw, swish-saw.

Suddenly Sharon felt light-headed. There was a tingle in her fingertips. She did not want to be here. She felt vomit rising. It had only been an hour since she'd eaten. It didn't matter, because it was coming up and nothing was going to stop it.

Now her feet were tingling as well. There was no way she was going to make it to the bathroom, but she struggled valiantly to get up and leave the room. She almost made it to the door. Turning away from the scene behind her, she retched as she'd never retched in her life, throwing up great gobs of her dinner, noisily, with a sickening gag. She smelled the sour stench of her vomit, but couldn't stop. The contractions came harder and harder until she was dry heaving. Her throat was scratched raw. No one moved to help her, no one said a word.

She glanced back at her associates. They were still staring at Zahira Kumba. By this time, the black girl had managed to extract her husband's heart, although the job was sloppy and there was more blood and viscous substances than before spread over the parquet wood floor.

Sharon had thought there was nothing left to throw up, but the weakness overwhelmed her again. Now the girl took the knife and gouged out the dead man's eyes. She rolled one of them around in her hand, like a soft marble. The other lay uselessly on Woodrow's cheek. Small rivulets of blood dripped from the empty sockets. Throughout it all, Zahira had a calm, almost playful, expression on her face.

Sharon Graham heard a loud gurgling sound. She didn't know whether it came from the dead man's body or whether it was her own moaning as she doubled up and fell to the floor, where she continued to heave. Her throat was raw. The reek of vomit had worked its way up into her sinuses.

She felt rage, shame, and cold, hard anger. Charles hadn't raised a finger to help her, and the Chinese woman, the goddam, fucking, shit-whore *Chink* just sat there like an impassive lump. *Get control of yourself, Sharon Graham. Get control of yourself. Toughen up, you hear? Toughen up.* Mercifully, these were her last conscious thoughts. The world went a soft purple, then a soft black, then a soft nothing.

Zahira, covered nearly head to toe with bodily excretions, completed her work. She put the organs she'd collected in a nearby bucket Cunningham had conveniently provided, and walked silently out the door, toward the kitchen.

"It appears that Ms. Graham was not able to stomach this part of our demonstration," Cunningham said, not unkindly. "I wonder if you two gentlemen can help me tidy her up and place her on the day bed in the corner of the room. As he stood up and flexed his long, perfectly manicured fingers, he saw that Lee Chung Lien had paled.

"Something wrong, Doctor Lee?" he asked.

"N-no," she stammered. "It's just that I've never seen it performed at close range. It's always been something that happened—offstage."

"Ah, like the American bombing of Syria that came into the living rooms of the world courtesy of CNN? It wasn't real so long as it was only on television?"

"I suppose so."

"I can understand your feelings, Chung Lien. You've been braver than most soldiers would have been. As a scientist, I trust you appreciate the need to visualize what you've accomplished, even though it may be painful. He noticed her hands were shaking.

"Well," he said cheerily, noticing that Kono and Prasad had concluded putting Sharon on the chaise. "Time to clean up this mess. Doctor Lee, Hitoshi, Raj, would you mind joining me downstairs so we can watch the last part of the demonstration."

The recreation room was fresh and airy. When they got there, Phineas was engrossed in reading the article on the Congo River in the November *National Geographic*. He hardly noticed their arrival. After a moment, he looked up. "Where are Woodrow and Zahira?" he asked.

In response, Cunningham said, "Little Bo Peep has lost her zebra and can't tell where to find him."

It took a moment for the trigger to take effect, before Phineas said, "Yes?"

"Phineas, there's a bit of a mess in our conference room. We're having a meeting there and we need to have it cleaned up before we resume. Woodrow died and made quite a mess in so doing. Just outside the room, you will find a large, sharpened axe and a hatchet. Please cut Woodrow's remains into manageable pieces and place them in a number of garbage cans which you'll find in the antechamber just off the conference room. When you're finished, please clean the room so that it is totally spotless, then go upstairs, take a hot shower, put on the new casual outfit you'll find in the bathroom, and return to the recreation room."

"Certainly, sir."

They followed Phineas up the stairs and watched as he took the implements with him into the room. Without so much as a look at the still-unconscious Sharon Graham, Phineas sized up his brother's corpse, picked up the axe and, with four sharp swings, severed the remains of Woodrow's head. He found it relatively easy to cut off the arms with the hatchet, and there was little blood. The well-muscled legs, however, presented a problem. Phineas stood again, reached for the axe, and brought it through his brother's thighs. It took several over-the-head swings to do it, for Woodrow's thighs were thick with dried gristle and solid bone.

When Prasad heard the splintering sound of metal shattering bone, he left the room quickly. He was more fortunate than Sharon. He made it to the nearest toilet, where he brought up most of what was inside him. Then he stuck his head under the bathroom shower and let cold water run over him for a long time.

When he returned, he saw that Phineas had cut the remains into small pieces and stuffed them neatly into garbage bags. Phineas started cleaning the floor and surrounding furniture with rags, mops, and pails of hot, soapy water. He went about his business whistling, proud of his handiwork. After every vestige of what had gone on was erased, Phineas took his leave.

Cunningham walked over to where Sharon was just regaining consciousness and wafted ammonia under her nose.

"Charles, I'm so sorry," she said, fighting back tears. "It's just that it was so—so awful."

"Nothing to apologize for," he said, patting her shoulder. "Death affects all of us in different ways. It's cleaned up now. You can look if you want."

She did, and was surprised to see absolutely no hint of what she knew had gone on in the room a short time before.

"How long was I unconscious?"

"Half an hour. You weren't the only one. We all felt squeamish toward the end. Do you feel strong enough to walk?"

"I think so."

"Perhaps we'd best adjourn to the library," Cunningham said, as he helped the unsteady woman to her feet.

The library, twenty by thirty feet, conveyed a sense of rich intimacy. Three of its walls were lined with leather-bound books, each a first edition, some dating back four hundred years. The Royal Bokhara carpet that covered the floor had taken three master weavers eighteen months to complete.

The fourth side of the room looked out onto a small, hedged garden filled with white marble Greek statuary. Immediately in the foreground was an original of Rodin's *The Thinker*. Two hundred had been made during and after the master's lifetime. When he'd died, Maître Rodin had considerately left the casts to the French government so that his work could be renewed and enjoyed perpetually by generations who succeeded him.

To the left of the window, a six-foot diameter illuminated globe, constructed a hundred fifty years before, was housed in a floating brass-and-wood frame. Cunningham always smiled when he looked at the then known world and found that the Preserve existed only in the heart of "Darkest Africa."

When everyone was seated, their host said, "What you have just witnessed, grisly as it may have seemed, is proof of the outstanding result you've achieved. The weapons work in practice as well as in theory. I have in my vault the only copy of a document that contains all the information on each of our time bombs, where each of them may be reached at any given time and, most important, their trigger sequences. This isn't the first use we've made of our weapons."

"Is that why we've had an influx of such substantial income during the past few years?" Prasad asked.

"Yes, Rajendra. By the time we were engaged in that business, money had started to become very, very good in that field. Five million dollars or more for each job, depending on the importance of the target."

"Won't it be easy to catch one of our weapons?" Hitoshi asked.

"To what end? The person seized will remember absolutely nothing. No one could prove otherwise. What would convicting and sentencing such a person achieve? Of course, we want to avoid the appearance of 'the perfect crime,' so we vary our operations. In some cases, a backup weapon eradicates the first one."

"Like when Ruby shot Lee Harvey Oswald?" Kono asked.

"Good heavens, no," the tall man said, smiling inscrutably. "That was way before our time. Of course, there has always been speculation—" He let the sentence hang in the air.

"In the next several months," he continued, "a large number of influential people will meet untimely ends. After a pattern emerges, I will discreetly approach those in power. Ultimately, I will advise them that there exists an unstoppable army of robots, programmed to do the bidding of a small, internationally moral organization that would like to 'assist' in bringing order to a chaotic world."

"You intend to control the entire world by ruling its rulers?" Chung Lien asked.

"Yes. Of course, we would have to be extraordinarily cautious, meticulously careful so that nothing could be traced back to us. That's not as hard as it sounds. One or more weapons will be involved in every operation," Charles said, assuming the role of general. "The only ones we can truly trust are one another. Each of us travels widely. I can contact each of you by limitless means. It is imperative that henceforth, in any communication between us that might even remotely be insecure, we speak with caution."

"What about your aide?" Chung Lien asked coolly.

"Sharon's as much a part of our team as you. She's been with me longer than the rest."

"Give us the logistics, Chief," Kono said.

"Simplest case: one of us gives a direct command to the weapon. Generally, we engage in more complex operations to shield us from any hint of detection. Suppose on May fifth it would be appropriate for a certain Turkish economist to meet his maker. I contact one of you. Whoever's called gets hold of the 'fuse' and gives the trigger sequence and command.

"This 'fuse,' in turn, gives the trigger sequence and command to the 'time bomb,' who then carries out the termination. Sometimes we eliminate the 'bomb' through a third weapon. The program must appear entirely random. The possibilities are limited only by the seven hundred fifty weapons in our arsenal. The apparently haphazard means of accomplishing our end, coupled with each of us being two, three, or even four times removed from association with the weapons involved, is our guarantee of anonymity."

"Ultimately we rule the world?" Prasad said. "Choking off free will?"

"The average human being will not have a scintilla less free will than he or she has now. The only thing such a person will know is security, peace, and order so that he or she might better be able to exercise that will."

"Almost Hitlerian," Prasad mused.

"Please don't equate me with the likes of Hitler. I have no intention of becoming king of the Earth. I only suggest that if we are in position to counsel the world's political leaders what they must do, and have them listen and obey, then the world will truly be a better place, a more secure place, a place in which everyone will be happier."

Chung Lien looked at the American with interest. "So we remain as invisible as we are now, but we control the rulers."

"No one will know where the power comes from. They simply and silently will be thankful they live in a better world. Most of the religious ones will probably thank God. Only we—and those under our control— know who that God really is."

APRIL - MAY

11

"Haakon Honigsson, Signor Haakon Honigsson, arriving passenger, please pick up the nearest red courtesy telephone. Haakon Honigsson, red courtesy telephone please."

"Why don't you take the call, darling? I've got to make a stop at the ladies' room. Besides, it'll be the last time you'll be 'Mister' without them adding 'Minister.'"

Honigsson laughed and hugged his wife of thirty years. "I'll be right back. I can see the phone from here."

He'd gotten halfway to his destination when a small, swarthy man in his late twenties addressed him in perfect, unaccented Swedish. "Excuse me, sir, have you the time?"

"Of course." Honigsson raised his left arm and twisted his wrist to look at his watch. It was the last move he ever made. By the time the carabinieri at Rome's Leonardo da Vinci Airport had discovered the tiny needle mark in Honigsson's side, his assassin, too, was dead, undoubtedly by his own hand.

The Island Floating Palace of Heavenly Delights was one of Hong Kong's premier restaurants. The elite of many nations met there each week. In addition to brotherhoods too numerous to mention, the Lions,

Rotary, and Foreign Press Club regularly dined on the succulent splendors created there.

This evening promised to be an auspicious one. The minister of culture of Peoples' Republic was to address a dinner meeting of the Hong Kong Commonwealth Club. Every one of the five hundred seats in the restaurant had been booked. Even tiny Israel had sent a delegation consisting of a single third deputy secretary for cultural exchange, and a short, nondescript man of middle age, by his looks a physically fit retiree on holiday, who'd been asked by the Israeli chargé-d'affaires to provide security, if any were needed, to protect the young, low-ranking diplomat.

"For which I'll receive?"

"The type of dinner even you would salivate over, Ezra. Not to mention all the Pellegrino water you can drink."

"I'm overwhelmed by your generosity, Chaim," Caen responded sardonically. "To what do I owe this gargantuan feast?"

"The fact that the host nation is footing the bill."

The crowd started arriving at six, in time to see the beautiful sunset from its upper decks.

Wong Lee Yin had mercilessly driven his crew of ten master chefs and thirty sous chefs since one that afternoon, preparing an awesome variety of delectables. Shortly before the first guest was to arrive, one of the sous chefs came up to Wong Yee Lin. "Yes?" the owner-chef snapped impatiently. "I've no time to waste, ignorant underling. What is it you want?"

"Hail, Britannia, Britannia rules the dust," the man said.

The owner-chef's features slackened.

"The plate covered with the silver dragon is to be set aside for the PRC minister of culture. You will make certain no one but the minister eats the food on that plate. You will dispose of any food he does not eat, instantly. Do you understand?"

"Yes, of course."

An hour-and-a-half later, after consuming his entire meal, Tsao Ping Do, the Chinese minister of culture, rose to address the assemblage. He spoke for close to twenty minutes before closing, "Gentlemen," he said, "In the next thirty years, I believe all economic systems will accommodate one another, and those businessmen who have temporarily taken up residence in Macao, Singapore, and Vancouver will return once they see that Hong Kong is a land of greater promise than ever."

The minister had started to call on a man in the back of the room when suddenly he grabbed his stomach. Without another word, he collapsed.

The coroner who performed the autopsy said it must have been a particularly virulent form of food poisoning. Although those who attended the dinner feared for their own health during the next ten days, not one other guest experienced the slightest discomfort.

12

The WhatsApp connection between Tel Aviv and Hamilton University was instantaneous and precise. Savage saw Ezra Caen's well-used face as clearly as if they'd been sitting across from one another.

"Your wildly aggressive theory may seem more realistic than I originally thought, Jeff. I was visiting Hong Kong a week ago and I witnessed something a bit odd. The Cultural Minister of the Peoples' Republic dropped dead in the middle of a speech. The local gendarmerie fed us some cock and bull story about food poisoning, but none of the other 499 people in the dining hall, felt even a tinge of discomfort. In my profession, you go with your gut feeling, and since I had no feeling in my *gut*, my antennae hinted to me there was something 'off' in this scenario. I didn't have rime to investigate, but I figured it was a local matter and they have law enforcement on Hong King island. Meanwhile, I trust you've been following these figures on your terminal?"

"I have, Ezra." Savage looked at the first page and made some markings with a highlighter pen.

| | _This Year_ | | | | | _Last Year_ | | | | |
	Jan	_Feb_	_Mar_	_Apr_	_TOT_	_Jan_	_Feb_	_Mar_	_Apr_	_TOT_
Political murders or suicides	5	9	15	26	**55**	2	3	3	6	**14**
Deaths where close associate of deceased was suspected of involvement in the killing and died within a week	4	8	10	21	**43**	0	1	0	1	**2**
Deaths where suspect was immediately identified and taken into custody	1	1	5	5	**12**	2	0	2	2	**9**
Deaths where suspect was taken into custody and denied killing victim	1	1	5	5	**12**	0	0	1	1	**2**
Deaths where suspect was taken into custody, denied killing victim, and passed all known lie detector tests	1	1	5	5	**12**	0	0	0	0	**0**

"There were five murders in January," Savage continued. "Nine in February, fifteen in March and twenty-six in April. If each of these figures continues to increase at the rate they're going, the numbers will be astounding."

May = increase of 12 (Number of killings: 38)
Jun = increase of 24 (Number of killings: 62)
Jul = increase of 48 (Number of killings: 110)
Aug = increase of 96 (Number of killings: 206)
Sep = increase of 192 (Number of killings: 398)
Oct = increase of 384 (Number of killings: 782)
Nov = increase of 768 (Number of killings: 1550)
Dec = increase of 1536 (Number of killings: 3086)

Total number of "strange" killings: 6,287

"That's geometrical. The chances of that happening are infinitesimal, but if you take those figures at face value, you have 6,287 public figures dead, one hundred times the annual average for the past five years."

"Can you come up with more realistic figures?" Israel's legendary counterterrorist, known internationally as "the plodder," continued.

"Let's assume that the unexplained killings have peaked out, and they'll remain at the same level, no increase, for the rest of the year," Jeff said. He wrote out more figures.

Flat level for the rest of the year: Number of killings		
Jan-Apr. This Year	Jan-Apr. Last Year	% Difference
55	14	392

Assume no further increase and 3.92 figure remains accurate.

Total killings last year: 64   Projected this year: 251

Ezra Caen made a series of keystrokes, which Jeff visualized. "If we take these figures a step further," he said, producing a printout, "here are the figures:

	Full Year: January - December			
	5 Years Ago	2 Years Ago	Last Year	Current Year
Political murders or suicides	59	62	64	**251 6,287**
Deaths where close Associate of the deceased Was implicated in the killing and died within a week	4 (8%)	5 (8%)	5 (8%) 196	4915 (**78%**)
Deaths where surviving Suspects were immediately identified and taken into custody	54 (90%)	55 (91%)	58 (91%)	**55 372 (22%)**
Deaths where surviving suspect was taken into custody and denied killing victim	2 (20%)	14 (23%)	13 (20%)	**55 1372 (22%)**
Number (%) of deaths where suspect was taken into custody, denied killing victim, *and passed all known lie detector tests*	(0%)	0 (0%)	0 (0%)	**55/1372 (100%)**

"Do you think we should go to the FBI with these charts."

"Not yet, Jeff," Caen responded. "It's probably best not to bring anyone else in until we've refined our evidence. By the way, that includes Mrs. Roth, since she might be in some danger if anyone found out."

"What about Ron Ames?"

"I leave that entirely to your discretion. Meanwhile, can you produce a complete list of victims, suspects, associates who died within a week after the killing? Maybe I'm asking too much, but how much information do you think you could get on each of these people?"

"With Ron's help, I could get lots. It's incredible how much anyone with access to sufficient databases can find out about any other human being. Nobody escapes the computer today. Computer databases record and store everything that goes on in a person's life. Every industry—insurance, banks, oil companies, department stores, credit reporting agencies—is linked by computer network to every other industry. Ditto government agencies. Anyone with access to that network can trace where a person was, and what he or she bought, said, did, or even thought, at any given time in his or her life. If that person becomes ill, the medical computer system ties in to the rest, because the illness is covered by insurance. By the way, I might be able to find a few extra clues by this time next week, after I've met with Amy Roth."

Jeff Savage looked appreciatively at the attractive woman with whom he'd be working during the next few months: early thirties, five-three, short-cut dark hair, beautiful skin, businesslike, but undeniably feminine. Just before they came to her office, a young man asked, "Amy, may I see you for a moment?"

"Sure, Jack," she replied. "I'll be right back, Professor Savage. Why don't you make yourself at home in my office?"

When he entered, Jeff looked about the office. Fifteen by twenty feet, he estimated, window view, a Chagall litho on one wall, two good quality Impressionist prints on another. The one behind her desk held her diplomas and certificates laminated on walnut bases. He turned toward her desk and saw three framed photographs: a picture of the woman he'd just met, her arms around a pretty, honey-haired child of six or seven. A baby picture that could have been anyone. A straight-on shot of the same little girl pictured in the first photo. Not your ordinary everyday killer.

He looked up and saw she'd entered the room. "Good morning, Lady lawyer," he said, smiling.

"Good morning, Gentleman actuary."

Amy visually sized up Jeff Savage: medium height and weight, thinning dark hair, intelligent, wide-set brown eyes. His features were by no means extraordinary, but he had a gentle presence, and a pleasant, boyish manner.

"Ms. Roth—?"

"Why not make it 'Jeff' and 'Amy'?"

"Fine by me," he said, grinning. "At your service, Amy."

"I take it you've read the preliminary workup?"

"Uh-huh. My job is to show that Portugal was not willing to—and did not believe it was—assuming the risk that the Hanagasa Maru would be anywhere near Cape Town, or that when it spilled, the Great Atlantic Insurance Consortium would go belly-up. I give you ammunition, you convince the jury."

"The other side will have an actuary as well."

"I surmised that. I can readily access the relevant networks."

She leaned back in her executive chair, closed her eyes for several moments, then gazed levelly at him.

"Something the matter, Amy?"

"I was just thinking. If I asked you to trace a person or an organization, how hard would it be?"

"That depends on a number of factors," he replied. "I trust you've tried Google already?"

"Uh-huh. Nothing."

"If you could give me sufficiently specific information, I'd probably be able to locate the person and provide you with information not readily available."

Amy bent down, opened her lower right-hand desk drawer, and extracted a thin file. "Jeff, could I ask you to do me a personal favor that has nothing to do with the Portugal case?"

"Sure, provided you didn't ask me to do anything immoral. Hey," he said, noticing the dark cloud that passed over her face, "that's a joke. Of course, I'd be willing to help."

"I'd hoped you'd say that. I have a rather substantial problem."

"Would this be a time for candor?"

"What do you mean?"

"Amy, Mr. Cunningham told me about your . . . tragedy." He heard her sharp intake of breath. "I knew about Melissa before Cunningham ever called me.

"I thought if we opened on a candid note, we'd feel more at ease with one another. If it's a matter of sharing secrets, my former wife ran off with her gynecologist five years ago. If you'd seen me the year after she left, you'd have written me off as a hopeless drunk. A friend of mine and I have recently been studying not only your situation, but some things that may or may not be related. You may also find I sometimes lack diplomatic skills. Present conversation a case in point."

"*Touché* and thank you. Now that you've knocked me off balance, may I ask my favor?"

"The knight's armor has been sufficiently tarnished. Go ahead."

"How much do you know about the . . . situation?"

"Melissa's an oddball. I don't mean that in a derogatory sense. Her name came up last month when my friend and I were chasing one of my harebrained suspicions.

Savage continued. "Melissa shouldn't be involved in these numbers at all. She didn't kill a political figure, but she fits several of the other categories, the most critical being she denies any knowledge of what happened and the tests prove she's not lying. Amy, is there anything unusual that's happened in Melissa's life?"

"No ... yes. Six years ago she disappeared for two weeks. I'm sure she was kidnapped." She told Savage about the incident at the Safeway market. "She was returned by an organization called *ChildFinders*. After what happened this past February, I tried to call *ChildFinders* to see if they'd noticed anything strange about Melissa when they'd picked her up. *ChildFinders* seemed to have dropped off the earth. Don't think I haven't been plagued by what happened. It hasn't been that long. Charles Cunningham has been the kindest man alive since Daniel's death."

"I can think of very few men who wouldn't be."

"It's not like that," she said, smiling. "He's old enough to be my father. What's haunted me since this—this *thing*—occurred is the piece of the puzzle that's missing from Melissa's life."

"The time she was away?"

"That and my inability to turn up anything about *ChildFinders*."

"You've checked with—"

"Everyone and every organization. They've never heard of *Child-Finders*."

"Why do you want to involve me?"

"Charles Cunningham told me I'd need someone with access to a huge bank of computer information if I wanted to trace down *ChildFinders*."

"And you waited three months to try and find someone?"

"Yes. One, I was too close to the situation, too involved in trying to get my daughter back. Two, I had to fight my own way back to some semblance of sanity, given the whole bizarre situation. And three, I didn't know anyone who'd have such access."

"So why now? And why me?"

"All the roads I've tried came to dead ends. Maybe that's just the way it is and I might have to live with the fact that there are some questions that never get answered. But you're here in town on legitimate business, the fates seem to have thrown us together, and I've got nothing more to lose."

"I'll work on your problem over the weekend, Amy. Suppose I call you next Tuesday after work?"

"I'll go you one better. I've got a court appearance and two depositions near Hamilton next week. I'll have my secretary reserve a room for me at the Montclair House for Tuesday, Wednesday and possibly Thursday night. I'll try to be there by six. Cunningham-MacLeish'll treat you to dinner."

"It's a date."

Later that afternoon, Charles Cunningham dropped down to her office. "How did it go with Professor Savage?" he asked.

"Wonderful, Mister Cunningham. I think we'll really work well together. Remember a couple of months back, when you told me the only way I'd be able to locate *ChildFinders* was through a computer search?"

"Yes."

"Jeff's offered to help me. He said Hamilton University is plugged in virtually everywhere. I can't thank you enough for all you've done. Tell me, Mister Cunningham," she said, smiling, "did you assign me the Portugal case just so I could meet a computer expert who'd help me?"

The tall man's eyebrows lifted. His face assumed an inscrutable look. "Ask me no questions, I'll tell you no lies."

"I thought so," she said, grinning. "If ever a lady had a better friend than you, I've never heard of it. You're a dear, dear man," she said. She walked around to where he was sitting and, on impulse, kissed him on the forehead.

He glanced at her with a sternness belied by a twinkle in his eye and a smile he seemed to be trying too hard to suppress. "Is that the way for a partner to act?"

"Yes, my beloved friend. If the senior partner is you."

"Rajendra?"

"Yes, Flanders?"

"An actuary named Jeffrey Savage at Hamilton University is curious about *ChildFinders*. He's going to start looking for some answers this coming Tuesday."

"Do you want me to alter the information?"

"No, but can you find a way to monitor whatever he pulls up?"

"It's relatively simple if I can get into the computer labs at Hamilton. You say you need to be online before Tuesday?"

"Yes."

"I'll be in town Sunday night. I'll need some help from your end to make my job easier."

13

By Sunday morning, Jeff was ready to start the search. "O.K., Superman," he said to his reflection in the mirror while he was running the Norelco over his face. "You've told the lady you're going to try and find the needle in the haystack. Only you're in the middle of a place that doesn't even have haystacks and you've got a world full of goddam haystacks in which to look." *Still,* he thought, *a lady in distress—particularly a bright, attractive lady in distress—merits at least an effort."*

"Cut to the chase, Jeff, what do you need?" Ron asked.

"A really hefty machine plugged into a lot of stuff beyond Google."

"Insurance stuff?"

"Detective stuff. Of course, you go-to-church every Sunday types wouldn't have time to join me?"

"Services don't start 'til eleven. It's nine, now. I'll treat you to coffee at Starbucks. I wouldn't want to force you to choke down the dishwater they serve at the cafeteria."

"Last of the big-time spenders, are you? I suppose you want me to pick you up?"

"No, I'll pedal over. Or you could come over here and ride on the handlebars."

"What's mama look like?" Jeff blushed. "I see," his friend answered. "Are your questions all programmed and ready to go?"

"Nope. I could go fishing at my own terminal. I just thought it would go faster if I could use some hardware over at the center."

"Tell you what. It's Sunday morning, the day of rest. How'd you like to go fishing with one of the world's biggest, most powerful trawlers?"

"The Cray Titan?"

"Uh-huh."

"That's like asking Albert Einstein to teach a bunch of first graders how to add three plus two."

"They say Einstein was quite slow as a first grader," Ames mused. "His teacher thought he was borderline retarded."

"I've heard that. But the Cray Titan is not designed to chase database networks. That baby's used to break down DNA molecules and reproduce the beginnings of the universe."

"Suit yourself. Just thought you'd like to say that once in your life you got to play one of the grandest concert grands of them all."

"You're serious?"

"You got two hours, on condition I join you after church and you share what you've got with me. As in immediately."

"You've got a deal."

A Cray Titan High-Performance supercomputer is not what one uses to search for an organization. The Cray is for scientists who want to know what the world was like exactly one-millionth of a second after the big bang, or who needs to project what a zygote would look like at the precise instant the sperm and egg united. What Jeff wanted to use the computer for was almost an insult to the Cray. But, he thought, it would sure be fun to tell his colleagues, "Well, the other day, when I was working on the Cray Titan—"

Mention the word "computer" and the general public thinks of HP, Dell, or Apple. But to those whose lives *are* computers, there is the IBM Summit with a peak performance of 200 petaflops, or 200,000 trillion calculations per second; the second fastest computer, the TaihuLight, which can reach 93 petaflops; and a few more. Until 2016, the Cray Titan was the world's most powerful computer, but it's now dropped to "only" #9.

Jeff Savage had secured two hours on the Cray. Although he could log into any number of networks by using his own password, Jeff became a superuser by employing Ron Ames's password, "wXndana5."

At ten a.m., after he had entered the magic door, Savage initiated his query for *ChildFinders*. In an eye blink, the following appeared on the monitor screen:

"PEOPLE WHO FIND CHILDREN. DO YOU WANT TO CONTINUE THIS SEARCH? (Y/N?)"

Savage pressed "Y" and waited a split second.

"PLEASE ENTER YOUR INDIVIDUAL ACCESS CODE."

"wXndana5."

The machine responded: ORGANIZATIONS. CONTINUE THIS SEARCH? (Y/N?)"

"Y"

"*ChildFinders* International. *Luftleben* S.A., VADUZ. SHAREHOLDERS UNLISTED. DO YOU WANT TO CONTINUE THIS SEARCH? (Y/N?)"

"Y"

"PLEASE WAIT."

Now we're getting into high gear, Jeff thought. Hamilton University's computers were tied into at least fifteen networks, in addition to the internet. Jeff watched the Cray as it silently crunched numbers. Although it was the ninth most powerful supercomputer in the world, it was only one more vehicle on the information superhighway that connected a trillion or more computers around the world. The following flashed on the screen:

"INTERPOL LISTING: NONE. ADDRESS: DRAWER 370-AG, VADUZ, LIECHTENSTEIN. BANK REFERENCE: BANK OF THE SOUTH PACIFIC, VANUATU. EMPLOYEES: NONE LISTED. NO FURTHER INFORMATION AVAILABLE THIS LISTING. CHECK OTHER ENTRIES DESCRIBED ABOVE? (Y/N?)

"Y"

"TYPE IN ENTRY YOU WISH."

"LUFTLEBEN, S.A."

The supercomputer coughed up the same information for Luftleben.

Seventy-two trillion pieces of information per second, and the goddammed machine had run into two brick walls less than a minute into the search.

Jeff punched up "ROTH, MELISSA."

The computer returned fifty entries by city instantly. Five were located in Amy's general area. A few more keystrokes and he accessed five pages of information on Melissa, everything from her favorite foods, height, weight, dress size, to her present situation.

Next, Jeff accessed similar information on every person whom he and Ron had identified on their charts.

By the time he'd printed out all the data, it was almost eleven. He'd have time to analyze the information when he got home. Even if he wasn't paying, the Cray was an expensive toy indeed. He knew that retail users paid the university thirty thousand dollars an hour to log into one of its two hundred ports.

On a hunch, Jeff punched up another name. Not unexpectedly, the Titan produced ten thousand single-space pages on Charles Cunningham.

Jeff had another flash of inspiration. He'd been working with one of the most effective weapons in the world's intelligence arsenal at nearly incalculable speed. He knew of a much slower mind, which, in the world of *useful* intelligence, was a perfect complement to the Cray.

"Ezra?"

"I hate to sound short, but it's nine o'clock on a Sunday night and all of Tel Aviv's asleep. At least all of it *was* asleep until you called."

Jeff heard a sleepy feminine voice in the background. "Who's interrupting what we haven't even started in the middle of the night, Darling?"

"Fellow from the U.S. with some interesting speculation. Go ahead, Jeff," he said, returning to the cell phone.

"You ever heard of the Cray Titan, Ezra?"

"The Summit's older brother? Sure."

"Don't ask me how, but I've been playing on it for two hours. I've got about half an hour left and it'll take me that long to download some awfully interesting stuff. Do you have anything over there large enough to retrieve it?"

"Give me twenty minutes. The Weizmann Institute in Rehovot has equipment that can catch anything the Cray can throw and it's up and running twenty-four hours a day. I'll text Shafi Goldwasser and Adi Shamir, both of whom have passcodes, and I'll have whatever you send before noon tomorrow, 6 a.m. your time. Can it wait that long?"

"Of course. Sorry to wake you, Ezra."

"טיישלוב"

"Cute, Ezra. Bullshit is pronounced the same in Hebrew as in English. Give your redhead goddess a kiss on all four cheeks."

Halfway around the world, Vasily Vasilievitch Kogan looked at his timepiece. The ferry from Vydrino should be arriving any moment now. He'd decided to take a few days' holiday before returning to Moscow.

His mission had been an unqualified success. By this time next year, the pollution spewing into the lake from the giant wood pulp plant at Baikalsk would be cut by ninety percent. Only five percent of the jobs would be lost the first year, tapering off to two percent for each of the following three years.

Ten months ago, Vasily had been sent to Lake Baikal and assigned the thankless but politically critical job of mediating between the management of the cellulose factory, the workers who felt their government had betrayed them, and a cadre of environmentalists who exhorted the locals to save the planet by destroying the plant altogether.

Vasily looked out onto the vast body of water, its gray color reflecting the leaden sky, caused by a combination of low cloud cover and incessant, belching effluent from the factory's array of smokestacks. Not for too much longer, he thought, and smiled to himself. Within a year, the vast, fir-covered hills beyond the town would stand out green and clear against the rich, dark blue of Baikal's southern shore.

The ice floes had broken a month before. He debated whether to store his heavy, woolen greatcoat in the trunk he'd brought to the dock. Not a good idea. Once on board the ferry, he'd remain on deck, watching the ever-changing aspects of this vast inland sea. No matter how warm it seemed now, he knew the arctic chill would cut through him once the boat left the dock and headed north toward Listvyanka.

He glanced at his watch again. Twelve-fifteen. The ferry had been delayed, a common occurrence. Time was an amorphous commodity to the Buryat and Mongol tribesmen who loaded and offloaded tons of white fish, *nerpa*, the freshwater seals prized for their oil and fur, who occupied the northern third of the Lake, and wood products destined for the pulp mill.

"Tovarisch!" he called out to a squat, mustachioed, Turkic-looking man who was punching tickets at the ferry gate. "Any idea when the northbound boat is due to arrive?"

"Who knows?" the conductor said, shrugging his shoulders. "An hour, a day, they don't tell me these things. Why? You want to eat dinner?"

"Yes."

"Plenty of time for that. The American-Russian expedition came in to restock this morning. They pay better than the government, so our dock workers give them preferential treatment. You're Kogan, aren't you?"

"Da."

"Word's out about the agreement you got 'em to sign last night. My wife works at the plant. I'm grateful."

Vasily smiled. That type of thing would go down well with the authorities.

"I saw them haul in a huge load of fish this morning," the conductor continued chattily, oblivious to a line building up at his station. "I'd recommend you go to the Yenisei and have the grilled pike there."

"Thank you, I will," Vasily responded.

"If the boat comes in before you get back, I'll send a boy to fetch you," he said.

"Thanks again."

Vasily arrived at the Yenisei in the middle of the dinner hour. "No room for a single," the host said with the rudeness he'd come to expect. "It'll be an hour at least."

Vasily was in the midst of trying to explain that he was awaiting the ferry when a voice cut through the din. "Vasily Vasilievitch! Yes, you, Kogan! *Strarstvootye!* Come join us, tovarisch!"

"Lev?" he said in wonder, as he spotted the bearlike man, his cheery, red face all but hidden by a full black beard. "Lev Lebedev?"

"None other, old friend. I just flew out from *Piter* to escort a bunch of Yankee scientists around the Lake. We've chartered the *Obruchovna* for ten days. I'm teaching them the proper way to drink vodka, they're teaching me American songs."

The big man pushed and shoved his way toward the middle of the dining hall. Vasily gratefully followed in his wake. When they'd reached their table, Lev made introductions. The company was well-lubricated and boisterous.

There were huge platters of pike, omul, potatoes, and tureens of borscht already on the table. Someone thrust an empty plate at Vasily and told him to help himself. Until then, he hadn't realized how hungry he was.

"Ah, but you must sing for your supper," Lev said, patting him heartily on the back. "You must first teach our guests a Russian song."

Vasily glared at his friend, then began to sing.

"Good! Very good!" one of the Americans said. "Now we can all sing together. He started the chorus, "Those were the nights, my friend, we thought they'd never end ..."

"I think you made a mistake," his companion said. "It's 'Those were the *days*, my friend."

But Vasily had heard only the part about the *nights*.

His attention was riveted on an angry male voice a few tables away. "To hell with the agreement. They're all a bunch of Nazis if you ask me! What you should do is find a machine gun, walk into the Chairman's

Board Room, gun down every one of 'em, then go out and shoot the environmentalists, too. Blast every one of 'em off the face of the earth!"

Which is exactly what Vasily Vasilievitch Kogan did.

Afterward, he walked calmly back to the dock to await the ferry. Of course, he had no idea what he'd done.

"Chung Lien, what is going on?" Cunningham sat in his private study, a snifter of cognac in his hands.

"What do you mean?" The Chinese woman's voice issued from the speaker on his desk.

"We've had another misfire," he said angrily. "It's taken every bit of my persuasive power and a significant amount of money to keep the story out of the press."

"Calm down, Charles. These things happen." Doctor Lee's voice was icy business.

"These things aren't supposed to happen." He took a gulp of cognac. "I thought we had triple safeguards."

"Perhaps someone else has the list?"

"No one has the list except me."

"Maybe someone copied it?"

"Impossible!" Cunningham slammed his hand onto the arm of his leather chair.

"Then the only explanation is that a trigger sequence was accidentally picked up by one of our weapons."

"How could that happen?"

"Charles, we take extreme precautions to assure that the subjects are not likely to hear their trigger signal in their expected environment. However, no system is perfect. An unexpected factor must have entered the time-bomb's life."

"How could Vasily Vasilievitch Kogan have heard the phrase 'Those were the *nights*' at Lake Baikal?"

She shrugged.

"Where is Kogan now?"

Charles looked at the notes on his desk. "Enroute to the State Security Installation outside Moscow."

"Can we intercept and dismantle him?"

"I'll think about it."

"Charles, there must be fifty programmed operatives between Baikal and Moscow."

"I said I'll look into it, Doctor Lee." Cunningham's anger had changed into a glacier.

"What about Melissa Roth?" Chung Lien's words were a pick, looking for a crack to widen.

Charles swung his chair around and leaned forward onto his desk. "You know very well why we must hold off on recovering that subject. The Roth child must be left where she is. We cannot afford any more attention on that front."

"I do not see how that follows. Without examining all of the misfired weapons, we cannot know that there has not been an equipment failure. Kogan was one of the early subjects. The dispenser unit had not yet been perfected."

"I said Melissa remains where she is. I will look into obtaining Kogan for you to study."

The connection ended. Cunningham sipped at his cognac, allowing its smoothness to defrost his anger. After a few swallows, he thought, "This is a challenge," and smiled.

14

On Monday morning, Ron Ames' orderly world was disturbed by his secretary's insistent buzz.

"Yes, Sarah?"

"Reginald Maharaj Punjabi is here to install the new network equipment."

The man who entered was small, about forty-five years old, slender, with coffee-colored skin. "Good morning," he said. "I am sorry to disturb you, Professor Ames." Rajendra Prasad forced a thick Indian accent, though he had in truth lost his own many years before on the streets of Vancouver. "I need your approval to enter the computer center—university rules they tell me."

"Ah, yes. Bureaucracy wins again. Even for the installation of new network equipment. How long do you need, Mr. Punjabi?"

"Not long, but I do need you to be there and verify that I have properly installed the units."

"Very well, then. I can't understand why they didn't simply send a technician down. Truth to tell, I know all about how these things work, but I don't know that much about connecting up the hardware to make them work."

The smaller man smiled easily. "Perhaps that's one of the reasons they want you to watch me. I'm afraid my services do not come cheap and the university wants to make sure they do not need to ask me to return any more than possible."

Prasad followed Ames down the hall and into the Computer Center. Students sat at terminals around the room, finishing up their final projects. The two men passed through a door at the far end of the center marked "Authorized Personnel Only." Beyond it, they entered a small room with white coats hanging on the wall. Each of them picked up one of the static-free lab coats and put it on. Prasad/Punjabi followed Ames through another door, and into the main computer room.

"Which one's your main server?"

"Actually we've got three of them for backup, plus one dedicated exclusively to the Cray Titan."

"Ah," the Indian sighed appreciatively. "The Stradivarius itself."

The hum of cooling fans was louder among the various network servers than it had been in the computer center. Prasad set his large briefcase on the floor, popped it open, and pulled out some tools and cables. Ron, like most men observing something he did not understand in the least, feigned interest, watched politely, and uttered the occasional, "Oh," and "I see." At one point, he said, "How come you're using so little cable? Last time someone was here, there was enough wiring to fill my office."

"It's all changed today, Professor Ames. Don't get me wrong, we continue to use all the wiring you already have, but now we use a lot of wireless connections to and from your central servers."

Prasad was as good as his word. It took less than an hour for him to complete the installation. He carefully packed away his equipment and left. As he climbed into his rental car and started the engine, the Indian took a deep breath.

That afternoon, rangers in the Angeles Crest National Forest near Lake Arrowhead, California, found the body of an unidentified, middle-aged East Indian who'd been shot in the back at close range. Within hours, through a routine check of fingerprints and dentures, they'd confirmed the identity of the real Reginald Maharaj Punjabi. Another weapon had struck home.

"What do you make of it Alexei?"

"More years ago than I care to remember, we were working on mind programming in a laboratory fifty *versts* north of the Korean border. Those were heroic days."

Fyodor silently willed the old man to go on. There were five of them on the team that had been appointed to unravel the Vasily Kogan mystery. Alexei Proznost, seventy-four, had been a pioneer in the use of brainwashing. His mind was somewhat addled by too many years on the bottle, the few teeth he had left were mottled and crooked, and one usually had to sit more than six feet away from him to avoid the sour stench of his bathing habit, which, Fyodor speculated, was a once a month thing. Still, the young bioneurologist thought, this wizened old man probably knew more than the four of them combined.

Sasha Vylukov, a middle-aged bureaucrat, had survived the demise of communism by his very blandness. His duty was to record and synthesize what the others said. If he'd ever had an original thought of his own, one would never have known it. He was a master at aligning himself with whatever the majority felt. If there were no majority, he always said that he needed more time to consider the matter carefully.

Fyodor was most attracted to Vera Galovna, the group's biotechnician. Although her face was square and plain, her skin was a healthy, rosy color, she had fine, large breasts, and there was a wonderful, earthiness about her.

Tadeusz Kolodny, a middle-aged Polish Jew, who'd never requested an exit visa for Israel, had retained his position as a State neurosurgeon. He gently nudged Proznost to continue. "Could there be a two-step mind regeneration process, Alexei Pyotrovich? Programming supported by a physical implant?"

"We were unable to perfect it in the Chinese laboratory because of internal disputes. Years later, I heard that Professor Lee's daughter proposed a multi-step process."

"Would a brain incision assist us in determining whether or not that had been used here?" the Polish neurosurgeon asked.

"It would be less intrusive to use virtual imaging," Fyodor replied.

There was bitter, collective laughter. In these days of moneyless Russia, there was a ten-month wait to use one of the eleven PET scan units still operating in the capital. Fyodor knew that the MRI was a dream that would not come to pass for another five years, and that virtual imaging was something akin to science fiction.

"Perhaps," Fyodor mused, "we might ask our American friends to observe him on one of their machines?"

There was an excited buzz within the group. Moments later, that excitement dampened when Sasha Vylukov, who'd excused himself to make a call, returned and indicated that State Security paperwork necessary to send Vasily Kogan abroad would take six months.

15

"Jeff? Amy Roth."

"Hi. I expected you'd be calling earlier."

"I'm sorry. Depositions ran 'til six thirty. I just missed getting a speeding ticket, but I managed to make it here in one piece?"

"Where are you?"

"The Montclair. Just checked in. Have you been able to locate *ChildFinders?*"

"I'm afraid not." He heard her discouraged sigh. "That doesn't mean I haven't found some information that might eventually lead me to it. Meanwhile, all I've got is a WAG."

"WAG?"

"Wild-ass guess. Have you eaten yet?"

"Nope. I'm famished."

"Tell you what. I know how anxious you are to get any information that might shed some light on your . . . problem. I'm not dressed for company, torn shirt, scuzzy pants, socks that don't match, but if you don't mind, I could order some take-out food, hop into the Mustang, pick you up and bring you back here."

"Sounds like an awfully un-original and not particularly charming way to get a girl over to your apartment."

"The way I look, and probably the way I smell, you'd better believe it's original. Look, if you don't want to, I'll understand—"

"What kind of food do you like best?"

"Why?"

"I'll get the food. I've got a Lexus, courtesy of Cunningham-MacLeish. Just give me your address."

Amy took in the front room of the apartment. Dark brown fabric sofa, flanked by two wooden captain's chairs. A driftwood table sat in front of the sparse assembly, bare except for an Oriental water pipe and a small brass figurine. A Panasonic stereo console, surrounded by floor-to-ceiling bookcases, occupied the wall opposite the sofa. Off to the side, an ebony-colored upright piano. Nothing quite matched.

"Early garage sale," Savage said. "When Connie split, I gave her everything except the Pakistani rug on the floor, the piano, and the Turkish water pipe. I scrounged up the rest. It's not much, but it's mine."

Amy noticed, not for the first time, his completely unaffected boyishness. She felt a pleasant tingle.

"I brought Chinese food if that's OK," she said.

"Fine. Want to eat it in the kitchen or the workroom?"

"Whichever."

"I'll get some plates and we'll go into the den. Might as well get started." He disappeared into an adjoining room. Moments later he reappeared, carrying a tray with two plates, cartons of food, and two cans of Diet Coke. "Follow me into my chamber of horrors," he said.

At the end of a hallway, they turned left and entered a twelve by fifteen-foot den. A tan, four-drawer, Steelcase file cabinet stood in an alcove, next to a small Samsung television set. Most of the large pine desk was occupied by a computer setup and a series of reference books. There was a six-inch-high stack of papers to the left of the computer and a similar pile on the floor beneath the desk. Four travel posters depicting Vienna, Venice, Cape Town, and Istanbul, covered the nearest wall. A fluorescent fixture provided the alcove with off-white light.

"The work center," Savage remarked.

"Care to tell me what you've found?"

"What I haven't found is *ChildFinders*. What I have found is a gigantic puzzle that might involve *ChildFinders*. If it does, God help us all."

"Would you like some food while you're explaining?"

"Now that you mention it, yes."

"Fried rice or chow mein?"

"Both, please."

Jeff laid out several sheets of cross-referenced deductions and conclusions. Amy listened as he summed up his findings. "We have a three hundred ninety-two percent rise in unexplained political deaths over the same period last year. Two of those killed had achieved the pinnacle of leadership."

"My late former husband certainly wasn't in a position of leadership anywhere."

"That's why I believe his death was an accident."

"I notice you avoided using the word 'crime.'"

"I don't consider any of these acts to be crimes."

He walked her through the lists, explaining as he went. "We have three kinds of cases: the deed where the actor is still alive—"

"Like Melissa?"

"Yes. There are six of those. Next, we have cases involving suicide victims. Then, there are deaths where a close associate of the victim died under mysterious circumstances. Of the six live suspects, each claims to have no knowledge of what he or she did. The tests show they're all telling the truth."

"So Melissa's not an aberration?"

"Except she didn't kill a public figure, she's typical."

He showed Amy a list of forty-eight names, ranging in age from eight to thirty-seven, that he'd picked from around the world. Only three were from the United States. The youngest of the group was Melissa. There were separately stapled sheets for each of the names.

"Do you notice anything in common?" he asked.

Amy paled. "Each one disappeared for a period of ten to fourteen days earlier in their lives. None recalled where they'd been or what they'd done during their absence."

"Do you see where I'm headed?"

"I think so."

"The oldest person involved in the killings is thirty-seven. If we deduct the age at which that person disappeared, seventeen, we project a twenty-year operation."

"Go on."

"If we take the information we've got on Melissa and add it to what we know about the others, it would be logical to suggest that while they were missing they were subjected to some kind of hypnosis."

"Don't tell me you believe in that *National Enquirer* stuff, 'I was kidnapped by little green men from Mars'—?"

"I don't believe or discount anything. I have too little evidence to come to any solid conclusions."

"What does your intuition tell you?"

Jeff looked at his watch and smiled. "That it's nearly midnight. If you need to go back to the hotel and get up early tomorrow—?"

"No," she answered. "This is more important to me than sleep. Please continue."

"Suppose Melissa wasn't the only person who was hypnotized. What if a lot of people disappeared? What if they each started out in different places and were returned, brainwashed, to those same places?"

"Sounds like science fiction to me."

"Things we called 'science fiction' a few decades ago are common today. The Chinese developed brainwashing to a high art in the 70s and 80s. Suppose there were someone—or some*ones*—who kidnapped people just to see how far they could take the technique?"

"I hate to rain on your parade, but you've taken some random events and projected a conspiracy theory like the Kennedy assassination. Even now, people don't let that poor man's death just die. It's like a little boy who picks at a scab and keeps picking. Unless it's left to heal, it'll never get well. I'm having trouble concentrating now. Would you like something to drink?"

"Tea, please. It's in the cupboard to the right of the fridge."

She left and returned momentarily with two mugs that didn't match.

"Suppose *ChildFinders* is such an organization," Savage continued, as though he hadn't heard her. "We're into the next generation of nasty games. We don't have a Soviet Union on the other side anymore, but we do have Russia, China, Iran, North Korea, and a dozen other countries or groups who'd profit from anarchy. Your friend Cunningham said it would harm *ChildFinders*' efforts if kidnappers knew exactly where they were operating."

"The man who brought Melissa back told me the same thing."

"That makes sense. Perhaps Melissa is one of the pawns in the dirty little games mind warriors play."

"You're telling me to stop looking for *ChildFinders* because I'm not going to find them?"

"Locating *ChildFinders* is not the end of the story. The main thing as far as you're concerned is to find out what really happened to Melissa and why."

"Whom do you suggest I ask?"

"Charles Cunningham."

"Why him?"

Savage picked up another sheaf of papers. "This is a deep search dossier on Mister Cunningham. Over ten thousand pages. Inherited his way into the practice, married to the same society woman for more years than you've been on the planet, no children, been on every committee that means anything to anyone. By the way, have you ever heard of the World Security Commission? It used to be called the Trilateral Commission?"

"Another sidestep?"

"Maybe. There've been rumors about it for years. It's supposed to be a tight clique of the most powerful people on earth. I'm not talking presidents and kings, I'm talking heavy-duty, across-the-board, around-the-world power."

"Secret?"

"Uh-huh. The Cray Titan might come up with a couple of names, but I'll bet you a thousand dollars to your one it won't come up with more than that."

"How does that tie in to what we're talking about?"

"Those reputed to be members of the Commission have been quietly speaking about a world government for years. Twenty-four years ago,

Charles Cunningham made overtures to gain entry into what was then the Trilateral Commission."

"And?"

"I don't know anything more than that."

"Where does that leave us?"

"If Cunningham's a member of the Group, or if he's friends with members of the World Security Commission, he'd have access to far more information than he's disclosed to you."

"About *ChildFinders*?"

"Yes."

"Why do you say that?"

"I've done some quick analysis. *ChildFinders* and *Luftleben* are both Liechtenstein corporations. That, in and of itself, is no big deal. Half of the multinational corporations in Europe that want to keep secrets are headquartered in Liechtenstein. Their corporate laws are the most protective in the world. Among other things, they have bearer stock. That means whoever holds the stock certificates owns the stock, and Liechtenstein doesn't check into who the owners are or what their connections might be.

"More important, both *ChildFinders* and *Luftleben* use the Bank of the South Pacific. Cunningham-MacLeish has represented the Bank of the South Pacific and one of C-M's partners, Donald Mangam, served on its board of directors from 2006 to 2010." Amy looked at Savage quizzically. "To answer your question," he said, "there's at least one lead connecting Charles Cunningham to *ChildFinders*."

"So what? Murderers, rapists, princes, and paupers all over the world have bank accounts."

"But Bank of the South Pacific is neither Bank of America nor Chase. It's a small, private, offshore bank, serving a select group of clients. Cunningham-MacLeish had somebody on its board for four years. Unquestionably, the firm has maintained connections with the Bank. Offshore banks don't deal with Federal regulators. The identity of their customers is easily kept secret."

"Are you suggesting that Charles Cunningham has connections who could trace deposits and checks?"

"Score one for the lawyer."

Savage noticed that although Amy was trying hard to concentrate, she tried to stifle a yawn. "Finally getting tired?" he asked.

"Does it show?"

"Uh-huh."

"I don't mean to put you off, Jeff. I appreciate all of your help more than I can tell you, but I've been up since five this morning. I'm absolutely exhausted. What time is it?"

"Almost one a.m. Actually, there's not much more I can tell you tonight. I hope you'll consider this in the way it's meant, but would you like to sleep over?"

"That's certainly the most direct proposition any man has ever made to me."

"It wasn't meant like that at all. I've only got one bed and a saggy couch."

"I really am much too tired to drive back to the Montclair at this hour. Do you at least have a spare toothbrush?"

"A toothbrush and an old bathrobe if you need it."

"Very well, Mister Chivalry."

Within half an hour, each had dropped off to sleep on opposite sides of the bed, using separate blankets.

The clock radio read 4:20 A.M. It was cold. Amy wrapped herself more tightly in the blanket and drifted into light sleep. She awoke when she heard the flush of a toilet down the hall. When Jeff returned to the bed, she kept her eyes closed and lay still, breathing softly. It was still cold.

Savage climbed into bed quietly, covered himself, and tried to ease back to sleep, so as not to disturb her. He chuckled to himself at the irony of the situation. He was sleeping with one of the most attractive women he'd ever met, close enough to inhale the soft, fresh, woman scent emanating from her body, close enough to realize he was feeling an incredible excitement, yet not sleeping with her at all. He longed to reach out and touch her, just to see if she was real or if he was dreaming.

He rolled over onto his side, reached out tentatively, and gently touched the spot where her hip rose under the covers. She sighed softly and moved closer to him. He could feel the warmth from her body. It was wonderful. It made it so much easier to relax. And it felt so nice. He was soon sound asleep again.

"Charles?"

"Yes, Rajendra."

"Savage has picked up Höffer, Bank of the South Pacific, and Mangam."

"Not to worry, my friend. Mangam's dead, hundreds of offshore companies all over the world use Höffer, and we're certainly open about using the Bank. They've cut things down from infinity to one chance in several million. Believe me, Rajendra, there's nothing to worry about."

"You're sure you don't want me to change anything?"

The American smiled to himself. "No, Rajendra, I don't think that will be necessary at this time." *Let them feel they're getting closer*, he thought. *The game's more exciting that way.*

16

Savage awoke to the smell of fresh brewed coffee and the sound of industrious banging in the kitchen. He looked over at the clock. Eight a.m. He showered, shaved, brushed his teeth, and emerged from the bedroom.

"How do you like your eggs?" Amy called out.

"Surprise me," he responded.

Even without makeup, she looked lovely.

"What do you intend to do today?" she asked.

"I thought we'd go over to the computer department. I'd like to introduce you to Ron Ames, try to steal some time on one of his mainframes, and see if you can give me a different slant on my questions."

"Why is that any better than working from here? You can access the mainframe for your home, can't you?" Amy asked.

"Yes, but our system administrator created a multitasking search program at the lab that will make gathering information much faster."

"Would you mind if I stopped at the Montclair and changed into something more comfortable and less ravishing?"

"Do I have a choice?"

"Nope."

"I can see why you decided to help the damsel in distress." Ames took Amy's hand and kissed it.

"That means at least two of us have eyes that still work," Jeff responded.

"Listen, you male chauvinists, I hate to burst your little balloons, but I was charmed into coming here by the promise of work to be done. I've got two days to do it."

They walked through the glass doors into the computer laboratory. Amy felt an immediate chill as they entered the air-conditioned environment. *Why do they always keep these places so cold?* she thought, as they walked through the computer center to the system administrator's terminal. It was in a cramped room with a terminal on a small desk, a high-speed printer in one corner, a file cabinet, and two chairs. Amy dropped her jacket over the back of one of the chairs. She looked around at Jeff, smiling.

"What's so funny?" Jeff asked. "You like small spaces?"

"No, it's just so typically college. I've been away from this world for a long time."

"Things don't change much around here."

"Where do we start?" Amy looked from the computer to Jeff.

"By cross-referencing the stuff we found last night."

Jeff spent the first several minutes cross-referencing Bank of the South Pacific and Karl Höffer. Fifty-one of Höffer's clients had utilized the bank since 1993. Forty were Cunningham-MacLeish clients.

"Isn't doing what we're doing a violation of the attorney-client privilege?" Amy asked, raising her eyebrows.

"Yep, but there's nothing here that's not readily available information," Jeff responded. "Unless all your clients pay cash, it's easy for anyone with a computer and the right database to learn exactly who they are. Attorneys make bank deposits, checks clear through the attorneys' accounts. Every court file is a public document that reveals who represented whom, in what kind of case, and when. I can usually access attorney-client information in less than ten minutes."

Of the forty entries, they paid particular attention to two, *ChildFinders* and *Luftleben*, but beyond the coincidence of representation, they uncovered no new information on either entity.

"Could I try a little 'wild-ass guessing?'" Amy asked.

"Be my guest," he replied.

"The link between *ChildFinders* and the outside world seems to be *Luftleben*, right?"

"Yes."

"*Luft* refers to something having to do with 'air,' such as an airline or an air carrier. '*Mit Luftpost*' means 'By airmail' in Switzerland and Austria. The German national airline is Lufthansa."

"You think *Luftleben*'s an airline or air carrier service?"

"Maybe."

Savage punched up a list of the world's commercial carriers and private air services. No *Luftleben*. He scowled. "Another blind alley."

"Not necessarily. *Luftleben* is registered in Liechtenstein. Can you access aircraft registrations in Liechtenstein?"

"Yes."

There was a knock on the door. Savage got up to answer it, surprised that he felt a tightness in his neck from the tension. He rolled his neck to the right, then to the left, and did a few stretching exercises to restore circulation. When he opened the door, he faced a smiling Ron Ames. "Hope I'm interrupting something."

"Hi, Ron," Amy said. "Do you need the computer?"

"No. I thought you two could use an extra brain."

"The more the merrier," Jeff said. "Join the hunt."

Within minutes they located five aircraft registered to *Luftleben*: a 1963 Cessna 205 Stationair, Congo Registration Q9-TLC; a Grumman Gulfstream IV, Liechtenstein Registration HB*7594; a Lear 50, HB*7242; and two Boeing 767s, HB*3647 and HB*3672.

"Let's track the reported flights of each of these aircraft during the past five years," Ames suggested.

Another few minutes and Amy, who'd quickly become adept at tracing information said, "The only data on the Stationair shows landing requests at Kamina and Lumumbashi, in eastern Congo."

"I've piloted small planes," Jeff said. "Unless that aircraft has nothing but fuel tanks everywhere, a 205's only got a range of six hundred fifty miles. Even though we've only got two reference points, we can triangulate by plotting seven-hundred-mile circles using Kamina and Lumumbashi as end points." While Savage produced the trace lines at one terminal, Ames worked at another.

"The other planes have a much wider flight range," Ron said.

"That's not surprising," Savage remarked, looking up from his computer-generated drawings. "They've got intercontinental capability. If they fly at normal jet altitudes, they're required to file IFR flight plans."

"Can you reduce the printout to a map?" Amy asked.

"Sure," Ames responded. "Why?"

"I've done a lot of commercial flying. All airlines publish in-flight magazines showing the routes they fly. You can spot their hubs by finding where all the lines converge."

"Good idea, Amy," Jeff said.

When the printout was finished, Amy said, "Most of the flights center within the area bounded by Jeff's two circles."

"All of these particular aircraft use Africa as a hub," Ron said. "There's nothing unusual about that. There are at least six African capitals within the radius you've drawn."

"Yes," Savage answered, "but, with the exception of Nairobi, not one of them's a major airline destination, and the point at which each of them closed out their flight plans is far from any capital. A private aircraft is free to cancel its IFR flight plan before it lands."

"Why not see if any of the aircraft were ever registered to anyone other than *Luftleben*?" Ames suggested.

The computer information showed that *Luftleben* was the original owner of the Grumman and the Lear. One of the 767s had been owned by United Air Lines and the other had been owned by American Airlines and Citybird before they'd been purchased by Luftleben.

"The Stationair puzzles me," Jeff said. "*Luftleben*'s owned the plane since 1983, twenty years after it was built."

"Can you think of any way to determine where it was before that?" Amy asked.

"The frame number's the only reliable reference," Jeff said. "Light aircraft change engines every two thousand hours."

Five minutes later, Savage found that 9Q-TLC, which had previously been HB*3537, had originally been registered in the United States as N8454Z. "I should have a list of owners back to Day One in another minute," he said. It took less than that. When the entry came up, Savage swore under his breath.

"What is it?" Amy asked.

"See for yourself," he said.

N8454Z, 1963 Cessna 205 Stationair, manufactured August 20, 1963. Registered owner: Charles Flanders Cunningham, III—

After lunch at the Co-Op, Ron excused himself to attend an early afternoon appointment. Jeff suggested that he and Amy walk around the campus until Ron's meeting was over. "I think we need to clear our heads, so we know there's still such a thing as sunshine, blue skies and ivy-covered walls. My brain's on overload."

The school had originally been built in the mid-1800's. Several of its structures were covered with ivy, but as Hamilton grew it kept pace with the times. Futuristic glass buildings were more numerous than their dignified predecessors.

"Hi, Professor Savage," Amy heard somebody shout. She turned and saw a tall, leggy blonde. The girl was wearing a short skirt and halter top.

"Hello, er, Tanya." Amy noticed the stumble in his voice, and saw the flames of embarrassment licking at his cheeks. "How are you?"

"Oh, not bad," the girl said. "I haven't seen you around the work-out room, recently. Have you changed your exercise regimen?" Amy noticed that the blonde was looking at her, not Jeff. She wasn't sure whether to laugh or feel insulted. Instead, she remained silent. Let the professor get himself out of this one, she thought.

"Uh, I've just been busy grading term papers. I'll be back on my old program, soon. Have a nice day, Tanya." Jeff moved to walk on. Amy paused a moment before following. Just enough that he had to slow down.

"See ya, Doc," the blonde's voice said from over their shoulders.

"A lady friend?" Amy asked.

"Hardly. A co-ed, probably not more than half my age."

"No need to feel embarrassed. May I ask a personal question, Jeff?"

"I reserve the right to refuse to answer."

"Fair enough. What happened between you and Connie?"

"We followed our hormones into a relationship. After three years of dating, it was 'What do we do now?' So, we married young. After three more years, Connie decided campus life was a bore and her gynecologist either made a lot more income or was a lot better in the sack, maybe both, and off she ran."

"You seem to be able to talk about it pretty easily."

"I wasn't for a long time."

"Seems you have all the opportunity you want for feminine companionship at Hamilton."

"I date. Mostly I have friends who happen to be girls, rather than girlfriends. No real attachments."

While they walked back toward the computer laboratory, Amy mused, "Daniel and I had a good marriage at first. Same story as yours, I suppose, except no one ran off with anyone, and there wasn't any rancor when we divorced."

"I don't mean to come off as sexist, but I think men would come out of the woodwork once they knew you were available," he said. "You're beautiful, bright, independent—"

"And not that naïve, Jeff. I've got an eight-year-old child who, at least until we can prove otherwise, may be a psychopathic murderer, a sweet little girl who killed her father and doesn't even remember it. I'm capable of making a good living on my own. I'd always be looking over my shoulder, even if a man wanted to marry me, and asking why."

"Eventually you've got to trust someone."

"I'm sure I'll get to that point. Now's just not the right time. Come on, friend. We've got some work to do."

"Yes, ma'am," he said obediently.

"The connection to Charles Cunningham is getting stronger," Ames said. "Whatever's going on is happening somewhere in central Africa.

Let's go over the other entries that tie Bank of the South Pacific, Höffer and Cunningham-MacLeish together and see if we can make progress."

After they'd carefully studied several additional printout sheets, Amy said, "Jeff, last night you mentioned something about mass hypnosis and brainwashing."

"I did."

"What kind of facility would you expect to engage in that kind of activity?"

"A government entity."

"Or a medical clinic?"

"Maybe."

"I think I may have come up with something."

She pulled one of the sheets. Savage read the entry.

CHILDREN'S INSTITUTE OF CENTRAL AFRICA

Address: Administrative Headquarters: Private Box 4840, Kinshasa, Congo. Physical plant: Manono, Congo.

Description: Charitable entity. 200-bed hospital and adjacent home for orphaned children. Funded through the Preservation Trust (Pty., Ltd.), Geneva, Switzerland. Bank Reference: Bank of the South Pacific. Qualified physicians and surgeons: 3. Nursing employees: 15. Other employees: 150.

Organization: Corporation registered in Vaduz, Liechtenstein. Box 370-AG. Shareholder: The Preservation Trust (Pty., Ltd.), Box 13100, Geneva, Switzerland. Registered Agent: K. Höffer, Box 370-AG, Vaduz, Liechtenstein. Reference in the Democratic Republic of the Congo: Hon. G. M'Bele, Office of the Interior Ministry, Kinshasa.

History: The Children's Institute was founded in 1993 by the Preservation Trust. The physical plant, in Manono (Pop. 2,500, est.) in Shaba Province, Southeastern Congo, is the most modern, well-equipped facility of its type in the area. It consists of a two-story concrete structure and numerous residential outbuildings. During its twenty-five-year existence, the Institute has served thousands of men, women, and chil-

dren. The Honorable G. M'bele, interior minister of Republic of the Congo, proposed the Institute for a Nobel prize on two occasions. Listed physicians are licensed in the Peoples' Republic of China, the United Kingdom, and the Democratic Republic of the Congo.

The Honorary Board of Trustees includes G. M'bele, Kinshasa, Congo; Doctor Lee Chung Lien, Beijing, PRC; Charles Cunningham III, USA; Doctor Rajendra Prasad, Calcutta, India; Hitoshi Kono, Lahaina, Maui, USA.

"The Democratic Republic of the Congo. Within the seven-hundred-mile radius. Cunningham. Bank of the South Pacific. Höffer. Five for five."

"Six for six," Amy said.

"What do you mean?"

"A hunch. Charles Cunningham's got a single photograph in his inner sanctum. A man named Guillaume M'bele. I wouldn't be at all surprised if that's the same person who's the reference for the Institute. Is the Preservation Trust on your list?"

"Yes," Ames replied.

"See if you can get more information on it. We may finally be closing in on the magnet that catches some of the needles in the haystack."

"Ron," Savage said. "I think it's time we called someone. Who'll it be, the Feds or

Caen?"

"Without question, Caen," Ames responded. "The choice is a no brainer. He's brighter than all the Feebies combined, and he can get through to them quicker than the president."

"They have identified the Institute. The flight charts make me nervous," the Indian said, as he handed his mentor the same sheaf of papers Amy, Jeff, and Ron Ames had been looking at minutes before.

"Rajendra," he said. "You worry too much. As long as the race is a tie, we win. Would you feel more at ease if there were two hunters instead of three?"

Prasad gave the tall man a questioning look.

"By the way, Rajendra, do you have the latest calculations?"

"Yes. Eighty-nine political deaths, two accidents."

"How many weapons have we used?"

"Two hundred twelve."

"So we have five hundred thirty-eight left?"

"Yes."

"Good."

The tall man found it prudent not to mention the additional operatives who'd been programmed since December and who did not appear on the current list of weapons.

17

The printout showed that Cunningham, Lee, Prasad, and Kono were Trustees of the Preservation Trust, but further research showed no more than that the Preservation Trust was administered under the laws of the Cayman Islands. Another dead end.

Savage looked at his watch. "Six o'clock. Time to quit for the night."

"What happens now?"

"I've retrieved sufficient input for my present purposes. Now I start building a wall of information by cementing in bricks.

"So I bow out for a while? Don't call me, I'll call you?"

"Not entirely, Amy. I feel extravagant tonight. I'd like some real food and the companionship of the loveliest woman within a radius of six feet. Are you up for a cowboy steak at Buffalo Ridge or are you one of those chicken, fish, and tofu types?"

"You're talking to a Midwestern girl who'll eat anything that doesn't bite back."

"Great. I'll drop you at Montclair House to freshen up and pick you up in an hour."

No sooner had Amy arrived at her room, she found the red, "message waiting" light flashing. She called the front desk.

"Four messages, Ms. Roth. Tomorrow's depositions have been changed from ten to eleven. Your daughter, Melissa, called at three this afternoon. She missed your wakeup call but says not to worry, everything's all right. Mister Cunningham called at four-twenty and again at five-thirty and asked that you call him as soon as possible."

"Thank you very much."

Amy felt a vague discomfort. Why would Charles call her now of all times? Ordinarily, it would not have disturbed her in the least, but she had just spent the day unearthing information about Cunningham that put an odd spin on their relationship. He'd told her he knew virtually nothing about *ChildFinders*. She, Jeff, and Ron had dug up evidence that demonstrated that if anyone had inside knowledge it was Cunningham.

Charles picked up the phone on the second ring. "Amy?"

"Is something wrong, Mister Cunningham?"

"Not at all. How are depositions going?"

Something was wrong, all right. He'd delegated cases to his trial teams for years and never gave a damn what was going on. All he wanted to hear was the final, favorable result. Charles Cunningham was not a man who dealt with minor details.

"We didn't have any today. Throckmorton's office had a law and motion matter that went all day."

"Oh? I didn't know that."

Of course he wouldn't know that. A one-day continuance of a deposition was "mouse nuts" on the scale of importance.

"So you had a day to see the sights, eh?"

"Actually, Jeff Savage and I got together."

There was a slight pause at the other end of the line before Cunningham said, "That's great, Amy, just great. How is he?"

"Fine. He sends his regards."

"Amy, I thought about you and Melissa today. Perhaps when you get back next week, we might sweep through the evidence once more. The thing with Melissa's been bothering me."

"I know how you feel, Mister Cunningham. The trail gets colder as time goes by. What I really want is to get my daughter out of that home," Amy said.

"That's exactly why I want to review the evidence. Anyway, I appreciate your humoring me, Amy. I'll see you next week. Give my regards to Professor Savage."

"Thank you, I will."

After she hung up, Amy's emotions were mixed. The puzzle had taken on an added dimension. She felt guilty for having suspected Cunningham of any untoward acts. Here he was, concerned for her welfare, still trying, three months later, to help her unravel the mystery. That was certainly above and beyond the call of duty. On the other hand, she was certain there'd been a hesitation when he heard she'd met with Jeff Savage. In the natural scheme of things, it was decidedly unnatural for Charles Cunningham to want to "review all the evidence" and embark on an investigation of Melissa three months after the fact.

"Hitoshi? We have two weapons within a hundred-mile radius of Hamilton University." Cunningham gave explicit instructions on what he wanted, then terminated the call.

He smiled inwardly. Life without challenge was a bore. It had always been a hollow victory when he'd trounced an easy opponent. He'd never considered there would be any opposition to his plan because it was so perfect, so foolproof. Now, he realized he might be the quarry. Even if his ultimate victory was a foregone conclusion, the pursuit might add a little spice.

"All right, Mister Savage," he said to himself. "If it's a game you want, I'll play along with it."

"Professor Ames, this is Templeman, night security. I hate to bother you, but we've had a break-in at the main computer room. Someone's done major damage to the Cray. I think you'd better come down."

"Who was that, darling?"

"Templeman, a night security guard at the university. He says there's been a break-in and a lot of damage. God knows what kind of damage has been done to the computer. I'd better go down there. Otherwise they'll only roust me out of bed in an hour or so."

"Want me to go with you?"

"No, Dana, I'll be back in a couple of hours." He looked at his watch. "With luck, I'll make the eleven o'clock news."

When he arrived at the Montclair, Jeff surprised Amy with a bouquet of long-stemmed roses. She surprised him by wearing a pair of tight jeans and an emerald green top, an outfit so flattering it left him momentarily speechless.

Buffalo Ridge was a sawdust-on-the-floor, oak plank table and bench place that served only one thing: steak. Twelve ounce, sixteen ounce, or the "Range Boss," a two-pound monster. "And all the beans, salad, and western bread you care to devour."

The restaurant commanded a view of the city below and the stars above. It was a warm, clear night. After dinner, they walked the "cowpoke's trail" outside. Their first kiss was an accidental thing they'd each unconsciously planned. It was delicious, garlicky, and sexy as hell, and they were both trembling when it was over.

"Is that how you treat all your visiting guests?" she asked, huskily.

"Only the beautiful ones." He tried to keep it light, but his own voice came out a croak.

"Come on, friend. Let's keep walking and talking before something happens that shouldn't."

"Why shouldn't it, Amy?"

"I'm not ready yet, Jeff, not that I don't find the idea incredibly appealing. During these last two days, you've made me feel alive again. It's just that more time has to pass."

"How much time, Amy?"

"Enough. I'll know when." She kissed him lightly on the cheek. "If you're around when the time comes, so will you. Now, good sir, I think it's time we were getting home. Maybe I'll be able to catch the eleven o'clock news before I fall asleep."

They entered the lobby of the Montclair House ten minutes before eleven. A crowd had gathered around the large television in the public room. The volume was turned up and the announcer's voice caught their attention immediately.

"We repeat, earlier this evening, there was a break-in and explosion at Hamilton University's computer center. Damage to the multimillion-dollar Cray supercomputer is believed to be extensive. In a bizarre twist to the story, Professor Ronald Ames, Chairman of Hamilton Computer Department, was en route to the scene when he was killed in a head-on collision. A car driven by Jason Antrim, sixteen, apparently wandered into Ames's lane of traffic. Police speculate that Antrim compounded the problem by accelerating instead of hitting the brake pedal. Antrim remains unconscious at Community Hospital. More details at eleven."

Two agents from the Bureau interviewed Jeff and Amy first thing the following morning. Abner Burchard and Donald Wilson looked so much alike they could have been mistaken for brothers.

"Neither of you is suspected of committing any crime," Wilson began. "If you'd like, you can have counsel present."

"That won't be necessary, Agent Wilson," Amy said. "I've talked to law enforcement personnel before. You're no doubt aware of the incident involving my daughter."

"I am. I apologize if I tread on sensitive toes by bringing it up."

"Not at all," she said. "What we've been working on for the past two days involved Melissa."

"Gentlemen," Savage said. "I asked Ron to call you about this whole thing over a month ago. He was my closest friend in the world." Amy could see he was close to tears. "Perhaps if you tell me how much you already know, I might be able to fill in some of the pieces."

Wilson looked at Abner Burchard, who nodded.

"We know you logged three hours on the Cray last Sunday, and that the two of you and Professor Ames spent most of yesterday in the lab.

"There was an apparent break-in at the center last evening. Mrs. Ames advised us that her husband got a telephone call from a security guard named Templeman. Professor Ames left home a few minutes later and said he expected to be home in two hours," Wilson continued. "There was no one named Templeman employed by the university security service."

"How badly was the Titan damaged?" Amy asked.

"It'll be down for at least two weeks," Burchard said. "Now it's your turn. Do you know any reason why what you've been doing would make someone want to destroy a hundred-million-dollar piece of equipment?"

"Yes, I believe I do," Jeff responded. "I trust you know my background?"

"Uh-huh," Wilson said.

"Good. That'll save time. Do you have a recording device?"

"Affirmative," Wilson replied.

"Then I suggest you turn it on."

Afterward, the four of them went to his apartment, where he led them through the printouts one-by-one, explaining his theory as he went along. When he'd concluded, Wilson said, "Everything you say makes logical sense, but how do you know you aren't barking up the wrong tree?"

"The simple answer is, I don't," Jeff said amiably. I've got access to information most people don't even dream about, but I'm still just one man."

"I'd hardly call Ezra Caen 'just one man,'" Burchard said, his tone mildly sardonic.

"Uh, I'd forgotten about that," Jeff replied, coloring slightly. "You've talked to him?"

"Of course. Dennis O'Brien was on the phone with the Agency within an hour after what happened. Since it was broad daylight in Tel Aviv, I'll give you one guess where the next call came from."

"So you've probably already got everything I've got and maybe then some."

"That's an affirmative. What I'm wondering is why you or Professor Ames didn't contact us before."

"You probably would have treated us like some kind of cranks."

"I'm afraid you're right," Wilson said.

"My turn to ask some favors?"

"I don't know if we can give them, but since you've been so cooperative with us, it doesn't hurt to ask."

"All right. Is Antrim conscious?"

"Mister Caen asked the same thing. Last thing we know, he wasn't."

"Is he under guard?"

"Yes."

"Good. I'd like you guys to run a check on him as soon as possible. In particular, find out if he's ever been away from home without explanation for any extended period of time. When he recovers consciousness, ask him what, if anything, he remembers about the auto accident that killed Ron Ames."

"Lots of people have no recall about a serious accident they've been in, Mister Savage," Abner Burchard said.

"Probably so," Savage replied. "But I'll bet if you get every psychologist, psychiatrist and hypnotist you can to talk to him, not only will he not recall the accident, he won't recall even being in the car. If what I speculate is true, I'm going to ask a lot bigger favor."

"Which is?"

"Get me every bit of information you can on every person and entity we've talked about this morning."

"We'd need approval from much higher authority, Professor Savage," Wilson said.

"I don't care what it takes. I gave you a lot of information on good faith. I've made a wild-ass guess that may come closer to the mark than anything your people have got. Deputize me, arrest me, put me under lock and key without telling anyone, violate my civil rights all you want—but get us that information."

"I'm glad you included us both," Amy said.

"Why shouldn't I? But for Melissa's tragedy we wouldn't be here now. In the words of our history books, she may well have fired the shot heard 'round the world."

"What do you mean?"

"Amy, I'm going to make an assumption I probably have no right to make. It's the wildest hunch of all. I believe Melissa is a weapon that accidentally misfired."

Amy paled. "Oh, my God!" she exclaimed softly.

"What is it?" Burchard asked.

"A few nights after Daniel's death, I went back to the office. I saw lights on in Mister Cunningham's suite. When I went up to see him, I heard him speaking on the telephone about a weapon that misfired. I forgot about that, until now."

Later that evening, after Amy had left for Winchester Township, Jeff visited Dana Ames. Her eyes were swollen and puffy from crying, but she was remarkably composed.

"Jeff, you were his best friend."

"Second best, Dana. You were always first."

"Do you really think it was an accident?"

"I don't know."

"Could it have had something to do with what you two were working on?"

At the mention of their weekly activities, Jeff's eyes teared and he felt a huge lump in his throat. What would Wednesday nights be like now? It hit him with a gut-wrenching realization that but for Ron Ames he really didn't have many friends. As he looked back on their relationship, he only now began to realize that he'd had major surgery. A very big part of his heart had been torn out.

He fought down the feeling of terrible loneliness, realizing he'd have to put on a brave face for the lovely woman who'd shared Ron's life and who'd be left more alone than he.

"Yes, Dana, I think it very much had to do with our Wednesday night stuff."

After he got home, for the first time since Connie left, he cried himself to sleep. Midway through the night, when he relived what he and Ron had been doing the past few months, he suddenly felt a cold, hard anger building within him. He muttered what he'd thought, but not voiced, to Dana Ames. "If what I believe is true, I'm going to make one monstrous sonofabitch pay dearly for this."

18

"Ezra, now I truly need your guidance. And even more, your help."

"All you need to do is ask, *boychik.*"

"How much do you know about computer research?"

"About as much as I know about anything else, which isn't all that much. But I've got friends who could help me."

"You told me about Adi Shamir's and Shafi Goldwasser. They're world-class heavyweights. The next question's harder. I know Ron Ames' password, which they've probably shut down by now. Is there any way in the world you can get into any of the supercomputers?"

"Which one do you want, the Summit, the TaihuLight, or numbers three, five, and six in the world?"

"This is no time for joking, Ezra."

"I'm not joking, Jeff. Two hundred sixteen of the top 500 supercomputers in service today rely on Mellanox Technologies' InfiniBand to accelerate their systems. Mellanox is an Israeli company and I know its president quite well."

As demoralized as Jeff Savage was from the tragedy involving Ames, he realized that Ezra Caen had just opened the door to the biggest toyshop in the world.

"How soon can we get together, Ezra?"

"Would a week be soon enough? Where would you suggest we meet?"

"If I had my 'druthers, I'd suggest Oak Ridge or Lawrence Livermore, but Hamilton University is certainly okay. The Cray's number nine, which would probably be enough to serve our needs. Next week works for me, Ezra. Do you want me to pick you up at Dulles?"

"Depending on what you send me, I may want to come early, call on a few friends in D.C., and get their input."

Five days later, a short middle-aged man, so nondescript he'd fade into the woodwork and be forgotten five minutes after he'd entered, came into the headquarters offices of Cunningham-MacLeish. He asked politely if he could speak with Charles Cunningham for a few moments. The receptionist, after ascertaining he did not have an appointment, asked if the man could leave a message and relayed that Mister Cunningham was overseas and would be returning the following week.

The visitor said, "Of course, I understand." He handed the receptionist a sealed letter marked, "Personal and confidential please," then added, "If Mister Cunningham wishes to contact me, I can be reached care of an address inside the envelope."

He thanked her for her time, left the letter, and departed. The receptionist, in turn, transmitted the sealed letter to Sharon Graham's desk.

When Charles Cunningham returned and was going through his correspondence a week later, he opened the envelope and read, "If you continue with your plans, we wish you luck. You'll need it. s/Secretary of the Trilateral Commission." There was no return address on or inside the envelope.

SUMMER

19

They were sitting outside the mansion, sipping iced tea and enjoying the cool afternoon breeze when Cunningham said, "It's been six months since the war started. The world needs stability more than ever. It's not a nice time to be alive. Interesting, perhaps, but not safe. With so much violence going on, one or two more deaths, even if they involve important people, merit little more than a column inch on page twenty-four." He turned to face his computer wizard. "Rajendra, what's the current count?"

"One hundred eighteen deaths, not counting the two accidents. We've used two hundred sixty-three weapons."

"Do any of you foresee any problems?" he asked.

"Yes," Chung Lien said. "The Russians have contacted their American counterparts over the Baikal affair. They hope to get Kogan to Johns Hopkins by mid-August."

"By that time, we'll have erased another forty-five people."

"Charles, I'm concerned you seem to be taking Savage so lightly," she said. "He seems determined to avenge what he perceives as his friend's murder. Don't you think it's time to bring the mother and daughter in?"

"No, Chung Lien. We must not ruin the experiment by bringing the mother in yet. I concur we should retrieve the daughter."

"The mother already suspects something," Chung Lien said.

"Perhaps," Cunningham replied. "But she has no idea of—" He

paused as Doctor Lee nodded. "Besides, we need every weapon in our arsenal available for instant use. "Kono," he said, changing the subject. "Are *Luftleben* and *ChildFinders* still operating normally?"

"Yes, but I'm starting to share Doctor Lee's concern, Papa-sama. I think we should suspend operations for now. Whoever's been conducting computer searches seems too interested in our air transportation arm."

The American glanced at a handwritten list. *ChildFinders* was still bringing in new subjects every ten days. Unknown to the others, he'd started bringing in four additional recruits each month from the surrounding tribes in southern Congo. There'd be fifty-four unaccounted-for weapons by the end of the week. He sighed. "You're right, Kono. It's an unnecessary risk. Effective immediately, we'll shut down *Luftleben* and *ChildFinders*."

"What about the weapons we've programmed since January?" Chung Lien asked. "Have you made a list of them?"

"Only a handwritten one, I'm afraid," Cunningham remarked, seeming embarrassed. "Maybe it's best I keep that list separate until we need those reserve weapons. Any objections?" There were none.

"What's our timetable?" Prasad asked.

"Mid-November."

"What if we can't address the world leaders by that time?"

"Trust me," Cunningham said. "We will."

"One hundred eighteen deaths that follow the same pattern. A seven hundred percent increase over the same period last year. Now do you believe me?"

"It's hard to refute your figures, Professor Savage," Burchard said. "Particularly when you were right on target about Antrim."

"If we're going to work together, would you mind if we use first names? I'd feel more comfortable. And since you probably know more about Amy and me than we do about each other, don't you think turnabout's fair play?"

"I don't see why not," Burchard said. Jeff guessed he was forty. The man stood six feet tall and was a series of squares, square face, unstylish crew cut, blocklike body. Only his eyes, gray-green, open, and intelligent, distinguished him.

"Not much to tell," he said. "I grew up in the hills of Kentucky. We were so poor we couldn't pay attention. I graduated Kentucky Law School. The FBI recruiters made it sound wonderful and it was, for the first couple of years." He looked down. "There are certain things they don't tell you when you're in training. Like how the adrenalin flows just before you walk into some sorry slob's house and tell him he's under arrest. Or when you crash into some poor woman's house with a search warrant and tell her that her boyfriend's forging hundred-dollar bills and in the process you trash a lifetime collection of clay pigs and toy dolls, and rip through her bras and undies looking for a stash of bogus bills while a pair of little kids look up at you in stark terror.

"They don't tell you that when you're combing the back hills for suspected bank robbers you might have to arrest your brother—"

"I'm sorry," Amy said.

"It's got nothing to do with you, Mrs. Roth," Burchard said. "I chose to join the Agency. That means I play by their rules."

"At first, it was a lot easier for me," Wilson said. He was an inch shorter and two or three years younger than his partner. He, too, was a solid box of a man. "I was the eldest of three sons of a Florida produce broker. I was all-state halfback the year I graduated high school, went to Louisiana on a football scholarship and ended up taking an accounting degree at Tulane. During my last year, the Bureau contacted me. What they offered was considerably more exciting than number crunching, so I came aboard and never looked back."

"The perfect life," Jeff said.

"It was, until I fired a little too slowly to save my first partner, did three months of therapy, and fell behind on my child support payments."

"I thought they frowned on that sort of thing," Amy said.

"They do," Wilson replied. "The public's image of FBI agents isn't always accurate. We're all supposed to be lily-white knights in shining armor, like the old TV show. Why destroy their image by letting them know we don't solve all the crimes and we suffer from the same weaknesses they do? Some of us screw around, some drink too much, a few have been bought."

"So now that we're working together, what do we call you?" Jeff asked. "Do you really go by Abner, Agent Burchard? No offense meant."

"Yes, I do. I know it sounds hokey as hell, but I figured if it was good enough for my parents, it's good enough for me."

"Don?"

"I prefer Buzz," he said, smiling. "Shall we get back to business?"

"Suits me," Jeff responded.

"We're trying to get the Russians to send Vasily Kogan to Washington for PET scan, MRI imaging, and even a virtual scan," Wilson said. "The Russians suggested surgery if we don't find anything."

"How come it's taking so long to get him here?" Savage asked. "The Baikal incident took place two months ago."

"Last winter took a lot out of the country. Food for the starving and medical services for the seriously ill take priority over an expense-paid vacation to the U.S., especially for the security group. The Russian government wanted the investigation completed as quickly and quietly as possible. They were not pleased at the specter of their limited funds being used for these kinds of expenses."

"Do you propose to perform surgery on Melissa?" Amy asked.

"No," Wilson said. "VanBurgh's available in Georgia."

"How secure is he?" Savage asked.

"What do you mean?"

"Suppose he was programmed. Wouldn't it be logical that whoever sent VanBurgh out would be concerned that their weapon was still floating around?"

"From everything we've determined, once these weapons have fired they're used up," Wilson said. We'll do a scan on VanBurgh at the same time we do one on Kogan."

Just then there was a muted ring on the intercom.

"Agent Burchard, there's a call for you."

"Thanks, Gladys." Burchard reached for the phone, pressed the flashing red button and listened. Aside from "Uh-huh's" and slight nods, he gave no hint of what he was hearing.

After five minutes, he hung up the phone and spoke in a low voice. "VanBurgh was stabbed to death and someone gave Antrim a lethal injection within the past hour. The Deputy Chief has taken us off the case. He implied in no uncertain terms that it was not his wish to terminate the investigation, but that pressure was coming from high up the line."

"What do we do now?" Savage asked. "We all know who's next on the hit list—the only living survivor in the United States. Have you been told to stop guarding Melissa as well?"

"Not exactly," Burchard said, a slow smile coming to his face. "We can't always fight City Hall directly. But remember, even old Joshua walked around Jericho for days before the walls came tumbling down."

"What do you mean?" Amy asked.

"The word I got was we *officially* stand down from this case. What I do on my own time's my own business. Buzz?"

"Count me in. How do we protect Melissa?"

"Suppose I were to call you know who?" Savage asked. "If he was able to protect an unwilling Ayatollah with a hundred thousand people on the square, he just might be able to keep a little girl safe. I'm sure he's got an idea how to do it." Turning to Amy, he said, "How close tabs can you keep on Cunningham?"

"He could be halfway around the world on any given day. Sharon Graham guards him like he's the Messiah."

"Any cracks in her armor?"—

"None that I know of."

"All right," Burchard said. "We'll ask some off-duty friends to monitor Cunningham. I have a feeling the orders from 'on high,' came from him. If that's true, you can be sure he's got a reason for it. We may be getting closer than we think to figuring out what the puzzle's all about. Meanwhile, Jeff, you seem to be the one with the closest connection to Ezra Caen. See if he can be available for a conference call a few days from now."

Half a week later, Jeff Savage and the two special agents met in Burchard's office.

"Ten in the morning. Should be early evening in Israel. O.K. to make the call now?"

"Sure," Jeff said.

Just as Abner was starting to punch in the number, there was a sharp rap on the door."Can it wait a minute, Ma—?" Burchard froze in mid-sentence as the door opened.

The three men stood slack-jawed, momentarily unable to speak in the presence of the apparition. She was not particularly tall, 5'6" or so, in her early forties, with long blonde hair, a mirror image of the German-American model Heidi Klum, widely reputed to be the most beautiful woman on the planet, and a body that famed personality could only dream about.

"Gentlemen," she said in slight central European accent, dazzling the room with her smile, "whenever you're through staring at the merchandise, we can start the discussion. It doesn't bother me in the least to have three handsome young men appreciating what's in front of their eyes," she continued, "but we really should get down to business sooner rather than later."

Moments later, Ezra appeared, with Dennis O'Brien in tow. "You'll excuse us barging in like this," he said, "but Mister Savage said you needed the best baby sitter available to protect Melissa, and I couldn't think of anyone more suitable than Hypatia, who's agreed to come out of retirement as a favor to me."

"Hy-PAY-sha?" This from Wilson, whose normally deep bass voice came out a croak.

"You won't find a deadlier agent in Israel, which means you probably won't find a deadlier agent in the world. She was deep cover in Iran for almost a decade, the most valuable asset we had. I'm not at liberty to discuss the role she played in the assassin operation, except to say it was absolutely critical, and I'd sure trust her to keep *me* safe."

20

"Good morning, Hillcrest School. How may I help you?"

Charles Cunningham picked up the handset of the phone, cutting off the speaker. "Good morning," he said. "Might I please speak to Doctor Dunsford?" Cunningham knew very well that academicians loved to be referred to by their titles.

"I'll see if she's available, Sir. May I tell her who's calling?"

"Charles Cunningham the Third."

He smiled at the pregnant pause. "One moment, Mister Cunningham."

The line was silent for thirty seconds before Emily Dunsford, Hillcrest's principal, picked up. "Good morning, Mister Cunningham. It's a pleasure to hear from you again."

"Good morning, Doctor Dunsford. I hope I'm not interrupting anything?"

"Of course not, Mister Cunningham. I'm delighted to take your call. How may I help you? I daresay, could it be that another of your clients has decided to assist our building fund?"

Sometimes it surprised him how easily people were bought. A simple fifty-thousand dollar endowment, and this woman was practically ready to lick his boots. "I'm sorry to say I don't have such good news today. Rather, I wondered if you could answer a few questions for me. One of my partners, Amy Roth, has a daughter who was in your third-grade class."

"Melissa. A sweet child, Mister Cunningham, bright, well-behaved. What a dreadful shame that—"

"Yes, of course. Since her father's untimely death, I've taken a personal interest in the family—in a grandfatherly way, you might say."

"Of course, Mister Cunningham."

"I'd like to find out more about the child," he said. "*Entre nous*, I'd prefer this be done quietly."

"I understand, Mister Cunningham. Am I to trust the mother is not to know of your interest?"

"You are a wise and perceptive woman, Doctor Dunsford." He was well aware that she thought he was chasing Amy Roth as a trophy wife. That would serve his purpose. Undoubtedly, the headmistress had seen several older men hunting young widows and single mothers over the years. She'd probably received calls like this more than a hundred times. "You know, now that I think of it, the trust has certain discretionary funds. I'm certain I could convince our board of trustees to provide additional funding for, shall we say, administrative expenses. Might you have some time to see me later today, so we might chat?"

"I'd be flattered, Mister Cunningham."

"In that case, Doctor Dunsford—"

"Please call me Emily."

"Very well, Doctor D— Emily," he said, as though he were embarrassed. "Might I suggest lunch at Top of the Globe?"

"Why, I don't know what to say, Mister Cunningham."

"How about a simple, 'yes?' My chauffeur will pick you up at quarter to twelve. It'll simply be two friends meeting for lunch. Discretion is always important, you know."

"Of course. I look forward to meeting you in person."

Abner stood in front of the secretary's desk. The small sign on the desktop read, "Helen Picard."

The woman picked up the interoffice phone and pressed a button. A moment later she said, "Doctor Dunsford? A Mister Abner Burchard is here to see you."

Burchard stood patiently while the secretary listened to the voice at the other end of the line.

"She says she's very busy at the moment and is already running late for a luncheon meeting. If you'd like to come back at around three this afternoon—"

"Thank you, ma'am, but this won't take a moment." He pulled out his card case and continued, "This is official FBI business."

The woman spoke into the phone. "He's insistent, Doctor Dunsford. He's from the FBI." After a pause, she said to Abner, "I'm sorry, sir, but she simply doesn't have time to see you—"

Abner grabbed the phone from the secretary and said calmly, "Miss Dunsford, I don't mean to disturb you. I know you're having lunch with Charles Cunningham and that his chauffeur is supposed to pick you up in a few minutes. Please rest assured what I have to say is important enough that you'll want to hear me out first."

A moment later the principal walked out of her office and beckoned Abner to follow her.

Once inside her office, Burchard said, "Miss Dunsford, I hope you'll forgive my bluntness. I'm aware that Charles Cunningham has recently contributed fifty thousand dollars to Hillcrest's building fund and that you hope to obtain additional money from him, which is one of the reasons you are lunching today."

"How dare you intrude on such things? Has the FBI taken to snooping on private schools?" Her voice was a mixture of outrage, shock, and a hint of nervousness. He'd heard the same from most subjects who were uncertain how firm their footing was. "We haven't tapped your lines, ma'am. There's nothing illegal about Mister Cunningham's contributions, nor his promise of more to come. Placed in your position, I'd be both suspicious and angry at what you'd undoubtedly term my 'nosiness.'" She stood aghast for a moment, so he continued, "I'd deeply appreciate it if you'd listen to what I have to say before you make any judgments."

"Go ahead, Mister Burchard."

"As you may know, at this point no one has been able to determine why Melissa Roth killed her father."

"I thought that thing had blown over." He noticed that the head-mistress seemed to have recovered her confidence quickly. He would need to work hard to keep her off balance.

"It had, ma'am. However, recent peculiar developments have brought out questions we didn't even know to ask before. It seems a co-incidence to you, and I assure you it seems strange to me, that Charles Cunningham and I appear to have reached you within moments of one another. Because of that circumstance, the Bureau is assigning you an undercover security guard detail for the next several days."

Emily Dunsford put her hand to her mouth.

Burchard continued, "We're concerned only with your safety, ma'am. Your private concerns will remain private."

"What do you mean?"

"I mean that the Bureau is not in the habit of spying on the private lives of those under protective custody."

She stared at him like his old grade school teacher had when he missed the point of a question. "Why are you concerned for my safety?"

"Ma'am, I honestly think the less you know the safer you'll be."

"Why should I cooperate if you won't tell me what's going on?" He could see her expression hardening. She was regaining her mantle of power that he had temporarily displaced. He knew he needed to shake her up a little more.

"We'll do what we have to do, ma'am. If you prefer, we'll go through the usual process of subpoenas and court hearings. I was simply trying not to subject Hillcrest to unnecessary embarrassment."

"I see." Her lip turned up in a wry smile. "So the FBI would stoop to blackmail?"

"Not at all, Miss Dunsford. Everything would be completely above-board and legal. All of the niceties required by law would be observed. It would slow us down some. By that time, you'd probably be dead."

"I'm listening," she said. He noticed the slight tremor in her hands.

"We've already got Melissa Roth's school records, report cards, and observations by her teachers, ma'am. I would like to talk to Melissa's third-grade teacher today. It would also be helpful to know the names and addresses of every person who most likely spent time with Melissa the day she killed her father."

"Do you expect me to have this information at my fingertips, right this moment, when I'm supposed to be at lunch with Charles Cunningham? I'll consider helping you if you'll answer some questions for me."

"I'll do the best I can, ma'am," he said smiling.

He watched as she thought through her questions. After a moment, she began. "Is Mister Cunningham in any kind of trouble?"

"Not as of this moment, no."

"Is Mister Cunningham courting Mrs. Roth?"

"Far as I know, that's the last thing on his mind, ma'am."

"Do you believe Mister Cunningham is involved in the murder of Daniel Roth?"

"Yes, ma'am." He gazed at her levelly.

"I see." She buzzed her secretary. "Helen, could you come in a moment, please?"

"Yes, Doctor Dunsford. Mister Cunningham's chauffeur, is waiting in the outer office."

She glanced sharply at Burchard.

"That's fine, business as usual," he whispered. "Give me a few more minutes."

"Tell him I'll be out in five minutes, Helen. Offer him a cup of tea while he's waiting, then come in, please."

When Miss Picard entered, Emily Dunsford said, "I'll be gone about two hours, Helen. Please give Agent Burchard everything he needs. *Everything*. Without question.

"Also, you may notice strangers around school and our home for the next several days. Agent Burchard seems to believe we need protection. I'll explain it to you later. Just cooperate with him, please."

"If you say so, Doctor." Miss Picard's professionalism impressed Abner.

The principal turned toward him and said, "How do you propose I behave on my luncheon date, Agent Burchard?"

"As naturally as you can, ma'am."

"Knowing what you've told me?"

"You are the headmistress of a prestigious institution. That certainly makes you the equal of Charles Cunningham. Listen carefully to what he has to say."

"Do I answer his questions?"

"Absolutely, ma'am. As candidly as you can. Mister Cunningham knows at least as much about your business as I do." He watched the headmistress blanch. She was obviously used to believing no one could touch her here at Hillcrest.

"What if he asks about your visit?"

He smiled, "You can tell him an FBI agent came to your school just before noon, elbowed his way in, and sought information about enrolling his children at Hillcrest. You might even mention it, first. That might convince him you really didn't know the purpose of my visit."

"Suppose he wants the same information I'm giving you."

"How long would it take you to gather it under ordinary circumstances?"

"Three to five days."

"That's all the time I'll need. Thank you again, Miss Dunsford, Miss Picard. I apologize again for my brusqueness. Unfortunately, sometimes it can't be helped."

The Top of the Globe occupied the penthouse of the tallest building in the city. It seated fewer than one hundred twenty-five patrons, quite small for the area's most exclusive and renowned restaurant. It had won more awards than any other dining place within a hundred-mile radius, and was reputed to be one of the top ten restaurants in the country.

The *Globe*, one of the nation's most respected newspapers, had moved the bulk of its operations to a nearby suburb ten years before. Its token occupancy of the old building was for prestige. The cost of renovating it would have been prohibitive. It would have been cheaper to raze the hundred-year-old structure than bring it up to code.

Charles Cunningham met the limousine as it arrived at the Globe building. "I'm sorry I'm late, Mister Cunningham." Emily Dunsford sounded, if anything, a little irritable. "A new parent applicant came by. An FBI agent, would you believe? He simply would not be put off."

"I understand only too well, Doctor Dunsford. I've dealt with that type far too often, myself."

He paused a moment, to end that line of conversation, then continued, "Why don't we get inside, out of this oppressive heat? I need to give some instructions to my chauffeur. I've arranged for a private dining room for us, if you don't mind." He looked elegant, patrician in a business suit she estimated must have cost ten percent of her annual base salary.

"It would be my pleasure."

When he entered the building a short time later, Cunningham led Doctor Dunsford into the attendant-operated elevator, which took them directly to the penthouse. Once there, the maître d' ushered them to a large room with a spectacular view of the city.

"Wine?" the man asked, a study in understated obsequiousness.

"Have you a preference, Doctor Dunsford?" Cunningham said to his guest.

"I leave it to you, Mister Cunningham," she responded.

Within moments the sommelier brought a 1984 Lafite Rothschild to their table. Shortly thereafter, their waiter appeared. The menu, dated today, was engraved, not embossed, in gold leaf on heavy, cream-colored, marbled paper. There were no prices anywhere on the page.

"If I might, Doctor, I should like to recommend the Cream of Truffle soup and the Caesar salad for starters."

"My goodness," she was unable to stifle a gasp. "That's more than I usually eat for an entire lunch."

"By all means, you must indulge yourself," Cunningham said, chuckling. "After that, I suggest the pressed duck *flambé*, scalloped new potatoes *en croûte*, and petite asparagus."

"It sounds as though you're familiar with everything on the menu."

"I dine here quite often." He winked conspiratorially at her. "I once drafted a will for the head chef and only charged fifty dollars."

She laughed heartily. It was reputed that Cunningham, MacLeish, Durgan & Whyte did not pick up a piece of tissue paper from the floor without charging fifteen hundred dollars for a junior associate's time consumed in bending to do it.

"I'll accept anything you recommend with pleasure."

After he'd ordered for them, Cunningham slid into the heart of the conversation as smoothly as if he'd been buttering the hot baguette they'd each been served. "As you know, Doctor Dunsford, Mrs. Roth has been a partner in my firm for some years. She's also been a, ahem, very special . . . friend," he dropped his voice. "If I might confide in you, Doctor Dunsford—and since you're a woman of the world, I believe I may—Mrs. Roth has been deeply disturbed over the inexplicable and tragic events of last February. Thus, I perceived if I were somehow able to come up with some answers I could ease her mind."

"I understand," the headmistress replied. She'd been advised to listen and that she might be in danger. Be polite, be cautious, be natural. She nodded at Cunningham to go on.

"Amy—Mrs. Roth—told me police authorities had investigated thoroughly, and they'd asked questions of you?"

"That's so," Emily answered.

"But they weren't able to determine anything. Doctor Dunsford, I flatter myself that once upon a time I was a pretty competent trial lawyer. I'd like to think that even if I've attained an age and position where I could relax my vigilance, I might not have lost all my talent for unearthing salient facts."

She sat mute, her attention goading him on.

"Perhaps you might be able to assist me?"

"How, Mister Cunningham?"

"If I might somehow speak with Melissa's teachers, students who saw her the day of the tragedy—?"

"You understand, Mister Cunningham, our students' files are confidential. The school could lose its accreditation and be subject to criminal prosecution should any private information be revealed to outsiders." There was neither shock nor condemnation in her tone.

"Of course, Doctor Dunsford. I would never entertain the thought of doing anything unlawful. I value your integrity and that of Hillcrest too highly ever to suggest such a thing. My only desire in this unfortunate situation is to assist if I can."

"What did you have in mind, Mister Cunningham?"

"Nothing more than your permission to speak with those who might have seen something unusual. I assure you I would be circumspect. No one need know where I'd secured names and addresses."

"No formal report cards, student information, that kind of thing?"

"Dear me, no."

The waiter brought their entrees. The succulent pressed duck looked superb. The steamed vegetables and crusted potatoes were served on separate, adjacent plates. The waiter departed.

"I apologize for my gauche behavior," he continued. "That certainly wasn't the main reason I suggested we dine together. My primary purpose was to discuss the establishment of a Daniel Roth scholarship at Hillcrest. I had thought to fund it with an initial contribution of thirty-five thousand dollars, plus fifteen thousand for administrative expenses. I'd be honored if you would consider serving as trustee. It would not impose unreasonably on your time, as my staff would handle the details. I'm certain there would be no conflict of interest if you accepted a reasonable trustee's fee?" He stabbed one of the pieces of duck with a fork and placed it in his mouth.

"I don't believe that would be too heavy a burden to bear," the principal replied. He could see the flush of blood reddening her neck and cheeks. After taking a bite of her own, she continued, "There might be ways I could assist you in finding the information you wanted with respect to Melissa Roth's teachers, her playmates— How soon would you need that information?"

He smiled. Greed overrides fear every time, he thought. "How soon could you get it?"

"Would three or four days be all right? It would have to be done discreetly."

"I understand." He nodded sagely. "Might I recommend the cherries jubilee for dessert?"

"That would be wonderful, Mister Cunningham."

After they'd been served, Cunningham said, "So tell me about this agent who came to harass you, today. Perhaps I might speak to his superiors."

"Oh, I don't think that will be necessary. He actually turned out to be quite charming." He could discern the tension in her voice. His chauffeur would find out the truth.

He glanced at his watch, "My goodness, it's nearly two. I know it's terribly rude of me, but I have an appointment with Senator Slaybaugh at two-fifteen. An appropriations measure she wanted me to discuss privately with one of her colleagues on the other side of the aisle. Would you find it terribly offensive if I arranged for my chauffeur to return you to Hillcrest in my absence?"

"Not at all, Mister Cunningham. I've enjoyed our time together immensely."

"Hitoshi, can you get me information on an FBI agent within two hours?"

"Yes, Papa-sama."

"Good. Here's the information I want—"

Cunningham glared at the receiver before replacing it. He didn't for a moment believe Emily Dunsford about a casual call from an FBI agent trying to get his children into Hillcrest, particularly since his driver had reported the car was still parked at Hillcrest when he dropped Miss Dunsford off.

Fifteen minutes later, Sharon buzzed him on the intercom. "Special Agent Kerlin, Federal Bureau of Investigation on the line, sir."

"Good afternoon, Agent Kerlin," he said.

"Good afternoon, Mister Cunningham. I understand you wanted information on Abner Burchard?"

"I don't want to violate protocol, Agent Kerlin. It's just that I heard he's interested in enrolling his children at Hillcrest Day School and I thought I might be of assistance."

There was a brief silence at the other end of the line.

"Boy, have you been misinformed, counselor."

"What do you mean?"

"Abner Burchard's has no kids that I know of. He's a confirmed bachelor, sir."

"I'm sorry to have troubled you, Agent Kerlin. Thank you so much for your help."

Twenty minutes later, Cunningham entered a crowded cafe, where he made a local call from a pay telephone. "Africa house," a young, male voice answered. "May I help you?"

"Might I speak to Gilbert Sethuli, please?"

"Hey, quiet you guys!" the young voice shouted. "One of you see if Sethuli is up in his room."

A minute went by before a deep, cultured voice answered, "This is Sethuli."

"In fourteen hundred ninety-three, Columbus sailed the wine-dark sea." Cunningham waited several seconds, then continued, "Gilbert, I want you to get in your car and drive to Hillcrest Day School. I have an errand for you. Here are your instructions—"

Within an hour after Emily Dunsford had departed for lunch, Abner Burchard located Mary Beth Horvath, Melissa's third-grade teacher, on Cape Cod. Mrs. Horvath had taken last year's calendar with her to the Cape, "so I could avoid the hassle of having to re-invent the wheel when I return to Hillcrest next week. It's a standard week-at-a-glance thing, Agent Burchard. I've been teaching at Hillcrest for eight years. I've gotten it down to a shorthand format."

"Can you tell me what you were teaching on February fifth this year?"

"We started that day with current events—the kids always bring in a small article from the daily newspaper. Then reading, mathematics, social studies. It's hard work for kids that age. By day's end they're exhausted. I spent the last half hour letting them make up 'fractured nursery rhymes.' That's a game where they change standard Mother Goose stuff by substituting silly words for the real ones. 'Peter, Peter pumpkin eater had a big, fat ox and couldn't keep her.' That kind of humor may not impress adults, but eight-year-olds love it."

Burchard scribbled on a pad, "Fractured nursery rhymes. Substitute odd words for the real ones."

"Did Melissa act differently in any way that day?"

"No. To the contrary, she enjoyed 'fractured nursery rhymes' more than most."

"Did you have a chance to observe the kids at recess?"

"Only to the degree that any teacher whose room is right next to the playground notices kids. Most of the time, the boys play on the jungle gym and the girls play jump rope."

"Ice cream soda, lemonade punch, tell me the 'nitial of my honey bunch, that sort of thing?" He smiled at his memories of the playgrounds of his youth.

"Nowadays, I'm afraid it gets a little more violent than that. Things like 'Jennifer, Jennifer, silly little goat. Jennifer, stab your father in the throat.'"

His blood went cold. "What did you say?" he asked, forcing himself to keep his voice calm.

"What, about the silly goat rhyme?"

"Yes." His mind was screaming at him. It took all his concentration to loosen the muscles in his shoulders and back.

"Unfortunately, it seems to be a part of life in the twenty-first century, violence and all. It's become too much a part of the kids' lives, even here in the suburbs."

"Thank you, Mrs. Horvath." Abner hung up the phone and immediately made a quick call to his office. Senior Agent Kerlin picked up the line.

"Tom? Abner Burchard. Is Buzz Wilson still around?"

"Yeah, Abner. I'll get him for you. By the way, a friend of yours, Charles Cunningham, called and asked about you earlier in the afternoon. He heard you were enrolling a kid at Hillcrest School and wanted to talk to you about it. Boy, did he sound flabbergasted when I told him you were a bachelor."

"Did you tell him anything else?"

"Nothing."

Good, Abner thought. Emily Dunsford had played it cool.

"Hold on, I'll get Buzz."

When Wilson came on the line, Burchard said, "I spoke to Melissa Roth's teacher. I think I may be on to something. When the kids went out to the playground she remembered they made up all kinds of rhymes when they were playing jump rope. Something about being a billy goat and stabbing your father in the throat. I've got the details written down on my note pad. Can you meet me for dinner tonight?"

"Sure, Abner. Where?"

"The Sherlock Holmes Pub in about an hour?"

"O.K."

As he hung up the phone, Emily Dunsford came out of her private office. "I'm sorry, Agent Burchard, but it's time for me to close up. Rules don't permit me to leave you here alone."

"That's all right, Miss Dunsford. Thank you so much for your help. You've saved me many days of searching."

"Have you found anything?"

"I think so. I'll know more, tomorrow."

"What about that security you were going to give me?"

"As soon as your car enters the street below Hillcrest, you'll see an off-white Chevy Malibu. One of them's already followed Miss Picard home. By tomorrow, there'll be four guards planted in places where you'd least expect them. Gardeners and janitors. You'll hardly notice they're here."

"I feel safer already. Are you coming?"

"Yes. I'll walk you out to your car."

She smiled up at him. "Thank you."

They'd just reached the bottom of the stairway to the parking lot when she said, "With all your talk about security, I forgot to set the automatic alarm on the administration office door. It'll take less than a minute."

"Shall I go with you?"

"No, that's all right. Wait for me in the parking lot."

Gilbert Sethuli owned a nineteen ninety-nine Plymouth with one hundred eighteen thousand miles showing on the odometer. Of course, the odometer hadn't worked when he'd bought the car for two hundred dollars a year ago, and the car made funny, scree-ly noises when it started, but it got him around the city with reasonable certainty.

Gilbert was not thinking about his car's condition as he pulled into a wooded area adjacent to the main parking lot at Hillcrest School. A neuropsychiatrist testing Gilbert Sethuli at that moment would have concluded he was essentially unconscious. He'd been given a set of orders over which he had no control. The target had been described to him with accuracy sufficient for his needs.

The student from whom he'd purchased the car, had sold him an unregistered revolver for another twenty-five dollars. Sethuli kept the gun in the trunk to ensure he'd be safe in this violent land so far from home. He parked the car, opened the trunk, and withdrew the weapon.

The trees were a hundred yards from the administration building, too far for accuracy. He would have to get closer. He slipped into the woods and donned a pair of coveralls and a gardener's hat. From his hiding place, he observed two cars in the parking lot, a light green Buick and a Chrysler sedan. The man who'd been described to him was walking toward the Buick. Still too far away. He edged out of the trees, the gun hidden between his right hand and the overall pant leg. One hundred feet. Seventy-five. At sixty feet, he could make out the target's features.

Slowly, he raised the weapon.

Just then, a woman in her fifties came down the stairs toward the man. She glanced in his direction and shouted, "Abner, look out!"

Everything happened in a blur.

Sethuli got the first shot off before Burchard's bullet whizzed harmlessly past his shoulder. Momentarily surprised by the noise, his shot went high and to the left of the target, who suddenly dropped to his stomach. Emily Dunsford was running toward Burchard when Sethuli's projectile struck her in the right eye. She screamed once in a mixture of shock and intense pain as she felt the blood rushing down her cheek, and crumpled to the ground. Within a moment, her agonized writhing stopped and her body stiffened.

It took Sethuli three seconds to aim and pull the trigger again. Just as he got the shot off, he felt a tearing fire in his throat as the bullet from the .38 caliber police special brought his life to an end. The projectile from his weapon punctured the Buick's tire less than four inches from Abner Burchard's shoulder.

21

"Jeff? Buzz Wilson."

Savage glanced over at Amy Roth, who was in the midst of preparing dinner. He'd splurged on a Lafite Rothschild Bordeaux and three dozen long-stemmed roses. Savage's intentions were of questionable honor, depending on what was meant by honor and who did the questioning.

"You couldn't have chosen a worse time to call."

"Someone tried to kill Abner Burchard an hour ago."

"What? I don't believe it."

"The FBI's back in with all four feet. I've ordered round-the-clock surveillance on you, Amy, and Melissa."

"Who is it, Jeff?" Amy asked.

"I'll tell you in a moment. Where are they, Buzz?"

"They'll be setting up across the street."

"What can we do?"

"Sit tight. We're checking out some leads. We'll set up a phone tap as soon as we can get a truck out there."

"Where do you suggest I sleep tonight?"

"See if the lady will let you sleep over."

"Thanks," Jeff said sourly. "Where can I get hold of you?" Wilson gave him a number and rang off.

Savage turned to Amy. "Someone tried to kill Abner Burchard. We're under a protective net for the time being. I don't have much in the way of details."

As they sat down to eat, the phone rang again. This time Amy answered. "May I speak to Jeffrey Savage?" A male voice.

"Who's calling, please?" she asked.

"A friend," the voice continued. "Don't worry, Mrs. Roth, neither you nor he is in any immediate danger. We know who tried to kill Agent Burchard and we'd like to help. Please put Mister Savage on the line."

Amy pointed to Jeff, then to the phone. "Savage."

"Listen carefully, Mister Savage," the voice commanded. "My principal finds you a worthy adversary. It's no challenge to win anything by default, do you understand?"

"Keep talking," Jeff answered, his tone flat. He'd signaled Amy for some paper and a pen. He started scribbling furiously as the voice continued.

"The man who tried to eliminate Abner Burchard was a Congolese graduate student named Gilbert Sethuli. As you may have already guessed, Sethuli had absolutely no idea what he was doing. The FBI has not yet tapped into this telephone. I simply wanted to tell you and your friend that you need not worry about premature termination. Happy hunting, tiger."

The line disconnected. No sooner the caller was off the phone, Jeff called Wilson and reported the conversation.

"Damn," Wilson swore softly. "The guy stays one step ahead of us at every turn. I'll double up the protection. Thanks for calling."

Amy's calm demeanor surprised Jeff. During dinner, she said, "You know, Jeff, we can spend our time worrying that this might be our last night, or we can live as naturally as anyone can under unreasonably stressed conditions. I've lived with pressure since I started trying cases. I survived Daniel's death and the whirlwind surrounding Melissa. I'm prepared to accept that whoever was on the phone was truthful when he said we're in no immediate danger. Tomorrow, maybe, but I can't always project what tomorrow might bring. Except that I now have an overnight guest, I'm prepared to go on with our evening as planned." She dimmed the lights and lit the five candles in the silver candelabrum she'd placed between them.

There was a sharp knock at the front door.

"Who is it?" Jeff called out, rising and moving toward the entryway.

"Sullivan, FBI."

"Do you have I.D.?"

"If you look out the front window, I'll shine the flashlight on my card case so you and Mrs. Roth can check it out."

"It could be a ruse," Jeff whispered to Amy.

As if reading Jeff's thoughts, the voice continued, "I thought Buzz Wilson would have called you by now." He flicked on the flashlight. Savage went as close to the window as he dared. The badge and card case looked official. "Look, Professor Savage, if you need further identification, why not call Agent Wilson? My name is Allan Sullivan, Number 106382. I've worked with Wilson and Abner Burchard. I'll wait if you want, or you can dial the van direct if it makes you happy. There's a gray Toyota Camry, license number 4GTY064 parked right outside your door. Feel free to check out everything I say. I've got the whole night."

"Do you think we should call Wilson?" Amy whispered.

"No. I think he's telling the truth. Let's stall for a little while to make him think we're checking up on him."

After two minutes of silence, Savage called out, "OK, Mister Sullivan. Wilson says you're clean." He opened the door. The man who stood there was six feet tall, late-thirties, with thinning hair and the same blocky build as Wilson and Burchard.

"I'd like to go through the house to make certain everything's secure. It would be a good idea if you follow me around to point out any specific areas that cause you concern."

They watched as Sullivan went through the house, turning on lights, making sure windows were locked and screened, opening and closing every closet in the dwelling. He took the better part of an hour to finish his task.

"Everything seems secure," he said, as he returned to the front door. "You can't be too careful, you know."

"Are you going to be outside all night, Agent Sullivan?"

"Yes," he said, as he stepped out onto the porch. "Oh, by the way, I almost forgot. Buzz Wilson said to give you this," he said, handing them a plain, white envelope. "The instructions in here are fairly detailed. You don't need to look at them right away. I'm sorry I interrupted your dinner."

"Would you like to stay, Agent Sullivan?"

"Thanks, but no, Mrs. Roth. I've got a sandwich out in the van and a whole night's work to do." He excused himself and left.

Amy said, "Perhaps we should call Buzz, just in case?"

"Good idea."

Wilson came on the line after the second ring. "I thought you two were all buttoned down for the night. I was getting ready to go home myself."

"Go right ahead," Amy said. "I just wanted to call and thank you for sending Agent Sullivan to check out the house. You don't know how much safer we feel."

"What?"

"Sullivan, Allan Sullivan? He said he'd worked with you in the past."

"Allan Sullivan?" Wilson said. "Is this some kind of a joke, Amy?"

"What do you mean? Agent Sullivan showed us his card case, badge number 106382. He's in his late-thirties, built like you—" She felt a chill as Wilson interrupted her.

"Amy, listen to me. I don't know where you got your information. There is no Allan Sullivan in the FBI. Until a year ago, he was an agent. He was quietly cashiered when internal investigation revealed he was on the take. There was no criminal action. He's simply not around anymore."

"You mean—?"

"The FBI takes care of its own. We also make sure our own name is never sullied by a rogue cop. Former agent Sullivan, same badge number, incidentally, died, apparently from natural causes, last November."

"Buzz, this is no time to be funny," she said, feeling weak. "He left us an envelope with instructions he said came from you."

"Better open it and read what it says."

Amy's hands trembled as she opened the envelope. Inside, there was a single sheet on which were typed the words, "You might want to question your FBI security. Have a good night's sleep. Happy hunting, tiger."

"I think it's time we called Charles Cunningham," Amy said after she'd hung up the phone.

"Why Cunningham?"

"You, yourself hinted he might be on the same trail we are, if for different reasons."

"I can't help but be suspicious—"

"Jealous, perhaps?" She smiled as he fidgeted. "Jeffrey Savage, let me remind you again, Charles Cunningham's married, thirty years my senior, and my law partner, even though that's the same as saying Bhutan is China's partner. He's old enough to be my father, which is exactly the way I view him."

"How do you feel about me, Amy?" he asked seriously.

"Different question," she smiled, "and one that's far more complex. Trust me, Jeff. I believe Charles Cunningham can be a lot of help."

She punched in Cunningham's private number and reached him several moments later.

"Amy?" The voice was warm. "Is something the matter?"

Without waiting for him to go on, she blurted out the story of Abner Burchard's close call with death, their conversation with Wilson, and the events that followed. Cunningham listened patiently, interrupting only with an occasional "Mm-hmm."

When she'd finished, he asked, "Is Jeff Savage on line with us?"

"No."

"How well do you know him?"

"Why?"

"No reason in particular. Does he seem more than normally interested in you?"

She glanced over at the rumpled-looking man sitting two feet away, who was pretending to leaf through a coffee table book. "Why, Charles?"

"Amy, I'm neither young nor unsophisticated. There are many ways for a man to inveigle his way into the heart—or the bedroom—of a lovely young woman like you."

"I'd hardly suspect him of something as elaborate as that."

Savage glanced up. "Mister Cunningham," she continued. "I picked up the phone when the voice called. I was here when the agent came in. This is serious. We're concerned and I'm asking for your help." She signaled Savage to come to the phone.

"I apologize for hinting anything, even as a joke," he said. "Might I please speak with Professor Savage?"

Jeff came on as soon as she'd beckoned. "Jeff, I'm afraid I owe you an apology," Cunningham chuckled. "As you probably heard from Amy's end of the conversation, I rashly suggested, in jest of course, that you might have some part in this bizarre situation."

He glanced over at Amy, who spread her hands in a gesture that meant, "Keep it steady, keep the peace." She blew him a silent kiss.

"Apology accepted, Mister Cunningham."

"Charles is fine."

"Charles, then."

"Listen, Jeff, telephone lines are not secure. Perhaps I should come over so we might review the evidence together."

"Before I can help, I've got to know what you've found."

Jeff glanced sharply at Amy. Her expression said, "Use your own discretion. It's your ballgame."

"Very well, Mister Cunningham," Savage said. "As I'm sure Amy told you, we started searching for *ChildFinders*."

"So I understand."

"I'm going to ask a number of questions, some of which may seem accusatory and unnecessarily intrusive. They're not meant to be, but if you're serious about wanting to help—?"

"You needn't bother explaining, Jeff."

"What do you know about '*Luftleben*?'"

"It's a Liechtenstein corporation that runs a private airline into and out of southeastern Congo. It has two 767s, a Lear, a Grumman Gulfstream, and a Cessna 205 that, once upon a time, used to belong to me."

"Why Congo?"

"The directors of *Luftleben* are long-time associates of mine. Some of them serve with me on the directorate of the Children's Institute. Undoubtedly your research turned this up?"

"Yes, sir. Guillaume M'bele?"

"One of my closest friends in the world. Interior minister of Congo. It was his idea that I start the Children's Institute. The Preservation Trust, a non-profit organization largely funded by me, charters *Luftleben* to bring in unfortunate children from all over the world so that my associates, Doctor Lee Chung Lien and, until his recent, untimely death, Doctor William Hensleigh, could help better their lives. You may also recognize the names Prasad and Kono. Doctor Prasad is one of the great computer geniuses of the world. Hitoshi Kono is a businessman who, like myself, has amassed a fortune so great that he feels morally bound to share his bounty with others. Prasad keeps all the records. Kono and I are financial benefactors."

Savage was disarmed by Cunningham's candor and by the direct, no-nonsense way in which he answered—even anticipated—the questions. He also knew Cunningham, the consummate trial lawyer, knew what it took to be a convincing witness. He might as well keep going and see how many more answers the fox anticipated.

"Where does *Luftleben* land?"

"The 767s land at Nairobi. From there, the smaller planes pick up the children and transport them to a small strip outside Manono, just south of the Institute."

"What about Bank of the South Pacific?"

Without blinking an eye, Cunningham answered, "I own twenty percent of that bank." That was a surprise to Savage. The computer had not unearthed that information. "Cunningham-MacLeish people have been on the board from time to time. *Luftleben* and the Preservation Trust are customers."

"And *ChildFinders*?"

"It might well be a customer too. I put my bank shares into a blind trust ten years ago. I can probably get you a client list. Since we both appear to be looking for *ChildFinders*, I appreciate the hint you've given me. You have my word, first, that I didn't know *ChildFinders* had an account there and, second, that I'll text a shareholder's query to the Caymans tomorrow." Cunningham seemed to be playing straight with them.

"Have you any idea who tried to kill Abner Burchard?" Amy asked.

"None."

"Does the name Gilbert Sethuli mean anything to you?"

"Yes. He's an orphan boy who was raised at the Institute. I sponsored him into our city's finest university. He won a graduate scholarship on his own. Have you met Gilbert?" Cunningham asked.

"No. His name popped up in connection with the Institute," Amy lied.

"He was our ambassador to a World Health Organization conclave a few years ago. Delightful fellow. I'm sure you've heard of some of our other distinguished graduates, Johannes Tshambala, Phineas Dhlumini, Emily Mabuti, Paulina Matanzima—"

Savage made a mental note to find out what he could about these people.

After another quarter hour, Cunningham asked, "Is it my turn to make inquiries?"

"Your witness, counselor," Amy said. She looked as though she'd shed five years.

"Thank you. Jeff, what information do you have about *ChildFinders?*"

"Hardly any, sir, but if we're looking for the same organization, there could be repercussions far beyond Melissa Roth."

"Meaning?"

Savage decided to bounce his theory about the raised elevation of violent homicides and kidnapped children off Cunningham. The lawyer acted neither shocked nor disdainful.

"You feel *ChildFinders* is involved in an organized plot to kill political leaders?" he asked.

"I'm not that far along yet, Mister Cunningham."

"Let's take your theory one step further. Why would they want to kill anyone?"

"Money."

"Or power?" Cunningham encouraged his two companions to come up with ideas.

"Yes, or power," Amy said. "Though God only knows why they'd want power in today's world."

"A little hard on society, aren't you?"

"Perhaps by adding to the chaos, these people could consolidate their power?"

"It's possible," Cunningham said. "But how would they be able to control these killers, assuming for one moment that our far-out speculation has any validity?"

"Hypnosis?"

"Not impossible. Have you read *The Manchurian Candidate*?"

"No," Savage replied, "but I saw the movie on Netflix a few months ago. Scary idea."

"Brainwashing," Cunningham said, in answer to Amy's questioning look.

"Could *ChildFinders* replicate such a scenario?"

"Quite easily. The technology's far ahead of what it once was. Doctor Lee, one of my associates at the Institute, has published several papers in the field. She'd certainly be able to give us her insights."

"You sound as though you believe there really might be something to Jeff's theory, Mister Cunningham," Amy said.

"I'm not saying yes or no," he equivocated. "We both know if the hypothesis were true, the result could be very ugly. Let's not rule it out. Would the two of you like to fly to the Institute, or should I bring Doctor Lee here?"

"How would we get to the Institute?"

"I'd make arrangements with *Luftleben*. Unfortunately, it will be three or four weeks before I can break away. Meanwhile, I suggest we keep in touch with one another and share information." He glanced at his watch. "My, my, ten thirty. I must be going. I've got a court appearance scheduled for tomorrow. No rest for the wicked," he said. "I trust you've got enough information to keep you busy for a while." He excused himself and left.

"What do you think about Cunningham now?"

"Smooth. I'll say that for him."

"And honest?"

"Facially, yes. But a salesman once told me if you can sell sincerity it doesn't matter whether you're telling the truth or not."

"Still the doubting Thomas?"

"Not doubting, Amy. Skeptical. I'd like to check out his answers. They correlated with my computer information so perfectly I'd almost swear he had access to my terminals. Would you mind if I used your computer for a few minutes?"

"Shall I warm up the roast while I'm waiting?"

"Holy mackerel!" he said, blushing. "I'd forgotten all about dinner." His natural use of the antiquated phrase was not lost on Amy who was having some very adult tinglings of her own.

Cunningham was mildly troubled as his chauffeur drove the slate gray Rolls back into town. He reached into his breast pocket, extracted the digital recorder with which he'd captured the entire conversation, and listened to it. He was certain he'd been convincingly frank. He hoped—but did not trust—that Savage would be satisfied with the information. Still, the promised trip to meet Lee Chung Lien might be enough to put the actuary off. He must remember to be more careful next time.

Ah, well, what's done is done, he thought.

When Savage returned to the kitchen, he said, "We have an inconsistency."

She looked at him quizzically.

"Cunningham said the 767s land at Nairobi and the smaller planes fly into and out of a small airstrip at Manono."

"So?"

"I just checked out his story on one of the appropriate bases. There are no records of *Luftleben* Boeing 767 aircraft ever landing at Nairobi. More important, there's no airfield of any kind at Manono."

"So Cunningham was lying?"

"I'll let you draw your own conclusions. He's on the board of the company that owns the aircraft. He undoubtedly flies there at least once a year."

Just then the phone rang. Amy answered it, thanked the caller, and hung up. "That was Buzz Wilson. He said everything's tied in. Sleep well tonight, your friendly Federal Bureau is awake."

"Sounds good to me. Do you have a spare toothbrush? I'm afraid I didn't come prepared to spend the night."

"Not even a toothbrush?" she asked, smiling at him.

"Not even."

"Shame. I guess you'll have to share mine."

"Didn't you ever hear that spreads germs?"

"So does this." She reached up and kissed him.

His arms went around her. It had been a long time, too long, since she'd been held, stroked, and caressed. She'd almost forgotten how good it felt. Their kissing became hungry, passionate. At the last moment before her control slipped, she pulled away. Her eyes were bright, glowing and she smiled at him.

"Amy?"

"Not yet, Jeff. But stick around for a while—and be my friend for now?"

"Separate rooms?"

"I think we'd better." She squeezed his hand affectionately. As he turned to walk down the hall, she said, "Jeff, Cunningham didn't say *he* flew into Lumumbashi or Manono. He said the Cessna picks up children at Lumumbashi and flies them to the Institute. They come from around the world. He also said his associate, Doctor Lee, published papers on brainwashing."

He was instantly alert. In a verbal collision, they both said a single word at the same time. "*ChildFinders.*"

22

He could always say he must have been tired, confused, that they'd misunderstood. The story about the 767's landing at Nairobi would not be hard to check out, and he'd flown over Manono often enough to know there was no landing strip there. A stupid, trivial, but potentially serious mistake, given the information Savage and Amy had uncovered.

He'd been a trial lawyer long enough to know how to salvage a bad situation: the ability to keep a poker face, to turn disadvantage to advantage, to make jurors believe black really is white, were the hallmarks of a good advocate. And Charles Cunningham was a *great* advocate.

He walked into the private bathroom adjacent to his office, washed his hands, and looked in the mirror. The face that stared back at him appeared younger than it had a few months ago. No doubt the adrenalin coursing through his body these last few months had fueled the fountain of youth. Almost sixty-three? He looked ten years younger.

He smiled to himself. Let Savage keep searching for answers. Cunningham enjoyed the chase, which he knew would end a shade too late. It was all part of the challenge. Soon enough he'd rule the world's rulers. What then?

He'd made love with Sharon two nights ago. It had been wonderful, as usual, but afterward he'd noticed that Sharon was starting to show her age.

Amy Roth? A younger woman, but—. His mind wandered to Lee Chung Lien, a deadly, single-minded scientist with an unlined face and a slender, youthful body. There was no difficulty getting Chung Lien into bed. The challenge would be to make her stay in his bed alone.

He pressed the intercom button. "Sharon, would you come in, please?"

He'd been right. She did seem to be aging.

"Yes, Flan?"

"Could you block out the next six weeks and get Doctor Lee on the phone. I'd like to meet with her at the Preserve this coming weekend to make sure everything's in order."

"Fine, sir. Will it just be the three of us?"

"This time I think I'll go alone."

Sharon arched her eyebrows. "I don't understand, Cha— Mr. Cunningham. It's always been you and I who've prepared for visitors." He could see the shocked anger and hurt in her eyes. Sharon was a wonderful woman, who should be enough to satisfy any man. But he wasn't just any man. He hadn't been alone with Chung Lien in the past ten years. He'd determined to see if the fantasy she presented was anything more than that.

"I know, Shari," he said smoothly. "And so it will be. I want to meet with Doctor Lee to ensure that the Center is functioning properly. I've been somewhat concerned since Doctor Hensleigh's death. You know how it is."

"No, I don't" she snapped. "I see no reason why Doctor Lee can't make sure the Center's functioning by her own little self."

"Now, Shari, it's not what you think. I just want to make sure."

"And I shouldn't?"

"No, you shouldn't." His tone was sharper than he'd intended. "I need you here to manage my domestic affairs."

"While you go about your *foreign* affairs?" Her voice was acid.

"Sharon, that's enough. We're not children. We're both old enough to trus—"

"Trust, Charles? *Trust?*" she shouted. She pulled back her shoulders, straightened up and said, "All right, Mister Cunningham. Go make your inspection of the Center. Fool around all you want with little Miss Lee Chung Lien. Get whatever disease she's passing around to anyone who'll have her. When you're done, you'd better think twice about coming back to old, faithful Sharon Graham with her wrinkles and her sagging body. And you can spare me your hangdog expression. I've seen the way you've watched me lately. I've seen myself in the mirror. What a shame I can't age as gracefully as His Majesty, Charles Cunningham, King of the World."

Summoning her last shred of dignity, she said, "Please call me if there's anything else you need, Mister Cunningham," turned on her heel, and strode out the door.

An hour later, when he felt she'd had sufficient time to cool down, he buzzed her again. Edith Wembley from the thirtieth-floor typing pool answered the intercom. "I'm sorry, Mister Cunningham, Ms. Graham reported ill and took the afternoon off. I have no idea where she went."

Damn, he thought. Of all the times to have Sharon throw a temper tantrum. He did not need extra trouble in his life at this moment.

He dialed her home number. Twelve rings. No answer. He replaced the receiver, impatiently. She'd reported ill. Sharon Graham was not the type to suddenly take ill. She was probably walking on the beach, cooling off, concluding that once he'd had his weekend with Chung Lien, he'd be better than ever. He called another number. "Melodee Florists? Good afternoon, this is Charles Cunningham. I'd like you to send five dozen long-stemmed roses to Ms. Sharon Graham, first thing tomorrow morning. Her address is—"

Charles Cunningham was only partly correct. Sharon was walking along the beach, but she wasn't cooling off. Every now and again she stopped, put her head in her hands, and sobbed silently. An attractive, fortyish woman who'd given up her life for a man she worshipped. A man who was trashing her with consummate charm, but trashing her nonetheless. The king of the universe. Smooth, elegant, and a rotten, three-timing bastard.

Did she deserve better? She'd known he was married when they'd first climbed into bed together. After twenty years, she and Margaret Cunningham, the brittle, non-entity crinoline queen, were sisters under the skin. Now it was her turn to feel what Margaret must have felt all these years. How many nights had Mrs. Charles Cunningham silently cried herself to sleep? How dare he? How dare he take up with that loathsome Oriental whore?

She had no awareness of when the man appeared next to her. He was her own age, perhaps a few years younger. Tall, broad, with workman's hands. His face was a shade too large, a little too square for his frame. How long had he been walking beside her?

"Is this a private beach, or can two lonely people walk with one another?"

The urge to say something dismissive like, "Get lost, Buster," died in her throat. His voice was remarkably gentle, the question framed simply. She said nothing for a few moments, kept walking. He made no move to rush her.

"Does it show that much?" What a silly pair of opening lines, she thought. Like two notes played out of harmony.

"Well, ma'am," he said, a slight country drawl coming through, "if you'll excuse my saying so, it sure doesn't seem like the happiest day of your life."

"How long have you been following me?"

"I haven't been following you."

"Walking alongside me, then."

"A while."

She shivered as a sudden gust of wind came off the ocean.

He took off the windbreaker he was wearing and offered it to her. She nodded appreciatively and put it on. "I know a coffee shop nearby," he said. "It's not much—you can't expect much near the beach—but they've got a heck of a nice cinnamon-apple pie and it might make life a little sweeter for you."

She smiled up at him. A tired, sad, smile. The woman was quite attractive. Whatever weight she was bearing seemed heavy on her shoulders.

"My name's Abner," he said, as they turned toward the boardwalk. "Abner Burchard. No nicknames and I'm not married." He looked sheepishly at her. "I thought you'd best know that before you went to a restaurant with a strange man."

For the first time that day, she laughed. Abner. *Abner?* "Hi, Abner," she said. "I'm Sharon Graham, single, and hurting. And since I walked two miles to get here, I've dreaded the thought of walking home. The coffee shop it is."

That evening, Abner Burchard took Sharon to dinner at a small, intimate restaurant a few miles from her home. He listened attentively as she spoke. "The other woman's always the villainess. If the straying husband goes back to the long-suffering wife, the story has a happy ending. Oh, I've been well provided for: a house of my own, travel to exotic places—" Her voice was bitter. "Girls with whom I went to high school got married to ordinary, everyday Joes, had babies, went through the heartache of teenaged subhumans. Some made it, some got divorced, some were left behind. I don't know that I'd trade with them."

"It's hard to comprehend someone else's pain when you're in the midst of your own."

"Yes, it is." She noticed he was looking directly at her, without judgment, without rancor. His eyes were dark blue.

The waiter approached them for their order. "Prime rib," he said. "Sharon?"

"The same, please."

He raised the glass of merlot. "Salud."

"Prosit. How about you, Abner? Divorced?"

"No, ma'am."

"Surely you're not—?"

"Absolutely not. I guess I just kinda' fell through the cracks, or got tied up in my work."

"Let me guess. A retired football player, now coaching a local high school team?"

"Nope."

"An astrophysicist at MIT?"

"Hardly."

"What, then?"

"Truth, the whole truth and nothing but the truth?"

"A lawyer?"

"FBI." He saw her stiffen perceptibly. "Maybe that's why I fell through the cracks. A lot of people think we're all looking for commie pinko anarchists under every bush, that we're all brawn, light on brain cells, or that we're after them for something suspicious they've done like fail to pay a parking ticket. The minute I tell a woman what I do, I usually get one of two reactions."

"Such as?"

"One is to run the other way as fast as they can. The other's the cop-lover syndrome, for want of a better phrase. Groupies, trophy hunters." He chuckled, trying to lighten the conversation. "Usually all body, light on the brain cells."

"People are uncomfortable because they think you know everything there is to know about them," she said. "Secrets they don't want to share with anyone."

"I'm sure that's part of it. For example, I know you're Charles Cunningham's private secretary, single, forty-five, have an ailing mother who lives in Phoenix, and that you were born in Tennessee, not too far from where I grew up."

She turned white. "I think I'd best be going."

"Please don't."

The simple sincerity in his voice held her.

"Sharon, one night out of my life, just one, I'd like to be part of the real world. A place where a very attractive woman might see me as nothing more than a human being, not someone to be tagged with a title, 'FBI, lawyer, doctor.' I'd like to talk about the latest novel I've read—Robertson Davies, by the way, not James Patterson. I'm forty-two and single with nieces and nephews running around Kentucky and West Virginia, colleagues in the Bureau I can call day or night, everything except a friend who'll say, 'Abner, I don't care what you do or what you are.' Someone who's a little lonely, like me. Someone who took the slightest wrong turn in life and missed the brass ring by a finger's length.

"I'd like to sit and listen to you pour your heart out, just because I want to hear you, not because it's part of an investigation. Do you know how many people listen but never hear what another person's saying? Maybe I'd like to talk about Anderson Cooper or how a dog did his duty in my front yard, or how you handled some smartass client day before yesterday. We can say goodbye at the door after the meal and each of us can go our own way, but at least I'd have been something more than a programmed automaton for an hour or so."

Sharon shuddered when she heard the words "programmed automaton." Could this sincere, unpretentious man know more than he was letting on? No, she said to herself. *Don't just listen. Hear what he has to say. To walk out on him would be needlessly cruel.* God knows she'd been a victim of intense cruelty earlier today. He'd walked alongside her, comforted her at her weakest moment. *How fair would it be to repay that kindness by dismissing him? And he really wasn't bad looking in a clumsy, funny sort of way.*

"OK, Mister Burchard, tonight you're just plain Abner. We'll see how you behave during dinner. Then I'll decide whether we part at the door on the way out." She smiled at him.

He smiled back.

"You really shouldn't smile, you know. You look much more dignified when you're serious."

They spoke for three hours, about theater, politics, books, religion—at the restaurant, in a nearby park, at Denny's, where they enjoyed a late-night dessert. She should have been exhausted. She was exhilarated. She'd devoted her entire life to Charles Cunningham, catered to his every whim and, like any woman drawn to a strong, dominant man, lived in his shadow. Sharon had never known a man who seemed to appreciate her for herself. She felt a pleasant stirring within her. Abner had become far better looking, more desirable as the evening wore on.

"Ms. Graham," he said. "This afternoon, I promised I'd give you a ride to your house. It's a little late for you to walk back now."

"What time is it?"

"Ten past the witching hour."

He walked her to the door. They both felt the awkwardness of adolescents, not knowing what to say or do. "Thanks, Abner," she finally said. "You've brought a wonderful end to a horrible day." She realized she hadn't thought about Charles Cunningham, Lee Chung Lien, the office, or the Preserve for hours.

He put his arms around her, almost clumsily, and she leaned against his shoulder. They stood that way for a while. Finally, she broke the silence. "Would you like to come in—for a cup of coffee or whatever?" she said softly.

"More than anything," he replied. "But not tonight. It wouldn't be right. Not yet." He felt her soft tears as she pressed closer to him. "Did I say something wrong?"

"No, Abner Burchard, you big, innocent lunk, you didn't say anything wrong." She smiled through eyes bright with tears. "You said something very, very right. Thank you. Thank you for one of the nicest evenings I've ever had in my life." She took his face between her hands and kissed him full on the lips. A moment later, she was gone.

23

"Good morning, my brother!" Byron Thomas stood in the early morning sun and waved to his friend, the Right Honorable Frank Joseph, prime minister of Dominica. "How are you this morning?"

"Quite well, old friend. How about yourself?"

The two men shook hands. Inches away, the traffic rolled along the bumpy, potholed Caribbean road.

"I can't much complain. Here," he said, producing a small plastic bag. "I brought you a present from my gardens."

The prime minister smiled and took the bag. "Looks like another mango. I do so love your mangoes." He opened the bag and looked down. "Only one this time?"

"Only one," Thomas said. "The last of the crop. But it is ripe and ready to eat."

"Then we must share it, as we have shared everything," the prime minister said. Reaching into the bag, he pulled out the small, orangecolored ovoid. A moment later, the two men were splattered across the road and adjacent foliage as the grenade exploded.

Melissa Roth fidgeted nervously, opened one eye, looked at the digital clock, and closed her eye again. Six thirty. Willie would be up in a few more minutes. No sense in disturbing her.

Her eyes were still closed when she heard a soft rustling at the door. "Willie?" she called out softly. "Is that you, Willie?"

No response. She turned and looked toward the nurse's bed. It was empty. Strange. Willie never got up before seven. After six months, Melissa Roth knew her caretaker's habits almost as well as she knew her own.

"Willie, where are you?" she called, louder this time. The bathroom door immediately adjacent to her room was open. She felt frightened. Aliens had taken over the home, just outside her door. She knew they were out there. She pulled the covers over her head. They'd never find her here. She was safe.

"Good morning, Melissa." The voice was kind, feminine.

Melissa peeked out from under the covers and saw a tall, pleasant-looking young woman.

"Who are you?" the child asked.

"My name's Miss Gray. You can call me Ida, if you'd like."

"Ida? That's a funny name."

"Yes, it is," the young woman said, laughing easily. "I didn't have much choice in the matter. My parents named me."

"Where's Willie?"

"She took the day off. We get the day off, too."

"What do you mean?"

"How'd you like to visit your own home today?" The child's eyes widened. Ida Gray put her fingers to her lips. "Shhh, we mustn't tell anyone. It's our secret, just yours and mine."

"Shouldn't we tell Doctor Evans?" Melissa whispered.

"I already have. He said it's all right, so long as no one else knows. How quickly can you be ready?"

"Right away."

The child walked to the bathroom, closed the door, and emerged five minutes later, wearing a pair of jeans, a multicolored t-shirt, and tennis shoes. Ida checked to make sure the corridors were clear. It was ten minutes to seven.

"OK, Melissa, let's go," she said, hurrying the little girl out the door.

"Can't we even have breakfast?"

"Later, at home."

"Does my mom know we're coming?"

"Of course."

"Then why isn't she here to get me?"

"It's a surprise."

"I don't get it," Melissa said. "If she knows about it, it's not a surprise."

"Never mind, she'll meet us at the house." Melissa noticed that the young woman seemed nervous. She kept glancing up and down the corridor.

"I think we should tell Doctor Evans."

"I told you I've already cleared it with him," Miss Gray said. Her voice was sharp.

"I don't believe you!" Melissa said. "I'm going to tell Doctor Evans myself."

"No!" Ida Gray snapped, pulling Melissa by the arm. "Come on. We have to leave right now."

"Where's Willie? I think you've done something to Willie."

Ida had been given her instructions and hadn't planned for this contingency. Just get the kid out the door and into the car, we'll take it from here, she'd been told. She stopped for an instant to think about how to handle the situation.

That was all the time Melissa needed to break away. "Help!" she shouted. "Doctor Evans, help me!" She ran blindly down the hall, faster than she'd ever run in her life. She started crying hysterically as she ran. "Mommy, mommy, mommy!" she screamed.

Five minutes before, Michael Flannery, the night orderly, had finished wet-mopping the linoleum floor outside Doctor Evans' office. He'd left the mop and bucket in the middle of the hall while he'd gone to the supply room to get the "Danger! Wet floor!" sign. Plenty of time, he thought. The kids won't be up for another fifteen minutes.

He heard a child's scream and ran back toward the hall, just in time to see Melissa Roth charging toward the area he'd just finished. "Look out!" he shouted, but it was too late. Melissa's feet had come out from under her. As she fell, her head would have hit a nearby steel bucket but for the fact that at that moment, a startlingly beautiful woman dressed in a nurse's uniform intercepted the child's fall, When Melissa opened her eyes moments later, she found herself looking into the woman's kind, brown eyes.

"Are you my fairy godmother?" she asked, calmly.

"You might say that, Melissa," the pretty lady said. "My name is Hypatia, and I'm here to make sure you're safe until your mom arrives."

In the commotion that followed, no one but me saw Ida Gray leave by a side door.

"What happened, Doctor Evans?"

"Mike Flannery said Melissa was screaming and running like she was frightened out of her wits. Fortunately, Hypatia was able to divert her fall."

"I was just getting dressed when I heard noise from the monitor we'd placed in Melissa's room."

"Where was Willie during all this?" Amy asked.

"Probably on her way to work," Dr. Evans replied. "She's on day shift, and would have been easy for whoever tried to kidnap her to get a job on the night shift as an orderly. Boring job, long hours, pay's not great. Mister Caen, you mentioned something about accelerating a schedule?"

"Yes, Doctor Evans," Ezra said. "In light of events that seem to be falling into place, I requested that Amy consent to having a neurosurgeon look at Melissa. The 'near accident' of earlier this morning provides a perfect excuse for what I'd like him to do. The investigating authorities agree with me."

"Who's the neurosurgeon, if you don't mind my asking?"

"Doctor Oriba."

"You can't do much better than Howard," Evans said.

An hour later, Jeff, Amy, Ezra, and Melissa arrived at a small private hospital ten miles from Border House. Howard Oriba, a man of fifty, Jeff Savage's height and build, who wore a camel's hair coat, open-necked shirt, and brown slacks, approached them as they arrived at the hospital's intake desk.

Doctor Oriba had been pre-advised what to expect and the real purpose of the visit. After greeting them all warmly, he turned to Melissa. "Now, then, young lady, what seems to be the problem?"

"I tripped and almost hit my head on a bucket."

"Poor bucket," he said. "Did you try to break the floor, honey?"

"No, Doctor," she said seriously.

"What happened?"

Melissa explained to Doctor Oriba the events of earlier that morning.

"Okay, Melissa, you've helped make my job much easier. Why don't you and your friends follow me into the examining room and let me take a look. I won't hurt you."

"Are you sure?"

"Word of honor."

They followed him through double wooden doors and into a small room. Doctor Oriba lifted the child easily onto the examining table. He poked and probed swiftly and surely, shined a light into her eyes, wrote a few notes on a pad.

"I don't think there's anything wrong," he said reassuringly. "We should do a PET scan just to make sure." He reached into his pocket and pulled out a lollipop. "Why don't you sit here and take it easy while I talk to your mom for a few minutes, Melissa?" he said.

"Yuck. I haven't even had breakfast yet."

"Okay, okay," he said, backing away, holding both hands up. "I know when I've done the wrong thing. Some O.J.?"

"Much better," Melissa replied.

When Amy, Jeff and Caen were alone with Doctor Oriba, who'd been thoroughly briefed about what had happened over the past six months, he asked, "And no one ever thought to do a brain scan?"

"They did a scan," Amy said.

"How far down did the scan go?"

"I don't know. Why?"

"Most scans cover the skull but don't go farther down. There's a serious tie-in between the brain and the spine at a lower level. I'd like to scan down to the base of Melissa's neck."

"Fine with me, Doctor," Ezra said.

By eight forty-five, Melissa, sedated and accompanied by her mother, was wheeled into the diagnostic imaging department. The room was dimly lit with large machinery on one wall and a control panel facing a leadedglass window. A tall, black man in his late twenties sat with his back to the controls. He had a broad smile on his face.

"Doctor Oriba up at this hour?" he said.

"Just cut the jokes and work your magic on that machine, Denzel."

Amy looked past the young man to where an attendant was strapping the sedated Melissa onto a long, metal bed. The girl's head was held down by a large, padded loop of metal, and her body was strapped in to prevent movement. The head of the bed was attached to what looked like a huge, white doughnut.

"Do you know how it works, ma'am?"

She looked at the young operator and nodded. "The bed is mechanically moved to precise locations," she said, enjoying the look of surprise on his face. "The emitter and receiver make a circuit of the toroid, giving you a picture of a slice of her brain."

" I'm impressed," the operator said. Turning to Doctor Oriba, he asked, "How far are we going?"

"To the base of the neck."

"You're the boss."

It took about thirty minutes to take the pictures. After that, they carefully went through and stored each of them to film. Oriba looked closely at one particular slice near the base of the neck.

"Is anything wrong?" Amy asked.

"I don't know," the doctor replied. "There's a small lesion at the base of her neck. I don't think it's a tumor. I palpated Melissa's neck earlier and couldn't feel anything, so whatever's there is buried deep within the fat, muscle, and nerve tissue."

He tapped several keys on the control panel and the display changed. "This is a greatly magnified view of Melissa's neck immediately above the lesion. As you can see, there are lots of wrinkles and skin folds, even in a very young child. They get more pronounced as we age." He pointed to a line that seemed slightly darker, more exact than the others. "Has she ever undergone surgery?"

"No," Amy said. She looked at him with a worried, quizzical expression.

"Strange," he said. "This mark was clearly made by a surgical incision."

"I don't understand."

"Amy, I'd like your consent to do exploratory surgery."

"When?"

"Within the hour. It's a relatively minor surgery and there's an operating room available."

"Is there any danger to Melissa?"

"Not from the surgery. I doubt there's any from whatever's in there, either, but I won't take chances."

Amy stared hard at Melissa for a few moments, then said, "Do whatever you have to do, Doctor."

Jeff squeezed her hand tightly. "I have a feeling we should have Ezra, Abner, and Buzz Wilson here when the doctor gets out of surgery."

Doctor Oriba emerged from the operating room holding a small, flat piece of soft plastic half the size of a fingernail with two dark nubs on top.

"Melissa's fine," he said, smiling. "I'd like to have this chip analyzed in the lab."

"Doctor Oriba, would you mind if our biochemists and computer analysts assist your people?" Wilson asked.

"Computer analysts?" He arched his eyebrows.

"Yes, doctor," Burchard said. "We have reason to suspect one of the nipples at the top of the sac is a computer microchip."

That evening, Jeff, Amy, Burchard, Wilson, and Caen met at the Bureau's district office.

"The biochemists found traces of clozapine, fluoxetine, and benzo-diazepine inside the container," Burchard said.

Jeff and Amy looked at him quizzically. "Nerve inhibitors." He continued, "By the thickness of the plastic sac, they concluded that most of it had been discharged."

"What about the chips?"

"One of them is a device that slit the container and allowed the chemicals to be distributed. We've sent that part to Syd Morris at NSA. She's one of the best computer minds in the country."

"She?" Amy asked.

"Now, look who's being sexist," Jeff chided her. "Sydney Morris— her real name—was a legend by the time she hit thirty. How did you guys meet her?"

"As I'm sure you know from watching the evening news on any channel, the country's gotten very sensitive to anything involving computer crime. Syd put together a crash course in 'Computers for Boneheads 101.' Buzz and I attended class for six weeks. Now you know why we got assigned to the case after Ron Ames was killed."

"What happens next?" Jeff asked.

"I suggest that Ezra put his people in touch with Syd and start speculating."

"What about you guys?"

"We'll get that Russian over here and do exactly what Doctor Oriba did to Melissa," Wilson said. "If we find what I think, we'll go to the U.S. Attorney and get an order to exhume the bodies of several people who died under mysterious circumstances during the past six months."

24

Rajendra Prasad glanced at his watch. Seven-thirty. The flight from New York was due to land any moment. He was unnerved by the call he'd received twelve hours earlier. "Twenty minutes after Lufthansa 72 touches down at Rhein-Main tomorrow, meet me in the men's restroom around the corner from the Ikarus bar. There are five stalls in the lavatory. Wait in the middle stall. I'll be in the one to your right. Don't tell anyone about this call under any circumstances."

"Hitoshi?" The line had gone dead.

It was totally unlike Kono to be out of touch for so long. Three days ago, Cunningham had advised each of his colleagues it was imperative they call in their whereabouts at least twice a day.

One hour before Kono's plane was scheduled to land at Rhein-Main, Cunningham received a call back from the police commissioner in Kahului, Maui. "We've located your friend, Mister Cunningham."

"Good. May I speak to him, please?"

"Afraid not, sir. He's on the Lufthansa flight to Frankfurt."

"Thank you, Koki. I appreciate your help."

He called Doctor Lee. "Chung Lien," he asked, his tone casual, "have you heard anything from Kono in the last twenty-four hours?"

"No, Charles. Is anything up?"

"We may have a small problem."

"What kind of problem?"

"I don't know yet. Stay at this number for the next several hours. I'm going to investigate."

No sense in trying to reach Prasad. He was attending a computer conference in Frankfurt. He had said he'd call a little after noon but didn't know a number where he could be reached.

Odd, Cunningham thought. It was too much of a coincidence that Prasad and Kono would be in Frankfurt on the same day.

He placed another call, to a discreet, not particularly reputable, detective to whom Höffer had referred him.

"Let me get this straight, Herr . . . Jonas. You say there's one thousand euros waiting for me at the Lufthansa ticket counter along with a description of the man I'm supposed to follow? I'm to watch until he has met an Indian gentleman, then call you back?"

"That's correct, Herr Finke."

Prasad had taken the early morning British Airways flight 902 from Heathrow to Frankfurt and landed an hour ago. He'd had no difficulty lying to Cunningham. There really was a computer convention in Frankfurt. He might well stop by and network with his colleagues. He'd booked a return flight for five-twenty that afternoon. As he alighted, he carried a laptop computer and a newspaper he'd taken from an empty seat as he was leaving the aircraft.

The transit lounge at Frankfurt International airport was a small, expensive city with every amenity, an island in the middle of jetways and runways. The duty-free shops had very few Japanese goods. Most products displayed were decidedly German, despite the push toward one European Community.

Local chunk salami went for twenty-six euros per kilo. When he saw the four-euro price tag on a can of Pepsi-Cola at the Ikarus bar, Prasad decided to wait until after he'd met Kono to have a snack in the city.

A gentle, three-tone chime rang and a pleasant, impersonal female voice announced the arrival of Lufthansa flight seventy-two. Fifteen minutes later, Prasad walked into the restroom.

The public lavatory was Teuton-spotless and smelled of fresh lemons. Prasad thought elves out of Grimm's Fairy Tales must pass through with mops, brushes, and buckets of lemon-scented, soapy water more than a hundred times a day. There were racks on the wall selling Erotim condoms. He ducked into the middle stall, sat on the toilet seat, and opened the London *Daily Mail*. While he detested the trashy tabloid stories, he secretly enjoyed looking at the scantily-clad women whose pictures adorned Fleet Street's "rag."

His hand shook as he read the headline and the lead story.

POLITICAL DEATHS MAY BE TIED TO BRAIN IMPLANTS!

Washington, D.C. The Daily Mail has learned from sources in the American capital that brain implants may be directly related to a rash of politically-related killings during the current year. According to our correspondents, joint American and Russian teams found sacs containing mind control drugs when they performed exploratory brain surgeries earlier this month on an eight-year-old child who mysteriously stabbed her father, and a political expert who, last May, ran amok and killed six people in Baikalsk after he had successfully worked out a labor-management agreement. Both suspects had passed psychological and lie detector tests administered by law enforcement agencies.

Daily Mail sources report that the United States Attorneys' office is trying to obtain court orders from the Federal Court for the Southern District of New York to exhume the bodies of fifty-seven men and women who have been involved in unexplained deaths in the United States this year. U.S. and Russian agencies declined to rule out a connection between the surgeries and a wave of apparently random, unexplained killings that have taken place since February. Deaths of political figures, ranging from first-term backbenchers to the president-elect of Albania, have increased by 600% from this time last year. Until now, no one has had an explanation for this series of bizarre coincidences.

The Indian trembled. If they'd found the sacs, they'd found the microchips.

"Rajendra?" The soft voice came from his right.

"Hitoshi?"

"Have you spoken to anyone?"

"No."

"We've got problems, my friend."

"The *Daily Mail* said as much."

"They've operated on Kogan and the Roth girl."

Prasad remained silent for a few moments. "Should we let our leader know?"

"I'm sure he was the first to know. He's better connected than most world leaders."

"So why not call him?"

"Because I think he's compromised the entire operation."

"Meaning?"

"He arranged for Sethuli to try to kill an FBI agent."

"What?" Prasad exclaimed. How did you find out?"

"A friend of mine at the FBI told me they were sure Sethuli wasn't acting alone." He slipped a piece of paper under the stall.

Prasad picked it up and read, "No more talk. You never know who could be listening. Stay here one minute before you leave. Meet me at Apartment 4, Stuttgarterstrasse 15 near the Hauptbahnhof at 11:30. Get rid of this paper immediately."

There was no one in the lavatory when Prasad left.

"When Mister Kono landed, half an hour ago, he went into a stall in the men's lavatory adjacent to the Ikarus bar and spoke to a man he identified as Rajendra about someone named Sethuli. They were in the W.C. for five minutes. A minute after Kono left the washroom, a brown-skinned man matching the description you gave me left the room. Is there anything further you want me to do, Herr Jonas?"

"Yes, Herr Finke. Have you still got either of them in sight?"

"The Indian."

"Good. Follow him. Call me this evening. You'll find an additional three thousand euros under the door to your office. You may call Karl Höffer in Vaduz if you have any doubt about my good faith."

"I have none, Mister Jonas. I'm grateful."

"If you are as astute as I have been led to believe, there will be substantially more business."

"Thank you, Herr Jonas," the detective said appreciatively. This was the most he'd received for so little effort in his entire career. Not that he believed for one moment that his benefactor's name was Jonas.

The weather report had predicted Frankfurt would be fourteen degrees Celsius. By ten, when the cloud cover broke and the sun came out, it appeared the temperature would exceed the forecast by several degrees. Rajendra, who'd worn a turtleneck sweater and summer sports jacket, started to perspire. It was not from the heat.

After he left the airport, he took a cab to the *Messeturm*. He'd never liked Frankfurt, which he found to be an arrogant city, made up of sharp angles and upthrust buildings, with a disdainful Germanic coldness that looked down on the rest of the world.

After he located Stuttgarterstrasse, about a fifteen-minute walk from the tower, he stopped at an international newsstand, picked up the London *Times* and the International *Herald Tribune*, and went into a decent-looking cafe in Baseler Platz. Both papers carried the news about the American-Russian discovery. If the FBI and Russian State Security were working together, the rest of the international intelligence community wouldn't be far behind. He knew they'd cooperated with one another, even during the most frigid days of the cold war.

In the world of advanced computers, a microchip designer's work was as individual as a fingerprint. He perspired more freely. How long would it be before someone implicated him?

As late as five-thirty this morning, Charles Cunningham had told him with calm assurance, "Every day we're eliminating several more targets. We're advancing our timetable to October first."

Prasad had been troubled by Cunningham's words. The plan had always been to wait until the American holiday season. Kono had told him there was no way Cunningham could not know about the press story.

Given his connections and the sophistication that had served him so well in difficult situations, Charles would almost certainly know what to do. But if that were so, why would he have had the audacity to unleash a weapon on an FBI agent?

Just then a middle-aged man passed by the window of the cafe and gazed directly at him. Prasad felt his stomach churn. He had seen the same man enter the men's room at Frankfurt airport just as he was leaving. Was he being followed?

Grab hold of yourself, Prasad, he thought. *Middle-aged men have a right to go to airports, they have a right to go to the water closet, and they have a right to walk down the Mainzerstrasse in broad daylight and stare at customers in a busy streetside cafe.*

The man entered the restaurant and came directly up to him. "Excuse me, sir," he said politely, in heavily-accented English. "Are you by any chance Rajendra Prasad?"

"Why?" Prasad snapped. Then, abashed at his own rudeness, he said, "I'm sorry. Yes, I am Prasad. Why do you ask?"

"I am Hans-Dieter Finke. I will the computer conference be attending this week and I was told you might be there as well. I wanted one of the world's computer legends to meet."

Rajendra smiled inwardly at the man's faulty English usage. Immediately afterward, he felt guilty at having perceived this man as a spy. "Would you join me for coffee, Herr Finke? I apologize for my discourtesy. I somehow thought I'd seen you before."

"Yes, that is so. We passed one another in the lavatory at Frankfurt Airport early this morning."

"You were there?"

"I was. The assistant manager I am, at a computer shop a few blocks from here. My employer, Gunter Krause, asked me to pick up the Philips representative, who was coming from Amsterdam, and bring him into the city. I wanted to speak with you when I first saw you, but that might both of us have embarrassed. After I'd dropped the Philips man off, I am strolling in the Leipzigerstrasse. Imagine my surprise when I see you here. I am certain I must have looked equally strange to you."

"You did." Prasad did not add that Finke had frightened him out of his wits.

After fifteen minutes, Prasad discerned that poor Finke would never amount to more than an assistant manager in a retail store, and his imperfect use of the language made it difficult to follow the man's conversation. Finke's knowledge of computers, which he parroted with great pride, was elementary and narrow, but the drone of the man's voice calmed Prasad's fears.

Shortly thereafter, Finke took out an old-fashioned pocket watch on a chain. "*Gott im Himmel,*" he said. In a man of more sophistication, this would have been a quaint anachronism. In Finke, it sounded natural. "I'm late in returning to my work. If Herr Krause returns before I'm back, he'll have my hide. He's a real *hochmüt* that. From Hamburg no less. Ah, but I forgot, Herr Prasad, you're not from Germany, you wouldn't know the type. It was an honor to meet you. God willing, our paths will cross again."

25

---

15 Stuttgarterstrasse appeared to have survived the war. Apartment four was on the fourth floor. There was no elevator in the building. Prasad knocked once.

"*Wer ist das?*" The voice was uncertain, suspicious.

"Prasad."

He heard the click of a bolt being unlocked. Kono signaled him in. The front room of the apartment had a high ceiling and was furnished in a style popular forty years ago. "A friend's place," Hitoshi said. "I've kept a key over the years. Are you sure you haven't been followed?" His voice was tight.

"I'm certain." *Unless you count Hans-Dieter Finke as following me around*, he thought.

"How long have you known Charles Cunningham?" Kono asked.

"Twenty-three years, why?"

"Did you ever find it strange that he lifted you from the gutters of Vancouver without even knowing you and gave you the ability to do anything you wanted in your profession?"

"I haven't given it much thought. What about you, Hitoshi?"

"With me, it was adventure rather than the need for money. I could have survived the rest of my days in comfort without lifting a finger. Cunningham is incredibly persuasive. There's something hypnotic about being close to so much raw power."

"I know," Prasad said. "It was as if I were a one-man Microsoft. Whatever equipment I wanted, it was there. Did I want a library? Up to date, state-of-the-art research tools? Available immediately. A staff of bright young men and women? Mine for the asking. I became wealthy enough to buy an entire city in India."

"Did you ever suspect Cunningham's motives before last December?"

"Yes. What about you?"

" Cunningham never impressed me as an altruist. Would you like some tea?"

"Please."

While Hitoshi was in the kitchen, Rajendra went to the window and looked down at the wide, busy street. A fat young woman walked by on the side opposite the apartment house, wheeling a large perambulator. An old man with wire-rimmed glasses tipped his hat to her and stepped out of her way. Farther down the street, a white Mercedes and an orange-colored Volkswagen were parked, half on, half off the sidewalk.

"Our colleague is a megalomaniac," Hitoshi said, as he reentered the room bearing a tray with china teapot, cups, and saucers. Prasad said nothing. "I believe Cunningham had Will Hensleigh murdered."

"I do, as well," Prasad said. Have you spoken to Chung Lien?"

"Don't be naïve, Raj. She's as amoral as he."

"So you see her as being on his side?"

"Lee Chung Lien's on nobody's side but her own."

"What do you suggest, Hitoshi?"

"I need time to think about it," the Japanese replied. "I've never felt myself to be a great moralist. I'm a pragmatist and a survivor. Life's been good to me. I'd like to stay on earth a while longer. Cunningham's tentacles stretch so far I imagine I'd be dead within twenty-four hours if he knew how I felt."

"Why did you tell me?"

"Because I intuited you felt the same way. Now that I know you do, we at least have some power. If one of us should disappear in the next two or three months, the other will know it wasn't accidental."

"How do you know I won't go straight to Cunningham with what you told me?"

"The same reason I won't."

"What do we do for now?"

"Play Cunningham's game. Stay alive."

"The Indian went to an old apartment house in the Stuttgarter-strasse shortly before noon. He left an hour later and went to the computer convention. He is booked on the 17:20 British Airways flight to London Heathrow. Herr Kono is taking the overnight Lufthansa to Los Angeles." Gone was the heavy accent, the unusual speech patterns. Finke's English was crisp, perfect.

"Thank you once again, Herr Finke. Your services have been commendable. Your bonus will be waiting when you return to your home this evening. I believe you'll be pleasantly surprised. You do like blonde women?"

The detective's eyes widened. "You know me far better than I know you, Herr Jonas."

"Karl Höffer told me about your tastes," the American said. "You may rest assured there will be plenty of money for all the beer and *Weiss-wurst* you'll ever need."

The American put the receiver down, smiled to himself, and made three more overseas calls.

Hilde Koch, twenty-five, was the stereotype sexual fantasy of every red-blooded German male over the age of twelve. She stood five-feet-eight inches tall. Her straight, platinum-blonde hair, which hung to her waist when it wasn't done up in pigtails, framed a face that had "Come and get it," written all over it. Long lashes, sultry brown eyes, full, sensual lips. Most men who'd stared at her open-mouthed, and there were many, kept their gaze going down to her extraordinary bust, then to a pair of long, beautifully turned legs.

Hilde knew the commercial value of her charms very well. She did not consider herself a common whore. At three thousand euros a night, she was a courtesan. As she was fond of saying, she would marry when she found a man rich and handsome enough, but how could she pick one flower unless she'd sampled the entire field? Her clientele was select: ministers, rock stars, ambassadors. It was not unusual for her to receive international calls weeks in advance of an expected visit. Often, she was already booked when those calls came in.

Hilde had raised her rates by half three months ago. She calculated that if she lost fifty percent of her business, she'd earn exactly the same as she had been making before and she would have the extra time for other pursuits. It hadn't worked. When word got around of the raise in Hilde's prices, she became more sought after than ever. She was in her apartment in the Grabenring wondering how much more she could make by raising her rates to thirty-five hundred euros a night when the telephone rang.

She picked it up with a musical, "Al-lo?"

"Friedrich Schiller once said, 'That nation is worthless which does not stake everything on her cowardice.'" Hilde Koch's eyes glazed over.

A moment later, a male voice said, "Hilde, I want you to go to the home of Hans-Dieter Finke. Here is his address and here is what I want you to do."

Penelope Preston decided to close her Brompton Road boutique early. The weather was untypical of London, a warm, sunny afternoon with the lightest touch of breeze, and Tony had called just after lunch. "Listen, luv, what say you and me play tourist and visit the Tower of London? Stroll along the Thames, rehearse for the wedding night afterward?"

She laughed merrily. Her twenty-eighth year was the happiest of her life. Penny's small shop had prospered beyond her highest expectations. Anthony Sikes-Burnham was every girl's dream, sensitive, intelligent, recently admitted to Lincoln's Inn, a killer in bed. They'd met ten months ago when he walked into the boutique, looking for a gift for a girlfriend. Within an hour, he'd walked out of her shop and into her flat.

Six months later they were engaged. Although they hadn't yet set a date, their constant wedding "rehearsals" continued to titillate and delight each of them several times a week.

She'd just stepped out of the shower when there was a knock on her door.

"Who is it?" she asked.

"Miss Penelope Preston, please? I have a telegram from Mister Anthony Sikes-Burnham."

The voice was familiar. She was sure it was Tony. She thought she'd give him a thrill. Dropping the towel from about her slender body, she opened the door. She scarcely had time to recover from her shock when the stranger, a pleasant-looking fellow her own age said, "If I lose mine honor, I lose my sixpence—. Penelope, there's a Lufthansa flight leaving for Los Angeles this evening. You will be on board that plane, in seat 4-B, first-class section. Here is your ticket and a syringe to put in your purse. You will be sitting next to a man named Hitoshi Kono. Here's what you are to do. . . ."

The knock on Finke's door had come at precisely seven o'clock.

The woman was an astonishing apparition, and what she was wearing was designed to make him see everything the vision had to offer. She had brought *Weisswurst* and beer. Her voice was smoky when she said, "Herr Jonas asked that I make sure you were well entertained."

This is the luckiest day of my life, Finke thought. *First I make more money than I've made in the entire month, now this.*

"Shall we eat something before we make you happy?" she'd asked, eyeing him with a combination of innocence and lust. "We've got the whole night. You'll need all the energy you have." She was wearing a red velvet choker from which hung a diamond pendant.

"Why not, Fräulein. . . . Fräulein. . . .?"

"Hilde, Herr Finke."

"Ach yes, Hilde. A beautiful name for the loveliest woman in the world."

"Why, thank you," she said demurely. "Would you mind terribly if I became a bit more comfortable? It's so warm in here." Without waiting for his reply, she undid the buttons on her white blouse.

Finke, who'd hardly finished the first few bites of Wurst and was downing a mug of beer, almost choked. He barely managed to chug the beer down.

"Would you like more to eat?" she asked, her cheeks showing high color, the double entendre only too clear. "I'll be happy to wait if you want dessert."

"I'm quite ready, Fraulein Hilde," he said, taking her hand and walking toward the bedroom.

"I know just what will excite you," she replied. "Have you a belt?"

"Why?"

"Perhaps you want to spank your naughty little girl?"

"Oh, you are a wicked one, aren't you?"

"Nothing more than you deserve, meine grosse Herr," she said. "Don't get up. Tell me where the belt is. I'll bring it to you. Let me be your love slave tonight."

He sighed heavily. "Ordinarily I'd get up and find it, but you understand this old man's a little winded."

"An old man? Where? All I see is a vigorous lion. Tell me where the belt is, then roar for me while I find it."

"In the closet, not two meters away."

"Good."

She found the belt, then returned, clad only in bra and panties. "Let me ride on your back before you hit me?"

"That's fine." He turned over on his stomach, then raised himself on his hands and knees. She mounted him and he started gently bucking.

"Faster, faster," she squealed. He bucked harder, breathing hard from the exertion.

Suddenly she wrapped the belt around his throat and pulled hard. His last living thought, as his vision dimmed was, "Oh, God, not a heart attack. Not now."

The 787's twin engines roared as the bird climbed into the sky north of Heathrow. The pilot set the controls on automatic for the computer-plotted course and radioed London Center for updates on the weather.

Clear, calm, a lighter-than-usual westerly jetstream. It was going to be an easy, boring flight.

The plane had been half empty on the flight from Frankfurt to London. Hitoshi wondered what kind of seat companion he'd have on the flight to Los Angeles. First class always filled up on these long hauls. Lots of airline personnel rode the evening flights. The young lady approaching his seat might be one of them. Slender, about five-feet-four, short-cut, brown hair, alert blue eyes. She had a pert face, was smartly dressed, and was wonderfully fresh-looking.

"Excuse me, but I believe I'm seated in 4-B." The voice was educated English. Kono's eyes widened with interest.

"Then this is my lucky evening," he said. "I'm Hitoshi Kono."

"Penelope Preston." She smiled. Her features crinkled warmly. She held her right hand out and he shook it, then rose as she sat down in the aisle seat. "I've never been across the pond before. How long does this flight take?"

"Ten hours," he replied. "Will you be staying in Los Angeles?"

"Yes," she said. "I'm . . . meeting a friend there." Kono's face dropped. "She's an old school chum." He brightened again. "I've opened my own little dress shop recently, nothing much to look at, but I hope to import a few American clothes and send some of mine to the colonies." She giggled.

This girl's charming, he thought. *The flight won't be so bad, after all.*

During the first hour of the flight, Penelope Preston, after asking that he please call her Penny, chattered about inconsequential things. Just like any first-time passenger across the Atlantic, Hitoshi thought. Her talk was soothing after his nerve-wracking day. The pressure he'd felt gave way slowly, like air escaping a small hole in a balloon. He ordered wine for them both, and set his watch back to Pacific time. "Miss Preston, it's been a very long day. Would you mind terribly if I dozed for a few minutes?"

"Not at all."

"Please wake me up when the food service starts? I didn't have a chance to eat dinner before the plane left Frankfurt."

"Certainly, Mister Kono." She extracted a Rosamunde Pilcher paperback from her purse. "Would you like me to summon the flight attendant to get you a pillow?"

"No, thank you," he said, leaning back in the wide seat. "This will be fine."

Within a few minutes, Hitoshi Kono was dreaming. He was in the Congo, in one of the Preserve's guesthouses. There was a knock on his door. He was surprised to find Penelope Preston waiting for him, dressed in blue shorts, sneakers, and crisp, white blouse.

She reached up and touched his forearm gently, then moved her hand up and down his arm. He felt the cool touch of her fingers. There was a sharp prick. Too late, he struggled to open his eyes, realizing this was not a dream.

As the ten milligrams of Digoxin took effect, he crumpled into a sleep from which he would never awaken.

Rajendra glanced over his shoulder continually between the time he left the Stuttgarterstrasse apartment and the time he boarded the return flight to London. *You are becoming paranoid*, he warned himself. *You've done nothing wrong, there's no reason to be concerned. If Cunningham's watching anyone, it will be Hitoshi, not you.* Another part of him, the alert, street-smart kid from Calcutta, said, *Yes, but you'd better make sure your own arse is covered.*

The British Airways flight was filled with businessmen returning after a day in the land of the Hun. After landing at Heathrow, he took a cab back to the Mayfair. Every so often, he glanced back. *Nothing out of the ordinary. Stop worrying, you're home.*

"Any messages, Tyrone?" he asked the night bell clerk.

"Just a moment, sir, I'll check."

When he returned from the front desk, the elegantly-attired Black man handed Rajendra a typewritten envelope. "Only this, Mister Prasad."

"Thank you." When he got to his room on the seventh floor, Prasad entered carefully. Still skittish, he checked the lavatory as well as under the bed. No one there.

He bolted the door and opened the envelope. Inside was a sheet of plain paper, on which was typed, "Hitoshi suffered a fatal heart attack on the flight back to Los Angeles tonight. What will you do now?"

The note was unsigned.

The uncontrollable trembling began.

Prasad felt cold. Very alone. And very, very frightened.

26

"There've been three hundred eleven deaths since February," Caen said. "Professor Savage's initial wild-ass speculation is starting to look awfully accurate. What do you fellows think?"

"I say we hire ourselves an actuary to make some more guesses, unless Buzz or I can do better than he's done," Burchard said.

"Thanks for your vote of confidence, guys," Jeff said.

Ezra continued, "Let's go over our latest information." He scanned the computer sheets in his hand. "One, there is no precise pattern linking any of the deceased to one another. So, we have no way of predicting who will be the next victim.

"Two, all roads appear to lead to an organization called *ChildFinders* and an individual named Charles Flanders Cunningham III, who denies knowledge of that agency. Charles Cunningham has an impeccable international reputation that would give him no motive to kill anyone. He's as 'inner circle' as any man could possibly be, and he has nothing to gain by political murders.

"Three, with the exception of misstatements concerning Lumumbashi and Manono, Cunningham's explanations coincide with our own findings.

"On the other hand, if there is no tie between Cunningham and *ChildFinders*, we're at a complete dead end. Have you special agents checked out the others?"

"Yes," Abner said. "Their reputations are clean. None of them seem to have any motive to involve themselves in planned killings. Two are dead. The other three. . . ."

"Wait a minute!" Savage interrupted. "Did you say *two* of them are dead?"

"Yes, I thought you knew."

"I didn't know there was a second one. Who is . . . was it?"

"Kono."

"The one statistically least likely to die. How did it happen?"

"He was flying from Heathrow to LAX on Lufthansa the night before last when he apparently suffered a massive heart attack."

"Did he have a history of heart problems?"

"None," Burchard said.

"Did they perform an autopsy?" Jeff asked.

"Yes. We should have the report within the next few hours," Burchard responded.

"Can you check the manifest? Find out the identities of everyone who was anywhere near him during the flight?

"Why, Jeff?" Wilson asked.

"Wild-ass guessing again."

"According to the coroner, Kono was given enough Digoxin to kill a horse," Wilson said. "The young woman who sat next to him on the plane doesn't remember a thing. The tests confirm she's telling the truth,"

"Tell-tale sac?" Jeff asked.

"We'll know by tomorrow."

"How are the tests coming on the bodies that were exhumed?"

"One hundred percent positive for chemical implant."

"A few months ago, Ron Ames let me use the Cray Titan," Savage said. At the time, I told him that using the Cray to hook into a database was like having Einstein teach math to a bunch of first graders. Just before I hooked in, he told me a lot more about what that monster could do. I think it's time we gave the beast a chance to roar"

"You are insatiable, Chung Lien! At this rate, I'll be dead in less than a year," he said, laughing.

"I'm surprised you didn't bring your watchdog along."

"She was not pleased. I'm sure she's back in the States plotting my demise as we speak."

"That's not funny, Charles. We're under attack on two fronts. We don't need a third."

"Hitoshi's gone. That'll keep Prasad in line."

"What made you decide to spare him?"

"We can still use him to advantage."

"How?"

"When it comes to computers Prasad's their equivalent or better. He can plant viruses in their systems and paralyze the hunters."

"What about their hard copies?"

He raised up on one elbow and lazily stroked her soft body. They still haven't got enough information to prove anything or stop any of our weapons. Without more, they won't be able to do much in the three weeks before the meeting."

"I accept the present need for Rajendra. What about Miss Graham? I certainly don't understand the need to leave that hole unplugged."

"A colorful turn of the phrase, Chung Lien. Perhaps it's just a sense of loyalty."

"Or weakness?"

"I've never understood the jealousy between you two."

"Jealousy?" she said. "I consider myself above that sort of thing. I'm speaking as a scientist. What further use can she be to us?"

"She wouldn't think to betray me."

"Don't be a fool, Charles. Your misplaced loyalty could prejudice the project. First the Roth woman, now Graham—"

"Let me think about it, all right?" he said sharply. "I don't intend to destroy what we've worked so hard to attain."

"Yes, sir," she said, standing and bowing. "Is there anything else the Master demands?"

"Not at this moment," he said coldly.

"Sharon, I need to speak to you."

"Where are you?"

"Local. There's a Shell station on the corner of Twenty-third and VanDevanter. Wait by the phone booth closest to the street."

As Sharon left her house and drove toward the service station, she suspected she was being followed. Since Charles would retain only the best surveillance, she might as well not even try to determine who was tailing her.

Shortly after Sharon turned the corner, a Ford F-150 picked up the steady beep emitted from a homing device in the trunk of her car. Its driver was so intent on pursuing her Toyota he didn't notice the green Jeep Cherokee that was following him. Its driver picked up a cell phone and pressed in a preset number.

"Wilson."

"Did you catch where she's going?"

"Affirmative, Leila. Abner already copied the numbers on both boxes. Verizon and AT&T have activated the tracers. They'll locate where he's calling from if he's on the line more than a minute."

"If not?"

"We'll follow her twenty-four hours a day. The bird's got to land somewhere."

Shortly after Sharon Graham pulled into the gas station, her own cell phone chirped. "Yes, Raj?"

"I'm sure Charles killed Hitoshi."

"How do you know?"

"I'll provide proof when I see you. Where is he this weekend?"

"The Preserve."

"Without you?"

"You guessed it. He and the bitch queen—"

"Are you all right?"

"No. Yes. I guess so. Why?"

"I think we're both in great danger. He's three weeks away from his meeting. We've become surplus baggage."

"You think he'd double-cross us? We've been with him more than twenty years." The monstrousness of what Prasad suggested began to sink in. She'd known Cunningham forever, inside and out. Despite his fero-cious need to make the plan work, she could not believe him capable of brutally turning on his closest associates. On the other hand, he'd been buttery smooth about his fling with the Oriental woman, long-stemmed roses or not.

She looked up and down the street. A beige Ford F-150 had parked on VanDevanter a few seconds ago. A man emerged from the van and walked into an adjacent restaurant. The driver remained in the car.

"Sharon? Are you still there?" Prasad asked.

"Mm-hmm."

"Do you know anyone to whom we could go?"

"Good guys or bad guys?" Sharon asked.

"The best of the good. Can you get to them?"

Sharon hesitated a moment, then smiled. "Yes, Raj, I believe I can."

"We've got to meet. Tonight, if possible."

"Where?"

"Best Western Pikesville, five o'clock, Room 361. I've made reser-vations there." He rang off.

The man who'd gone into the restaurant came back to the van with two white cups. She saw him hand one to the driver. The door closed and they drove off.

"Did you get the whole conversation?" the first man asked.

"Yes. He'll be checking into the Pikesville Best Western."

"Did you locate Prasad?"

"Yes. He called from a cell phone five minutes away from the Pikes-ville Best Western. He'll be checking into Room 361 within the next few minutes. How far away are our people?"

"Twenty minutes. We'll grab him the moment he opens the door. He asked Sharon if she had any contacts in the Bureau," Abner said. "Boy, does she ever!"

"Don't tell me old, dyed-in-the-wool bachelor Burchard's getting sweet on her."

"Wilson," he replied. "You are one nosy sonofabitch, you know that?"

"Uh-huh."

Less than ten minutes after he hung up the phone, an Uber dropped Prasad off at the motel entrance. Rajendra looked at his watch. Four fifteen. Sharon would meet him in forty-five minutes in 361. He looked out the door. No one had followed him.

"May I help you, sir?" the desk clerk asked. He was in his late twenties and wore black slacks and a plaid shirt.

"Musarahman Abora," Prasad said. "Three sixty-one."

"Ah, yes, Mister Abora," the clerk said. "Will this be cash or credit card?"

"Cash."

"How many nights will you be staying with us?"

"Just the one."

"Thank you, sir."

Prasad handed him four twenty-dollar bills.

"I'm afraid we don't have change yet. People usually don't start checking in until five-thirty or so. I'll go into the back office to get it. Why don't you fill out the registration while I do so?"

The man disappeared into an adjoining office just as two large men came up and firmly grabbed Rajendra's arms. "Good afternoon, Mister Prasad," the taller one said. "We've been waiting for your arrival."

"Where the hell is Prasad?" Wilson radioed down.

"Damned if I know," the disembodied voice said. "We thought he'd taken the inner hall up to 361."

"How many agents have you got down there?"

"Four."

"Sweep the place. He couldn't have gone far."

Moments after the agents discovered the clerk's bludgeoned body, an effeminate looking musician wheeled a cart bearing a large string bass case toward a 2008 Chevrolet Suburban parked adjacent to Room 115. Two large men dressed in Best Western staff shirts emerged to help him load the case into the back of the wagon. "Don't you ninnies understand a *thing*?" he berated them in a strident voice, three registers above normal. "This is a valuable instrument. You don't just throw it around like it's a piece of meat. Rehearsal starts in less than an hour. If I'm not up to snuff for the performance tonight, I'll be mortified. Careful! Don't you dare look at me like that. I'm paying good money to have you help me. I could just as easily have stayed at the Hilton, you know."

The porters shrugged and ignored him. Each lifted an end of the case and shoved it into the cargo hold of the station wagon. The effeminate man made a great show of tipping them three dollars each and drove off.

Sharon arrived promptly at five, parked her Toyota in a space marked 362, and got out. No sooner had she punched the elevator button than Abner Burchard appeared at her side.

"Abner?" Her eyes widened.

"Don't say anything. We're taking you to a safe house. Rajendra Prasad's been kidnapped. From right under our noses."

SEPTEMBER

27

Jeff Savage and Ezra Caen watched as the Cray printed out its conclusions.

1. *Since the beginning of this year there have been 351 deaths of political figures. This represents a deviation of 617% above the norm.*

2. *The deaths appear to be random and occur with regularity worldwide.*

3. *419 persons of 594 persons connected with these killings (70.53872%) were physically examined for lesion at the base of the neck. 100% of these persons show positive for implantation of a 12mm x 7mm x 3.6mm wide slit plasticene sac containing trace residue amounts of tricyclics, m.a.o. inhibitors and serotonin uptake inhibitors, consisting of corticotropin-releasing hormone, clozapine, fluoxetine, and benzodiazepine. The closed end of the sac is attached to a Subminiature Electrical Dispenser 2mm x 2mm x 2mm dmzo-32686 miniature microchip slaved to chemical cutting of the sac and nerve direction or inhibition, etiology unknown.*

4. *CONCLUSION: All persons responsible for the 353 deaths listed above were subject to implantation.*

The next four pages printed out a single-spaced statistical jumble analyzing the connection between *ChildFinders*, *Luftleben*, the murders, Cunningham and his associates, then continued:

The center for operations appears to be in Eastern Congo. Jeff had arrived at that conclusion days ago.

The printout revealed that the Children's Institute appeared to be a front for the real operation, that there were between 716 and 1,792 persons so programmed, 54% male, 46% female.

Now the supercomputer got into personalities: Lee Chung Lien, an expert in intracranial reconstitution, engaged in brainwashing at least 594 known persons, 320 males, 274 females. William Hensleigh, deceased, an expert in biochemical medicine, had been engaged in formulating and implanting the medical sacs those subjects. Rajendra Prasad, an expert in computer design and technology, engaged in designing and implementing the computer microchips in those who had been programmed, while Hitoshi Kono, an expert in logistics, had arranged for transportation to and from Congo by an operation known as *ChildFinders* and/or *Luftleben.*

Each subject tested had undergone a single, unexplained absence, 10 to 14 days' duration, between their second and twentieth years.

Now came the heavyweight identification. The computer stated that Charles Flanders Cunningham III, Sharon Graham, and Guillaume M'bele, interior minister of the Republic of the Congo, were most likely implicated in the project.

The supercomputer suggested that each programmed person was subject to a triggering mechanism, such as a password, that activated the brainwashing and chemically cut the medicated sac; that the microchip enhanced the brain's receptor centers; and that after release of the medication the microchip, through an unknown mechanism, erased the mind's recollection of what happened.

Jeff had suspected Cunningham's involvement. The Cray appeared to confirm his suspicions. Three big questions remained:

Q. IDENTIFY THOSE WHO WERE PROGRAMMED.
EVIDENCE INSUFFICIENT TO FORMULATE RESPONSE.

Q. IDENTIFY PASSWORDS TO PROGRAMMED PERSONS.
EVIDENCE INSUFFICIENT TO FORMULATE RESPONSE.

Q. WHY WERE THE PERSONS PROGRAMMED?
TO OBEY ANY COMMAND WITHOUT QUESTION OR MEMORY.

Q. WHY?
EVIDENCE INSUFFICIENT TO FORMULATE A RESPONSE.

Jeff swore to himself. The computer had gone as far as it could go. Now it was time for a combination of old-fashioned human investigation and an actuarial leap of faith.

Charles had known the answer to almost every question he'd asked. It was almost as if he'd been given the script and had time to rehearse his responses.

Hensleigh was dead. Kono was dead. Sharon had escaped, but someone had kidnapped Prasad, reputedly one of the great computer geniuses of the world. Shortly after Ron's death, the FBI had interviewed Sarah Martin, Ames's secretary, to find out if there had been any unusual visitors to Hamilton's computer lab during the week preceding the damage incident to the Cray supercomputer.

The sign-in log revealed that a Reginald Maharaj Punjabi had signed in three days before Ron was killed. Punjabi's body had been found three thousand miles away from Hamilton the same afternoon that he'd allegedly been at the lab. Sarah remembered only that the man who had identified himself as Reginald Punjabi was brown-skinned, short, slender, and in his late forties.

At three-fifteen, Jeff signed off the Titan and went into the laboratory's outer office. "Excuse me, Sarah," he said, "do you remember when the FBI asked you about the brown-skinned man who called himself Reginald Punjabi, the one who came here a few days before the big fire at the lab?"

"I don't know, Professor Savage. It's been months."

"Do you think if you saw a photograph of him it might refresh your memory?"

"I'd certainly be willing to try. Do you think he had anything to do with the explosion?"

"Possibly," Jeff said.

Jeff excused himself and text-messaged the all-hours number Wilson and Burchard had given him. "Can u pdf me foto of Prasad?"

When the photo arrived, Jeff showed it to Sarah Martin. "What do you think, Sarah? Is this our man?"

"It's hard to say . . . I . . . wait . . . yes, that's him all right."

"How can you be sure?"

"I recognize the mole just above his upper right lip and the other one on his forehead."

"Thanks, Sarah. I'll be in the lab if anyone wants me."

Once there, another piece of the puzzle started to fit into place. Charles Cunningham had known the answer to virtually every question. *It was as though he'd had a script. But who could have given him the script?* Savage thought.

He glanced over at the huge, tanklike machine, all bells, whistles, and speed, the greatest thinking mechanism man had yet devised. Yet it was totally without a soul, without morals of any kind. When it came to answering properly phrased questions, the Cray Titan did not differentiate between Adolf Hitler and Mother Theresa.

Jeff called Wilson back. "One more favor, Buzz. Can you get Syd Morris on the line?"

"Sure, Jeff. Why?"

"I've run into a roadblock with the Cray. Not only that, but my intuition tells me our supercomputer has a big mouth. You told me one time Syd's the best computer expert the FBI's ever used. I think it's time to bring her in. She's got the reputation, the smarts, the knowledge, and the authority to move very quickly if what I surmise is true."

"I'll call you back in a few minutes."

Prasad is one of the great computer geniuses in the world, Savage thought. He had been here only once, for the better part of a day. Could Syd Morris help the supercomputer diagnose whether it had an illness? If so, perhaps he could make the Cray turn into a moralistic tattle-tale.

His thoughts were interrupted by Ames's secretary. "Professor Savage, Mister Wilson and Ms. Morris on six-five-one."

After Wilson had made the introductions, Syd said, "Frankly, Professor Savage, I'm not surprised you wanted to speak with me. The

FBI told me to expect a call from you any day. I've already spoken with Shafi Goldwasser, thanks to Ezra Caen's intervention." Her voice sounded warm, but businesslike. He tried to picture the face on the other side of the telephone line. Probably had short, mousy-brown hair in a severe cut, and wore huge horn-rimmed glasses.

She listened, with only an occasional "Uh-huh," as he described what he was looking for and Wilson filled in some of the blanks.

"So you want to find out if someone is hacking into your system in a highly sophisticated way, and, if he or she has, where's the information going? Let me give you a few commands to type into your server. I'll set up a conference call and get back to you in a few minutes. You might want to take the call in the lab so you can strike the appropriate keystrokes while we're talking."

Q. IS ANYONE HACKING INTO ANY OF YOUR SYSTEMS?
A. THERE IS A 1:1,000,000 DEVIATION IN CONNECTOR CABLE 7ZX41857.

He directed the Cray to proceed to fuzzy logic and enter a series of graded answers. Slightly over fifty percent of the responses were in the affirmative.

Q. IS THIS UNIT SENDING OUT WHAT I AM TYPING NOW TO ANY OTHER USERS?

The graded answers demonstrate a sixty-five percent probability.

Q. WHERE IS IT SENDING THIS INFORMATION?

The computer triangulates the area between Philadelphia, Baltimore, and Washington, D.C., but is unable to give more detailed information.

Q. DO YOU THINK THE HACKER WILL GO OFF LINE WHEN HE FINDS WE ARE TRACKING?

After a series of ever more imaginative queries, aided by two of the top computer geniuses in the world, the computer reluctantly, and with a bare fifty-one percent probability rate, suggested that this particular hacker would try to disable the computer by virus.

After he'd disconnected from the conference call, Savage called Syd back. "My intuition says it's got to be Prasad," he said. "Assuming he's the one planting the virus, do you think you can help?"

"I'll try."

"Good afternoon, Rajendra. Looks like you were a bad boy again." Cunningham's face appeared on the video monitor.

"Where are you?" Prasad choked.

"That is no concern of yours. Have you been in touch with Ms. Graham?"

"Why do you want to know?"

The large man bent back his right pinkie finger. Prasad winced in pain. "Y. . . yes," he responded.

"I thought so."

Rajendra was strapped into an armchair. He could wiggle his fingers, but little else.

"What did you tell her?"

"I suspect you killed Kono."

"What else?"

"I believe you're going to kill us."

"Really? Prasad, I'm disappointed you'd suspect such a thing of me after our twenty years together."

"Stop playing games, Charles," Prasad said huskily. "I think you and Chung Lien are planning to take this whole thing over yourselves."

"Oh, do you?" Cunningham asked smoothly. "I resent your mistrust, Rajendra. I think you should be punished. Gentlemen, please execute step one."

The larger of the two behemoths approached Prasad with a sharpened butcher knife. The Indian twisted and turned violently, to no avail.

Two quick chops and he was minus two pinkie fingers. The smaller of the two men quickly stanched the blood.

Prasad vomited all over himself before he fainted.

"What now, Mister Cunningham?" the larger man asked.

"We disconnect. Please call me when he regains consciousness."

"Will do."

"Any word on the girl?"

"Yeah. The Feds grabbed her."

"Do you have any idea where she's been taken?"

"Andrews Air Force Base."

"Damn!"

"What?"

"Nothing. Call back when he comes to."

28

They had been in the air two hours. He'd given her a mild sedative, but she was still alternately shaking and crying.

"Wh . . . where are we going, Abner? she asked, between sobs.

"Far away, Sharon."

"He'll find me. You know he will." She shuddered.

"Not if we can help it. You'll be staying at a government safe house, under twenty-four-hour-a-day surveillance."

"Do you think that will stop him?"

"I hope so."

"Stay with me, Abner. Please?"

"For a little while," he said, taking her hand gently. "How'd you get involved with Cunningham in the first place?"

"Twenty-four-year-old secretary working in the typing pool at one of the largest, most powerful law firms in the world makes good. Actually, much more than good."

"How long were you lovers?"

"More than twenty years."

"How do you feel about him now?"

"Ambivalent. You don't devote your life to someone for that period of time and have it evaporate just like that."

"Even if you know he'd kill you to achieve his ends?"

"I still can't believe he'd—" She had difficulty choking back the

---

tears. "There's a sense of unreality about all this. It's like a nightmare. Somehow, I know I'll wake up and find myself back at work on Monday morning, or I'll walk the gardens of the Manor at twilight."

"How do you feel about the whole thing?"

"Honestly?" She paused for a moment. "I feel guilty. Don't ask me why. I feel I've betrayed everything he stood for. Maybe I wouldn't be in the position I'm in now if I hadn't met you."

Burchard looked out the window. The faint lights of a small town caught his attention. One of ten thousand small towns throughout the country. He turned back toward the woman and sensed a great inner resolve beneath the tears. "Don't forget, you wouldn't have met me but for the way he treated you."

"How do I know Lee Chung Lien wasn't merely a momentary fling? A vain attempt to catch and hold the wind?"

"Isn't that the same person you called—?"

"Oh, I've called her lots of names in her time. Never to her face. Perhaps if I hadn't made such a fuss about her, nothing would have happened."

"What's she like?"

"Chung Lien? Objectively, she's one of the most brilliant human beings on earth. A nymphomaniac who swings either way, probably for experiment rather than excitement. If I were to tell you she's completely amoral, would that say anything to you other than that I was feeling the sting of rejection?"

"The ultimate 'dragon lady?'"

"I think that's a fair assessment."

"Would you like something to eat?"

"Yes, please. Where are we going, Abner?"

"Somewhere in the hills between Roseburg and Coos Bay."

"As far west as I could get and still be in the country."

"We could fly you to Hawaii, but there's not much chance to hide there. Besides, it might remind you of Kono."

"You guys know almost everything."

"Sometimes the good guys win."

"You heard me on the phone with Prasad?"

"Uh-huh."

Suddenly, she trembled again. "Hold me close, Abner. Hold me very close. What do you think they're doing with Rajendra? He's a good man, you know. Like Hitoshi and me, he got trapped by the promise of having the whole world."

"I don't know what will happen, Sharon. All I know is we're looking."

"Rajendra, listen carefully to me. You're minus two fingers. Consider yourself lucky. Next, it will be your testicles, then your tongue, then your eyes. Do I make myself very clear?"

The prisoner nodded.

"You're in the basement of one of the larger computer complexes in the state. You've got access to every network you'll ever need. Thanks to you, we've been monitoring the Titan at Hamilton University. Savage is getting too close, too quickly. I want you to program a virus that will infect that Cray and every other system Savage might conceivably use. If you're a good boy, I may let you survive. Do you understand?"

Prasad nodded. He hoped in vain that Cunningham couldn't see the tears that were rolling down his cheeks.

"Buzz, how soon can you get down here?"

"Two, three hours, why?"

"I've got some important computer information to show you."

"Can't you e-mail it as an attachment?"

"Sure. But I think we should talk face to face, the sooner the better. I need to be here for damage control, if nothing else, in the event Prasad should somehow get in."

"I'll try to round up Amy. I can't bring Abner, though."

"Why not?"

"I'll tell you when we get there."

"Mommy, am I really going home next week?"

"You sure are, darling."

"I can't wait."

"Neither can I. They've only got a couple more tests to do."

"Willie was very nice. She said somebody must have drugged her. I'm glad she wasn't hurt."

"So am I, Melissa." The phone rang. Amy picked it up.

"Amy? Buzz Wilson. Jeff says he's found a lot of important information. He wants us to come down to Hamilton right away."

"Can you give me fifteen minutes?"

"Sure."

"Who was that, Mommy?"

"Agent Wilson. He wants me to go down to Hamilton University and meet with Professor Savage."

"Are you going to marry Professor Savage, Mommy? I like him."

"No time to talk about that now, darling. My first job is to get you home."

"I love you, Mommy."

"I love you, too, darling."

Rajendra broke out in a cold sweat. Perspiration ran down his face. It had been easy enough to log into Hamilton's computers as a superuser, but no sooner had he tried to slip the virus in than the Cray responded:

UNABLE TO RECEIVE PROGRAM. 1) RETRY? 2) CANCEL?

He pushed **R** to retry.

UNABLE TO RECEIVE PROGRAM. 1) RETRY? 2) CANCEL?

R

UNABLE TO RECEIVE PROGRAM. 1) RETRY? 2) CANCEL?

R

SYSTEM FAILURE. PLEASE ENTER YOUR PASSWORD TO TRY AGAIN.

The system simply refused to swallow the virus. Cunningham had warned him his life was on the line. He'd better succeed.

"He's been knocking at the door, Syd. How were you able to devise the antidote so fast?"

"You said it was Rajendra Prasad, right?"

"Yes."

"The human mind gives out its own fingerprint. Just after you called, we had the Summit analyze all of Prasad's known work. We asked it to determine the most likely virus Prasad would try to plant. Then we told the big guy to devise an antiviral program."

"How long will it take you to immunize the networks?"

"It's already done."

"Thanks, Syd."

"Not me, chum. Thank the miracle brain."

29

Cunningham watched with growing frustration as Prasad's program met brick wall after brick wall. "Damn!" he said to Chung Lien. "Somebody must have gotten word we'd try to get in. The computer told Savage he didn't have enough information. It pointed to us as suspects, but admitted it couldn't go much farther with what information it's got."

"Why are you upset then?" she asked.

"We might have to advance the schedule again."

"Your secretary typed the lists of the names and passwords of our weapons. Could she have kept any information?"

"Not a chance," Cunningham said. "The last update was nine months ago, back when she was my loyal, adoring slave."

"Could she have committed anything to memory?" Chung Lien asked.

"How many names, addresses, and trigger phrases can you remember off the top of your head?"

"Perhaps twenty."

"A minuscule percentage. We've used six hundred ten weapons so far. Four out of every five gone. She'd be able to lead them to two live weapons at best. Which reminds me. . . ."

He picked up the phone and dialed a number in the United States. A soft female voice answered at the other end and identified herself as Noelle Woods.

"Humpty-dumpty sat on a fencepost."

"Excuse me?" the voice said. "I think you must have a wrong number."

Cunningham quickly put down the phone.

"Damn, Chung Lien. What's going on here?"

The Chinese woman glared at him. "What are you talking about, Charles?"

"That weapon just failed to activate. How is that possible?"

"Perhaps you dialed a wrong number," she said.

"No. The weapon identified herself."

She thought for a moment. "There are only two possible answers. Either she must already have accidentally fired, like Kogan and the Roth girl…"

"Or?"

"Something much worse. They may have discovered a list and are deprogramming weapons."

"Impossible!" Then he thought *"Or maybe not."* Out loud he said, "How many more of these failures are there going to be?" His face was flushed red.

"I'm certain the failure rate is very low."

"But not zero."

"My dear Charles. There is never an experiment with zero failures. By the way, what about Prasad?"

"I almost forgot. Thank you, Chung Lien." He dialed a familiar number in the United States. "Cunningham, here."

"Did you wish to speak with Prasad again?"

"No. That's quite all right. Terminate him." As a final kindness, Cunningham said, "Quickly."

"What's our agenda from here, Charles?" she asked.

"I've set up a private dinner with the president and the prime minister outside London this coming Thursday evening. Once I get their commitment to attend the summit, I'll fly to Paris, Berlin, and Moscow over the weekend, Tokyo on Monday, and Beijing the following day."

"And they said Kissinger invented shuttle diplomacy," she said, laughing. She ruffled the white hairs on his chest. "Don't you think it's time we made a serious attempt to retrieve our first little misfire as insurance? She's supposed to leave Border House next Friday."

"What about the mother?" Cunningham asked.

"We can pull that trigger whenever we want."

"I've invited her to the Preserve, just in time for the meeting."

"Clever, very clever," Chung Lien said.

He relaxed and lay in her arms, feeling a warmth emanating from her body that belied the icy coldness of her calculating mind. "Have you ever considered marriage, Chung Lien?"

"Surely you know better than that Charles."

He frowned. "I'm serious. With Sharon out of the picture, there would be only you and me."

She looked at him, smiled mysteriously, then burst out laughing.

"What's so funny?" he asked.

"You know I'd never be satisfied with one man, not even you, my dear. It's not in our natures to trust anyone, not even each other. You'd find it fascinating to try to conquer me for a while. When that didn't work, infatuation would turn sour and you'd be looking for ways to rid yourself of me, just like you did with the others."

He looked at her sharply. "Surely you don't believe—?"

"Cut the bullshit, Charles," she said, not the least daunted. "We've always leveled with one another. We're two of a kind. The end justifies the means. You've said that yourself. While you'd be trying to eliminate me, you'd best look over your shoulder knowing my plans for you were no different."

He smiled. She certainly was the ultimate challenge, he thought. Try and catch the wind in your hand, but be careful lest you end up with a knife in your back.

"Truce," he said, palms up. "You're right. All the more reason our partnership works so well. So, what do we do?"

"For now, we've a world to conquer and we'll have a lot of fun in the process. In the future, knowing exactly how the other operates may be the balance that keeps us from destroying what we've put together."

30

With Sharon's help, Abner had written down more than twenty-five names by the time they approached Coos Bay.

"Can you remember any more?"

"I wish I could, Abner."

"From what I can see, these are all weapons who've already been expended," he said. "I wish you could think of some new ones who haven't been used yet. That way we could put those people under surveillance and potentially prevent more murders."

"Is this list enough evidence for you to ... bring him in, I guess you call it?"

Abner shook his head. "It's still only a series of vague clues, wild-assed guesses—"

"And the word of a jilted woman." She looked thoughtful. "Would knowing some of the trigger phrases help?"

"Couldn't hurt. Explain the whole thing to me one more time, would you."

"Each trigger was a phrase," Sharon said. "Some very familiar to the listener, others less so. Each phrase contained a specific error. 'I regret that I have but two lives to give for my country,' 'To err is human, to forgive yellow.'"

"Are those actual trigger phrases?"

"Yes."

The plane began its descent. Sharon became quiet and introspective. She said little as they made their way through the airport, to a nondescript car being driven by an equally nondescript man.

"You probably know the names of those weapons who've been expended already," she said, as they entered the hidden safe house.

"That's true."

"How many new ones did I give you, Abner?"

"Three."

"Not too great, I'm afraid."

"The trigger phrases will be more valuable in the long run. To think it all started with one little girl, Melissa Roth." He noticed Sharon had turned white. "Is something wrong?"

"I just remembered one more name. The very first American we programmed—"

"Jeff? Abner Burchard. What have you found?"

"A lot of statistics that point toward Cunningham."

"I have direct confirmation," Burchard replied.

"Sharon Graham?"

"Affirmative."

"Does she know where the bodies are buried?"

"A few of them. Who's with you?"

"Buzz, Amy, and Ezra."

"Get them on line. I've just learned something that will blow your minds."

Time had lodged the sac securely. It took the surgeon two hours to extract it. Amy Roth was discharged from the hospital that afternoon.

During the following week, there were no new political murders.

31

Abner left the Oregon safe house for Washington, D.C. in the early hours of the morning. One look at the Special Agent who was waiting for him at Dulles Airport sufficed to tell Burchard that the man was not the bearer of good news.

"You've got to be kidding," he exploded, after hearing what the Agent had to say. "Are you sure you've searched the house, the grounds?"

"Absolutely. Sharon's gone."

"How could it have happened? You guys were supposed to have monitored everything that came within a mile of the place."

"Abner, no one has even come close to the barricades since she got here. Did you tell her about the hidden exit?"

"Of course."

Although the government had done everything to ensure that the safe house was secure, there was always the remote risk that someone could violate its integrity. To protect against that contingency, the Agency had constructed an escape passage that tunneled under the foundation of the house and emerged half a mile beyond the perimeter, in a thick forest.

Sharon had still been sad and ambivalent when he'd left. What he had not anticipated was that his leaving would turn all of her mixed feelings into rank fear. Although she'd said nothing to him, she harbored no false illusions. With Charles Cunningham's connections, he'd learn exactly where she was and infiltrate the safe house within twenty-four hours.

Left alone with her thoughts, her anxiety turned to anger. It was not enough that Flanders had dumped her like so much garbage. Now he wanted to dispose of her as well. And for that slut, that nymphomaniac. Well she might not have the Chinese woman's brilliance or body, Sharon thought, but she was a survivor. She'd been with Charles Cunningham at the beginning and had managed to hang on to him for more than two decades.

There was only one way to protect herself; one way that made sense. She'd have to convince him she'd been needlessly jealous, play up to him in any way she could, meet him face to face, on his own turf, and then get rid of him before he wasted her. An appropriate word that she thought: Wasted. Like what she had done with her life.

Just before dawn, she used the emergency exit from the safe house.

By the time Burchard learned of her absence, she had hitched a ride into Eugene, taken the early morning puddle jumper to Bend, rented a car, and gotten halfway to the Idaho border.

At eleven that morning, she placed an international call over WhatsApp to the Manor. Lee Chung Lien answered the phone and immediately pressed the record button on the adjacent monitor.

"Doctor Lee, this is Sharon Graham. I don't have much time. I need to talk to Mister Cunningham immediately. It's very important."

"I'm sorry, Miss Graham," the voice was cool, distant. "He flew to London early this morning."

"Listen, Chung Lien, this is urgent. I know you and I haven't gotten along in the past, but this is critical to the entire operation. I need to talk to Charles. I'm not concerned about this past weekend. If he's not there, can you please have him call me? I'm calling from my cell phone over WhatsApp. I'll stay here for the next hour." She gave the number.

"Very well, Ms. Graham. I'll see what I can do."

It was a comfortable seventy-one degrees in the high desert east of the Cascades. Sharon Graham noticed perspiration stains forming under her armpits. Seventeen minutes went by. Each time she heard the mechanical roar of a vehicle her eyes darted toward the highway. She jumped when the phone rang.

"Sharon? Are you all right?" The voice was warm, assured.

The bastard was as smooth as ever. All right, Flanders, she thought, let's see how you deal with a simpering, weepy dishrag. "Yes. No. I don't know. Charles, I need your help."

"Of course. Calm down. You sound terribly upset."

"Oh, Flanders, Flanders—" she started to sob into the phone. She told him how Abner had reeled her in during her hour of weakness.

"Did you give them any information, Shari?" he asked gently.

Now she must be extremely cautious.

"Nothing they didn't already know, according to Agent Burchard." She'd thrown out the bait, she thought. Even Charles would want to know just how informed his enemies were. "I . . . I did remember several trigger phrases, though."

"No matter. Probably all but two or three of them have been expended."

She had to steel herself for the next part. "Oh, Flan, Flan, my darling, can you ever find it in your heart to forgive me?" Her voice broke.

"Shari," he said, reassuringly. "There's nothing to forgive. You acted bravely in the face of unreasonable pressure. Fortunately, you gave them nothing of value."

"How . . . how was y .. your weekend, Flan?"

"Just as you suspected, Shari. Doctor Lee and I had our little roll in the hay. I needed it to find out how much you mean to me, darling."

She felt sick to her stomach, but the game was on now, and she had no choice but to play it. "I . . . I want to come to you, Flan. Right now. I need you. You'll never leave me again, will you?"

"No, Shari, I won't. It'll be all right. It'll be fine."

"Just like it used to be, my darling?"

"Of course. Even better."

"Can I join you in London, Flan? It would be a honeymoon." *A honeymoon in hell for Mister Charles Bastard Cunningham III*, she thought, an idea forming in her head.

"I see no reason why not," he said. "Where are you?"

"Thirty miles west of Pendleton, Oregon."

"Just a moment while I consult my iPad and book you." Moments later, he said, "Shari, there's an Air Oregon flight from Pendleton to Portland leaving at twelve-thirty your time. I've reserved space for you on that flight. Can you make it?"

"Uh-huh."

"Good. It'll get you into Portland an hour later. There's a two-fifteen Alaska departure to San Francisco that'll connect you to a British Airways nonstop flight to Heathrow. Got that?"

"Yes, Flan." She sounded like an obedient child, the prodigal daughter come back to the arms of her protective father. "You're sure everything's all right?" The flights would give her plenty of time to think, to jog her memory. One unused weapon and the right unused trigger phrase, and she was in business.

"I'll be at Heathrow to pick you up, myself."

"Thank you, Flan, my darling. I'll be with you as soon as I can."

"Godspeed, Shari." He hung up the phone and placed a call to Portland. When the voice at the other end answered, he said, "Peas porridge hot, peas porridge lukewarm—" He waited a second to make sure that a voice answered.

"A woman named Sharon Graham will be flying into Portland International Airport on the one thirty Air Oregon flight from Pendleton—"

At her end, Sharon hung up the phone and stared at it for a moment, wondering whether she should try calling Abner. No, you sweet, innocent lunk, she thought. This is one piece of dirty work little Sharon will have to do all by herself.

By the time Sharon was fueling her car a few miles out of Pendleton, Abner Burchard had traced her as far as the car rental agency in Portland. The license number was transmitted to every police department in the state. He'd accessed Creditnet to determine any food or gasoline purchases she'd made. At quarter after twelve, he traced her to a Shell station in Moro. There, the trail came to a dead end.

At twelve forty-five the Umatilla county sheriff's office reported that Sharon's rental car had been turned in at Pendleton airport. By one, he knew she was on the Air Oregon flight, fourteen thousand feet over Hood River.

He called the district director in Portland and explained the situation as succinctly as possible. "The Air Oregon flight is ten minutes out of Portland. It's too late to recall it," he said. "Any ideas?"

"No problem," the other drawled. "I'll call Portland tower and have them keep the plane circling while I get our people in place."

"Could you have your agents check the arrival area, just in case someone's set her up?"

"Done."

"Thanks. I owe you." Burchard was just about to put the phone down when he thought of one more thing. "Don't hang up," he said. "I have another request. When you have her safely out of the airport, call me. And have her standing by. There are a few choice words I'd like to say to Miss Sharon Graham."

"Maybe you should just fly over here and spank the lady, Burchard," the district director said, chuckling at the irritation in the Special Agent's voice. I'd like to be a bug on the phone during that conversation, he thought. Then he issued his instructions—too late to keep the plane circling over the airport.

"Ladies and gentlemen, this is your captain speaking. We've been cleared to land. You'll be happy to know we're arriving almost ten minutes early."

Good, Sharon thought. She looked at her watch nervously. Forty-five minutes between flights was cutting it close enough, even if Portland wasn't the biggest or busiest airport in the world. She felt reassured when the small plane touched down and pulled into the Air Oregon landing area, even more so as the pilot feathered the propellers and she saw the wheeled stairway approach the stationary aircraft.

"Ms. Graham?"

The flight attendant bent over Sharon and looked at her curiously. "Yes?"

"Are you all right?"

"Why shouldn't I be?"

The flight attendant smiled. "The captain just got a message saying you weren't feeling well and needed some assistance getting off the plane. Why don't you—?"

"I'm fine." Sharon unbuckled her safety belt and stood up.

The flight attendant put a gentle but firm restraining hand on her passenger's shoulder. "That's good news," she said. "Nevertheless, why don't you let everyone else get off first and I'll give you a hand with disembarking? You have a connecting flight, don't you?"

Sharon's earlier nervousness turned to panic. "Let me off this plane!" she said, her voice a shade too loud.

The flight attendant glanced up toward the cockpit. The captain was framed in the doorway. He shook his head and made his way toward Sharon, against the stream of passengers.

"Miss Graham," he said quietly. "I'm Captain Carlson. I'm sorry, we didn't want to alarm you, and now it seems we have. I had a call from security. It appears you may be in some danger."

Charles, Sharon thought. This had to be related to that sonofabitch. She sat back down and thought of Abner. Okay, Agent Burchard, she promised herself, you've just earned your chance to help me hoist Charles Flanders Cunningham to his own petard.

"I'm waiting for word from inside the terminal," the Captain said, interrupting her thoughts. "Polly here will stay with you. I'll let her know when it's safe to get off."

Sharon moved over to the window seat and pressed her nose against the thick plexiglass. The small plane was parked some distance away from the terminal and there was nothing more interesting happening outside than the removal of baggage from the hold.

Meanwhile, inside the terminal, a man in an Oregon State Patrolman's uniform headed at a halfrun toward the inspection station that led to Gate 17. "Sharon Graham is a bad woman," he said softly, repeating what the voice had told him. "You must eliminate her."

"What seems to be the problem, officer?" The checkpoint security woman seemed more curious than alarmed.

"We've received word that a female accessory to a bank holdup is coming in on the Air Oregon flight. I just heard it arrived early. Have all of the passengers disembarked?"

"No way to tell," the woman said. She looked at the man more closely. "Are you sure you need the gun? Security doesn't allow anyone into the terminal area with a firearm."

"I appreciate that, ma'am, but this is an emergency. I've got my orders. If you want to argue with my superiors, you can call Oregon State Police headquarters, or I'd be happy to speak to your supervisor, but first I've got to get to Gate Seventeen."

The woman hesitated.

"Look. You'd better let me through. Now. Jobs aren't that easy to find, you know."

"Well, go on then," the woman said, waving him through. "I suppose it's okay, you being a cop and all. I'm not gonna' risk no eighteen dollar and forty-three cents an hour job arguing with no cop."

At a full run now, the policeman headed toward the arrival gate. At the last moment, he sidestepped to avoid barreling headlong into a slender, dark-haired woman who seemed to have deliberately stepped into his path.

"Excuse me, Officer," she said. "Do you know if the Pendleton flight has arrived yet?"

"No, I don't," the policeman said sharply.

"I'm waiting for my boyfriend," she continued, trying to make light conversation. She glanced at the police special in the holster at his right side. "Isn't it unusual for an officer to carry a gun inside the airport?"

"I wouldn't know," he replied. "I don't usually work the airport beat. I hate to be rude, Miss, but we're expecting a prisoner transfer on this flight, and I was held up in traffic. The guy I'm supposed to pick up has a history of violence."

"Oh?" she said. "I was told you were here to pick up a female accessory to a bank holdup."

"What?" He turned to face her, pulling out his gun as he did so.

He was too late. Special Agent Sarah Cavassa wrestled him to the ground, and his firearm slid harmlessly away.Of course, when they interrogated the rogue police officer later on, he said, truthfully, that he didn't even remember going to the airport.

32

"Without question, you are the ultimate host, Charles."

"Thank you. I try to consider my guests' needs, particularly when they're among closest friends. *A vôtre santé*," Cunningham said, lifting his snifter in a toast to the British prime minister and the president.

The cognac glowed in the light of a roaring fire. Outside, a cool, misty rain dampened the ground around newly planted rose bushes. *Not a bad life*, Cunningham thought.

"Time to spring your news, Charles?" the president asked. "I must say, the anticipation's getting to me."

"And to me," the prime minister said. "When the quiet diplomat speaks, Kings and commoners listen."

"You do me too much honor," Cunningham replied. "Or have you been watching the ads for an American stock brokerage house?"

They laughed, relaxed in the camaraderie of old friends.

"Getting down to business," Cunningham continued. "What would you say if I told you I've been able to negotiate an arrangement whereby the Japanese will take down all their tariff barriers and announce a plan to award American companies thirty billion dollars in contracts for the development of agriculture in Somalia and Haiti over the next decade? Or that I've orchestrated a deal wherein a consortium of Saudi sheiks, Iranian oil interests, and Swiss bankers will give Russia a similar amount in loans, grants-in-aid, and guarantees, provided their government agrees to move ground forces into Iraq and allow market competition in Russia?"

The president grinned. "I'd say you were a crackpot dreamer."

"Let's take my dream a few steps farther. Prime Minister, suppose I told you that the EU was prepared to pay all costs to complete the automobile tunnel to the Continent in exchange for a ten-year option to buy all the North Sea oil that Britain can produce at today's market price, and that the EU was also prepared to send a peace-keeping force to Belfast, at its expense?"

"I'd say you belonged on a soapbox in Hyde Park," the prime minister said.

"To the contrary, I am quite sane. How long have each of you known me?"

"Twenty-four years."

"In that time, have I ever lied to you, or made a promise that I haven't delivered?"

"Never."

"You're aware that I operate quietly, opening doors that aren't available to most?"

"I am," the president said. "I've availed myself of your services on more than one occasion."

"Very well. Trust me when I say that I have spoken with the highest powers. There is substantial consideration to be exchanged everywhere on the planet.

"Your economies are both reeling. You need infusions of capital and your people need jobs. Brushfire wars like Syria don't work anymore. You can't use one match to warm the entire house. The U.S. looks to China, England looks toward the EU, but each of you mistrusts those necessary trading partners. Every country has its own agenda. Amazingly, those lists fit like pieces in a puzzle. Let me show you what I mean."

Charles Cunningham spent the next hour explaining the simplified trade and nonaggression agreements he had worked out. "All these conditions are provisional, of course."

"They all trust you to keep your own counsel?" the president asked.

"Don't you? The world is psychologically primed to move forward now. There's got to be something far more dramatic than undersecretaries meeting with deputy chiefs of mission for months on end, arguing over every meaningless comma in a hundred-page document. What we need is for the heads of state themselves to come together for a single day, away from the glare of publicity and the press, and emerge with simple, meaningful, signed accords."

"You no doubt have a plan?"

"I do."

"Which is?" the president asked.

"Switzerland has functioned as a neutral meeting ground for centuries, but Geneva is identified with European conservatism. Unknown to the two of you, unknown to virtually everyone, I have my own hideaway in an insignificant area of eastern Congo. It has all the amenities you'll need for a summit meeting. I should like to propose that a week from this coming Saturday, the two of you join me at my residence. The following day, we'll host the rest. It will be a very brief, unannounced meeting, so that the world press does not become suspicious.

"There's a twelve-thousand-foot, uncharted, all-weather airport adjacent to my estate, and ample security to obviate anyone's worry. I suggest each of you bring a small retinue of your own, should you have any concern for your safety."

"The idea's fascinating, Charles," the president said.

"Do you honestly believe you can pull it off?" the prime minister asked.

"If I have your commitment to attend, I'll personally travel to Paris and Berlin tomorrow, Moscow on Sunday, Tokyo on Monday and Beijing five days from now. Each of the others has agreed to meet with me, but I've told them nothing about the proposed African summit."

"Count me in," the president said.

"Then the *ayes* have it," the prime minister chimed in, smiling.

"Wonderful," Cunningham said. He picked up the bottle of cognac and filled, first the president's glass, then that of England's prime minister. There was just enough left at the bottom of the bottle to pour a few drops into his own glass. He glanced over at the unopened bottle that stood on a silver tray, decided against it, and said, "This'll do for me. We've polished off one bottle and, besides, I feel drunk with anticipation." He savored the last drops of amber liquid in his glass.

Looking first at one leader, then at the other, he said, "I've always believed that the best resolution of a problem is that which makes all sides happy."

With Jeff's help, Amy had redecorated Melissa's bedroom with pale, pink curtains, a matching pink canopy over Melissa's bed, a huge dollhouse, and a bookcase filled with her daughter's favorite books. The room was fresh, bright, and ready. Enough of the old to be familiar, enough of the new to be exciting. The only thing missing was Melissa.

Thursday afternoon, the law enforcement agencies advised Amy they saw nothing more to be gained in keeping Melissa under observation. Amy and Jeff stayed up 'til midnight, blowing balloons and drawing gaily decorated "Welcome Home, Melissa!" signs. They hid special gifts for her in every room and placed photos of the child all over the house. The homecoming would be the grandest day of Melissa's life.

As soon as Melissa awoke on Friday morning, she raced to the bathroom, showered and dressed, so she'd be ready. She packed her own small valise, propped Teddy on top of it, and pretended to leaf through *Where the Wild Things Are.*

At seven-fifteen, Willie entered the room. "I can see you're all ready to go home," she said, smiling cheerfully at the child.

"Uh-huh," Melissa said, barely able to conceal her excitement. "Is my mom here yet?"

"She's on her way. Are you sure you've packed everything?"

"Yes. Oh, Willie, I'm going home! I'll miss you, though. Promise you'll come and see me?"

"Of course I will, darlin'. Oops, I almost forgot, we've got one last blood test to do, before they cut you loose."

"Aww, no, not another shot," the child said, frowning. "I thought they were all over."

"Just this last one, honey."

"Oh, all right." Melissa held out her right arm, closed her eyes and scrunched up her face, waiting for the prick of the needle.

The shot was gentler than she'd remembered. She felt herself go all relaxed. She was dreaming, dreaming—

Three hours later, a faded Cessna Skyhawk landed at a private field in Alma, Georgia. Its pilot filled the aircraft's reserve tanks with hundred octane low-lead aviation fuel and made sure that the small bundle in the back, which was covered by a brown, canvas tarpaulin, had not stirred.

As he taxied out for takeoff, the pilot smiled to himself. Ten thousand dollars to deliver the kid to her father in the Bahamas. Found money. And a lot cleaner than running drugs. As long as he stayed VFR and communicated with no one, he'd be fine.

Just before he reached the coast at Brunswick, the pilot descended to five hundred feet, set the twin VORs, and turned southeast toward Freeport.

Within hours after he'd landed, the pilot was one of the few nonpolitical persons who was deliberately dispatched by one of Cunningham's "weapons."

"No!" Amy screamed. "I don't believe it! How could you let it happen?"

"I'm certain we'll find her," Buzz Wilson said. "We've got an all-points bulletin out everywhere. There's no possible way the kidnappers can escape."

"Good evening, Amy, this is Charles Cunningham."

"Where are you calling from, Mister Cunningham?" She'd been warned she must keep her voice under control, no matter the terror she felt.

"Berlin. I've taken Melissa into protective custody. You needn't worry. She's perfectly safe. Earlier this week, I discovered that a terrorist organization was attempting to kidnap her."

"Why Melissa?"

"They knew I was on a mission for the president. Although I couldn't say anything about it before, I can now tell you it had to do with *ChildFinders*. I had no child of my own they could abduct, but apparently they found out you and Jeff were searching for *ChildFinders*. They concluded if they could hold her hostage, they'd subvert some of our secret plans. For reasons of national security, and I know that sounds like a holdover from the Trump days, I can't discuss those plans with you now."

"Where is she?"

"At my private residence in Congo. When I found that law enforcement agencies in the United States weren't able to protect my associate, Rajendra Prasad, I decided to take the law into my own hands because I know how much she means to you."

"Keep him talking," Wilson whispered. "We're recording it all."

"When can I get her back, Mister Cunningham?"

Jeff extended his hands, palms down, raised and lowered them gently. "Easy, easy, it'll be all right."

"The danger should be over by next week. By that time, my informers within the organization will have provided me with enough evidence to go to your friends in the Bureau."

"Can I see her?"

"Of course. If you recall, I suggested a few weeks ago that you and Jeff visit me in Africa. Suppose I arrange for the two of you to come next Thursday? It'll be first class all the way."

The agents nodded at her.

"All right."

"Wonderful! I'll be traveling in the Far East for the next few days, so it won't be possible for me to meet you before then. I'll have Doctor Lee call you next Wednesday to firm up the plans. Don't forget to bring your swimsuits." He chuckled merrily. "I promise you a good time will be had by all."

"Good morning, Mister President. It was kind of you to see me on such short notice. Monsieur M'bele, I'm privileged you could attend as well."

"You're aware, my predecessor, President Kabila, has a very special relationship with your countryman, Dan Gertler."

"I am, President Tshisekedi. I assure you I would not have asked for an audience unless this was a matter of extreme urgency."

"Your reputation precedes you, Mister Caen, even in the absence of Mister Gertler's response. I assume you asked that Minister M'bele attend for a reason?"

"Correct, Mister President. On the one hand, this may be a painful meeting for Monsieur M'bele, but since he is known to be a genuine patriot and an honest man, and since our meeting concerns a very intimate personal friendship between Minister M'bele and the man of whom I speak, I wanted to assure that this would be a very private meeting, so that no one will be shocked, surprised, or embarrassed by what I have to say."

The three men met privately for more than four hours. At the end of that time, they reached agreement, shook hands, and the Israeli departed N'djili International Airport for Brussels and thence to Washington Dulles.

33

At eight o'clock Monday morning, Jeff received a call from Abner Burchard. "A 2010 Dodge Challenger will pick you and Amy up in ten minutes. No questions." He hung up.

The FBI's choice of transportation was hardly unobtrusive. The candy-apple red chariot bounced as though it were on rubber legs. When the driver, who looked as if he'd just gotten off the boat from Jamaica—coal-black skin, shoulder-length dreadlock hair, blue sunglasses, and oversized straw hat—jarred the quiet of the neighborhood by hooting the four-tone mega-decibel air horn and turning the reggae music to full blast on the car's overloaded speakers, Savage grinned and said, "Abner Burchard is truly a man of style and class."

He cracked the front door open.

"Eee-yy, mon!" the driver called. "You comin' or not? We got a lotta' road to cover and I gotta' get goin'!"

The car peeled rubber as it pulled away. As they rounded the corner, Jeff noted they were being followed by a conservative Chevrolet. Three minutes later, the bouncing stopped, the driver shut off the stereo unit, and the car accelerated onto the freeway.

"OK, what's this all about?" Amy asked. "Who are you, anyway?"

"Special agent Mike January at your service, Mrs. Roth. I operate out of Miami. Buzz and Abner knew I was vacationing up here and asked me to help out." He pulled off the hat, the wig, and the blue sunglasses. "You don't mind if I get rid of the accoutrements?"

"Not at all. Where are we going?"

"Classified." He handed her a slip of paper that read, "We're probably bugged. We're going to Headquarters Conference Room at Fort Meade."

When they arrived at their destination, Wilson, Burchard, Ezra Caen, and two other people rose to greet them.

"Jeff, Amy," Burchard said, turning toward an attractive woman of thirty, who had the straight, blonde hair and clear, fresh skin of a 'California girl,' "I'd like you to meet Sydney Morris."

"Syd?" Jeff said, his eyes widening. "We've been telephone buddies for a while, but I never imagined this. I expected you to be fifty, fat and frowzy. Computer geniuses aren't supposed to be young and beautiful."

"Miserable sexist pig." She winked at him. "Not only that, but a two-timer as well."

"I have a habit of saying things that don't come out right."

"No need to apologize. Your reaction's not unusual. I kind of get a kick out of it, myself."

Buzz and Syd began to laugh. Despite herself, Amy joined in.

"Ahem." The other person in the room cleared his throat. Everyone turned toward him, a man of medium height, in his midfifties, who projected an aura of power. He extended his hand toward Jeff and said, "I'm Carlton Farrell, the president's personal security advisor. And this is a serious meeting."

Burchard's face became stony. "The man's right," he said to the group. "Let's get down to business."

When everyone was settled, Farrell said, "I'm here because I was told there is a possibility that the president's life may be in danger. So far, all I've really learned is that Charles Cunningham—a longtime close personal friend of the president and a powerful man in his own right—has managed to arrange a private meeting of some of the world's most powerful leaders, a meeting scheduled to take place this weekend." He stopped speaking for a moment and looked around the room. "Certain other information comes, I'm told, from Cunningham's personal secretary, a woman he recently jilted."

He paused again, this time to pour himself a glass of iced water. He drank from the glass, waited as if to give anyone who wished to do so an opportunity to add to what he had said, and continued. "This woman apparently believes Cunningham is a megalomaniac whose plan is to take over the world. Based on that, you want me to go in and interfere with what is, to all intents and purposes, a summit meeting taking place somewhere in Africa, and arrest this man. The word of a jilted lover is hardly enough—"

"Wait a minute," Abner's soft drawl entered the conversation. "I spent Saturday putting together a report which you, sir, have had almost twenty-four hours to consider. Look at the confluence of events. There are a lot of public figures, and a few other innocents, dead—killed by an apparently undetectable army. The only connections we have been able to find is the fact that each killer had been kidnapped during childhood, and that each one was returned home by an organization named *ChildFinders*. Amy's daughter, Melissa, was one those kidnapped and returned by *ChildFinders*. She," he paused and looked over at Amy, who nodded as if to tell him that she was all right. "She killed her father," he said simply.

He paused again, and Wilson took over. "That same child was recently abducted by Cunningham and taken to his Preserve in Africa on the pretense that he was taking her into protective custody for alleged top secret national security reasons."

"My turn," Syd Morris said, looking at Farrell. "I assume Agent Burchard's report also contained the information that a strange implant was found in the necks of the *ChildFinders* killers. If you wish, I'll repeat the specifics."

"No need." The security man shook his head and looked at Jeff.

"I guess that leaves me," Jeff said. "Three of Charles Cunningham's closest associates died in the last seven months, all under mysterious circumstances. Someone tried to kill Abner, someone who—by Cunningham's admission—was a student from his Children's Institute. My best friend was killed by an alleged 'accident' caused by a brain-implanted driver. Finally, someone tried to have his administrative aide and former lover murdered in Portland airport, soon after she fled from protective FBI custody."

"All this evidence is nonetheless circumstantial, Professor. You have a series of events, related by the fact that Mr. Cunningham's name has cropped up on the periphery of each event. The only direct evidence you have remains the word of Miss Graham."

"Gentlemen." Syd set her hands on the table and stood. "This is not a testosterone-driven ego competition."

"Quite right, Ms. Morris," the president's security chief said. "Despite your report, Burchard—which I did read—and despite what has been repeated here, Charles Cunningham is a man of impeccable credentials. He's a respected, world-renowned attorney. The only questionable mark is that he was refused entry into the Trilateral Commission a little over twenty years ago."

Caen stared quizzically at him and said, "I thought the Trilateral Commission was a myth."

"No, it's not a myth," Farrell responded. "By the way, it's no longer called the Trilateral Commission. That's a Cold War anachronism that no longer applies. The group consists of wealthy and very influential persons from around the world—an infinitely more exclusive Bohemian Grove if you will—who discuss policy and sometimes advise leaders. What is a myth is that they're an evil, power-hungry organization." Farrell stood up and paced around the table. "Nothing I have heard or read so far is convincing enough for me to walk up to the president and say that one of his most trusted friends is a power-mad lunatic."

"So, what happens now?" Amy asked.

"You and Sharon are the pivotal points around which our case revolves," Abner said. "I believe Cunningham took Melissa to determine why she misfired. He's also using her to get you there. As far as I'm concerned, it can't be a coincidence that he wants you there at the same time as this meeting of leaders, so it follows he has some specific reason for wanting you there."

"But why would he invite me to come along?" Savage asked.

"That part does make sense," Wilson said. "You yourself said you've been told several times that you've proven yourself to be a worthy opponent. If Cunningham is the man behind all this, he'll want to show you in person he's won the trophy."

"This is all well and good, ladies and gentleman, but you still haven't given me anything rock solid I can take to the president and seriously ask him to stop the meeting in Africa." Farrell sat with his hands clasped on the table and glanced at each of the people assembled. "Doctor Morris, why don't you tell me about this microchip?"

Sid looked from the security man to Burchard and back. "Mister Farrell, this is an amazing piece of equipment. It receives input in the form of vibrations. From what the physician said about the placement of the implant, it would have to be pretty damned sensitive, too. If those vibrations match a preset code, it sends out several other signals. One of these causes a little tool at the other end of the implant to move, slitting the sack in the center."

"How does it slit the sac?" Farrell asked.

"That piece extends into the sac and has a very sharp edge. When it moves, the edge slices through the membrane. The microchip has one more function. It sends out a scrambled electrical signal to certain portions of the brain. What you'd call the reason centers. These signals block out the weapon's natural thinking and memory functions, turning them into what is basically a machine."

"All well and good, but how does Charles Cunningham connect to that? Certainly you can't say he designed it." The president's man stood again and paced.

"No. But these were made close to ten years ago. At that time, there were only half a dozen men in the world who had the expertise and creativity for this sort of project. One of those was Rajendra Prasad."

Abner touched Farrell on the arm as the man passed. "As we all know, Mr. Farrell, until his very recent death, Prasad was an associate of Cunningham."

The man stopped his pacing and looked over the group. "You've almost got me convinced," he said, "but it's still not enough for me to convince the president. I know the man. His loyalties are fierce. I'll step up the security, I'll mention what we've discussed to the president, but that's the best I can do." Farrell said his goodbyes and left.

"What do we do now?" Savage asked, a hangdog expression on his face.

"Ladies, gentlemen, that simply makes our jobs a little harder," Ezra said. "Even if Farrell could have kept the president from that meeting, Cunningham would still have the prime ministers of Britain, Germany, and France, and who knows who else, at his estate this weekend."

"What about Melissa?" Amy asked angrily. "How are we going to stop this monster? He has my daughter over there in his Preserve."

Jeff rushed over and set a hand on her shoulder. "Calm down, Amy. We're not giving up, just regrouping. Right Abner?" he said, looking up at his friend.

"Right. Wilson, I'm gonna' call in and see about getting some backup so the FBI can do this one on its own." Burchard walked to the phone in the corner of the conference room.

While Abner was engaged in conversation, Buzz spoke quietly with Jeff and Amy.

"So you see Amy as the trophy?" Jeff asked.

"Yes, I do. It would have been easy for Cunningham to turn her on you or on Ron Ames, as the simplest solution to all his problems. With you out of the way, there would have been no one to pursue him. My instinct tells me he's saved Amy for bigger things."

"Such as a 'demonstration weapon' when the leaders are gathered together?" Syd asked.

"Something like that," Abner said. He'd hung up the phone and returned to the group.

"Then he doesn't know she's been deprogrammed," Jeff said.

"Neither do we."

"What do you mean?"

"We removed the backup system—the chemicals and the computer chip—but the mind programming is still there."

"So, I'm still a weapon?" Amy asked. Savage could see that she was trembling.

"I'm afraid so, Amy," Abner said. "However, Sharon also told me that once the weapon was activated by the trigger phrase it wouldn't repeat."

"We don't know that for certain," Caen said. "The chemical reinforcement would only kick in once, but the erasure was accomplished by a computer chip which we've removed."

"Do you have any suggestions?" Amy asked.

"In order to deprogram you, Mrs. Roth," Syd said, "we've got to find your trigger phrase. We've got forty-one phrases to work with. While we don't have a significant database to work with, the computer plots 'fingerprints' by comparative data analysis. I believe the supercomputer could analyze similarities in phrases."

"When I talked to Melissa's teacher, she told me on the day Daniel Roth was killed, the kids made up 'fractured nursery rhymes,' during the last hour of class," Burchard said. "Sharon told me each trigger phrase was discreetly skewed by throwing in a phony word. So, the fractured nursery rhyme could have turned into an accidental trigger phrase."

"Anything else, Abner?" Syd asked.

"She recalled that the kids sang some sort of a jump-rope rhyme that ended 'Stab your father in the throat,'"

"Oh, my God." Amy turned white. "That explains it all."

"What do you mean?"

"The day Melissa killed Daniel. I remember the rhyme, now. It must have gotten frozen in my subconscious—

'Ice cream soda, lemonade punch

Tell me the 'nitial of my honey bunch

Melissa, Melissa, silly little goat,

Melissa, stab your father in the throat!'

"I didn't think of it at that time, but I remember that evening she kept asking when Dan was going to arrive."

"Do you have any suggestions as to what we do now?" Burchard asked.

"Yes," Syd said. "If Cunningham experimented with mother and daughter, he probably used the same class of phrase, maybe even the same phrase, so Amy's trigger is most likely a 'fractured nursery rhyme.' One-third of the forty-one trigger phrases fit that category. The Cray has the ability to analyze and sift through the phrases we've got, establish correlations, and produce words, phrases, and bits of phrases. I suggest we put you into a light sleep, Mrs. Roth," Syd continued. "While you're unconscious, we'll use electrodes to transmit words and phrases to your brain at twenty times the speed that you'd consciously be able to absorb. The mind emits discrete electric recognition waves when reacting to certain inputs. We'll connect the electrode sensors to the computer. The Titan can determine that discrete signal infinitely faster than we can."

"So you're going to make me a human computer?" Amy said.

"Yep. A computer with a virus. We're going to try to find that virus and knock it out," Sydney Morris said.

On Monday, just before he left Moscow for Tokyo, Charles Cunningham deposited eight hundred American dollars with the Russian PTT and telephoned Marrakech, Morocco.

The male voice at the other end said, "Yes?"

"Mister Khalili, this is Flanders. We spoke some time ago."

"Eight years, four months, seventeen days, Mr. Flanders."

"You keep excellent records."

"In my business one needs to be both discreet and cautious."

"I understand. Do you remember when I asked you about the most expensive commodity of all?"

"Of course."

"Do you still deal in such commodities?"

"Yes. At present I have a male and a female, totally attuned to one another and delightful to watch."

"At what price?"

"Three million United States dollars, apiece. Five million for the matched pair."

"How would they feel about a third player?"

"They've been trained to be very — compliant."

"How old are they?"

"The male is twenty, the female eighteen. Beautiful specimens."

"I'm not sure I will need them immediately. Might I propose a deposit to reserve their services?"

"One hundred thousand dollars a day, to a maximum of seven days. Should you exercise the option, the deposit would, of course, apply to the purchase price."

"Fine, Mister Khalili. I shall wire the hundred thousand to your Swiss account each day. Will that be sufficient?"

"Quite."

"What if I decide to exercise the option?"

"The balance must be in my account before they're picked up."

"Excellent, Mister Khalili. Please hold them in readiness. I will transfer the funds to your account within the hour."

34

By the time Amy's session at the Fort Meade Medical Center was finished, it was dawn Wednesday morning in Beijing.

"Is everything in place?" Chung Lien asked. The connection between the Democratic Republic of the Congo and Beijing was scratchy. Every so often, there were loud whistles on the line.

"Yes, older sister. I finished an hour ago."

"Are you sure no one suspects?"

"I'm certain. I've been a line mechanic for twenty-five years."

"What if the pilot inspects the aircraft?"

"He'll find nothing. The plastique looks like any of five thousand almost identical wires. The explosive is slaved to the altimeter. It will go off the moment they pass through eight thousand feet."

"Very good. The money's been posted to your account in Hong Kong. You can check if you want."

"I already have, older sister."

Four hours later, Cunningham's crew performed a thorough preflight inspection of the Citation X+. Everything functioned normally. The pilot looked at his watch. Eight-thirty. Their employer was due any moment.

At ten minutes before nine, Cunningham appeared. "There's been a slight change in plans, gentlemen," he told the crew. The Premier asked that I stay on and attend a State banquet. For me not to do so would be a breach of etiquette that would undo all I've accomplished here. I need you to fly Doctor Lee to Baltimore-Washington International Airport to pick up Professor Savage and Mrs. Roth. Would you mind calling her from Mumbai to advise her of your arrival time?"

"Certainly, Mister Cunningham," the pilot said.

"Meanwhile, I'd like to ask another favor."

"What's that, sir?"

"I've got a wager with the Premier that this plane can climb to fifteen thousand feet in five minutes. If I win the bet, there's an extra ten-thousand-dollar bonus for each of you."

Cunningham watched as the gleaming, silver bird trundled slowly down the taxiway, turned, and shot into the sky. Four minutes after take-off, there was a sound like distant cannon as the aircraft exploded in an angry ball of orange and black smoke.

Charles Cunningham looked up as pieces of the wreckage drifted silently down. He smiled, clapped his hands together in mock applause, and said, "Very good, my dependable Lee Chung Lien. Very good, in-deed. You almost made it."

He entered the terminal building and placed a call to Marrakech. "Mister Khalili, I've decided to exercise the option. A Lear 50 aircraft will be at the airport within the hour to pick up the merchandise. The funds will be on deposit within fifteen minutes."

"Luftleben 07 sixty-two knots out," the pilot radioed.

"Doctor Lee here," she said.

"Good afternoon, Doctor Lee. We're inbound to the Preserve with the latest shipment. Please inform Flanders it arrived on time."

That, Chung Lien thought, would be a very long-distance call in-deed. Earlier, she had checked with her agent in China, who confirmed that the Citation had exploded in the air. There were no pieces bigger than a man's hand and no way to determine who had been on board.

"I will do that, Captain," she said. "And I'll be there as soon as you land."

The Embraer pulled up to the terminal. Lee Chung Lien sat in an upstairs office, watching as the plane unloaded. The young people who deplaned were conscious and incredibly attractive, a boy who looked like a Greek god, and a girl who matched him in physical beauty. Their skin was a dusky, gold color.

She felt a flush move up from between her thighs. Perhaps there might be other uses for this couple before the brainwashing begins, she thought.

After the boy and girl had entered the guest cottage, Chung Lien flipped on the monitor. No sooner had the front door closed than the couple started kissing and fondling one another. They removed each other's clothing and went into the bedroom. Once there, they became oblivious to anything other than their own delicious lovemaking. It was as sexually titillating a performance as Chung Lien had seen in years and she longed to be part of it. She was already panting as she made for their cottage.

The young man, Lehti, and his mate, Daiwanna, were delighted to welcome her to their nest, and suggested by smiles and gestures that Chung Lien disrobe and join them. The Oriental woman rubbed fragrant oil all over her body and bade them do the same. They shook their heads. Their own sweat had an intense smell of love excretions, honey and almonds. Chung Lien could not wait to be a part of this and immersed herself in their ecstasy.

Suddenly, something was very, very wrong. Chung Lien felt a searing pain. She clutched at her eyes and tried to scream, but all that came out was a muffled gag. She felt a massive explosion in her stomach, and smelled the escape of her own excrement. Her body twisted in a grotesque parody of sexual climax. Within moments, she was paralyzed. Lee Chung Lien knew she was dying, knew with certainty that Charles Cunningham had not been on the plane. And that he had won.

The couple quietly arose from the bed, their job accomplished. They smiled at one another, left the corpse, and showered in the adjacent bathroom.

At just about that same time, Cunningham, who was enroute to Baltimore-Washington International Airport, placed a call to Marrakech from the plane. "Mister Khalili?"

"You've no worry, my friend," the familiar, oily voice responded. "Pursuant to your instructions, a private aircraft will retrieve them within the hour."

"I don't mean to intrude on the details of our business, but just as a matter of personal interest, how do they manage to—?"

"Lehti and Daiwanna are *venefici*," the Moroccan replied. "Their tradition goes back six thousand years. From infancy, they were fed wolfsbane and elaterium, two of the world's deadliest poisons, first in minute amounts, then in increasing doses. By the time they were ten years old, their bodies were completely immune to those substances. Of course, anyone else partaking of the natural body juices of a *veneficus* or *venefica* will die a horrendous death within a very short time. Are you certain you won't have need of them again? After all, you have paid for them, and there are no refunds for returned merchandise."

"No, thank you, Mister Khalili. What will you do with them?"

"They will stay with me for a few days. Then, I will offer their services, again. Of course, I am willing to divide the profits with you."

"That will not be necessary, Mister Khalili. Goodbye, sir, and thank you once again."

Cunningham replaced the receiver, then called a number in Rabat. No sooner had the voice answered than Cunningham said, "There'll be bluebirds over the white cliffs of Paris." He waited a few moments, then continued, "Mr. Dudley, there's a foul slave-trader, Hakim Khalili, who transacts his loathsome business in Marrakech. He has two particularly obscene love slaves whom he keeps in his home. Tomorrow morning, I want you to eliminate the three of them and burn the building where Mister Khalili keeps the records of his outrageous trade. His address is—"

Sharon had arrived at Fort Meade the night before. They insisted she remain under wraps until the *Luftleben* 767 had departed Baltimore-Washington International Airport.

By noon, the computer had fed Amy over a hundred thousand phrases and word combinations. They still hadn't found the word sequence they needed.

An hour later, Jeff and Amy joined Burchard and Wilson in the headquarters conference room for a final briefing. When they arrived, Sharon Graham was waiting there with Mike January and another man whom they hadn't met before. He was close to Abner's size, but without the naturally gentle expression.

"You know Mike already," Buzz Wilson made the introductions. "This is Jimmy Stevens. They're our backup."

Silence hung heavy in the room.

"The president's taking four Secret Service men with him," Abner said, finally. "They've been briefed that you two will be there. They know nothing of us."

"Then why are you going?" It was Sharon's voice. "You know the chances are you'll lose. Charles always stacks the odds that way."

"Look, Sharon, we've done this before. If we don't try, Cunningham wins by default. If you don't want to be a part of this, you're free to leave." It was obvious Abner wished she wouldn't come along.

"You couldn't find your way in there without me."

"Amy?" Wilson looked at the other woman. "We're going in there to get Melissa. No sense in endangering your own life."

"I'm a mother. Unless you've been there, you really don't have any conception of what it's like to carry a child inside you for nine months, to harbor a life. If I stay here and something happens to my daughter, I'll feel responsible—even if I'm not."

"No fear?" Abner asked gently.

"Of course there's fear," Amy snapped. "Would anyone in her right mind be looking forward to this?"

Jeff could see she was close to breaking. "Let's just stick with the plan," he said. "Remember, Cunningham is in it for the game. We can show him there's a lot more to this than his moving his pieces around."

Sharon thought over their plan for a moment. She knew the Preserve well enough to get Abner and the other agents onto the property, but she doubted they could really get to Charles. It was a good thing she had another way to deal with him. She just hoped Jeff and Amy could pull off their parts.

"Look," Mike said from where he stood by the window. "Professor Savage is right. We have more to lose by staying home, so I say we go.

Besides, I always wanted to see my homeland." The agent chuckled and his partner joined in.

Abner smiled around the room. "Right. Let's have a quick lunch and go over the plan before I get Jeff and Amy to the airport."

After the briefing, everyone checked their gear and prepared to go. Abner took care of Jeff and Amy. Sharon, Buzz, and the other two agents were busy packing their own equipment. They were all dressed like tourists.

"Where's Ezra?" the FBI agents asked, almost as an afterthought.

"Gone back to the sunny beaches of Tel Aviv," Jeff replied. "He left last night. Told me too many cooks spoil the broth."

"Pity," Burchard said. "He was a big enough player I thought he might enjoy seeing how it ended."

Indeed, the Israeli counterterrorist had departed the day before. But contrary to what he had told Jeff Savage, the unobtrusive middle-aged man was, at that very moment, landing in Nairobi.

As they drove into the Baltimore-Washington International Airport parking lot, Jeff winked at Amy and said, "Apparently Cunningham told the truth all along. Burchard and Wilson have been told to stand down permanently."

"I'm so embarrassed I even suspected Charles after all these years. I should have known better. Sharon Graham turned out to be the classic woman scorned."

Three cars behind them, the driver of the Honda Civic pressed the "Send" button on his two-way radio. "Luftleben 767, did you copy?"

Cunningham's rich baritone came over the speaker. "Yes, thank you. I'll be waiting for them when they get here."

"Amy, Jeff!" Charles Cunningham greeted them effusively as they climbed the ramp and boarded the huge aircraft. "I'm so glad I was able to conclude my business in time. We've much to talk about. I'm sure you have all kinds of questions. I have only one. Did you bring your swim-suits?"

"Yes, sir," Jeff answered.

"Melissa?" Amy said simultaneously.

"Your daughter's fine, Amy. Just fine. She can't wait to see you." He put his arm around Amy's shoulders and was not particularly sur-prised when he felt her stiffen. "I'm glad you remembered your swimsuits. They're *de rigueur* in that part of the globe. I hope you're hungry. My chef has prepared many surprises for us along the way."

"How long will the flight take, Mister Cunningham?"

"Charles. Will you ever remember, Amy? To answer your ques-tion, the flight takes about fourteen hours. Not to worry, this plane's a luxury liner, patterned after Air Force One. It's got offices, bedrooms, a full kitchen, and an entertainment center. Am I intruding or should I anticipate you'll be sleeping together? Oh, my, I fear I've trod where I shouldn't have. I do that occasionally, but then again we're all adults." He smiled. Jeff could see why Cunningham had succeeded in whatever he'd undertaken. The man could charm the skin off a snake.

"Well," Cunningham continued, "There's no reason why we shouldn't take off. We're cleared to Kisangani. From there, we'll proceed direct to our private airport. En route, I promise I'll answer all your ques-tions. Then we'll relax with an excellent wine, your choice of some of the most current movies or Broadway plays via satellite transmission, and the knowledge that we'll have a wonderful weekend at one of the most beautiful places on earth."

True to his word, Cunningham wasted little time in presenting them with what was obviously a well-configured fabrication, designed to put them at ease.

". . . so that's why I had to keep *ChildFinders'* mission secret, even from you," Cunningham said, apologetically, when he had finished.

"You mean, the government knew about it all along?" Jeff asked, trying to sound like a believer.

"Knew about it and sanctioned it. Next time you see your friends Burchard and Wilson ask them about it."

"I still don't understand why Melissa—?"

"That's the hardest part of all, Amy, and one for which I accept full blame. I don't know if you can ever forgive me. I give you my word of honor I never knew, nor in a million years would have dreamed, that your daughter was targeted for use until after it happened."

"Let me get this straight, Mister Cunningham," Jeff said. "The United States government was trying to avoid chaos in the Mideast by a series of predirected political killings throughout the world, just so it could keep things in balance?"

"Yes. It was higher than top secret. Imagine how it would have looked had our government spread the word even to its allies. That's why everything was channeled through a private operation. You're aware, of course, that such things have occurred in the past?"

"I've heard rumors," Jeff said. "The Iran-Contra stuff, suspicions that Israel and some of its Middle East neighbors were secretly collaborating on things, the Trilateral Commission—"

"What about the Trilateral Commission?" Cunningham interrupted sharply.

"I don't even know that it exists, except in fertile imaginations," Savage responded. "I've heard it's a take-over-the-world group that's said to operate beyond national borders. It sounds like science fiction if you ask me."

"Ah, yes, a fiction indeed," Cunningham replied, smiling. "I'm sorry I raised my voice. I fear that all the traveling I've done during the past week has made me more tired than usual."

Keep him talking, Burchard had advised. Draw him out. You might be able to catch a critical hint.

"Will there be many more killings?"

"No. The meeting will bring the deaths to a close."

"Meeting?" Amy asked.

"Yes. I'm afraid that once again I've been less than candid with you. We're having company at my retreat this weekend. The president and the British prime minister will be joining us Saturday. Three other world leaders will fly in on Sunday morning. I assure you they won't interfere with your weekend. The three of you may even choose to go home by Sunday morning. I promise you won't be disturbed."

"Disturbed?" Jeff said, his eyes wide. "Five of the most powerful men in the world, no doubt each bringing an army of security personnel, and you say we won't be disturbed? How come you didn't postpone our visit if you knew there was going to be a conclave this weekend?"

"Matters jelled more quickly than I thought they would. My friends consented to this meeting on very short notice. Amy, I couldn't possibly delay your being with Melissa simply because a bunch of old fossils wanted to meet with me."

"I appreciate that," she replied.

"I regret I'm not at liberty to advise you of the nature of the gathering. That would betray the trust of several people I hold dear."

"I understand," Amy murmured, yawning. "It's been a long day for me. I appreciate everything you've told us, Charles. Would you mind terribly if I slept for a while?"

"Not at all. How about you, Jeff?"

"Same with me, sir. What you've told us is mind-boggling. We certainly owe you an apology for suspecting you'd be involved in anything that was not for the greater benefit of all."

"Think nothing of it," he said, smiling paternally. "When you get to be my age, it's quite flattering when younger folk think of you as an . . . adventurer."

35

The supersonic Air Force plane took off from Meade Air Force Base an hour after the 767 left Baltimore-Washington International. Two hundred miles east of Philadelphia, the pilot turned southeast. Six hours later, the plane put down at Bujumbura. Its passengers, a contingent of agents detached for special assignment outside the United States, and the lone female with them, boarded a hydrofoil, which transported them down Lake Tanganyika to Kalemie, eighty miles from the Preserve.

An hour later, an ancient, wooden vessel that looked as though it would barely make the journey upriver to Nyunzu, the closest village to the Preserve's unguarded northern perimeter, departed the rotting timber dock. No sooner had the battered, creaky craft rounded the bend and lost sight of Kalemie landing, than the agents stripped away the tired boards, revealing a cutter equipped with twin Chrysler engines. They arrived at the final staging area two hours ahead of the 767.

"M'tumba, Mister Cunningham is due in half an hour. I need to make certain everything's in order before he lands."

"Miss Graham, when you arrive? I get no word from de airport." The elderly black seemed agitated. His hand shook, as if palsied.

"I came in over the road to the Institute and took the tram out, M'Tumba."

The answer seemed to satisfy him. "I so happy you're here, Miss Sharon. I been wanting to find Master for two days, ever since—"

"Ever since what?"

"I think you speak with Regina, Miss Sharon. Better fast." The woman he referred to entered the room. She was Sharon's age, tall, graceful, and better educated than M'tumba, thanks to Charles Cunningham.

"Who is it, M'tumba?" She stopped and put her hand to her mouth when she saw Sharon. "Oh, Miss Sharon. There was a dreadful accident two days ago. Doctor Lee, she . . . she . . . she *dead*, Miss Sharon."

Sharon made no attempt at telling the staff she was sorry. "How did she die?"

"She was cursed, Miss Sharon." The woman shuddered and passed her hands over her eyes.

Sharon gave her a moment to recover her composure. "What did you do with the body?"

"We call truthsayer from my village. He tell us to bury Doctor Lee's body in far-away place, so devils leave other bodies in peace. Last night, the shaman and four deathtakers come. Please don't be angry with me, Miss Sharon. Don't let the Master harm us." The queenly Regina was begging like a small, frightened child.

"Don't worry, Regina," Sharon replied. "I'll make sure the Master knows you did everything you could. During this weekend, he'll be having many guests. It's best you not say anything about it to him. One more thing."

"Yes, Miss Sharon?" M'tumba asked.

"The Master doesn't expect me to be here when his company comes because the meeting is supposed to be secret. Since he does not know what happened to Doctor Lee, he should not be disturbed by you telling him I am here. You understand? I will tell him about Doctor Lee at the right time and in the right way. You know that the Master and I—" She hesitated. Odd that even now she felt embarrassed.

"Know what, Miss Sharon?" Regina said, stone-faced. Then she broke into a grin. "You'll help us?"

"Of course."

Regina uttered an incantation in a foreign tongue. In answer to Sharon's questioning gaze, M'tumba said, "She ask the gods to bless your work, Miss Sharon. I join in her prayer."

"Amen," Sharon replied. "Now, just in case the Master asks about Doctor Lee, here's what you must tell him—"

The 767 landed at ten o'clock local time. The pilot shut down the engines just outside the terminal. Jeff and Amy looked around, amazed. "I can't believe it!" Amy said. "You've managed to build this airport and keep it a secret all these years?"

"Southeastern Congo is not exactly a tourist Mecca," Cunningham said. "This is only the beginning. Wait 'til you see the rest. The others won't be coming for several hours, so you'll have the full treatment."

He called the Manor. "M'tumba, would you please arrange for the carriage and four to pick up Mrs. Roth, Mister Savage and myself. Thank you." He rang off.

"The Master has arrived," the black man told Sharon and Regina. "He not ask about Doctor Lee."

Shortly afterward, the two women watched as M'tumba, outfitted in a Nineteenth Century footman's uniform, drove off in the burnished, wooden carriage drawn by four gray horses.

"I'd best hide in the basement for now," Sharon said. "Remember, Regina, nothing about my being here."

Once Sharon had descended to a small storage room, she closed and locked the door, took a pocket transmitter from her purse, and said, "They've arrived."

"We know. The president will be here by two this afternoon. How are you feeling?"

"Exhausted. Doctor Lee is dead."

"Pity. Birds of a feather and all that. It won't be too long, now. Do you think you can pull it off?"

"Are you sure you'll be there, Abner?"

"You know I will. "

"Abner?"

"Yes?"

"Nothing." She turned off the transmitter and sat in the darkness, listening to the silence and trying not to wonder what was going to happen to her when all of this came to an end.

Above her, outside in the sunshine, Amy couldn't stifle a gasp when she saw the Manor from the tunnel of moss-laden trees. "How beautiful!" she said. "But I expected to see Melissa. Why didn't she come with M't . . . M't—?"

"M'tumba," Cunningham said. "I'm sure Melissa was swimming when he left to come and get us. You'll see her soon, I promise. Meanwhile, enjoy your surroundings. The rainy season is always the loveliest time of the year in this part of Africa. The gods have been gracious to us this year. The flowers are in bloom. The trees are fully leafed. The greensward is at its most luxuriant."

He showed them around the elegant villa that had been prepared for them. Barely minutes later, he said, "I'm afraid I must excuse myself. My guests will be here shortly. The servants will see to your every need. Simply press 322 on any of the telephones in your cottage to call them. There is food, wine, anything you like on hand, at all times. This villa is here for your pleasure."

"What about Melissa?" Amy asked, her eyes narrowing.

"She'll be here in five minutes. I understand your feelings, Amy. One request, though."

"Yes, Mister Cunningham?"

"Please come to my dinner party this evening. And if you're worried about Melissa, she will be well cared for in your absence."

"Dinner with the president of the United States and the prime minister of England?" Jeff said. "I wouldn't miss it on a bet."

"Okay," Amy said. "As long as it's all right with Melissa." Five minutes later, Melissa bounded into the villa like a young pup. The child seemed to have dealt with the strain better than her mother. She looked tanned and well. By six-thirty, when she was getting ready for the dinner party, Amy felt more refreshed and confident than she had in a long time.

Outside, the four agents reconnoitered the estate. Mike used his training in electronics to find and bypass the few alarms their opponent had bothered to put in. It seemed obvious, at least at first, that Cunningham had never expected anyone to invade his compound.

As dark settled in, they found that wasn't entirely true. They were moving into position around the windows Sharon had described to them, windows which were lit and showed signs of activity behind them. Suddenly, two figures jumped from a nearby tree onto their backs. In the first instant, Wilson silently disabled one and Stevens smashed the other into a trunk.

"So much for subtlety, eh Jimmy?" Mike said to his partner.

Abner glared at the black man. "Keep it quiet and pay attention."

Inside the Manor, Charles rapped his knife on a crystal glass. "My friends, if I might have your attention for a few moments, please?"

The president gave a loud, theatrical sigh. "Oh, God, Charles, you don't intend to ruin this perfect day with an after-dinner speech?" The others laughed appreciatively. It had been a wonderful meal. The leaders' security agents had unobtrusively eaten in a room immediately adjacent to the dining hall, and had now returned.

"We'll adjourn to the library in a few moments. Right now, since I recognize the need for security, particularly in company such as this, I ask that each of you who have been selected to protect your leaders take the time to search each of us and satisfy yourselves that my library is entirely safe for our meeting."

The guards had been trained to trust no one, regardless of the circumstances. It took them a full half-hour to complete their search of the library. They hesitated to search the heads of government, but approached Amy, Savage, and Cunningham.

"That won't be necessary," the president told his Secret Service agents. "I've known Charles Cunningham for more years than I care to say. If I can't trust him, there's no one in the world left to trust." The agents nodded, frisked Amy and Jeff, and returned to their seats.

Shortly before nine, leaving Jeff and Amy sipping liqueurs on the terrace, Cunningham, the president, and the prime minister entered the library.

"My friends," Cunningham began. "I've told each of you the purpose of the meeting tomorrow. I must now admit I haven't been completely candid with you."

The president and prime minister glanced uneasily at one another.

Cunningham continued, "I wanted to meet with the two of you first because you are the leaders of the two most influential nations in the world. Now I'd like to show you a short film I've put together which will, I believe, explain the real purpose of this weekend's conference."

Cunningham started the video machine and ran the DVD he had made of the operation and its purpose. The two world leaders became more and more agitated, shifting in their seats, rearranging their hands in their laps.

"That's outrageous!" the prime minister exclaimed at the end of the film. "You don't think for one minute you can get away with this? I've never heard anything so preposterous since Hitler!"

"Don't you *dare* compare me with Hitler!" Cunningham said sharply. "He was a charlatan, a bigot, and a racist. What I propose crosses the lines of culture, color, and religion. It makes no difference to me what foolishness people subscribe to."

"The man who would be God," the president said, coolly. "With no army, no force other than your will? The idea's insane, Charles."

"Don't tell me I have no force, Mr. President. How dare you suggest I cannot bring this about? You've already witnessed the deaths of dozens of political figures worldwide. More than five times the number killed last year. And all your law enforcement agencies were useless against my army. More sophisticated and far more clever than 9-1-1, wouldn't you say?" he chided.

Out on the terrace, Jeff glanced toward the library and mentally urged Abner to hurry. He reached out and took Amy's hand.

"Lest you think I've used anywhere near my army of time bombs, I've prepared two demonstrations for you." Cunningham switched on the television monitor again. A camera zoomed in on Parliament house in Ottawa. "The seat of government of your nearest neighbor," Cunningham said. "The leader of the French Canadian separatist movement is to address Parliament at three o'clock, Ottawa time. He is one of the most heavily guarded human beings in the Western Hemisphere. Ah, I see he is now arriving."

A black Citroën sedan pulled up to the steps of the building. Four agents surrounded the car as its passenger opened the rear door and started to emerge. Suddenly there was a bright, orange flash. When the smoke cleared, there was no car, no passenger, no guards, only wreckage.

"If either of you think this did not happen, please feel free to call your embassies from a telephone in this library."

"Let us say you're telling the truth." The prime minister rose to join the president, who was already standing." To what purpose?"

"To demonstrate that no political leader on earth is immune. My weapons are completely unconscious. The most elegant part is that you never know who the murderer will be, a Secret Service Agent, a high-ranking member of the Sûrete, a sous chef somewhere in the Forbidden City." He chuckled. "You never know. It could even be someone in this room."

"Why have you done this, Charles?" the president asked.

"Many years ago, it became apparent to me that national governments were a thing of the past. The world had become too large, too cumbersome, too dangerous to leave to a large number of politicians, each with his or her own ego to salve."

"We've heard that before," the prime minister remarked in a steady voice. "Those science fiction tales about the so-called Trilateral Commission—"

"*I don't want to hear about the goddammed Trilateral Commission!*" For the first time, Cunningham allowed himself a display of anger. "It *is* a fiction, don't you understand? A fiction! A bunch of fractious, holier-than-thou hypocrites pretending they know what's best for the world! Where have they gotten this world today? Is it any better than when they embarked on their wonderful crusade? Well? Is it? *Me! I* embody the *real* spirit of what the Trilateral Commission—the World Security Commission—is all about. What you have seen on the TV monitor is what that idiotic Commission is *really* supposed to be about!"

He'd raised his voice several decibels. No one said a word. Realizing he'd almost lost control, he lowered his voice and continued, choosing his words carefully.

"The world is in chaos. There is no longer a moral right or wrong. Everything's out of control, out of balance. A week ago, when I proposed certain ideas to each of you, you were all smiles, all happiness. Trade barriers down, war a thing of the past, one world working together toward the same goal: peace, harmony, food, security for everyone on the planet. Suddenly my idea shocks you. Why? Each of you would continue in your present position, secure for the rest of your lives, if you so desire. Mister President, you, more than anyone, know how archaic the American system is. You must run for reelection every four years, face taunts and humiliation from someone who has neither your experience nor your grasp of world affairs."

The president looked thoughtful.

"Prime Minister," he said, "you worry every day about the next scandal that will erupt. You're terrified that with a single computer keystroke the lords of Japan can force Britain to its knees.

"Each of you is a slave to the vested interests who put you where you are and you know it. The only thing different about my program is that there will be a single person to whom you owe allegiance. A single, mature voice who has proven over long years of public service that he knows what truly is best for the world."

He paused.

"What if someone were to assassinate you?" the president asked.

"I am more than competent to attend to my own safety."

"So you're asking that we be slaves to you?" the prime minister said.

"Not at all." Cunningham smiled. "Rather consider yourselves as you always have—servants of the people. With only their best interests at heart."

"Provided the heart that beats is yours," the president said.

"Whatever. I have one last demonstration." He pressed a buzzer. "M'tumba, please ask Mrs. Roth and Mister Savage to come in for a few moments."

Shortly, there was a quiet knock on the door.

"Come in," Cunningham said.

Amy and Jeff entered the room, accompanied by a nondescript stranger whom none of them appeared to recognize. Cunningham looked momentarily nonplussed, but recovered his composure quickly. He continued, without missing a beat. "My friends, and the gentleman I've not yet met, I will now prove what I mean when I say anyone could be a soldier in my army. Fortunately, the president vouched for my character, so the Secret Service found it unnecessary to search me for a weapon." Cunningham pulled a .38 special out from under his jacket and held it loosely in one hand.

Turning directly to Amy, he said, "Hey diddle-diddle, the cat and the fiddle, the cow jumped over the other cat."

Amy's head swam. She saw a flash of a late winter day, girls playing jump rope, a phone ringing, a knife.

"Amy, I am going to hand you this gun," Cunningham's voice continued. Amy glanced uncertainly at Ezra. He nodded. She took the gun. Her hands were steady.

"Amy, what I am doing is for your own good." Cunningham paused, breathing in deeply. "I want you to kill Professor Savage."

36

She felt a weight in her hand. Lifted it experimentally. "*Hey did-dle-diddle, the cat and the fiddle, the cow jumped over the other cat*," she said softly, repeating what was obviously meant as her trigger phrase. Her heart beat fast as, again, a sense of *deja vu* brought flashes of a late winter day, girls playing jump rope, a phone ringing, a knife. But the phrase didn't affect her. *So I, too, was a weapon*, she thought. *Why doesn't that surprise me?* And then she knew.

That had been Melissa's trigger phrase. She had been triggered with the same phrase as her daughter, which was why she had forgotten so much of that afternoon.

She looked up at Jeff, then over to Ezra. She turned to Cunningham. He was confident. Fatherly—

—And a megalomaniac who had caused Dan's death and caused her daughter to commit patricide.

Jeff looked at her, his eyes gentle, his voice calm. "Amy, Charles Cunningham is a very bad man, I want you to—"

"No!" Cunningham screamed. "Not me! Not me, Amy, you know who I am! Not me!"

Amy stood between the two of them, her eyes calm.

"Amy," Jeff said, quietly. "I want you to shoot Charles Cunning-ham."

"No!" Cunningham cried out.

The ear-splitting blast of the gun was magnified by the small space. There was a shattering of glass as the library window behind Cunningham exploded. Then there was silence.

Cunningham, who'd covered his face, looked up to see Amy standing in front of him, the gun pointed at what had, until an instant before, been a Chagall stained glass window.

At that moment, security agents crashed through the door. A side wall of the library turned outward, revealing Special Agents Burchard and Wilson, and Sharon Graham, who held several sheets of paper.

"Sharon, you're not supposed to be here," Cunningham said. "You're supposed to be dead." He immediately realized how ridiculous he sounded.

"No, Charles. I'm sorry to disappoint you, but I'm very much alive. It's your friend Doctor Lee who's dead. As is Will Hensleigh, Hitoshi Kono, and Rajendra Prasad. All your colleagues are gone, Flanders. You're all alone. You've lost the game."

"That's where you're wrong, my dear," Cunningham said, quickly regaining his composure. "You see, there's only one copy of the list and I have it."

"And what do you think I'm holding?" She started reading a series of names, dates of the programming, voice signals.

"You're bluffing," the tall man said. "You've reconstructed a few names from memory, most of them already expended. I specifically had you type the only list there is in my presence, to make sure it would go no farther."

"I suppose you watched every character I typed?" she said, her eyes blazing. "Or that you made sure I didn't save the list on my computer terminal?"

"No, Shari, I didn't watch you every minute of every hour. You were my trusted aide, you and I were—are—"

"Lovers, Charles? Is that what you wanted to say? Does a lover arrange to have his mistress murdered? Does an honorable man liquidate his colleagues of twenty years? What do you know of love or honor, Charles Flanders Cunningham? What have you ever known about anything but your own selfish interests?"

The others watched the exchange in silence.

"What do *you* know of honor?" he shot back. "I picked you up out of the gutter, made you a wealthy woman, gave you power beyond your wildest dreams, gave you love."

"That button doesn't push anymore."

"Very well. I accept you may have some of the names and even some of the phrases, but you've no idea how many time bombs are out there."

"Wrong, again, Charles," she said. "You set precisely seven hundred fifty of your 'goodwill ambassadors' loose on the world. As of this moment, you've used six hundred fifty-seven. There are ninety-three left."

"Yes, but no one in this room knows where they are or when they'll strike." He turned to face the president and the prime minister. "You may or may not choose to believe Ms. Graham. That, of course, is your prerogative. Ms. Graham may indeed have parts of an outdated list. I guarantee you I have the only current list of where the remainder of my time bombs are located. Whether there are fifty or five hundred makes no difference. What it all comes down to is I need only two and each of you becomes history. So, my friends, I would say we are at an impasse."

No one spoke. *High noon at the OK Corral,* Jeff thought. He looked over at the president, then toward Abner Burchard, who nodded almost imperceptibly at the Israeli counterterrorist.

At that moment, they were interrupted by unruly commotion and noise as more than fifty men broke through the front door of the mansion and entered the room. Cunningham gasped as he saw Guillaume M'bele enter in their wake.

?"

"Guillaume? You—?"

The dignified black man cast his eyes down.

"Mister Cunningham," Ezra said. "Permit me to introduce myself. My name is Ezra Caen. I was born in what was then known as the Republic of South Africa. I am now a citizen of the State of Israel, and I have, as the Americans say, no horse in this race and no dog in this hunt. I have been asked to act as spokesman for the group."

"An officious intermeddler?" Cunningham sneered, trying to goad the newcomer on.

"You might well say that, Mister Cunningham. Since it's most likely true, I am not disturbed by your statement. But to get back to the subject matter of our little chat, you seem to believe that you and your adversaries hold equally high cards."

"That's correct."

"You concede it would be easy for any of the security agents or Congolese soldiers in this room to kill you right now."

"Which would avail you nothing at all."

"Mister Cunningham, with all due respect, I believe you're bluffing."

"Perhaps," the tall man said, an inscrutable smile on his face. "But you'll never know, will you?"

"No, we won't," Ezra said. "But then again, neither will you."

"What do you mean?"

"I believe we may hold the high trump card."

"I don't follow you," Cunningham said.

"This has all been a game to you. There are several people in this room who would enjoy killing you in an instant, Mister Cunningham. Professor Savage, whose closest friend you murdered for no justifiable reason. Amy Roth, whom you abused in the most inhumane way imaginable. Sharon Graham, for obvious reasons. Guillaume M'bele, whose trust you betrayed. If anyone deserves to die, it is a cold-blooded monster like you. But to kill you quickly and relatively painlessly would not only be a useless act of barbarism, it would be declaring the game over before the showdown. We'd never know who really won.

"Lee Chung Lien was one of the world's experts in brainwashing, but she wasn't the only authority in that field, any more than William Hensleigh was the world's greatest biomedical genius, or Rajendra Prasad was a unique computer wizard. There are others.

"Until the last few moves, you had every advantage. Your weapons were in place, only you knew where they were, and you stayed one step ahead of us so long as you tapped into Hamilton's supercomputer. The difference between the way we functioned and the way you operated was your undoing, Mister Cunningham. While you isolated yourself by eliminating those around you, we put together a team that cooperated in devising the final moves.

"You deserve to die, Mister Cunningham, but slowly, painfully, with full knowledge of the enormity of your crime. So, we propose the following as our final move." He glanced over at the president, who smiled and started speaking quietly.

"Charles," the American leader said, "It was my suggestion—my command, in fact—that you not be immediately dispatched. Although it may cost the taxpayers a little more than had you been killed right here in the Democratic Republic of the Congo, I believe we can put you up at an appropriate 'Club Fed.'" The president chuckled at his small joke. "After we put you through a slow, steady, brainwashing program of our own—without the time pressure of having to return you home within two weeks—after we inject you with the same solution Hensleigh devised for the others, you will become the ultimate time bomb, just like the rest, with one exception."

"What is that?" Cunningham asked, his voice hoarse.

"The difference between you and the others is that you will know you are programmed. We'll remind you of that fact every day of your life. So you'll know that any moment, all we have to do is say a critical phrase or show you a series of alternating colored lights, or even invite you to play a game of cards—you do remember *The Manchurian Candidate* I trust?—and off you'll go to do our bidding. Of course, you'll never know what the phrase is, and you'll spend the rest of your life trying to figure out what it is."

Cunningham was silent for several moments as he pondered what the president had proposed. Slowly, barely perceptibly at first, he nodded his head. "A simple, but elegant private taste of hell." His voice was husky. "I applaud your cunning and your sense of aesthetics, my dear president. What's your deal?"

"There's no 'deal' to make, Mister Cunningham." Ezra looked at the president, who nodded.

"First, you will turn over the entire list. I trust you have that on the premises?"

"I do."

"Next, you'll remain under arrest and constant supervision, at a federal institution commensurate with your station, for the rest of your life. During that time, we will systematically deprogram each and every remaining person on the list. If there is any difficulty in doing this—any difficulty whatsoever—the United States government will carry out the initial proposal."

"Whatever happened to due process of law, the right to a fair trial?"

"You chose your own due process when you chose to go outside the boundaries of any civilized law. Do you think if you were tried by any court in the world, you'd end up with less than a life sentence?"

"Go on."

"You've scattered a lot of pain and sorrow around the world. A five-billion-dollar fund, provided by the Preservation Trust, should ease some of that hurt. Your heirs will still be left with a substantial fortune. Ms. Graham will undoubtedly be granted clemency, having turned State's evidence. The Trust will pay her fine. It will make an outright gift of the Children's Institute to the government of the Democratic Republic of the Congo, and it will furnish the funds necessary to operate the Institute and continue to fund scholarships for the next twenty years. There are many graduates of the Institute who are well qualified to administer the worthwhile work you've started here. Of course," he added, "we'll make sure that any of those who'd undergone intracranial reconstitution were deprogrammed."

"What about the Center? The Manor? The billion dollars I've spent?" Cunningham asked.

"Those leaders who are coming tomorrow will make equitable division of whatever can be used to better their nations, or they may choose to give these things to the government of the host nation. Your servants will be given pensions sufficient to enable them to go about their lives in peace—and with the dignity you've denied them. The rest will go up in smoke, Mister Cunningham. As sad as it seems to destroy such an incredible manifestation of elegance and luxury, it must be done. The surface beauty hides the ugliness below. So long as the Manor stands, so long as your airport cuts a gash across the landscape, they will be symbols of evil and a blot on nature's way. Even were we to leave them intact, the rainforest would reclaim the land within a few years. By burning them down and planting seedlings, we'll accelerate the healing. The fact that you once lived here will actually benefit the earth. Unless, of course, you gentlemen disagree," Caen said.

No one raised an objection.

"Finally, Mister Cunningham, the four large aircraft will be turned over to the International Air Relief Foundation and your passport will be lifted."

"You'd leave me with nothing?"

"I'd hardly call the remaining two billion dollars 'nothing,' Mister Cunningham. Oh, and you may keep the TLC. I understand it has always been one of your favorite toys."

"I trust there's no room for bargaining?"

"None."

"How long do I have to give you my answer?"

The president glanced at his watch, then looked around the room at the others. "Thirty seconds should be sufficient. That's about as long as it takes to deal a new hand."

Cunningham stared straight ahead. At the end of the time allotted, he walked over to a nearby chess table, knocked over the black king, and smiled. "Checkmate, Mister President. I never did much care for card games, but chess—" He looked over to Savage. "I suppose you play chess, Professor Savage. I'll bet you'd be a worthy adversary there, too. Pity I did not think to invite you aboard as a colleague."

He looked around the room, then back at the president. "I accept your offer. Now, may I suggest we end the evening on a note that befits the occasion." He walked over to the library's intercom and pressed a buzzer. "M'tumba, Regina, would you bring in several bottles of our finest champagne, please? We're about to drink to a new relationship."

EPILOGUE: SEVEN YEARS LATER

Sharon was shocked when Abner called to tell her they were granting Charles Cunningham clemency. "Guillaume M'bele's death hit Cunningham hard," he said. "Our friend had been depressed for several weeks before his stroke."

"I didn't know he was ill. How serious was it?"

"He can speak, but according to the specialist who treated him, he's permanently paralyzed. The authorities concluded no purpose would be served by keeping him incarcerated at the honor facility. The new president apparently agreed."

"So he won after all." Sharon's voice was bitter.

"What do you mean?"

"He never believed they'd put him away for life."

"Aren't you being a bit harsh?"

"After what he tried to do to me? To you?"

"I'd hardly call a man who'll be a paraplegic for the rest of his life a winner. Seven years ago, he came closer to ruling the world than anyone knows. Now he's nothing more than an unknown footnote to history. He's asked to see you."

"How dare he?"

"Perhaps he sees his own mortality and wants to make amends."

"You believe that? You of all people should know that a megalomaniac like that doesn't change."

"I don't speculate on those things, Sharon," Abner replied quietly. "Would it hurt you to visit him?"

Although she'd never forgiven Charles Cunningham, a small spark within her still recalled the joy they had shared, the wondrous, heady days when they'd contemplated the greatest challenge of all. Despite her initial anger when she entered the minimum security prison, she couldn't help but feel an overwhelming sense of sadness when she saw what seven years had done to the once patrician Cunningham. The shock of iron-gray hair she remembered had been replaced by a few wispy strands of white. He'd lost fifty pounds, his pants were hiked high on his midriff, his shirt was spotted with food stains. His once magnetic eyes, sunk into deep sockets above his hollow cheeks, were faded, infinitely sad. He'd become a shabby, dilapidated old man.

"My God, what happened, Flan?"

"Life caught up with me, Shari." His voice was tremulous. Gone was the confident, rich baritone. Despite her bitterness, she felt her heart wrench when she saw two tears roll down his right cheek. "You know, I've not had one visitor in the past five years? Not that I wasn't allowed guests. The world simply forgot about me. They dropped my name from the letterhead after I was disbarred."

"I know."

It was an awkward meeting for two people who had shared the better part of their lives with one another. They were quiet for several moments. Finally, Charles broke the silence. "The new president was kind enough to grant me clemency."

"So I've heard."

Cunningham tried to raise his arm, failed, then gazed at her. "Do you ever … think back?"

She gazed directly at him while she pondered her answer. "I've relived our time together, Charles. More in anger than anything else. What you tried to do to me makes it hard to remember the good times."

"I'm sorry, Shari. I wish you could forgive me."

"Sorry?" She'd raised her voice in anger. She consciously lowered it again. Why vent her fury on this pathetic shell? "Don't you think that's rather an inappropriate thing to ask after all that's happened?" she said, more quietly.

"I shouldn't have asked your forgiveness," he said. "Perhaps if there were some way to let you know how far I've come since—. Margaret died the year after I came here. Did you know that?"

"Yes."

"No matter what you might think, you were the only woman I ever truly loved."

He closed his eyes.

Sharon fought back tears. Don't be taken in by this master manipulator, she thought. Not again. Not after so many years. She swallowed hard. "I have to go now, Charles."

"I understand. Thank you for coming. May I call you next month when I get out?"

"I'd rather you didn't."

But he did, two months later. When she heard what he proposed, she told him she'd call him back the following day. When Abner came home that night, she told him about the bizarre telephone conversation.

"He wants me to go to the Congo with him, to take one last look at what's left of the Preserve."

"What did you say?"

"That I'd call him back."

"Do you want to go?"

"Why would I possibly want to do that?"

"Curiosity. What harm would it do?"

She walked over to the front window and looked out at the lawn, turned brown by the summer sun, the flowers of spring long gone to seed. In her mind's eye, she wandered back and gazed at the endless greensward that led to the mansion, the flowers that bloomed each day of the year. She heard the crunch of gravel and the clucking of M'tumba's tongue as he urged the dapple-gray horses toward the entryway. She pondered Abner's question for a moment. What harm would it do? Perhaps the destruction of a memory I might want to keep intact, she thought.

He gazed at her levelly. "Perhaps you should go, if for no other reason than to close the circle and let us get on with our lives. I love you, Sharon. Wouldn't you say we've waited long enough?"

They kissed long and hard, then gently, and she nestled in his arms.

"You're right, Abner. Maybe it's time I did close the circle. I still don't trust him, though."

"Even in his present state?"

"Even in his present state."

"Perhaps if I gave you some extra security?"

"Meet me in London on the way home?"

"If that's what you want."

"Have you ever been there?"

"No."

"You'll love it. It's as far from Kentucky as you could possibly imagine. The theater season's just starting. We could see five plays in as many nights." She became more excited as she told him of the wonders of the English capital.

Next day, she called Cunningham and told him she'd accompany him to Congo, but that she intended to stop off in London—alone—on the way home. He seemed delighted and agreed to her condition immediately.

Once in Nairobi, Cunningham's trustee chartered a Shorts 300 for the trip into the Democratic Republic of the Congo. The boxy aircraft, originally built in Ireland to ferry automobiles across the English channel, was large enough to accommodate the custom-built all-terrain vehicle they'd need to drive around the Preserve.

Although the Preserve's airport had been bulldozed, the plane was able to land without difficulty on the gravel airstrip, which was potholed and overgrown with new grass. After the pilot lowered the rear exit ramp of the aircraft, Sharon drove the land vehicle onto what had been the runway.

They were amazed at the changes time had wrought. No one could tell there had ever been a Manor, ancient magnolia trees, or fountains. There was no sign of a rolling greensward, a circular entryway, beautifully tended gardens. Everything was gone except the dense virginal forest that had been there when he first set eyes on the place thirty years ago. Hundreds of young, sturdy trees thrust their branches to the sky. Below and between, there was leafy undergrowth. The rainforest had returned to reclaim the land.

"Shari, could I ask you to drive me into the old part of the forest. I'd like to remember things the way they were."

"How long will you need, Flan?"

"Long enough to relive the shattered dreams."

There was a decided stoop to Cunningham's shoulders. It had been half a dozen years since the authorities had defused the last of the time bombs on the list he'd given them.

Just inside the first row of trees, she saw three white rocks, each the size of a small dog. Inside the triangle formed by the rocks, there was a tall growth of scruffy grass.

"Please stop here, Shari."

She watched with shock as Cunningham suddenly stood up, moved stiffly to the center of the triangle and pawed at the grass until he had exposed the round plate.

"Y—, you can't walk," she said, immediately realizing how foolish she must sound.

"Oh, but I can," he said, smiling. "It's amazing how just the right amount of curare can cause temporary paralysis and weight loss."

"But surely the doctors knew?"

"Of course. It wasn't hard to persuade them to overlook one or two tests and arrive at certain perfectly rational conclusions, particularly when each was advised he would have a million dollars in an offshore Caribbean bank on the day of my release."

She sat in stunned silence as he unscrewed the disk, opened the ground safe, then carefully extracted a sheet of single-spaced, typewritten words. He read the sheet carefully and smiled.

"Sixty entries, Shari. A good start. A very good start. All the names, addresses, and trigger phrases of the time bombs we programmed *after* the war started. The list of names I somehow forgot to give to the authorities."

Cunningham folded the paper, placed it in the back pocket of his pants, then screwed the disk back in place. He stood up and kicked dirt over the plate, obscuring it once again.

"Shari," he said. "I'm so glad you came back. You must have known. So now we begin the game again, just like before. You and I." He reached out to take her in his arms.

"No, Charles," she said.

"What are you saying?" he asked. His smile froze as he saw her pull out the small weapon.

Realizing what was about to happen, Cunningham turned and started toward the clearing. The curare had not entirely worn off and his movements were clumsy. He'd gotten no more than a few feet when the potassium-cyanide-filled dart hit him in the neck. He fell to the ground. Moments later, he clutched at his chest, trying desperately to draw breath.

As he stared up at Sharon, his eyes wide in terror, gasping like a fish out of water, she said, "The game is over, you miserable sonofabitch." Her eyes hard and dry. "I loved you so much. We could have had the whole world, but you threw it all away. Hensleigh, Kono, Prasad, Chung Lien, finally you. Now I'm the only one left."

After he'd stopped writhing and lay still, Sharon bent over the dead man, took the list from his back pocket, removed the small dart and rubbed dust over the back of his neck, leaving no trace of what had happened. An autopsy would show that Charles Cunningham had suffered a fatal heart blockage. That was truly unfortunate, but in his aged, weakened condition, it was only to be expected.

It took her several minutes to dispose of the small weapon and drag Cunningham's body back into the vehicle. In a few moments, she'd start driving back to the plane. She'd have tears in her eyes as she told the crew of the death of her beloved old friend. She'd help the American Embassy in Kinshasa arrange for his remains to be returned home. Then she'd excuse herself because she had an appointment in London she must keep.

Just before she started the vehicle, Sharon removed the list from her pocket and read it carefully once more. She recalled what Charles had said only a few minutes before. "*A good start. A very good start.*"

Perhaps he wasn't so far off the mark after all. She mused about the title of the play she and Abner were scheduled to see the following evening. *She Stoops to Conquer.*

Her eyes took on a brightness that had not been there a moment ago. *It might work*, she thought. *It just might work at that.*

Sharon turned on the ignition, put the vehicle in gear, and started back toward the plane. She glanced over at Cunningham's body. "Let the game begin," she said softly as the vehicle emerged into the clearing. She was smiling.

The End?